I0670344

Firefly Mountain

by

Christine DePetrillo

This is a work of fiction. Names, characters, places, and incidents are either the product of the author's imagination or are used fictitiously, and any resemblance to actual persons living or dead, business establishments, events, or locales, is entirely coincidental.

Firefly Mountain

Cover Art by *Angela Anderson*

The Wild Rose Press, Inc.
PO Box 708
Adams Basin, NY 14410-0708
Visit us at www.thewildrosepress.com

Publishing History
First Faery Rose Edition, 2012
Print ISBN 978-1-61217-359-7
Digital ISBN 978-1-61217-360-3

Published in the United States of America

"Patrick's a fire investigator," Jonah told Gini. "Got an amazing dog around here somewhere too." Jonah scanned the vehicle bay looking for Midas.

Patrick pointed a finger under the stairs where Midas was curled up. As if knowing people were talking about him, the dog's head popped up. He rose to all fours and scuttled out from his sleeping spot. Once Midas was in full view, Gini let out a breathy sigh.

"He's absolutely gorgeous." Her eyes flashed to Patrick for a moment, then she walked over to Midas. She gracefully bent, offering a bonus view of one toned thigh, and cupped the dog's muzzle in her hand. After setting her oversized purse down, she let both hands rub Midas from ears to tail. The dog flopped down onto his back and made little satisfied doggy noises as Gini scratched his belly.

Patrick watched, wishing she'd give him some attention like that. Jonah elbowing him in the gut snapped him out of his fantasy.

"Knew that dog could rake in the ladies. What did I tell you?" Jonah went to join his sister in spoiling Midas.

Gini let Jonah take over and rose to her feet. As she walked back to Patrick, he watched her eyes comb down the length of him. What did she see? What would she think of what she couldn't see?

"You just move here?" Gini asked.

Patrick nodded, watched her chew on her bottom lip. If she thought she was going to get to know him, she was wrong. He couldn't allow it. She wouldn't like what she got to know anyway.

Dedication

To everyday heroes
who save lives in countless ways.

Chapter One

Surely Hell couldn't be hotter than this. A wall of orange flames surrounded him, dared him to approach. The roar of the fire pounded between his ears as thick, black smoke strangled any attempts at taking a deep breath.

This is what death is, Patrick thought. *It's going to take us. Raina, Julianne. Mom, Dad. Me.*

Still, he pushed through the angry blaze. Let it jab at his exposed skin as his sisters' screams rose above the fire's thunder. Getting to them was all he could think of, all that mattered. Twice, he had to pat out flames that jumped to his sweatpants and caught them on fire. He shielded his face with his bare arm and slammed his shoulder into the door of his sisters' bedroom. Inside, they were cowered in the corner. Julianne held the quilt from her bed over Raina and was about to get under it herself when her gaze connected with her brother's over the line of fire dividing the room.

"Get us out of here!" she screamed.

He didn't see any way to get to them, but knew he couldn't leave them. He grabbed Raina's sweatshirt from the chair at her desk and wrapped it around his face. Before he could think about what he was doing, he ran into the inferno. Pain, instant and knife-sharp, tore through his skin, but he made it to Raina and Julianne. Broke the window above their hiding bodies. Boosted Raina out. Moved on to Julianne.

The explosion behind them knocked his body

and Julianne's into the wall beside the window. The last thing he heard was Julianne's gurgled scream and the crumbling roof as the monster of heat swallowed them whole.

****

Patrick Barre woke with a choking gasp. "Shit."

He wiped the sweat from his forehead and stretched out his long limbs. He stopped when the flesh on the left side of his chest and down to his thigh tightened. Its elasticity was gone, taken twenty years ago. He ran a finger over the jagged folds of skin as he exhaled a slow, even breath.

Man, he hated that dream. Made it seem as if it all happened just yesterday. The heat was right there. The pain. His sisters' terror. His parents' charred bodies. How was a guy supposed to forget when it could be relived whenever he closed his eyes?

Maybe he'd give up sleeping. Stay up around the clock. That'd do wonders for his attitude.

The phone beside the mattresses he was using as a bed rang into the silence as Midas, Patrick's all black German Shepherd, jumped up next to him. Patrick pushed to sitting, gave Midas a vigorous scratching between the ears, and let the sheets cover the scars on his left thigh. The ones on his chest stared back at him in the mirror on the wall opposite the makeshift bed. He'd told his sister, Raina, it was a stupid spot for a mirror. He'd have to move it. Couldn't wake up every morning looking at the mess he had become.

The phone rang two more times before Midas barked. Patrick reached over and picked it up.

"What took you so long?" Raina didn't wait for him to speak. "First night in a new old house go all right?"

"I guess." Patrick yawned and finger-combed his short, brown hair, scratched at the scant beard framing his jaw and lips.

"Were you sleeping?"

"That is what people do at this hour on a Sunday, Raina."

"People who want to waste the day maybe, but not me and not you."

"Why not me?" Patrick stretched out his legs again and considered staying in bed for the rest of his life. Only thoughts of the dream had him peeling back the sheets and rising from the mattresses. Midas hopped down and waited at the bedroom door, his long black tail swishing along the floor.

"Because you have a few boxes to unpack and a willing volunteer to help you," Raina said. "I'm heading over with coffee and muffins so get your ass up."

"My ass is up."

"It wouldn't have been if I didn't call you."

"Don't be annoying."

"I think what you mean to say is, 'Thank you, all loving and perfect sister.' Right?"

"Sure."

Patrick pressed his feet to the cool wood floor and stood. He walked to the window in the bedroom he was using until he finished remodeling the master bedroom. Yawning, he peered out to the sprawling woods around the house. Lush and green from basking in the August sun, the trees offered a barrier between Patrick and the small Vermont town of Burnam. This fifty-acre plot of land was his sanctuary, and he had tons of ideas on how to make it his own version of Eden.

"What time are you coming?" he asked.

"Now. Put on some pants."

Raina hung up, and Patrick cursed at her impulsiveness. It was the one thing he both loved and hated about his baby sister. She had convinced him to move to Vermont from Rhode Island and take a job at the local fire department with one fanciful suggestion. A good thing. She had urged him out of bed this morning with one pushy order. Not a good thing.

And now he had to dig out some pants.

****

Gini Claremont held her camera steady as a hummingbird hovered over a honeysuckle bloom. These little guys were tricky to capture on film, but she'd been stalking the bird for nearly thirty minutes now. No sense in giving up.

She waited until the bird was absorbed in collecting nectar. After brushing her honey blond hair out of her face, Gini focused the camera lens so the bird was sharp and clear. She snapped photos from every angle, then the bird darted off in search of something more interesting. Some of the pictures ought to be good enough to send to *Leaf*, a nature magazine she did freelance work for from time to time.

Something furry rubbed against Gini's bare feet. She found Saber, her Maine Coon cat, weaving between her ankles. As Gini kneeled, Saber's puffy, striped tail tickled her skin when he jumped into her lap, and his large paws kneaded the denim covering her thigh.

"I've got tons of pictures of you, Saber. Don't be such a ham." Gini scratched under the cat's chin until his eyes became slits and a deep purr rumbled in his throat. He hopped down to the grass and stretched out all his limbs at once.

"That must have felt nice." Gini stood and raised her hands above her head. She reached skyward with her palms while pressing her feet deeper into the grass. "Not as graceful as you, Saber, but I think it had the same effect."

Gini turned toward the barn and put her camera on the shelf in the tack room. Moon, her all white

4

Andalusian, poked her head out of the stall. It only took a minute for Nyx, Gini's solid black Azteca, to do the same.

"Good morning, gals." Gini opened both stalls, and the horses meandered out to sniff and nudge her. They hung around long enough to eat the carrots she offered, then both horses trotted to the lower field for some lazy Sunday grazing.

"Breakfast. A good idea. What do you say, Saber?"

Gini grabbed her camera and headed back to the rustic farmhouse that once belonged to her grandmother. It was home—safe haven—to her now. With fresh coats of paint, electrical improvements, and appliance upgrades, Gini had managed to keep the country charm of her grandmother's decorating but add modern conveniences. In the kitchen now, she pulled open the stainless steel refrigerator and extracted a grapefruit. She sliced it in half, wrapped one half in plastic wrap, and returned that half to the refrigerator.

"When are they going to make grapefruits for one, Saber?"

As she cut the fruit into segments, Saber jumped up to the counter and tilted his head at her.

"Yes, I suppose I could have gotten a cat that ate grapefruit. Be better to have a man—a tall, sexy one—who ate grapefruit."

Saber let out a loud meow and hopped off the counter. He sauntered away with his tail flicking back and forth in annoyance.

"Sorry," Gini called, but the cat did not reappear. "So touchy. Maybe you *are* a human man, Saber." She laughed at her own joke and finished her grapefruit half.

With a whole Sunday stretching out before her, Gini was eager to get out to the south garden. She'd been so busy taking pictures at graduations, weddings, and family reunions this summer she hadn't been able to spend the time she usually did in that garden. Cardinals and jays would finish off her blueberries if she didn't get out there and pick some soon. Her father had been bugging her for tomatoes.

"Salad's not a salad without my Gini's tomatoes," he'd said last week.

Smiling at the look in her father's eyes as he thought about fresh garden tomatoes, Gini went out to the potting shed and gathered a basket, clippers, and a shovel. The path to the south garden was trimmed with wild violets, so purple in the August heat. The breeze carried the scent of the lavender growing around the fringe of the fruit and vegetable patch. Inhaling, Gini let the tranquility surround her. Let it keep any tension away.

No angry thoughts here. Angry thoughts were dangerous. Angry thoughts weren't allowed.

Gini lost herself in weeding, trimming, collecting. With dirt caked under her fingernails, she hauled a full basket back to the house. She headed up the back porch stairs but stopped when tires rolling along the gravel driveway sounded behind her.

"Hey, Gini." Jonah, her brother, smiled from the open window of his Mustang convertible. He hopped out without opening the car door and took the heavy basket from Gini before she could stop him.

"What are you doing here?" Gini held open the porch door, and Jonah scooted in.

"Thought we could get in a ride. Not too hot this morning. Horses shouldn't mind." Jonah dumped the basket on the counter by the sink. He automatically washed the fruits and vegetables. Gini couldn't understand why he hadn't landed himself a smart gal to settle down with yet.

That wasn't true. She knew why. Smart gals didn't marry firefighters. They drooled and lusted after firefighters, but didn't marry them. Too risky. Too many things could take a firefighter husband away from you. Gini had watched her mother worry about her father too many times to count. She'd once asked her mother why she'd married her father.

"He's my soul mate," her mother had said. "That overrules the danger of losing him."

Gini didn't see how that was possible. Best to stay away from firefighters. Go for a safe office man. Only office men in Burnam were a rarity. Most of the guys she knew were firefighters or some other brand of reckless male.

She was better off alone anyway.

"A ride is a perfect idea," Gini said. "I'll go round up Moon and Nyx."

"Great." Jonah grinned, looking so much like their father. "I'll meet you out there after I finish washing these."

Nodding, Gini went outside. On a short whistle, Moon and Nyx galloped back up to the barn. They cooperated as she saddled them both and led them to the trail that snaked through the woods on the west side of her property.

Jonah did his best cowboy swagger over to Gini and the horses. By the time he tipped his imaginary ten-gallon hat, Gini was nearly on all fours laughing. Could always count on Jonah to keep her dark thoughts at bay.

If it weren't for her brother—her entire family really—life would have been difficult. Impossible even.

Chapter Two

"Come in, Barre." Chief Warner gestured to a chair in front of his desk. Maple with a block of walnut where the legs met the top. Patrick thumbed a rounded corner of the desk as he sat. Couldn't help himself. He'd worked with maple before. Good and solid. Maybe he'd make his kitchen cabinets out of maple. Maple trees constituted a large portion of the forest surrounding his property. Only seemed fitting to use the hardwood in his remodeling.

"You settled in on that chunk of land up there?" Chief Warner asked.

"Good enough. Yesterday my sister helped me unpack the few items I brought with me to Vermont." More like *made* him unpack. He would have been content to live out of his perfectly organized and labeled boxes for a few weeks, but Raina wouldn't hear of it.

"It'll be too easy for you to load these boxes back into your truck and go back to Rhode Island," she'd said. "If you unpack, you're more likely to stay."

"I'm staying, Raina."

She'd looked at him for a long, silent moment. "I hope so, Patrick. I've missed you."

Raina was one of the few people who could make Patrick smile. Really smile.

"Missed you too."

And before he'd known what was happening, Raina had wrapped her slender arms around his waist and squeezed as if she were ten years old again and Patrick was sixteen.

He'd protected her. Saved her. But Julianne. Julianne was a different story.

"You're a certified career firefighter, right?" Chief Warner's voice brought Patrick back to the present.

"Yes, sir. Ten years with the Providence Fire Department, four of which I worked consulting with the police as fire investigator." Putting out fires had kept him busy, but helping solve fire-related crimes or determining how a fire had started had challenged him.

"Got your own dog too? Trained and everything?" Chief Warner glanced outside his office window at Patrick's gray pickup truck where one large black German Shepherd sat in the bed, its muzzle resting on the tailgate.

"That's right. Midas is certified as well."

Chief Warner glanced at the file folder of papers on his desk. "That dog's resume is almost as impressive as yours. I think the Burnam Fire Department is getting a good deal with the two of you."

He stood and offered his hand to Patrick. With a tight-gripped handshake, Chief Warner nodded at Patrick's humble silence.

"We're a small outfit, but the only fire department in the area who has full-time firefighters. The rest operate with volunteers. Do a mighty fine job, but we're expected to do even better work. I think you'll like it here, Barre."

"Hope so, sir." Patrick stood and followed the chief to the door.

"Claremont!" Chief Warner hollered into the vehicle bay. A tall, athletically built man with wavy blond hair looked up from where he was replacing air cylinders on the oxygen tanks.

"Yeah, Chief?"

"Jonah Claremont, this is Patrick Barre, aka

The New Guy," Chief Warner said. "Pretend you know what you're doing around this place, Claremont, and give him a tour."

Though sarcasm laced the chief's words, the grins on both men's faces were playful, teasing. Patrick had heard about fire stations where the fighters were like brothers. He'd never experienced the sensation himself. Not because the guys in Providence weren't nice and hadn't tried, but because he preferred to keep to himself. Maybe here things would be different though. If he let them be.

"Grab that good-looking dog of yours, Barre. He's earned a right to Claremont's tour as well." Chief Warner gave him a wave as he disappeared back into his office.

"That dog's yours?" Jonah asked. "I've never seen an all black German Shepherd. He looks like a wolf."

Patrick followed Jonah to the station's parking lot. As soon as they reached the truck, Midas stood on all fours and whimpered.

"We're coming for you, buddy." Jonah opened the tailgate and the dog jumped down. "What's his name?"

"Midas." Patrick watched as Midas licked every square inch of Jonah's face.

Jonah chuckled when the dog pawed at his shoulders almost knocking him over.

"Midas, *asseyez*." Patrick pulled on the dog's collar until Midas sat on his haunches. "Sorry. He's not usually so…friendly."

"It's okay. I'm an animal guy. He probably smells my sister's horses or cat on me. Was by her place this morning for a ride then helped her fix a broken barn door. You handy, Patrick?"

"You could say that." Patrick thought of all the woodworking he'd done during his lifetime. Furniture, sheds, houses. He'd tried building it all.

He couldn't wait to dive in on his house. It had potential. A little rundown and outdated, but nothing he couldn't handle.

"Good," Jonah said. "You can trust a guy who knows how to use a hammer. I mean really use it, not just carry it around in his tool belt, you know?"

Patrick supposed it was a good way to measure a man. If his own gauging system were any good, he'd say this Jonah guy was all right.

"This way." Jonah led Patrick back to the station. Midas trailed after them both, stopping only to sniff at random spots on the floor.

"How long have you been with the Burnam Fire Department?" Patrick asked. Small talk made him uncomfortable, but he figured the situation called for it.

"Pretty much forever." Jonah looked back and grinned as he took the stair steps two at a time. "My daddy was chief here before Warner. I grew up in this station. Lost my virginity in the parking lot right out back."

He turned down a narrow hallway that dumped into a tidy kitchen area. The walls were knotted pine and smelled of outdoors. Patrick breathed deeply, feeling oddly at home in the space. Pine cabinets hung above and below a dark green countertop. Stainless steel appliances broke up the golden wood that flowed from wall to wall. A long, sturdy table with chunky legs and benches on both sides sat in the middle of the room.

"This here's our dining quarters, obviously. My mother sees that the fridge is always packed and sometimes, if we've all been good, she'll make us a home-cooked meal. When we can, all us fighters sit together, as long as there's no fire burning somewhere, and have us a family-like banquet. Lots of nice guys work here. You'll see."

Jonah's blue eyes softened when he talked about

the fighters. "Suppose you had some nice guys back where you came from. Where was that anyway?"

"Providence." Patrick shifted his weight from foot to foot. The guys in Rhode Island had always been kind to him, but he hadn't gotten to know any of them on a personal level. Hadn't ever eaten dinner family-style with them. Hadn't even considered it.

"Spent some time visiting in Rhode Island," Jonah said. "Nice beaches. Good frozen lemonade."

Patrick laughed and the sound startled him. It had slipped through his lips with no effort at all. He cleared his throat and followed Jonah.

With more small talk and stops to introduce some of the other fighters, Jonah prodded Patrick and Midas into the dorm then moved onto the workout room, followed by the classroom, equipment storage, and vehicle bays. Every area was spotless and organized. Just the way Patrick liked it.

When Jonah showed him the lavatory complete with showers, Patrick kept walking, pretending he wanted to see the rest of the station. He'd managed to never use the station's showers in Providence, and he planned to do the same in Burnam. His body was his business, and he'd stick to cleaning it in the privacy of his own home where no one could judge him.

"It's not enormous," Jonah said, "but it's functional and efficient. We get to the emergencies in record speed and always have what we need. That's the point."

"Agreed." Patrick turned in a small circle below the fire pole Jonah had insisted on using to get back to ground level.

"You starting today?" Jonah asked. Midas nosed at his hands until Jonah gave the dog a back rub.

"Tomorrow," Patrick said. "Midas and I need to check in with the police department today."

"Well, I guess I'll see you bright and early tomorrow morning then." Jonah held out a hand. "Hope the tour was helpful."

Patrick shook Jonah's hand. "It was. Thank you."

"No problem." Jonah bent to get eye level with Midas. "Pleasure meeting you, doggy. I look forward to working with you. Both of you." He glanced up to Patrick.

"*Secouez*, Midas." On that command, Midas lifted a paw to shake hands, and Jonah laughed as he accepted it.

"He must rake in the ladies for you," Jonah said as he stood.

Patrick hesitated, not sure what to say. Jonah didn't give him the chance to respond. Instead, he motioned Patrick over to the back doors of the station and pointed.

"See that shiny, red Mustang over there? The convertible? That's how I rake in the ladies." Jonah wiggled his eyebrows. "I'll take you for a drive soon. You'll see." He elbowed Patrick and again the urge to laugh surprised Patrick.

"Unless you've already got a lady," Jonah said.

Patrick shook his head and snapped his fingers at Midas, who immediately gave up sniffing at Jonah's boots. "See you tomorrow, Jonah."

"Later."

Outside, the summer air was motionless. Patrick opened the door to his truck and let Midas scamper over to the passenger seat. After climbing in himself, he spent a few moments hanging on to the steering wheel in the suffocating heat. How was it that he'd only spent about thirty minutes in that station, but felt more at home than he'd ever felt in Rhode Island?

Shaking his head, Patrick started the truck and headed to the police station down the street. He had a meeting with the detective in charge of fire-related cases that he didn't want to be late for. Something about this silly little town had him wanting to make a good first impression. Never concerned him before. He was good at his job. He knew that. But for some reason, he had the urge to be better.

****

Gini held her breath as she did whenever she developed pictures in the darkroom at her studio in town. Something about watching an image appear on the photo paper that was magic to her. Always had been. Each picture, even though she'd been the one to take it with her camera, was a surprise, a gift.

She smiled as the little hummingbird emerged on the photo in her hands now. Its body hovered outside the honeysuckle bloom, needle-like beak poised above the petals. Her patience in capturing this shot had paid off. The editors at *Leaf* would love this picture.

A series of four short knocks on the darkroom door made Gini clip the almost completely visible picture to the drying line. She turned off the equipment she'd been using and opened the door.

"Sorry to bug you," Gini's assistant and general best friend, Haddy Thetford, said, "but Chief Warner called and said...yes." Haddy's eyes opened wide as her lips turned up in a huge grin.

"Yes? He said *yes*?" Gini clapped her hands then grabbed on to Haddy's arms. The two of them square-danced back to Gini's office. Giggles echoed off the high ceilings and wide-planked wood floors.

"I didn't think he would go for the idea," Haddy said.

"Me neither. Did you see the way his brows furrowed down to his nose when I suggested the notion?" Gini chuckled as she pictured the chief's face.

"I think it's the cause that got to him. He's got

three dogs and four cats. Says they belong to his kids, but I've seen him in town walking the dogs. They're as much his family as his wife and kids are. Maybe more so." Haddy sunk into the leather reading chair across from Gini's desk.

"A calendar of hunky firefighters is the perfect way to raise money for the Burnam Animal Shelter. It's going to stir things up in this sleepy town." Gini patted herself on the back and bowed as if in front of a crowd.

"You are a genius," Haddy said. "I kneel at your feet. Figuratively, of course. This skirt is new, and I'm not about to ruin it worshipping your brilliance."

Gini grabbed a sheet of paper off her desk, crumpled it, and tossed it at Haddy.

"I bet you'll want to be involved in every aspect of this assignment though, won't you?" Gini pointed an index finger at Haddy.

"Hell, yeah. If you think I'd miss a chance to put sexy firefighters in seductive poses while you take longer than necessary to photograph them, you, my friend, are sadly mistaken."

"Okay, we need to plan the shoots so no one is inconvenienced, and Chief Warner doesn't regret his decision."

Haddy grabbed a notebook off the end of Gini's desk. Pen in hand, she wrote down everything Gini said. When they were done, they had a solid course of action mapped out.

"I'll go by the station tomorrow and talk to the chief," Gini said. "I'd like to have the fighters come to my farm for the photo shoot. Between you and me we've got plenty of animals so we can play up the firefighters-are-compassionate-to-animals angle."

"My bird, dogs, and bunnies would love the chance to pose with some hunks," Haddy said. "Come to think of it, *I'd* love the chance to pose with some hunks. Maybe we can take a few extra shots, ones that aren't necessarily calendar appropriate?" Haddy licked her lips.

"You and my brother think so much alike." Gini let out a long breath. If it wasn't Jonah making a lewd but funny comment, it was Haddy.

"Your brother is an outstanding guy," Haddy said. "Deliciously outstanding."

"When are you going to come out and say you want him?" Gini laughed at the way Haddy's mouth dropped open. "You know you do. I think you two would make—"

"Was that the door?" Haddy popped up from her seat and scurried out of the office.

Left alone, Gini shook her head. Though teasing Haddy was fun, who was she to tell someone else how to handle their love life? She didn't know the first thing about relationships. She had her farm and her pictures. That's all she needed.

That's all she could have.

Chapter Three

"Here comes trouble." Jonah angled his chin to the station's front doors where a woman—perhaps an angel—with long, wavy hair the same color as Jonah's entered.

Patrick nearly dropped the hose he was inspecting for splits. He fumbled around, got tangled, then relaxed long enough to set the hose down without looking like an idiot. He hoped.

The woman's smile lit up the station, and her legs, impossibly long and shapely, balanced on a pair of sandals that crisscrossed leather straps over manicured feet. The slim-fitting tank dress she wore made her eyes sparkle a deep shade of blue. A simple necklace of small white seashells gave her a carefree summer look. Patrick could almost smell the ocean as he looked at her.

Stop looking. He forced his attention back to the hose at his feet.

"Hey, sis," Jonah said. "Looking good."

Patrick glanced over in time to see Jonah spin this goddess around in a circle. When she laughed, his heart pounded in his chest. The dimples gracing the smooth skin of her cheeks captivated him. He actually took a step away from the hose and closer to her before he caught himself.

What's wrong with you? Patrick turned toward the equipment storage room. He'd get some supplies and continue with his task. He'd focus.

"Patrick, wait up," Jonah called.

Patrick swallowed, his throat desert dry, and

turned around. A crowd of fighters had come to surround the woman now. Patrick's jaw tightened as the men laughed with her. Some of them even touched her, and she smiled along with them, teased, flirted.

And then her eyes connected with his, and she nudged playfully past the wall of fighters to come to him.

Patrick flicked his gaze to Jonah, who stood right in front of him now.

"Gini, come here," Jonah said. When she sidled up next to Jonah, he slung an arm around her shoulders and ruffled her hair.

What did that hair feel like? Silk probably. Patrick stuffed his hands in his pockets afraid he'd try to touch the golden waves.

"Knock it off, Jonah." Her voice was music, perfectly suited to that jolly expression on her flawless face. She edged Jonah away with her hip.

"Patrick Barre, this is my older sister, Gini Claremont." Jonah barely sidestepped the punch Gini launched into his shoulder.

"I told you to quit calling me your 'older' sister," she said. "It's not necessary. We're only two years apart." She turned that smiling face to Patrick and held out a slender hand. "Nice to meet you, Patrick. You sure you want to join this band of uncivilized brutes?"

Patrick stared at that outstretched hand, let his gaze travel up that tanned forearm to the subtly sculpted bicep and finally, to the bare shoulder where curls of sun-streaked hair feathered over her soft skin. It had to be soft. It just had to be.

Gini's wiggling fingers snapped Patrick out of his dream. He took her hand and confirmed what he'd been thinking. She was an angel. No doubt about it. When her fingers closed around his hand and she shook lightly, Patrick had a wild notion to stop time and hold her hand forever. Stupid notion because now he wanted to do so much more than hold her hand. That's why he dropped her hand and took three steps back to put some distance between his hormones and her perfection.

Hormones. That's what it was. He'd been alone for a long time, but he was still a man with needs. She was a beautiful woman. Only natural he'd be attracted, stirred up, by the sight of her. It would pass.

"Nice to meet you too." Patrick jammed his hands back into his pockets, but leaned against the wall beside him. Casual. He could be casual.

"Patrick's a fire investigator," Jonah told Gini. "Got an amazing dog around here somewhere too." Jonah scanned the vehicle bay looking for Midas.

Patrick pointed a finger under the stairs where Midas was curled up. As if knowing people were talking about him, the dog's head popped up. He rose to all fours and scuttled out from his sleeping spot. Once Midas was in full view, Gini let out a breathy sigh.

"He's absolutely gorgeous." Her eyes flashed to Patrick for a moment, then she walked over to Midas. She gracefully bent, offering a bonus view of one toned thigh, and cupped the dog's muzzle in her hand. After setting her oversized purse down, she let both hands rub Midas from ears to tail. The dog flopped down onto his back and made little satisfied doggy noises as Gini scratched his belly.

Patrick watched, wishing she'd give him some attention like that. Jonah elbowing him in the gut snapped him out of his fantasy.

"Knew that dog could rake in the ladies. What did I tell you?" Jonah went to join his sister in spoiling Midas.

Gini let Jonah take over and rose to her feet. As she walked back to Patrick, he watched her eyes comb down the length of him. What did she see? What would she think of what she couldn't see?

"You just move here?" Gini asked.

Patrick nodded, watched her chew on her bottom lip. If she thought she was going to get to know him, she was wrong. He couldn't allow it. She wouldn't like what she got to know anyway.

"From where?" Her hands tightened on the strap of her purse.

"Rhode Island."

Her fingers fascinated him. Though they were clean and her nails obviously cared for, her hands also looked used as if they'd seen some hard work. His own hands were a total disaster. Calloused and scarred—not as bad as other parts of him, of course—his hands had been splintered, sliced, pricked, skinned, and once, broken from pinkie fingertip to wrist. He flexed his left hand thinking about that incident.

"I went to school in Rhode Island. RISD, Rhode Island School of Design," she said. "Master of Fine Arts in Photography." She dug around in that mammoth purse and extracted a complicated camera.

Every muscle in Patrick's body tensed at the sight of that camera. He hated, no, loathed pictures. He always looked like a miserable prick in photographs. Something about having that lens zoom in on him made him think it could see through his clothes. To what was hidden underneath them. To what he tried so hard to forget.

"Ah, the more attractive Claremont." Chief Warner broke the silence Gini's camera had caused.

"Hey," Jonah said. "I heard that."

"Sorry, kid, but it's true. Your parents definitely gave all the beauty to this one. Don't you think so, Barre?" Chief Warner asked.

The corner of Gini's mouth curled up as she

waited for Patrick's response. He was in a sticky spot, and she knew it.

"Indeed." He hoped that was a safe answer. Judging by the fact that the dimple deepened in Gini's cheek, Patrick assumed she approved of his response.

"Does that make me the smart one?" Jonah asked.

"No, it makes you the ugly one." Gini stuck her tongue out at her brother and sent the chief into a fit of laughter. She let Chief Warner lead the way to his office.

As the door closed, Patrick let out the breath he'd been holding. The breath that was keeping him from going to pieces.

"My mother wouldn't say I was the ugly one." Jonah cuffed Patrick on the shoulder and went back to his duties.

Patrick studied Jonah for a moment. Jonah and Gini had no idea what ugly looked like. He could show them. He wouldn't, but he could.

****

Inside Chief Warner's office, Gini unrolled her plan of attack on the calendar idea. The chief did a great deal of nodding and smiling. Encouraged, Gini filled in all the details hoping she and Haddy hadn't left out anything important.

"So I can photo the fighters in rounds of two so I'm not leaving you understaffed at any given time," she said.

"Sounds okay to me." Chief Warner leaned back in his chair. "Your daddy came to see me the other day."

Gini's shoulders tensed. "He did?"

The chief nodded. "Told me how important the animal shelter is to you. I mean, I knew you volunteered there. Heck, everybody knows that about you. But, I didn't know pet therapy is what helped you with your...your, ah...you know, situation."

Gini hated that the chief knew about her situation. She hadn't wanted to tell him, but once her daddy retired as chief he insisted they sit the new chief down and explain it all to him. It was the safe, responsible thing to do, her daddy had said. And he'd been right. Damn him, he was right. Didn't make sitting there across from the chief any less uncomfortable though. The way he was looking at her with a mix of sympathy, curiosity, and a touch of fear had her feeling like a monster.

She'd kept it in check though. Hadn't had an incident in nearly ten years. She kept things light and fun. Didn't get involved with people who pissed her off. Meditated, practiced yoga, gardened, worked with the animals at the shelter and on her farm. All of that kept her balanced, peaceful. She loved her work, her clients, her assignments. Never had an angry thought at the studio or behind her camera lens.

Still, the possibility was there. Always lurking beneath her calm, centered exterior. The chance of her temper rising and...

Gini shook her head to chase away the negative vibes. She cleared her throat and said, "I'd do anything to help out the shelter. They've been good to me over there. Giving me my own keys, letting me work and visit there whenever I want. I think this calendar will pull in a lot of money. Money that can go into expanding the shelter, adding more full-time vets and a clinic perhaps."

"A good cause, Gini. A real good cause. I'm sure all the men will be willing volunteers, but I haven't told them yet. Figure they'd be more likely to say yes to a sexy little thing like you than an old geezer like me."

Gini let the "sexy little thing" comment go. After

all, hadn't she worn this dress—one she knew made her eyes electric—to be more persuasive? To get the men in a generous sort of mood? A questionable tactic, but Haddy had talked her into using it. It had already worked its magic when she'd come into the station. The compliments had flown around the vehicle bay like moths to a bright light.

Smirking, Gini stood. "I hope they all agree. You've only got twelve of them, and I need all twelve to make the calendar." She paused and sent the chief a grin. "Unless you want to pose."

"My posing days are over, sweetie." He patted his generous stomach. "Since I've been behind this desk, I've let the years catch up with me."

She shook hands with the chief, thanked him, and stepped back into the vehicle bay. Chief Warner was right behind her. He whistled loudly, causing her to wince and cover her ear.

"Gather around, men. Miss Gini here has a favor to ask all of you."

Jonah was the first to stand in front of her. He winked encouragingly. Gini had already discussed the calendar with him over coffee in her kitchen this morning. Of course he was all for the opportunity to get shirtless and be photographed. She knew he wouldn't have any objections. He'd offered several posing options as he fixed her barn door, some of them involving exposing a tease of butt crack. The two of them had laughed until tears ran down their cheeks.

Gini waited until all the fighters were in range. She scanned the assembly and noticed the new fighter, Patrick, at the back of the crowd, hands in his pockets again. She judged he had to be over six feet tall, and every inch appeared muscled and fit. His dark hair and beard were neatly trimmed, his navy uniform pants and polo shirt spotless. Something in the broody hazel eyes told her there was more than a superhero firefighter there.

She offered him a smile, and Patrick obliged with a slight nod of his head. Something also told her he didn't smile much. That it took a big effort to get him to smile.

"Well, fellas," she began, "I come to ask for your help."

"I'll help you with whatever you want. Whatever you need," one of the fighters called.

"William, we've been over this," Gini said. "I don't date married men."

Laughter circulated among the men until Gini wagged a finger at all of them. Like schoolchildren, they hushed and gave her their full attention.

"I'm looking to raise money for the Burnam Animal Shelter. To do so, I want to photograph all you sexy guys. Yes, even you, Chuck." She smirked at the fighter standing nearest to her, who narrowed his eyes and held up a fist, pretending he was going to sock her.

"I want to make a calendar, sell it, and give the proceeds to the shelter. We'll have a calendar-signing event when it's finished, and women will drool all over you for twelve solid months. What do you say? Who's with me?"

Hands flew up in the air, and Gini applauded. "I knew I could count on you, my heroes. I'll set up a schedule of when each of you will head over to my farm and bare your lovely chests for photographing." She was about to say more when Patrick slipping from the group caught her attention.

"More info to follow, boys." She weaved through them and stood over Patrick who'd crouched down over the fire hose snaked out on the floor. "Don't want to hear the details?"

"Nope." He dragged the hose over to the nearest truck. The muscles in his arms flexed, and Gini was mesmerized for a moment. She'd put his picture in

July, her birth month. Definitely.

"Why not? I'm—"

"Not going to take my picture," Patrick finished. He busied himself with the hose.

"What? Come on. I need all twelve of you for the calendar." Gini put her hands on her hips.

"You'll figure something out," he said. "I don't photograph well."

"Doubt that," Gini said before she could stop herself. Toying with the strap on her purse again, she tried another tactic. "You like animals, don't you, Patrick?" She angled her head toward Midas, who had taken up residence under the stairs again.

"Sure, but—"

"Then you'd succumb to a little harmless picture-taking to help them out, wouldn't you?"

"Look. I'll give you a donation if you'd like, but no pictures." He neatened the hose he'd been loading.

"Are you serious?" Gini couldn't believe he was refusing.

"Totally serious."

Gini touched a hand to his forearm and he froze. "Please?" she asked.

"I. Don't. Do. Pictures. End of story, Blondie." He peeled her hand off his arm and turned back to the truck. "You've got enough willing guinea pigs for your little project. Leave me alone."

****

Patrick could actually hear her mouth drop open though he didn't turn around to see. Instead, he squeezed his eyes shut and sent a silent prayer of forgiveness to whoever might be listening. Not that he believed anyone answered prayers. Not his anyway.

He hated pulling out the bad guy, but he'd do it to keep her off his back. Had to.

He waited for Gini to walk away, but she didn't.

Just stood there behind him instead. Only when someone shouted, "Fire!" did Patrick turn around. Gini's face was white, all the healthy blush in her cheeks drained away.

When Patrick saw one of the bushes lining the walkway to the fire station burning furiously, he ran past Gini to help extinguish the blaze. Once the flames were doused, blackened twigs were all that remained of the shrub.

Patrick looked up to see Jonah guiding Gini toward a black SUV parked at the curb. Her beautiful legs wobbled as Jonah appeared to be supporting most of her weight. He was murmuring something to his sister when he settled her into the passenger seat. Jonah hopped into the driver's seat and sped away.

"Know anything about landscaping, Barre?" Chief Warner tugged Patrick back toward the bush.

"Yeah," Patrick said. "I know bushes don't burst into flames all on their own."

"Around here, kid, sometimes they do. Go with Chuck, pick out another bush, and replace this one."

Patrick bit back the dozens of questions circling his mind. Somebody had a secret here. He knew something about secrets.

Chapter Four

"He made me so mad." Gini brushed the hair out of her face as she gazed out the car window.

"I know." Jonah's hands tightened on the steering wheel. "I'm sorry, Gini."

"Not your fault, Jonah." Gini touched a hand to her brother's elbow.

Jonah shook his head. "No. I should have tested Patrick out better. He seemed so nice. Easy going. I should have made sure before introducing him to you."

"You can't screen everyone. Besides, I'm the older sister, remember? I'm supposed to take care of you."

"And you do. We take care of each other." Jonah sent her a quick glance and a smile.

He was right. Her entire family took care of each other as if it were the only job they had. Family came first. There wasn't anything she wouldn't do for her parents or Jonah. They had done so much for her through the years. Tried to understand her situation. Kept her calm and happy. Put her back together when things went to Hell. Lied to keep the curious from discovering what she was capable of.

Gini counted the handful of small shops lining Pinecrest Avenue. One bookstore, charmingly cozy. One café, sandwiches and salads. One flower shop, lilies in full bloom. One hardware store, nuts and bolts. One bakery, her mother's pride and joy.

Gradually, Gini settled her stirring emotions. Seriously, what had Patrick done that was so bad?

He didn't want his picture taken. That was fair. He had a right to refuse. But why did he refuse? And why was he such a jerk about it? Did he actually call her *Blondie*?

Her stomach burned as the tone in Patrick's voice echoed in her head. She went back to counting shops as Jonah turned her SUV onto Maple Grove Court. Now she counted houses, and with each exhale, she released the anger. Let it seep out of her and vanish into the atmosphere. By the time they pulled onto her parents' driveway, she was centered again.

"I have to get back to the station," Jonah said, "but you shouldn't be alone or go to work yet."

Gini cupped her brother's cheek. "Once again, you have come to my rescue. I don't know what I'd do without you, Jonah."

"Me neither. You're such a handful." Jonah jutted his cheek toward her and accepted the kiss she dropped there. "Get Ma or Pop to take you to the studio, and I'll pick you up there later so you can have your car back."

Gini slid out of the car. She waved as Jonah backed out of the driveway. He saluted her and drove out of sight around the corner. Gini stood on her parents' front walkway for a few minutes until the door opened behind her.

"Gini?"

"Hi, Daddy." Gini turned to face her father. The look in Walter Claremont's pale blue eyes told her he already knew what had happened.

"Chief Warner called."

Probably wants you to keep me on a leash. Gini toyed with a pebble on the walkway with her sandal.

"Come in here, honey." Walter wrapped his arm around her shoulder and prodded her inside the house.

"Where's Mama?" Gini accepted the chair her

father dragged out from the kitchen table.

"She stopped at the bakery. You know how she still likes to get her hands on the dough from time to time." Walter smiled as he poured them both glasses of lemonade and sat across from her.

Gini took a long swig, and the remaining residue of the morning's disaster washed away.

"What happened?" Her father rested his hand atop hers.

"Nothing, Daddy. It was foolish. I let someone get under my skin."

"Who?"

"A new firefighter, Patrick Barre." She watched Walter's hand curl into a fist. "Down, Daddy. It was my fault, not his."

"Anyone who upsets my girl deserves a good beating."

"No, no. I let my guard down. He seemed pleasant enough, but when I mentioned taking his picture, he refused. Strongly."

"Why wouldn't he want his picture taken?" Her father's eyebrows lowered. "Maybe he's in trouble with the law or something."

"I don't think so. Probably wouldn't be a firefighter if he was a criminal or in the witness protection program. He'd pick something lower profile to blend in better."

Walter nodded. "Suppose that's true. You'd better stay away from him. You've gone a long time without a—"

"Flare up."

Her father's wry smile made her heart ache.

"Happy thoughts, baby. Happy thoughts." He patted her hand and finished the last of his lemonade.

Happy thoughts. Right. She could do happy thoughts. They had gotten her this far, and she wasn't about to let some smug jerk who didn't "do" pictures make her lose control. She'd avoid him. Simple.

****

Patrick wiped the sweat from his forehead and studied the newly planted bush. Chuck had gone off to get the hose to water it. Looking at the work they'd done, no one would ever know the former resident of this particular spot had been charred to an untimely death.

What the hell had happened? Patrick leaned his chin on the handle of the shovel as he thought back to the morning. Jonah's hot sister visits. She unveils her ridiculous calendar fund-raising plan. She gets all over his case about having his picture taken. A bush explodes into flames. Jonah escorts shaky sister off the grounds. Patrick was missing something in this whole scenario, but he couldn't for the life of him figure out what.

"Let her rip!" Chuck called back to the station. A gush of water rained down on the new bush. The soil around it was drenched in no time, and the branches splayed open.

Patrick waved and the fighter manning the hose cut the water. Droplets dripped from the branches, and the earth had that wet, summer sun smell. He breathed it in and put thoughts of Gini aside. That's where such thoughts belonged anyway. Aside. Way aside.

As he turned to follow Chuck into the station, Patrick noticed the black SUV shooting to the back parking lot. He'd caught a glimpse of Jonah in the driver's seat. The passenger side was empty.

"All set out there, boys?" Chief Warner asked.

"Yes, sir," Patrick said. "What hap—"

"Good, good," the chief interrupted. "Dorm and kitchen cleaning duty is yours, New Guy. Hop to it."

Patrick opened his mouth, but caught the tension in the chief's jaw. "Yes, sir." As he climbed the stairs, Jonah came in through the back doors.

"Claremont, my office. Now," Chief Warner said.

"Look, Chief," Jonah began. "She didn't mean—"

"Office, son. Get."

Jonah threw up his hands and marched into the chief's office. The door closed and Patrick couldn't hear anymore. He was curious though. So curious.

Let it go, man. None of your business. He'd keep his distance from Jonah Claremont and his mysterious, annoying sister. He'd gone this long without close friends. He could go longer. Too bad. Jonah seemed like someone he wouldn't mind getting to know better. Whatever. He lived closer to Raina now. Family would have to be enough.

****

No better color in the world. Inferno orange. Vibrant and alive. She loved the flecks of yellow and red that chased each other through the blaze. Reaching higher, gaining strength, throwing a scorching heat that melted everything in its path.

Such power, such divine power. It filled her. Scared away the dark shadows threatening to swallow her at every turn. Nothing could touch her when a fire burned. It surrounded her, protected her, made her feel real. She was a candle, and without the flame, she was useless.

This particular fire flickered in time with her pulse. The smoky scent of old wood caressed her nose. Made her think of all those campfires she didn't enjoy as a child. Those campfires where her father told her she was a no good mistake. Told her the world wouldn't ever accept her. Never understand her.

He'd been right, but she was changing that. The fire made it possible. If she could cause such destruction, the world would have to notice. Have to deal with her. Have to try to stop her.

As if they could.

31

The warmth from this blaze reddened her cheeks. Couldn't get too close. Close was dangerous. Windows smashed with the pressure. Glass sprayed, a million heated shards catapulting into the cosmos. Walls crumbled. Family photographs curled and turned to ash. They'd rebuild, but that wouldn't stop the next fire from being born. Wouldn't stop the reverence they'd now have toward the strongest of the elements.

Fire was king and she its loyal subject.

****

The alarm echoed through the fire station and sent everyone into a flurry of action. Gear was donned, engines started, sirens sounded. Two quint trucks raced to Cloudson Drive where fire engulfed a raised ranch. Neighbors crowded the streets as they shook their heads and held their families close.

Patrick hopped out of the truck as soon as it screamed to a stop in front of the blaze. The heat blasted him, and he threw on his helmet, face mask, and air cylinders. He signaled to Jonah that he was going in. Jonah confirmed the signal and followed right behind him.

Dispatch had noted it was unknown whether or not the house was occupied. Patrick and Jonah had been assigned to find out. They broke some windows that hadn't already shattered to let some of the smoke out as they searched. The first floor was empty as was the second. Patrick found a door leading to the basement and when he opened it, a wide-eyed older woman met his scanning sweep.

"Get me out!" she screeched.

Patrick grabbed the tablecloth off her kitchen table. He doused it at the sink and threw it over the woman. Covering her face—always careful to cover their faces—he scooped the little grandmother up and bolted for the stairs. The front doors had been hacked away by other fighters and his path was

32

clear.

Outside, Patrick handed the lady off to a waiting paramedic. He ripped off his helmet and face mask.

"Ma'am, is there anyone else inside?" he asked.

The woman shook her head and covered her mouth with a shaky hand as she coughed. "N-no. My daughter and her family are at a friend's house."

Patrick nodded. "Okay. You're safe now. This nice paramedic will take you to the hospital. Tell them how to contact your family."

The woman clamped a bony hand onto Patrick's coat. She let loose another round of hacking before she could talk.

"Thank you. I could have died in there."

The color had returned to her face, and Patrick knew she was going to be okay. Probably wouldn't sleep for a while, but she'd pull through. She was safe and so was her family. That's all that mattered.

Patrick turned back toward the house. Fighters crawled around it like ants. The hoses were spraying full blast, and one truck's ladder had been extended to cut ventilation holes in the roof. Thick, black clouds of smoke plumed out of the holes, but most of the flames had been extinguished. Some of the fighters were pushing neighbors back from the scene, gently encouraging them to go home.

Jonah clapped Patrick on the back, his helmet wedged under his arm as Patrick's was.

"I was right about you," Jonah said.

"Excuse me?"

"You followed protocol in there like a pro. You stayed calm. I knew my first instincts about you were right." He walked off before Patrick could say anything.

If Jonah thought he knew him, he was mistaken. Hugely mistaken.

Chapter Five

"Suspicious." Patrick leaned his elbows against his truck as he examined his map and notes. He'd made an initial sweep of the burned raised ranch with Midas.

"How so?" Detective Mason Rivers patted the dog at his feet.

"I'll have to comb through it again," Patrick said, "but newspapers and cotton rags were stuffed under the back porch door." He tapped his meticulously drawn map of the site. "Midas definitely picked up a trail of gasoline leading into the house too."

Mason nodded. "Okay. I've called in our photographer to document the scene. Should be here any minute. Once that's taken care of you can bag up any evidence you think is relevant and we can have it tested."

"That'd be good." Patrick put his papers in the folder he'd brought and dropped it on the driver's seat of his truck. He turned to face the ashy remains of the house.

"Shame, isn't it?" Mason folded his arms across his chest. He angled his head at the skeleton of surviving beams and let his brown eyes settle on the blackened cherry tree at the corner of the house.

"Any fire is a shame," Patrick agreed. "Especially if it isn't an accident."

"What happened to the times when parents told their kids not to play with fire?" Mason shook his head.

"Like kids ever listened."

"True. Something seductive about fire to some people."

"She's a dangerous lover." Patrick shrugged and grabbed his notebook. "I'm going to interview some of the neighbors. See if they saw anything unusual."

"I'll go with you."

With Midas trotting ahead of them, Mason fell into step beside Patrick, but stopped when a car honked behind him. After turning around, he said, "The photographer's here. Let's hold up on questioning the neighbors until she's done."

Patrick turned around as well. His notebook dropped from his hands as he watched Gini get out of her SUV. She shouldered her camera strap and started to walk toward them. Patrick bent to pick up his notebook that Midas pawed at and when he stood, Gini froze.

What was that flitting across her face? Fear? Anger? Both? Patrick regretted the way he'd had to speak to her at the station, but he had to protect himself. No way he was going to take his shirt off for her stupid calendar. Didn't matter how fantastic she'd looked in that blue dress and those sandals. He wasn't going to give in. She'd think him grotesque once she saw what he was hiding under his shirt anyway. Definitely not picture-worthy.

"I think I'll get a head start on the neighbors," Patrick said. "Catch up with you later."

Before Mason could agree or disagree, Patrick nudged Midas and marched away from Gini, who had changed her course as well to head toward the house. He couldn't deny he had more questions for her than he did for the neighbors, but he'd made the decision to stay away from Gini Claremont. Planned on sticking to that decision. Apparently, she had come to a similar conclusion. The way she'd looked at him before turning toward the house told him she didn't want to see him either.

Made sense. He'd acted like a first class jackass to get her to drop the picture-taking request. He wouldn't want to be around him either. Not a great first impression but necessary. Calling her *Blondie* probably was over the top, but he couldn't take it back now.

For the next two hours, Patrick buried himself in conversations with the neighbors of Cloudson Drive. None of them said anything helpful. No one saw anything out of place. No suspicious people had been milling about that they'd noticed. The family who owned the house was a model family. No known enemies. He'd have to go through the house again and study the photos.

Photos Gini took. Hopefully, he could get the pictures from Mason. Back in Rhode Island, the photographer the Providence Police Department used had been an old man with a face like a squirrel. No nonsense and obsessed with capturing every facet of the fire scene. He certainly didn't have the legs Gini had.

Patrick let out a breath, disgusted about catching himself thinking about Gini's legs, and walked back to his truck. Both Gini and Mason were gone. Excellent. He fished around in his evidence collection kit and extracted a flashlight and some evidence bags. One more peek before it got too dark. He could review his map and notes at home tonight.

As he walked to the back of the house, Midas sniffing along the way, his cell phone buzzed in his pocket. Patrick pulled it out and read the text message Mason had left him.

PHOTOS TAKEN. CAN BAG EVIDENCE AT SCENE. MEET ME TOMORROW MORNING. MY OFFICE. WILL SEND COPIES OF PHOTOS WHEN GINI DEVELOPS.

When Gini develops. Why did that phrase have his mind wandering?

Didn't matter. He was on the job, and she had obviously done hers. After flipping the phone off, Patrick started at the back porch door where he'd found the newspaper and rags. Pushing aside what remained of the door, he stepped inside. He'd entered from the cleared front door earlier with Midas. The dog had found the remnants of a gasoline trail through the first floor and leading upstairs. Someone had been inside to get the blaze to travel throughout the house.

Midas detected the gasoline again and paced along it as he'd been trained to do.

"Yep, *bon*. Good boy. I see it. Again." Patrick scratched the dog's big black ear.

After donning a pair of plastic gloves, he used his pen to sift through the soot at the threshold of the porch door. He collected some of the charred cloth although he'd seen enough like it to identify what it was. Still, in a new town, he'd play by the rules, do it by the book. Didn't want the first case he consulted on to not hold up in court if that's where it ended up.

While on his knees, bagging debris samples, his gaze fell upon something blue and oddly shaped under what remained of a wicker rocking chair on the porch. He shuffled back outside and shined his flashlight on the object.

A blue candle. At least it used to be. It had lost its rounded edge, reduced to a glob of melted wax, the wick totally spent. Patrick slid it out from its hiding spot and put it in a fresh evidence bag. He got a whiff of cinnamon as he sealed the bag. Certain the candle was the point of origin, he scrawled some notes in his notebook and gave the rest of the house another run-through with Midas.

Content he had enough to work with, Patrick headed back to his truck. Midas jumped into the passenger seat and after a quick stop at Maury's

Pizza Haven, the two of them were on their way home to dine and work. As he drove, Patrick mentally composed his official report—the one he'd turn over to Mason in the morning. Cut and dry. Someone poured a line of gasoline, stuffed newspapers and rags under the door, lit a candle, and poof.

The questions that remained were why and, more importantly, who.

****

Gini finished the last of her dinner and dumped the dishes in the sink. She'd get to them later or con Jonah into doing them the next time he stopped by. Tonight, she didn't have time for dishes. She had to develop the fire scene pictures for Mason. Not for Patrick even though Mason said he'd need a copy too.

No, she'd develop them for Mason. She'd known him a hell of a lot longer than Patrick Barre, and he never caused her to have an incident. Polite, sophisticated Mason. Upstanding citizen and intelligent detective. She'd put aside whatever else she had planned to do tonight for Mason.

Not for Patrick.

He'd certainly scurried off in a hurry at the scene this afternoon. Just as well. Made the stay-out-of-Patrick's-path plan easier to follow. She didn't even know why it bothered her so much that he didn't want to help her with the calendar. She would have been short a fighter if she'd hatched the fund-raiser idea last week before Patrick had joined the Burnam Fire Department. So why did his refusal scratch at her skin like thorns?

Breathe. She had to remember to breathe. A night in her home darkroom would settle her. Make her forget what Patrick had pushed her to do.

A bush at the fire department. How ridiculous. At least it had been at a location where people qualified to handle a spontaneous blaze were on hand. No one had gotten hurt. Not this time.

Gini shook off the chill rippling through her and shut off the kitchen light. She padded down the hallway on her bare feet and scooped her hair up into a loose bun. As soon as she opened the door to the darkroom, she let the shadows swallow the darkness inside her. In the silence of that room, she could focus on her work and not worry about anything else.

She developed the two rolls of film she'd used at the fire scene and uploaded the digital photos she'd taken as well. After scanning the traditional photographs into her computer, she emailed them and the digitals to Mason. Usually she didn't pay much attention to the details of the pictures she took for Mason. Freelancing for the police department wasn't art. It was business. She didn't have the same reaction to photos of footprints in mud or a pile of burnt debris as she did to a beautiful bride all smiles on her wedding day.

Gathering the hard copies now, however, Gini's gaze settled on a blue blob under the wicker rocking chair in the top photo. She turned the picture around and looked at it from all angles. Had to be a candle. Must be the fire's starting point. Mason would be glad to find that in the photos. Would make solving his case easier hopefully. Anything she could do to help made her feel a little less like a beast. Less like an anomaly that probably shouldn't exist.

Gini shook her head. "Enough, Claremont. Positive thoughts only, girl."

She cleaned up her workspace and went outside. The purple dusk kissed the mountaintops in the distance, and she breathed in the fragrant summer air. Lavender, mint, roses, and peaches combined to clear her head. Fireflies twinkled in the tall grass by the barn, and Gini had to smile.

Firefly. Her daddy had called her that when she was a little girl. He didn't realize how fitting the nickname would be until Gini was seventeen. That was the year she'd fallen in love. Fallen pretty hard too like all seventeen-year-old girls do, she supposed.

Gini sat on the arbor swing overlooking the west field. The sun had put itself to sleep, and the moon cast a white spotlight on the little pond bordering the field. Saber jumped onto her lap and circled until he found the perfect spot. As she rubbed the cat's silky fur, Gini closed her eyes.

****

"God, Gini, you're so beautiful," Cameron said. "I could look at you forever."

Gini blushed at Cameron's words. He always said just the right thing. She was a fairy tale princess whenever she was with him. He was her prince.

"We've been together for a long time now." Cameron slipped his hand over Gini's shoulders and squeezed her closer. He'd parked his dad's car by the river, and all the stars were out, ready to take wishes.

"It's been wonderful, Cameron." Gini leaned her head on Cameron's shoulder, and he kissed the top of her head. She soon found herself angling her face to him, seeking his lips, finding his familiar spearmint chewing gum taste, and getting lost in it.

Cameron broke away and slithered into the back seat. He dragged a giggling Gini into the space next to him, and his lips sought hers now. The seat beneath her was sticky with something she couldn't identify in the dark, but she pushed that aside and focused on Cameron. His scruffy black hair complemented the fact that he played electric guitar in a small band. His blue eyes always reminded Gini of a perfect summer day, one where the water and sky made a perfectly blue sandwich of anything between them.

Cameron's arms encircled her waist, and he tugged until her long legs could only separate to either side of his body.

"Your hair smells like peaches." Cameron burrowed his head into the curve of Gini's neck. "I love peaches."

"I know."

Gini's favorite pastime was making out with Cameron. His lips were so full, so soft. Whenever he kissed her, she felt as if she were flying. Time stood still. Her blood pumped like liquid fire when his breath tickled her neck, when his hands slid under her shirt, brushed over her skin.

She felt like a woman in Cameron's arms, not like the awkward teenage giraffe she usually felt like.

"I love you, Gini." Cameron's voice was a hoarse whisper. "I want to see you. I've got to see you." He lifted her T-shirt, prepared to take it off.

"Wait." Gini curled her fingers around Cameron's wrists.

"I can't wait, Gini. I don't want to wait anymore."

Cameron had been saying things like this for a few weeks. Each time Gini had been able to distract him or give him enough that he backed off. A quick fondle here and there. She was pretty sure his friends were giving him a hard time about not having sex with her. She didn't care what his friends thought. Most of them were morons anyway. Cameron was smarter, cuter, funnier, better than they were.

But still, she wasn't ready to have sex with him.

They kissed for a few more moments until Cameron started wiggling her shirt up again.

"Knock it off, Cameron." Gini swatted at his hands, but leaned in to start kissing again.

Cameron slid away from her and folded his arms across his chest. "When, Gini? When?"

"I don't know," she said softly. Suddenly that

sticky spot on the seat mattered. She knew its diameter, felt the border between sticky and not sticky. Inched over to get in the not sticky zone.

"You're killing me here. Really. I mean, I said I love you. What else do you want me to say?" He faced forward now. All the cuddling instincts gone to ice.

"It doesn't have anything to do with you saying something." Gini shifted to face forward now too. She felt ridiculous with them both in the back seat as if they were waiting for a chauffeur to take the driver's seat and whisk them away somewhere.

"Then what can I do to convince you that we're ready to do this?"

"Nothing. I'll just know when I'm ready, Cameron."

"Great. Don't I get a say?"

Not knowing what else to do, Gini put her hand on Cameron's and yelped when he grabbed her arm. He pinned her down on the seat, right in the sticky spot, and pressed his length against her leg.

"I'm done waiting, Gini. We need to do this. We're going to do this."

His lips crushed down on hers, and she tasted blood. Gini shoved at Cameron's shoulders, but he only pushed against her harder. She tried to maneuver around him, but the back seat of the car was already tight. She had no room. She couldn't yell. She did the only thing she could.

She bit.

"Son of a..." Cameron sat up, straddling Gini. He wiped at his bleeding bottom lip, and in a lightning quick move, he slapped Gini across the face.

Sparks exploded before her left eye, and her ear rang. She couldn't believe she was with the same boy who'd just told her he loved her. He'd never been violent with her before. Who was this kid? Anger that he would treat her this way swirled deep in her belly.

"Now you owe me, bitch." Cameron unzipped his jeans and grabbed the waist of Gini's shorts.

The explosion was what stopped him. Flames burst from the hood of the car. Cameron screamed when the windshield shattered, and the flames rushed in. Shock had them both paralyzed. When the fire jumped to the front seats, Gini snapped out of her hypnosis.

"Open the door, Cameron! We have to get out."

Cameron didn't move. His eyes were transfixed on the fire as it inched closer to them.

"Cameron!" Gini pushed the passenger seat forward and opened the door on that side. "C'mon."

She pulled on his arm as she fumbled out of the car. When he didn't follow right behind her, she poked her head into the back seat.

"Let's go. Hurry!"

Slowly, he turned to face her. She reached out her hand, and as he shifted to take it, the back of his T-shirt caught fire.

Somehow finding the strength, Gini clamped onto his forearms and yanked Cameron out. They tumbled to the gravel roadway, and Gini kept them rolling until the flames were snuffed. When she looked up, the car was engulfed in an orange fury. They had to get away.

Gini pulled Cameron to his feet. He moaned in pain. How bad was he hurt? She didn't have time to investigate because another explosion sent metal hurtling toward them.

It happened in slow motion.

She tried to push Cameron out of the way, but she wasn't quick enough. Red-hot steel rammed into his legs and sent him careening to the ground like a bowling pin.

The sweep of headlights had Gini whipping around. A car pulled over, and a woman jumped out.

"Are you all right? I called for help when I saw

*the flames." She stuffed a cell phone into her pocket.
"Let's get him a little farther away from that." The
woman motioned to the inferno that had become of
the car.*

*Together, Gini and this Good Samaritan
maneuvered Cameron toward the woman's parked
car. He cried out with each movement, and tears
streamed down his face. Gini tried not to look at the
bloody trail his body had left in the gravel.*

"What happened?" the woman asked.

*"I...I don't know," Gini said, although the feeling
in her stomach told her she did know. Knew exactly
what had happened. Exactly what she had done.*

****

Gini snapped awake on the arbor swing, and
Saber let out a hiss as he was jostled off her lap. She
rubbed the palms of her hands over her face,
brushed away the tears that had come in her
slumber, in her remembering.

Cameron had healed, but it had been a painful
journey. Multiple surgeries to repair the damage to
his legs had him missing most of his senior year of
high school. He'd had to repeat it. He and Gini didn't
talk much after the accident. Or incident, as Gini
called it.

She'd gone around for a while denying she had
caused the fire that exploded the engine. She went
over the scene thousands of times, replayed every
angle, analyzed every detail she could remember.
The anger was what stuck out in her mind. The
words Cameron had said. What he had planned to
take from her. But anger couldn't start fires. Could
it?

Her father had combed through the remains of
the car himself, several times, and with forensic
consultation. No obvious cause for the engine to
blow. No recognizable malfunction with the vehicle.
No foul play. Nothing.

Nothing but Gini's anger.

When she'd mentioned her theory to her father, he refused to believe her.

"Nonsense, Gini. Total nonsense," he'd said. "I've been fighting fires for a long time, and there is no way you could have started it like that. Stop blaming yourself."

She hadn't mentioned what Cameron was trying to do at the time. Hadn't mentioned how deeply he'd hurt her with his words and his actions. If she didn't talk about it, perhaps she could pretend it didn't happen.

Her daddy's not believing her had stung. Her own flesh and blood telling her she was talking nonsense. Before she could stop herself, she'd stirred up some fresh anger. The mailbox at the end of their driveway had gone up like a firecracker as she and her father sat on the front steps of their house.

Her daddy believed her then and had been helping her keep this ability—this curse—under control. Her family had managed it rather well. She'd filled her days with happy thoughts and felt normal most of the time.

Until Patrick Barre.

Chapter Six

Patrick and Midas sat on the bench outside Mason's office. He was early, but that was the way he'd planned it. He hoped to get the formalities over with so he could put in most of the day at the fire station. Though his paperwork was always in order, every detail checked and rechecked, Patrick didn't have an affinity for forms. He'd rather be at the station or building something.

He'd spent most of last night examining the photos Mason had emailed him. Though he had some mixed thoughts about Gini, he couldn't deny she had a gift when it came to photography. Patrick had been studying incident photographs for years. Most of them merely showed the facts. Gini's were pieces of art. As if she'd thought about angles and lighting, foreground and background, while she snapped her camera. The photos captured things he hadn't noticed when going through the actual house, and he liked to think he was an observant guy.

Cookie crumbs on a patch of unmelted linoleum. Burn rings rainbowing across plywood. Blackened fringe on a Navajo-print blanket scrap. Shards of mirror, like glass snow sparkling on tile.

And the blue candle, its waxy, lopsided edges hiding beneath sagging white wicker.

"Morning." Mason strode over with a coffee in his hands. "Sorry if I kept you waiting, but I'm no good without one of these." He raised the cup and pointed to it with his other hand. "Want some?"

"No, thanks." Patrick never touched the stuff.

Never understood the fuss over coffee. He liked his water pure and unspoiled.

"Come on in." Mason opened the door to his office and let Patrick enter first. Patrick would have liked to call the room messy, but that wasn't the right word. Not at all. Words like "hurricane," "devastation," and "catastrophe" came to mind instead. He felt as if he needed a hard hat to sit safely in the crowded disaster that was Mason's office.

"Dump those files off that chair there." Mason stepped over three boxes of files on the floor next to his desk to get to his own seat. "I know what you're thinking."

"That your office needs caution tape?" Patrick gathered up the files and held them as he decided where to place them. Even Midas, who wasn't particularly choosy about his hunkering down spots, didn't know where to go.

"Funny. No, you're thinking that there's no way I can possibly solve any cases in this mess."

"Yeah, okay. That was my second thought." Patrick settled for resting the files on the top of a low bookcase under the only window in the office.

"Don't worry. This all makes sense to me and I'm the one who has to work here." Mason sat and placed his coffee atop his littered desk.

"As long as it works for you." Patrick shrugged and gripped the file folder he'd brought as if he were protecting it. He didn't want his papers to catch whatever had infected this office. He finally sat, and Midas nosed a box aside until a clear spot of floor appeared.

"So did talking with the neighbors turn up anything?" Mason asked.

"No, but I dropped off evidence bags at your lab. One of them includes the remains of a—"

"Blue candle."

Gini walked into Mason's office. She scooped up the papers on the chair beside Patrick's and made herself comfortable without the blink of an eye. She was used to Mason's mess.

How used to his mess was she? How well did she know Mason? Patrick didn't like the flash of unexplained jealousy that zipped through him.

Gini faced Mason and offered him a sunny smile, but didn't toss one Patrick's way. She didn't look his way at all.

Okay. We can play it that way.

"Hiya, Gini," Mason said. "What blue candle? I don't remember seeing it in the photos you sent."

Patrick cleared his throat to answer, but Gini already had a photo from her ridiculously big purse in her hands. She got up and leaned over the desk as she put the photo in front of Mason. Patrick's pulse stopped for a moment as the hem of Gini's army green shorts edged up a little higher. The back of her thigh summoned his fingers, but he clenched them into a fist and forced himself to look away.

"It's right here." She tapped the photo.

Mason picked up the picture and studied it more closely. "Point of origin, Patrick?" The detective looked at Patrick over the top edge of the photo. Gini still didn't look at him as she sat back in her chair.

The bad guy act worked. She genuinely hates me. Going to pretend I don't even exist. Why did that make his stomach ache? It was what he'd wanted. No Gini, no calendar photo to worry about.

Shaking his head, Patrick focused on the business at hand. "Definitely. That candle is the point of origin. Coupled with the gasoline trail Midas found, it ignited that blaze. No doubt. It had a scent too. Cinnamon."

"Cinnamon?" Mason and Gini repeated together.

"Yes."

"Cinnamon is an aphrodisiac," Gini said.

Patrick wondered just how much Gini knew about aphrodisiacs and had to shake his head clear of the thought.

"We'll wait for the lab results, but I agree this candle is our starting point." Mason took the rest of the hard copy photos Gini handed him and fished around in his desk drawer. "There are empty folders in here somewhere." He shuffled around in the drawer, scattered the rubbish on his desktop, and mumbled to himself.

Unable to take it a moment longer, Patrick offered his file folder. "Here, Mason. Use this one. It's already got case-related information in it." Patrick reluctantly handed over the folder.

"Thanks." Mason slid the photos inside. "Look at this. It's all labeled and everything."

Gini chuckled, and Patrick's gaze shot to her. *Was she laughing at him?*

She swallowed, and the dimple in her right cheek faded as she put her serious face back on. Her hand clasped the straps of her purse, twisted, wrung. She struggled to not look his way. Patrick knew it.

"I've got to go." Gini stood. "You're all set, right, Mason?"

"Yeah, Shutterbug. Your work here is complete. As usual, you have proven most useful."

"Oh, go on, Mason. The things you say." Another easy smile for Mason. "Don't know why the gals aren't lined up to hear your poetic words."

Mason grinned. "Me neither."

"Could be this office scares them away." Patrick rarely joked around, but he wanted to see if Gini would laugh again.

He was richly rewarded. She let out a full giggle this time and almost looked at him. She caught herself though and averted her gaze to the window instead.

49

"Later, Mason." Gini slipped out of the office.

She hadn't said Patrick's name once, but she'd known he was there. Gini Claremont was a bigger mystery now and damn if Patrick didn't love solving a mystery.

****

Gini leaned against the wall outside Mason's office. The walls had threatened to close in on her in there. That had never happened before. She had always been more than comfy in Mason's office. He was a sweetheart. True, he was a sloppy sweetheart, as Patrick had noted, but she could always be herself with him. He was her brother's best friend. One of her best friends. Easy to be around.

Patrick Barre was another story, but her plan had worked. She'd considered him invisible and kept her feelings neutral. Okay, maybe it was a little funny he was so out of place in Mason's disorder. That the chaos had eaten at him. How could he be so rude one minute and humorous the next? And why did he smell so good? Like sawdust and blueberry muffins. She hadn't expected it to be so hard to ignore him. Hell, she'd spent most of her life ignoring feelings of attraction to men. Wouldn't be fair to reel one in and risk hurting him. She wouldn't let what had happened to Cameron happen to anyone else.

But it had taken every muscle straining in her neck to not look at Patrick. All her focus to not speak directly to him. She was drained, but at least she wasn't angry.

A wet nose pressed into her kneecap, and Gini looked down. "Hey there, pup." She scooted down to pet Midas.

"So you see him. Can talk to him."

Her eyes fluttered to Patrick's face as he stood in the doorway of Mason's office.

Damn, he tricked me.

"He hasn't been an ignorant thug." Gini focused back on Midas. The dog buried his face in her lap as she scratched between his ears.

"Look, we got started on the wrong foot. I'm not an ignorant thug. Just a camera shy one."

Gini lifted her gaze, and the smile on Patrick's face had her breath hitching in her throat. The smile made the golden flecks in his hazel eyes glint, and his lips looked as if they were capable of real danger. Anger wasn't the only emotion she had to worry about around Patrick.

"I suppose I can be a tad pushy when I don't get my way," Gini said. "I want the calendar to be perfect, for it to raise a ton of money for the animal shelter."

"It can do so without my picture," Patrick said.

"Sure, but—"

"Don't." Patrick shook his head. "You won't change my mind, Gini. Why don't we call a truce and go from there?"

Gini strangled her purse strap as the sound of her name out of Patrick's mouth sent tingly ripples throughout her body. Why did he have to be so tall?

"A truce?" She chewed her bottom lip. A truce had to be easier than ignoring him, which wasn't going so well at present. "Okay, deal."

Patrick held out a hand and Gini took it. They shook and maybe held on a bit longer than necessary before Patrick broke the connection. "I won't be an ignorant thug, and you won't pester me about pictures."

"Right," Gini said.

"Good." Patrick slipped his hands into his pockets and stepped around Gini. "See you around." He patted his thigh, and Midas trotted after him out of the police station.

Gini leaned against the wall again and brushed her hair out of the way. Had she made a deal she

51

couldn't keep? It wasn't like her to back down when she wanted something. And now she'd proven she could be around Patrick without setting things on fire. He could be civilized. She could be cordial. It could work.

Why did she feel as if it wasn't that simple?

"You're still here?" Mason tapped her on the shoulder, causing her to jump.

"Just petting Patrick and talking to Midas." She coughed on her mistake. "I mean...petting Midas and talking to Patrick." She busied herself looking for her car keys in her bag.

"He's something, huh?" Mason asked.

"Yeah, that dog is amazing." Gini pulled out her keys and studied her sandals.

"You know I didn't mean the dog, Gini." Mason tipped her chin up with his index finger. "You want to tell me why you were trying so hard to make Patrick nonexistent in there?" He gestured over his shoulder to his office.

"I don't know what you're talking about, Mason."

"Shutterbug, it's me. Don't forget I know you almost as well as your family does."

Except he didn't know everything about her. He didn't know the secret. She would never tell him.

"Okay, I'm caught, Mr. All-Knowing Detective." Gini held her hands up in mock surrender. "I met Patrick yesterday and we...clashed. I figured ignoring him was the best plan of action."

"Mature." Mason swerved out of Gini's reach as she tried to shove him.

"I didn't say it was a good plan. I've abandoned it anyway."

"Oh?" Mason's eyebrows rose as a teasing smirk slid across his lips.

"If you weren't armed right now, I'd kick your ass, Rivers," Gini said.

"Lucky for me." He tapped her on the nose.

"Stay out of trouble, Claremont." He laughed and went back into his office.

Stay out of trouble?

Easier said than done.

Chapter Seven

Working out always cleared Patrick's mind. Lift a weight, inhale. Lower a weight, exhale. Cleansing. Balancing. After his encounter with Gini, he'd felt all jumbled up, as if he were a bottle of soda someone had shaken, dropped down a flight of stairs, and thrown in a clothes dryer. Things were quiet at the station, so he'd headed to the training room determined to regroup.

He'd completed his last rep on the weights and started on some abs work when Jonah came in.

"For a working dog, Midas sleeps on the job a great deal," he said. "He's curled up on one of the bunks in the dorm."

Patrick sat up on his mat. "I like to think he sleeps so much so he'll be sharp when he's on a case. Besides we ran four miles this morning. He's allowed to be tired."

"You ran *and* you're in here. You training for the Olympics or something?" Jonah grabbed the chin-up bar and pulled himself up, lowered, pulled himself up again.

"No." Patrick started some crunches. "Just trying to get centered."

Jonah stopped his chin-ups and let his feet drop to the ground. "Centered?"

"Yeah, you know, get all those crazy thoughts whipping through your mind to shut the hell up. Centered." Patrick studied Jonah's face. Worry lines appeared at the corners of Jonah's mouth.

"What kind of crazy thoughts?" Jonah stood over

Patrick on the mat.

Crazy thoughts about your sister. "New town, new job, new house crazy thoughts," Patrick said instead. "A possible arson case. Take your pick."

Jonah let out a breath and tapped his sneakers together. "Right. Everyday stuff. I got ya. Where's the new house?"

"Actually, it's an old house," Patrick said. "Up on Hope Hill Road."

"That place practically swallowed by the woods?"

"That'd be the one."

"No offense, man, but if I remember correctly, that house is a shithole."

Patrick laughed. So easy to do around Jonah. "You do remember correctly, but I know how to use a hammer, right?"

"You'd better know how to use way more than a hammer, dude." Jonah walked back to the chin-up bar. "You got a master plan for the place?"

"Of course."

"Let me know if you need a hand. I work for beer."

"Good to know. I might take you up on that. There's a ton to do up there."

"Why don't we get started on the beer tonight, and you can show me the plan?"

A social invite? So soon. So casually delivered. Patrick's gut tensed. He wasn't good at this being buddies thing. He didn't have a degree in male bonding. Hadn't even taken the first class. It couldn't be too late to learn though, could it?

"Sure. It'd be good to get another set of eyes on the plan. Make sure I didn't miss something."

"Great." Jonah smiled like a little boy. "Down the street from the station is a bar called Wolf's. You'll see why when you meet the owner. Anyway, meet me there at eight-ish and we'll talk studs and nails."

Patrick went back to his crunches. Jonah flew through his chin-ups and hopped on the treadmill. No more conversation between them necessary, though Patrick started planning out what he'd say over beer that night.

How far would he let Jonah in? How far could he afford to?

****

"Only eleven fighters signed release forms." Haddy sat across from Gini at the studio's rectangular work table. They had ordered eggplant sandwiches from Maury's and ate lunch as they scheduled firefighter photo shoots.

"I know." Gini bit into her sandwich and let the flavor keep her from getting annoyed. "The new guy, Patrick, won't let me take his picture."

"Really? How come?" Haddy stopped chewing.

"Camera shy, or so he says." Gini gulped her lemonade.

"Is he hideous or something?" When Gini spilled lemonade and fumbled around to wipe it up, Haddy pushed her lunch aside and raised her eyebrows. "Oh, I see. He's super-hot, isn't he?"

"Yes. No. I mean, I don't know." Gini mopped up her drink and kneeled on the floor to catch the puddle forming there. When she rose, she whacked her head on the edge of the table. "Ouch. Dammit."

"Gini, Gini, Gini," Haddy said. "I know a love struck gal when I see one, and you, my friend, are—"

"Not love struck," Gini finished. "I don't know the guy. How could I be love struck?"

"That's what 'love struck' means, sister. Struck by love so instantly that it doesn't make any logical sense. It happens to people all the time." Haddy went back to eating her sandwich.

"Yeah, well, it doesn't happen to me. It didn't happen. Patrick is an attractive man, I'll admit that, but he's too...too...I don't know. Too something that's not for me."

"Mmm-hmm." Haddy wiped her mouth with her napkin, but didn't wipe the smirk away.

"Cut it out, Haddy, or I'll bust you up about Jonah."

"Go right ahead. There's nothing between Jonah and me."

"And if he waltzed in here right now and said, 'Haddy, want to go for a ride in my Mustang?' I suppose you wouldn't jump at the chance, right?" Gini threw away her lemonade-soaked napkins and folded her arms across her chest.

"I'm not your brother's type." Haddy combed her fingers through the end of her straight, chestnut brown hair. Her pale green eyes hid behind wire-rimmed glasses. The burgundy blouse she had on today made her olive complexion look a little on the exotic side. Her flowing skirt with tiny burgundy flowers on it fell to the knee and revealed a long, shapely line of leg. She'd be anyone's type.

"Don't be silly. Jonah doesn't have a type." Gini sat back in her seat and finished her sandwich.

"Yes, he does. He only dates red-heads." Again, Haddy fingered her own hair. "Think I should go red?"

"Absolutely not. If you dye your hair because you think it'll get my brother's attention, I'll fire you." Gini wagged a finger at Haddy. "Besides, I wouldn't be so sure you don't already have my brother's attention."

"Why? What did he say?" Haddy gripped the end of the work table and leaned forward far enough that her shirt grazed the sandwich in front of her. Sauce dotted a section around her left nipple. "Oh, crap." She dabbed at it with her napkin, but sauce on a shirt never turned out well.

"For someone who isn't interested in Jonah, you seem really interested."

"Shut up." Haddy marched off to the studio's bathroom, but laughed most of the way there.

Gini reviewed the fighters' photo release forms while she waited for Haddy and stared at the last one in the pile. The blank form. Patrick's form.

"How can I get your photo, Patrick? How?" There had to be a way to get him to agree. She'd convinced other camera-phobics to let her capture them on film. Generally, they were happy with the results too. Camera-shyness usually came from the belief that one didn't photograph well. All it usually took was one good picture to convince someone that they were photogenic. She had a hard time believing that Patrick thought he didn't photograph well. He had to have seen himself in the mirror and been pleased with what reflected back. It looked pretty damn good to Gini.

And she knew picturesque muscles rested beneath his shirt that would make any woman who bought her calendar foam at the mouth. How could he deny the women of Burnam such a show?

He couldn't, Gini decided. He'd made her lose her cool once, but now she'd be nothing but charming. He'd be unable to deny her this one small photo request.

"Stop thinking so hard, Gini. You'll pull a muscle."

Jonah sauntered into the studio and leaned his elbows on the work table.

"What are you doing here?" What had her face looked like when Jonah snuck up on her? Would he know she was picturing Patrick shirtless?

"Lunch run for the station. Ma made us all sandwiches at the bakery."

"Okay, but that doesn't answer what you're doing *here*." She smiled when Jonah stuck his tongue out at her. When they were kids they used to stick their tongues out at each other all the time. Mama would yell and say something like, "You two ought to be thankful you have each other. I had no one as a little girl and it was awful lonely."

Mama had hated being an only child, and Gini was pretty sure she would have hated it too. Of course, that didn't stop Jonah and her from sticking their tongues out at each other.

"You know anyone that likes nipples Italian-style?" Haddy came out of the bathroom still rubbing at the wet, red-orange stain on her blouse. When she looked up and saw Jonah standing there, her face reddened. Beads of sweat actually dotted Haddy's brow.

"Every guy in Burnam likes nipples Italian-style," Jonah said. "I like extra cheese on mine."

"I didn't know you were here." Haddy reached for one of the old, flannel shirts they kept in the studio for the messy projects they sometimes did. She slipped it on and folded in across her front like a robe.

Jonah sent her a smile, and Haddy flushed deeper. Gini watched the two of them stare at each other and shook her head. Some people didn't see what was right in front of them.

"Are you going to tell me why you're here, Jonah, or are you here to gaze dreamily at Haddy?"

"Huh? What?" Jonah closed his eyes, while Haddy shot Gini a look of death.

Gini stifled a chuckle and stood. "What do you want?"

"Oh, right. I'm heading over to Wolf's tonight. You want to come?" He glanced over to Haddy. "Both of you?"

"Oh, tonight?" Gini pulled at her lower lip. "Let's see. Haddy, can you check our schedule for tonight? Are we free?" She sent her friend an encouraging grin.

"Y-yes," Haddy said. "I'm free. I mean, we're

free."

"Great. Okay, Jonah, see you tonight." Gini nudged him toward the door.

"Right, tonight. Eight o'clock." He opened the door. "Bye, Haddy," he called over his shoulder.

Gini closed the door and skipped over to Haddy. "Well, well, well. What a turn of events. What a turn."

"What am I going to wear?" Haddy asked. "I can't go. I don't have anything to wear." She hung up the flannel shirt and swallowed loudly.

"As soon as we get this schedule of shoots done, we're going shopping, girlie. There is no way you are not going tonight."

Haddy nodded and threw away their lunch trash. She picked up her pad, and Gini grabbed the release forms. Studying the blank one again, she thought about Jonah. Maybe she could recruit him to help her convince Patrick that having his picture taken wasn't the worst thing in the world. She'd ask him tonight at Wolf's. After a beer. After a few beers.

****

Wolf's Pub was a knotty pine-paneled cave at the end of Center Square Street. Stonework on the lower portion of the building made the outside look as if it'd been carved from a mountain. Two hulking pine trees stood like soldiers on either side of the front doors. The small parking lot was nearly full.

Patrick parked his truck and walked up the stairs to the pub's entry. He studied the sign above the door, which had been carved from a stout piece of mahogany. The words "Wolf's Pub" were embossed on the dark wood. The "o" in "Wolf's" had been painted to look like a full moon and howling wolf heads adorned the two ends of the sign. Fine craftsmanship with a witty, decorative slant. Patrick already liked the feel of the bar. Maybe this evening wouldn't be painful after all.

When he opened the front door and stepped inside, the familiar crooning of a woman singer warmed something inside him. He turned the corner, and Raina sat before a piano on a small stage. Patrons huddled around circular tables that looked as if they'd been hacked from enormous tree stumps. Everyone's attention was focused on Raina and her jazzy melody. She carried a note to a place Patrick had heard her reach before, and the pub erupted in applause.

"Thank you." Raina stood and bowed slightly, blew the audience a kiss. "I'm going to take a short break, and then we'll continue our date." She winked and stepped off the stage.

Patrick watched several male customers get up from their seats and target his sister. Before he could think about what he was doing, he pushed through the crowd and stood next to Raina. With one look, each of the guys backed up.

"Raina."

She swiveled around, sipping wine. Her eyebrows shot up as she put her glass down on the bar.

"Patrick!" She threw her arms around him. "What are you doing here?"

"Meeting a...friend." He guessed he could call Jonah that.

"Deciding not to be a loner in Vermont? How wonderful." She tugged on his black T-shirt and grinned. "What do you want to drink?"

Patrick ordered a beer and, because Jonah wasn't there yet, sat with Raina at a table. He took the seat facing the door so he could watch it.

"If I'd known you were going to be so social, I'd have invited you to come hear me sing, brother." Raina waved to some men at a table across the pub.

"I wasn't planning to be social. And don't toy with them, Raina." Patrick pointed his bottle toward the men.

"They like when I toy with them." She fluffed her hair then took another sip of wine.

"I'm sure. But don't—"

"Patrick," Raina interrupted. "I'm a big girl. You don't have to protect me. I can take care of myself." She placed her hand over his and squeezed.

"I can't help it." Patrick shrugged.

"I know."

Patrick took another swig of his beer and glanced around the pub. The interior walls were pine-paneled similar to the outside. The floor was wide-plank, reclaimed barn wood, if he wasn't mistaken. Above him exposed beams gave the place a timber-frame feel. A giant wall of stone housed a fireplace that must throw serious heat in the winter. Patrick hoped it was properly ventilated so as not to be a fire hazard.

As he scanned the rest of the bar, the front door opened and Jonah walked in. Mason was right behind him. Jonah's gaze swept the room and when he saw Patrick, he waved. He and Mason headed over after stopping to chat with a few folks along the way.

"Hey, Patrick." Jonah plopped down in the seat across from Patrick.

"Jonah, Mason." Patrick gestured to Raina. "This is my sister, Raina."

"Nice to meet you." Jonah extended a hand.

Raina swirled the wine in her glass and accepted Jonah's hand. "Likewise." She glanced up at a still-standing Mason. "You going to sit, honey, or take our dinner orders?"

Mason's cheeks flushed, and Raina smiled. Patrick shook his head, knowing how much his sister loved the shy ones.

She pushed out the chair across from her with her foot. "Sit, cutie."

And Mason did. The brown of his eyes was almost completely lost to the dilated black of his pupils. A clear sign of attraction. Patrick was sure Raina noticed too. She picked up on subtle, social cues like that. For some reason, though, Mason ogling Raina didn't bother him as much as when other guys did it. Mason appeared to be a clean-cut man of the law. The kind of guy Patrick would pick for Raina. But would she pick him?

"So what do you fellows do?" Raina finished the last of her wine and glanced at the clock over the bar.

"I'm a firefighter like your brother here," Jonah said. "And Mason is a detective with the Burnam PD."

Raina's gray eyes widened. "A detective? Like putting the pieces of a puzzle together, do you, Mason?"

"I like catching the bad guys," Mason said.

"Keeping the town safe for gals like me, huh?"

"Definitely."

Patrick looked between the two of them then to Jonah, who gave a slight nod.

"The next song is for you then, Mason." Raina held out her hand, which Mason took. "Pleasure meeting you both." Her gaze only fell on Mason.

After letting her hand slip from Mason's, Raina dropped a kiss on Patrick's cheek and headed back to the piano. Jonah signaled to the waitress and ordered beers for Mason and himself.

"You want another, Patrick?"

Patrick shook his head. "Still working on this one." He glanced at Mason, still transfixed on Raina. She'd started her song, something about looking for a hero.

"Any word on the lab results for the evidence I took from the fire scene, Mason?"

Mason didn't take his gaze off Raina. He took a

63

long gulp of his beer, but his attention on her didn't waver.

"Mason?" Patrick repeated. He looked at Jonah, a little concerned now. "His head always this easily turned?"

"No way. For the first few months we knew Mason, Gini and I thought he was gay. Then we figured out he's extremely shy around women, especially attractive women. It took him almost a year to talk to Gini."

Patrick was dying to know if Gini and Mason had dated, but didn't dare ask. He didn't care or at least he could pretend not to care.

"Mason." Jonah shoved his friend and the detective jumped.

"What?"

"Snap out of it, man. You're getting drool all over the table." Jonah laughed at the frown lines around Mason's mouth.

"I am not." Still, he reached for a napkin at the center of the table and wiped his mouth. "God, she's beautiful though."

"Raina got lucky in the looks department," Patrick said. He and Julianne hadn't been so fortunate. His scars were at least hidden. But Julianne. Patrick's fingers tightened around his beer.

"Speaking of good-looking women." Jonah pointed to the front door where Gini and another woman talked to an older gentleman with a dark gray beard and long hair. His sharp, golden eyes flickered as he laughed at whatever Gini was saying. "That's Wolf, the owner of this pub. If werewolves exist, he's one for sure."

Patrick tried to laugh, but all his senses zeroed in on Gini. She wore light blue jeans that hugged her fit body. A silver tank top that flared out at the bottom gave her a curvy outline that made all the blood in Patrick's body rush to one spot. Her hair was pulled over her shoulder in a low ponytail, a cascade of curls resting at her neck. Silver hoop earrings sparkled at her ears.

Shaking his head, Patrick told himself to get a grip as Gini led her friend through the bar to their table. She faltered a little when her eyes met Patrick's, he noted, but she recovered quickly and tossed him a bright smile.

"Hiya." She pulled a chair from a nearby table and sat between Patrick and Mason. She could have sat anywhere, Patrick thought, but she chose that spot. Interesting.

"Hey, Shutterbug," Mason said. "Isn't that singing fantastic?"

Gini glanced to the stage and nodded. "Yeah, Raina is wonderful."

"You've heard her sing before?" Patrick was getting drunk on the wildflower scent wafting off Gini.

"Sure, lots of times. She plays here often. Don't you like her?"

"I love her." Patrick enjoyed watching the muscles in Gini's face tense.

"Raina is his sister," Jonah said.

Now Gini smiled as she looked at Patrick. "I see. How nice. She's very talented." Her face was completely relaxed now. Completely beautiful. What would that face look like waking up next to him?

Patrick cleared his throat and took another sip of his beer.

"Patrick, this is Haddy," Gini said. Jonah had plopped a chair down next to him, and Haddy was sitting in it, a permanent grin on her lips. "She's my assistant at the studio and my BFF."

Jonah rested his arm on the back of Haddy's chair. Haddy leaned ever so slightly toward him.

"Nice shirt, Haddy." Jonah fingered the beads

adorning the straps of her raspberry-colored tank top. "Though I liked the one with the stain too."

Haddy elbowed Jonah, and the two of them shared a chuckle. Patrick wondered what was going on there too, but again, kept his questions to himself. If he didn't want to answer questions, he shouldn't ask any.

"So you two were right," Mason started as he pointed to Patrick and Gini. "The lab results confirmed the blue blob to be the remains of a candle."

"How'd it get under the rocking chair?" Gini asked. "Don't people generally burn candles on tables or countertops?"

"Not unless they're trying to start a fire." Patrick watched as Gini shifted in her seat, toyed with the silver cuff bracelet on her wrist.

"Arson." Jonah shook his head.

"Looks like it," Mason said. "We've got a couple leads we're working on now."

"You'll catch them, buddy," Jonah said.

"We always do." Mason clinked his bottle to Jonah's.

After ordering some appetizers and drinks for the ladies, the group enjoyed some pleasant small talk. Patrick hadn't thought such a thing existed, but it was easy with these folks. Conversation pinballed from town news, sports, movies, to some funny family stories. Patrick commented on most of the topics, but stayed clear of family stuff. His family stuff wasn't comedic. Not in the least. He wasn't about to bring the light-hearted mood of the evening to a screeching halt.

When the waitress cleared away their dishes and Raina came back to join them, Jonah asked, "Okay, so where's the house plan?"

"Left it in my truck," Patrick said. "Be right back."

****

Gini watched Patrick weave through the bar. She hadn't done anything tonight to implement her picture-taking plan, but man, was she enjoying herself. When she'd first seen Jonah sitting with Patrick, the desire to flee swept over her. What if he made her angry again? She didn't want to endanger a bar full of innocent people. Only Haddy pushing at her back kept her walking into the bar.

Okay, maybe it was the prospect of sitting next to Patrick and spending an evening with him that had kept her walking. Whatever.

"So what do you do?" Raina asked Gini while Patrick was gone. She had been watching Gini since she'd returned to the table after her last set.

"Photographer."

Raina laughed. "You try to photo my brother yet?"

"He won't let her," Haddy said.

"Of course he won't." Raina leaned forward as if she were about to say something, but her eyes flitted up to the opening front door. "Be careful," she whispered instead.

Gini had a million questions. She half-contemplated asking Raina to visit the ladies room with her, but knew that wouldn't be subtle enough. Her questions would have to wait.

When Patrick joined them, he unrolled the blueprint he'd drawn of the house and smoothed it over the table. Raina stood when she saw it.

"This is my cue to say good-night," she said. "I've already seen these brilliant designs." She patted Patrick's shoulder and sent a smile to the rest of the group. "Pleasure meeting all of you."

"Lovely to hear you sing," Haddy said.

"We all enjoyed it," Jonah added.

"Thank you." She shouldered her purse as her gaze settled on Mason. "Maybe I'll see you again soon, Detective?"

Mason nodded dumbly, and Gini put her hand on his forearm. He tore his eyes from Raina and looked at Gini.

"Maybe you should walk Raina to her car, Mason. It's late." Gini gave his arm a little squeeze to propel him into action.

"Yes, of course."

"That would be lovely. Thank you, Mason." But Raina's gaze fell to Gini, and a silent nod passed between them.

Mason got to his feet. "Evening, folks." He turned and led Raina to the door. When he paused to hold it open for her, Gini knew he'd be all right.

"Hope you don't mind me nudging Mason," Gini said to Patrick.

"Not at all. He'd be good for Raina. She deserves someone nice."

"Don't we all?" Jonah shot a quick glance to Haddy, who edged a bit closer to him. She'd be in his lap before the night ended at this rate.

Didn't they all deserve someone nice? Sure. Would they all be allowed that wish? Gini doubted it.

She took in a deep inhale and focused on the blueprint. Patrick's small, neat handwriting labeled all the rooms. Two-car garage, three bedrooms, two baths, dining room, an enormous kitchen, and a great room with a floor to vaulted ceiling stone fireplace.

"Wow, man." Jonah pushed his drink aside and flipped the drawing so he could examine it more closely. "This is some space."

"Yeah." Patrick shrugged. "Too much space for me, but it'll keep me busy."

"No such thing as too much space," Haddy said. "Or maybe only girls feel that way."

Gini tapped the design where the fireplace was

drawn. "Love this." Pointing to the fireplace in Wolf's Pub, she added, "That is my favorite part of this bar. Looks like you'll have your own version."

"The fireplace is already there. Just needs some cleaning up," Patrick said. "Thinking I'll put a wood stove in front of it though. They're safer."

"Said the firefighter." Gini elbowed him in the arm and liked the feel of his skin against hers.

"Fire safety in the home is the most important thing." Patrick's expression was suddenly serious and...far away.

"Couldn't agree more," Jonah said. "What's your flooring plan?"

"Tile in the kitchens and baths. Wood in dining room, hall, great room. Carpet in the bedrooms."

"Logical." Jonah nodded. "What are these lines?" He pointed to dotted red lines on the print.

"Those, Jonah, are all the walls that need to be demolished before I can start building this plan." Patrick sat back, and a fleeting thought of massaging his exhausted muscles after a day of knocking down walls surprised Gini.

"Wow, man. Good thing I'm going to help you," Jonah said.

"You're going to need a team of help if you want to ever finish this," Gini said.

"Don't you love volunteers?" Jonah winked at Gini.

Gini's eyes sprang open wider. "I'm not volun—"

"Of course you are. Gini, we can't let our newest Burnam citizen do all this work by himself. Haddy'll help too, won't you?"

No fair. Haddy would agree to anything that involved being around a tool-carrying Jonah.

"Sure. I'm good at fetching tools."

"That's the spirit." He turned to Patrick. "Gini's handy too. She built an arbor and swing for her backyard." Jonah looked back at Gini. "C'mon.

Patrick needs you."

Gini peered at Patrick, who sat perfectly still as if he were holding his breath. Did he want her help? Need it? What else did he need?

"Look, you don't have—" Patrick started before Gini held up a hand.

"No, I'll help. If you don't mind, that is."

Patrick studied her for a long moment. The lights in the pub made his eyes a darker shade of green-brown, like grass mixed with maple syrup. Gini waited, holding her breath now.

"I'd never say no to free labor," he finally said.

"Oh, we'll figure out a way to make you pay," Jonah said around a grin.

Gini exhaled and worried more about what helping Patrick might cost her.

Chapter Eight

Patrick and Midas arrived early at the station the next morning. He'd slept better than he had in a long time. No dreams. Just the smell of wildflowers. He told himself it had nothing to do with spending the previous evening with Gini. He was tired from getting organized at the house and starting over in a new town so he'd needed the sound sleep. That's what it was. That's what he'd believe.

But the time he'd spent with Gini—with all of them really—had been more fun than he'd expected. The conversation had been easy, and their genuine interest in his building plans had made him feel like one of them. He'd never felt like one of anything back in Rhode Island.

Well, maybe one of the circus sideshow freaks.

At the station, he was on dorm duty again, which was fine. Gave him a chance to think. Besides, he liked cleaning. The order of it, the sterility. Freshening a room calmed him. Scrubbing, sweeping, dusting. The method to all of it was logical and efficient.

So when Jonah came in wearing the muddiest pair of boots in history, Patrick nearly blew up. He jerked his arms toward the gloppy, brown trail of sludge Jonah had left behind.

"What are you doing?" he asked.

"Huh?" Jonah looked to where Patrick pointed. "Oops. Sorry, man."

Patrick was already on his hands and knees wiping at the mess. On the white of the tiled floor, the tracks were particularly harsh. He grimaced as he wrung out his rag and muddy water sloshed into his bucket.

"Where were you before work? A pig pen?" Patrick continued scrubbing until the brown streaks disappeared.

"Almost actually." Jonah sat and peeled off his boots. He held them in his hand and wavered over where to put them. The look on Patrick's face told him nowhere in the dorm would be an acceptable place.

Patrick held out his hand. "Give them here."

Jonah shrugged and handed over the boots. Patrick carried them to an open window. He clunked them together until most of the caked-on mud dropped off. Then he set them down on another rag. Jonah watched the entire process while standing in his socks.

"Do I get those back?" He smiled when Patrick glared his way.

"On your way out." Patrick dumped the contents of his bucket and stowed the cleaning supplies. "Now how were you 'almost actually' at a pig pen before work?"

"I was at Gini's farm. She's photographing for the calendar today." Jonah stood and struck several manly poses with his arms flexed. Patrick didn't know what his reaction to that was supposed to be, and Jonah dropped his arms. "Okay, right. Anyway, I was over there this morning, first thing, to have my pictures taken. Haddy made me stand in the middle of the dirt field beside Gini's barn while one of Haddy's dogs stood on hind legs with its paws resting on my back. Freaking huge dog."

Patrick started down the stairs to the vehicle bay. Jonah hopped off the chair and went after him. Remembering his boots, he stopped back in the dorm and grabbed them. He slipped them back on and met

Patrick downstairs.

"You're really not going to let her take your picture, huh?" he asked.

Patrick's shoulders slumped. Was he going to have to make a deal with Jonah too?

"No pictures." He shook his head.

"It'd make her so happy though." Jonah took a step closer to Patrick. "It's best to keep Gini happy."

Before Patrick could ask a question, Jonah turned on his still slightly muddied heel and walked away. Patrick followed, but Chief Warner got in his path.

"Just the guy I was looking for," the chief said. "Mason called. Wants to chat about your report for the arson case when you get a minute."

"Sure." Patrick stepped around Chief Warner and headed for Jonah.

"Patrick, 'when you get a minute' means now," the chief said.

"Right, of course." Patrick dug out his cell phone and dialed. He gave the chief a nod and walked to the classroom to get some privacy. He sat at the first conference table and drummed his fingers on it. He needed to get to the bottom of what was going on with Gini. Why did his picture mean so much? Why was it best to keep her happy? What did she eat for breakfast? How did she like her hamburgers cooked? Did she like to be on top or the bottom?

"Rivers." Mason's voice cut into Patrick's wayward thoughts.

"Mason, it's Patrick. What do you need?"

"I need to know your sister's favorite flower," Mason said.

"What?" Patrick wasn't sure he'd heard him correctly. "Chief Warner said you wanted to speak with me about the arson case."

"Well, yeah. That's what I told him. I am a professional, you know. But cut a guy a break. Don't

73

make me guess and get it wrong. I want everything to be perfect."

"Everything?" Patrick pictured Mason walking Raina out of the bar last night. What else had he done?

"Our first date. Somehow I found the balls I'd thought I'd lost and asked Raina to dinner tonight. By some series of cosmic events, she said yes. Now are you going to tell me what flower she prefers or do I have to haul your ass in to the station?"

Now Patrick laughed. "You sound a little desperate, Mason."

"I am. I won't hide it. I *really* like Raina. She's beautiful, and smart, and can sing, and—"

"Okay, okay," Patrick said. "I get the idea. Raina loves tulips."

"Tulips? That's it? Nothing exotic? Nothing impossible to get? Tulips?" Mason's voice got higher and higher.

"Tulips. She's loved them since she was a little girl. Used to draw them all over everything. Got in trouble with her fifth grade teacher for drawing them on her homework." Patrick smiled as he remembered Raina crying about that.

"But they're so pretty, Patrick," she'd said. "Why doesn't Mrs. Glickson like them?"

Patrick had thought it had something to do with the fact that Mrs. Glickson probably hadn't received real flowers from anyone in quite some time.

"You're sure it's tulips?" Mason said.

"Positive. Bring her tulips and you're set for the night." Patrick never envisioned the day he'd be telling a man how to win his sister over. He'd spent so much time keeping men away from her. "Look. You seem like a nice guy."

"Uh-oh," Mason said. "Is this the part where you tell me to keep my damn hands off your sister? Because I don't know if I can do that, man."

"No. This is the part where I tell you to *be* a nice guy, or things could get ugly."

"Fair enough. We haven't gotten to know each other that well yet, but I am a nice guy. I'm also extremely inexperienced in the dating department, so I'm more scared than anything else right now."

"Takes a real man to admit that," Patrick said. "Don't worry, Raina comes off a little pushy, but she's scared too."

"Thanks for the inside info."

"No problem. Any case related stuff?"

"I'm heading out today on some leads. Hopefully my foraging will turn up something."

"Keep me posted." Patrick hung up and stuffed his phone back into his pocket. When he entered the vehicle bay, he saw four fighters standing beside one of the trucks. As he approached, their conversation floated to him.

"I got to sit on one of the horses," Willy said. "Gini said she was going to use an up-close shot that had me from waist up and the horse's head in it.

"That's because she was trying to hide your chicken wing legs, Willy," Chuck said. The other two fighters roared in laughter along with Chuck.

"Shut up." Willy folded his arms across his chest but was laughing too. "At least I didn't have to snuggle up to a fluffy bunny. You're lucky it wasn't pink."

More laughter as they ribbed each other. The joking ended with the other two fighters taking off for Gini's farm.

What would Gini have made him pose with? How would she try to hide his...flaws? Patrick had worse features than chicken wing legs to hide.

Doesn't matter. Gini wasn't getting anywhere near him with her camera no matter how much fun the other fighters were having.

****

"Tuck the pup under your chin, Steven." Gini adjusted her camera lens. "That's it right there. Perfect." She looked at the current firefighter model and enjoyed the way the sun made his skin all golden. He had a ripped chest and arms so corded with muscles she was certain he could crush her with a hug.

Haddy fanned herself as she stood next to Gini. "The temperature escalated like twenty degrees back here when he took that shirt off," she whispered.

Gini giggled and snapped her camera. She pulled it off the tripod and went in for some closer shots, experimenting with the light and perspective. Haddy's golden retriever wiggled in Steven's oversized hands, but his grip surrounded the small pup easily.

"This calendar is going to be awesome," Gini said.

Steven smiled then sneezed.

"Bless you." Gini pulled her camera from her eye. "Steven, are you allergic to dogs?"

He nodded, long eyelashes fanning across his cheeks as he looked down.

"Yikes. Haddy, get that pup away from him."

Haddy rushed in and scooped up the dog. Gini put her camera back on the tripod. Steven slipped into his shirt.

"Why didn't you say something, Steven?" Gini asked. "I could have given you another animal."

"Wouldn't matter. I'm allergic to all of them." Steven shrugged and dug his heel into the dirt.

"Well, why did you agree to do this then?" Haddy asked. "Not that we're sorry you did. You looked amazing holding Spike." She bounced the puppy in her arms.

"It was only for a few minutes." Steven sneezed again and Haddy offered him a tissue. "I didn't want to let you down, Gini." He blew his nose.

Gini patted his cheek. "Thanks, Steven. I appreciate it."

"You appreciate it enough to kiss me?" He stuffed the tissue into his pocket and grinned.

"Nice try." Gini waggled a finger. "How about a kiss on the cheek?"

"I'll take what I can get."

Gini rose to her toes and pecked Steven's right cheek. He kept his hands by his sides like a gentleman and tipped his head.

"Thanks. That should carry me along." He gave Haddy a quick hug and headed for his car.

"Tell Nick and Drew they're up next."

Steven waved a hand in acknowledgement and slid into his car. As he drove off, Haddy sidled up beside Gini.

"I could photograph firefighters for the rest of my life." Her voice was light and dreamy.

"We're already halfway through unfortunately." Gini tapped the schedule stuck to a clipboard.

"Pity. Such beautiful scenery." Haddy shook her head. "I loved the way Jonah looked next to my Titan." She rubbed her Doberman's silky black back as the dog pushed his nose into her leg.

"I'll put Jonah in May for your birthday."

"That'd be nice. Who are you going to put in July for you?" Haddy reloaded the film in Gini's second camera so it would be ready for the next round of shots.

"Haven't seen anything I truly like yet." Gini pulled the saddle off Nyx, figuring she'd do some bareback poses with the next guys.

"Or," Haddy said, "you've seen what you truly like, but he won't let you take his picture."

Gini brushed Nyx's ebony coat until it shimmered like a puddle in moonlight. "Don't think I've given up on photographing Patrick. I have a plan."

"What kind of plan? Sneak attack?"

"No, that wouldn't be fair. I'm going to reel him into my net of charm then persuade him to let me take his picture."

"Net of charm? Sounds devious," Haddy said. "I like it."

"He's just shy being new here and all." Gini thought about Patrick's rudeness when they first met and knew that wasn't the kind of guy he was. Not after spending time with him last night. She'd come on too forceful that first meeting. Now she knew how to handle Patrick. He required gentle, subtle, sweet. She could be those.

Probably.

"Once he's more comfortable around us, he'll open up," Gini said.

"He'd better do it fast though. We don't have a lengthy timetable for this fundraiser. If you're going to turn him around, you need to work quickly."

"I'll start this weekend when we're helping him at his house. What better place? He'll be more at ease on his own turf. He won't even see me coming."

"Devious, for sure." Haddy pointed at Gini. "Makes me wonder what I've agreed to without knowing it."

Gini rubbed her hands together as if she were a mad genius. "You'll never know, my friend. Never know."

But Haddy was easy. Patrick was a bigger challenge.

Chapter Nine

Fuel. Heat. Oxygen. These three ingredients were all that were needed to make a fire. To create something so lovely, so magical, so powerful. The simplicity of it never failed to amaze her. That she could light a candle as mommies did on their babies' birthdays and have such radiance at her fingertips. Ripples of pleasure vibrated throughout her body at the thought.

She looked to the candle cradled in her hands. She'd made this candle special. Melted the paraffin wax herself. Added chamomile oil to get rid of the tension that followed her every moment of every day. Poured it into a tin can. Slipped in the wick. Waited. Waited for it to be ready. To take shape. The finished product was a thing of beauty. All perfectly cylindrical and smooth. That wick itching to be lit.

And she'd be the one to light it. To let the candle fulfill its destiny. The flame and wick would meet in an instant blaze like meant-to-be lovers, wild and carefree. Everything in their path would be obliterated by their passion, their heat. What man had erected, fire would demolish in a smoke-filled dream.

The roar of it, the primal thunder of the blaze, was music. A symphony that only few appreciated. Only the ones who were listening. Who could hear the elemental notes and understand the true necessity of it.

She listened, heard, understood. And she craved more. So hard to resist the flame's call.

But not yet. Patience. The time would come and she'd be ready.

****

Saturday arrived before Patrick was prepared. Sure, he had all the materials, all the tools, the know-how, but having people here touching his tools, being in his way, worried him. He'd always worked alone, most of the time in silence. Just the bang of a hammer, the whir of a saw to fill the void. But today, there would be conversation to make, lunch to share, and who knew what else.

He gripped his drill as if it were the soft blanket he'd carried around as a little boy. He could do this. He could allow these few people into his circle. He'd let them into his home, share his building dreams with them, maybe laugh with them as he had at Wolf's Pub.

But he'd be careful too. Especially of Gini. He wouldn't let his guard too far down. He had to keep his distance, maintain the boundaries. For his sake as well as hers.

When the doorbell rang—more of a buzz with a couple of crackly chirps than a ring—he drew in a huge breath and somehow willed himself to answer the door.

"It's just me," Raina said. "No need to be anxious yet." She patted his shoulder and stepped past him into the house.

"I'm not anxious." Patrick closed the door.

"Patrick, please." Raina unloaded the muffins and juice she'd brought with her and turned to face him. "I know having people over is not your thing, but it won't hurt. I promise. You can put your weapon down." She motioned to the drill still clenched in his hands.

Patrick shrugged and pulled out one of the muffins. Blueberry, his favorite. As he chewed, he followed Raina into the great room. She stopped at the three massive windows spanning the far wall.

"Now this is a view." She spread her hands out to encompass the panoramic mountain scene. "I could look at this forever."

Patrick finished the muffin. "It is something, isn't it?" He couldn't quite describe the feeling looking at those distant mountains gave him. The sun shimmered over them, some patches bright green, others shadowed. Anything could be out there beyond the peaks lining the horizon. Maybe the feeling was hope.

The doorbell chirped again, and Raina glanced to Patrick. "You want me to get that?"

Patrick shook his head. "No. I'm okay." He headed for the door. If he was so okay, why were his palms sweaty? Why did that muffin feel like a baseball in his stomach? He couldn't leave them out there. He had to answer the door.

"Turn the knob, Patrick," Raina called from the great room.

He put the drill down, took the last steps to the door, and opened it. Jonah, Mason, and Haddy stood on the other side each carrying something. Jonah had some tools, Mason had coffee, and Haddy had a cooler.

"Morning," they said in unison as if they had rehearsed it.

Patrick's worry lost some of its fizz. "Come on in."

Hellos and how-are-yous passed around. Some tool admiration between Jonah and Patrick. Some paint color talk between Raina and Haddy. Some serious coffee drinking on Mason's part. Still, Patrick couldn't resist wondering.

"Where's Gini?" he asked.

"She'll be around," Jonah said.

"Fussing with the calendar," Haddy added.

"She wouldn't have to fuss much if she'd made it

a Burnam Police Department calendar instead of a Fire Department one," Raina said as she winked at Mason. He stopped mid-sip, and his lips turned up in a grin on either side of his coffee cup.

"You know it's only a matter of time before Gini thinks of doing a police one," Jonah said. "She's always raising money for some animal cause."

As if following their conversation, Midas rose from his napping spot in front of the fireplace and trotted to the door. He sat and angled his head, his tail thumping on the cracked linoleum.

"What's he doing?" Mason asked.

"I don't know." Patrick kneeled down and patted his thigh. "*Venez*, Midas." The dog didn't budge even when the doorbell rang.

Jonah opened the door because he was the closest. Gini stood on the front step, her arms wrapped around a large pot with tall grasses splaying out of it.

As soon as he saw her, Patrick crossed the few steps to get to her. He couldn't have stopped himself if he tried. She rested the pot on her thigh, one foot on the first step, and brushed the curls out of her face. That single motion made Patrick's blood roller coaster through his veins.

"Howdy," she said. "I brought you grass." Gini's smile beamed brighter than the sun, and Patrick had failed to apply the proper sun block. She was penetrating through all his defensive layers with that smile. *Damn.*

Raina nudged Patrick's arm, and he snapped out of his basking. "Thanks." He took the pot off her thigh. His hand brushed against her leg for a second, but in that second he wanted to touch so much more. Instead, he used his hands and arms to put a death crunch on the pot.

Gini stepped into the house and wiped soil off her jeans. "You're welcome. Fireflies like that grass."

She pointed to the pot.

Fireflies?

"Oh, Patrick used to be fascinated by fireflies," Raina said. "Remember that, Patrick?"

He nodded, but didn't take his eyes off Gini. He was fascinated right now.

"I like them too." Gini stepped a little closer, and Patrick blinked out of his enchantment.

"I'll find a good spot for it." He set the pot down under some windows in the kitchen where sunlight pooled on the floor. Midas trotted over to sit beside it.

Jonah turned around in a circle and clapped his hands together. "Okay, Boss, where do you want to start?"

Patrick got his construction mind in gear and pushed his hormonal male mind into the corner. "I've marked the walls that are getting ditched with white chalk. We can start with any of those."

"All right. I brought my reciprocating saw so two of us can be cutting, while the rest cart debris. Sound okay?" Jonah asked.

"Fine with me," Raina said. "I'm here more for moral support."

Mason laughed. "I'm with her. There's not enough coffee in the world to make me pick up a saw."

"And here we have revealed Mason's fatal flaw," Jonah said as he hung his head. "The man will wield a gun, but not a tool."

"I thought you judged a guy by his ability to hold a hammer," Patrick said.

"In most cases, I do. Mason passed the other parts of my interview process. I let the tool thing slide in this one instance."

"How fortunate for us." Gini gave Mason's arm a squeeze.

Mason tipped his cup toward Gini. "Thank you."

"Any time." Gini pulled out a pair of safety glasses from her back pocket and used them as a headband to corral her hair. She wandered around the house checking the walls Patrick had marked. Within moments, Jonah had his saw plugged in and roaring away to cut a starting point for taking down drywall. Midas barked at the noise and took off to find a quieter spot.

"I'm going to move this food to the other end of the house," Raina announced over the buzz. "I don't like sawdust and drywall bits in my muffins."

"I'll give you a hand with that," Mason said.

"Take this too." Haddy handed her cooler to Mason. "Some lunch time goodies."

Mason and Raina disappeared down the hall as Patrick caught up with Gini. Her jeans fit so perfectly that he again had to remind himself to look but not touch.

"You know," Gini said as she turned around, "this is going to be something."

That's what most of his body was hoping for—to be something with Gini. Then Patrick realized she was talking about the house.

"Hope so," he said, but now he wasn't sure what he hoped for.

"The view is amazing." Gini had stopped by the windows in the great room to look outside, but she was beginning to like the view indoors better.

"That's why I bought the place." Patrick came to stand next to her.

His T-shirt hugged his biceps, outlined his chest, and disappeared into a pair of jeans that stretched down two long legs. Gini angled her head up to take in his face and the dark, stubbly beard around his mouth and jaw. How would it feel to have that beard brushing against her face? Those lips against hers?

When Gini realized she'd been studying Patrick a little too long, she shifted her gaze to his and found those hazel eyes examining her as well. What did he see? Was he fooled by the ever-present smile on her face? Or did he know that each day was a struggle to maintain control?

"No furniture?" Gini gestured to the room around them.

"When I sold my place in Rhode Island, the couple who bought it offered to pay extra for the furniture. They were just starting out, and the furniture would be in my way here while I worked, so I took them up on their offer. Made sense at the time."

"And now?"

"And now I miss my stuff." Patrick shrugged. "I'll get new stuff that fits in better here."

Gini tried to picture what Patrick's tastes would be. Leather and wood instantly came to mind. She could almost smell the two intermingling in the giant great room. Why did she want to see the finished product so badly?

"We should get rolling," Patrick finally said.

"Right." Gini picked up his reciprocating saw. "Can I drive first?"

Patrick's eyebrow rose, and he studied her for a few more silent moments before Gini pulled down her safety glasses, her hair spilling back into her face. She put the saw down to reach into her pocket and dig out an elastic. Gathering the curls, she smoothed them back and captured them into a low ponytail.

"Do you think I can't handle the saw because I'm a girl?"

"No, not at all," Patrick said. "I'm sure you can handle it. Jonah said you built an arbor with a swing, right?"

"Uh-huh. Came out damn good too."

"If you do say so yourself." Patrick plugged the saw into an extension cord.

"Other people will say so too. You can ask them."

"Maybe I will."

Gini couldn't help imagining the calendar shot she'd use for Patrick once she got him to agree. He'd have to pose with Saber. That cat would totally soften those sharp firefighter edges, and his furry tail draped across that muscled chest she was sure Patrick was hiding from her would be a nice contrast in texture. She chewed on her bottom lip as she thought about positioning cat and man on her swing. It'd be perfect.

"What are you doing?" Patrick's voice made her suck in a breath.

"Huh? Nothing."

"You looked like you were thinking really hard."

"Sometimes I do think really hard."

"About what?"

Dangerous territory. *Not going there.* Gini shook her head. "Lots of stuff." She stuffed earplugs into her ears, pulled the trigger on the saw, and it revved to life. Conversation impossible.

Gini attacked the nearest marked wall and made an opening in the drywall. Soon they were both ripping off the wall board in bits and pieces. Mason and Raina, back from their food organization, took turns carting the trash out to the pile in the driveway. Somewhere else in the house, the metallic screech of Jonah's saw sounded as he cut through nails. He was already onto removing studs. She'd be that far along too if she hadn't wasted time inspecting Patrick.

But she wasn't used to guys like him. So quiet. So serious. She'd spent her entire life around firefighters, most of which had been loud jokesters either teasing her or flirting with her. Patrick's stoic observation, however, left her in uncharted territory. She wasn't sure how to handle him or even if she should.

Damn, she wanted to though.

With the last of the drywall peeled away from their section, Gini picked up the saw again and hacked at the studs. Patrick gripped the loose wood and twisted until each stud came free of its ceiling mount. They had a tall pile of two-by-fours in no time.

"Where are those trash collectors?" Patrick gestured to the stack.

"Probably making out somewhere," Gini said.

Patrick laughed, and Gini let the sound wash over her. She had a feeling he didn't laugh easily so when he did, it felt as if she'd accomplish something. She found a piece of chalk on the window ledge and made a tally mark on a piece of drywall. Gini propped the drywall up against the window.

"What's that?" Patrick shook sawdust from his shirt.

"I'm keeping count."

"Of what?"

"How many times I make you laugh today." Gini drew a smiley face next to her tally. She shaded in around the mouth to make a beard, which made Patrick laugh again. He took the chalk from her hand, his fingers hesitating for a moment around hers, and added another mark to her tally.

"You're off to a good start." He hoisted up three of the discarded two-by-fours, balanced them over his left shoulder, and headed for the garage. The way his legs strode powerfully across the disgusting linoleum floor made Gini feverish. His ass filled out those jeans as if someone had poured him into a denim mold.

Maybe she didn't have to worry so much about setting things on fire around Patrick. Maybe she had to be concerned about being set on fire instead.

Chapter Ten

By the time lunch rolled around, Patrick counted sixteen marks on Gini's tally board. He hadn't ever laughed that much in so short a time. He wasn't sure how she was managing it. She revealed some fun childhood stories about Jonah. Talked about her parents. Shared a few interesting photography tales. She weaved humor and wit into every topic. He had no choice but to laugh. Had to be magic or something.

Even Raina stopped in her debris hauling with Mason to furrow her brows at Patrick.

"Who are you and what have you done with my brother?" she whispered as she tugged him aside.

Patrick sobered, and Raina shook her head. "No, no," she said. "This guy is preferred. He looks...what's the word I'm looking for? Oh, I know. Happy. You're allowed to be that, you know."

He nudged her away and turned to find Gini inspecting her ungloved finger. As he walked over, a drop of blood rolled down her perfect flesh and landed on the plywood floor.

"What happened?" He automatically went into full rescue mode and took her hand in his.

"Nothing. A splinter got me. A mammoth one. Right through my glove. Got some of it out." She held up her index finger, but blood covered the slice again.

Patrick guided her to the small bathroom off the master bedroom. Pointing to the toilet, he said, "Sit." He pulled a few tissues from the box behind her and made her press them to her finger. "I've got some first aid stuff in the other bathroom. I know this bathroom is ugly, but it's clean." He gestured to the cracked white tile on the floor and the hideous, wicker-like wallpaper. "Be right back."

The instinct to take care of Gini was immediate. As he grabbed the first aid kit, Patrick told himself it was because he was a firefighter. Helping people was what he did. As much as he tried to believe that, he knew other factors were at work here. He should call Jonah. Have him tend to Gini. He was her brother. She'd want family to help her. When Patrick emerged from the other bathroom, however, he turned toward the master bathroom instead of toward the kitchen where Jonah was working.

Inside the bathroom, Gini appeared small, fragile. Patrick knew she wasn't. God, he'd seen her brandish his saw like a knight with a sword. She didn't flinch when drywall or sawdust spit back into her face. She'd used raw physical strength, grunting louder than Patrick sometimes, to free some of the studs. She wasn't delicate.

And yet, she was.

Patrick kneeled beside her and pulled away her hand holding the tissue. Fresh blood pooled in the cut.

"I washed it," Gini said, "but I'm a slow clotter."

"That's better than being a fast bleeder," Patrick said.

Gini laughed. "Okay, tally mark for you on that one."

Patrick smirked and pulled on some gloves.

"My, my. Aren't we prepared?" Gini let him rest her hand, palm up, on his knee.

He looked at the gloves as if not realizing he'd donned them and shrugged. "It's automatic."

"I see. Standard procedure." Gini squirmed a little when Patrick used tweezers to remove the sliver of wood still in her finger.

"I follow the rules." He disinfected the cut and bandaged it in under a minute.

Gini wiggled her finger, testing its mobility with the bandage. "Ever break the rules?"

Patrick looked up at her then. Some part of him wanted that to be an invitation, and maybe it was. One dimple showed in her cheek as she grinned at him, her blue eyes unwavering. It would be so easy to lean in and taste her lips, sample what she had to offer, swim in it.

No, most likely, you'd drown. Then there would be no turning back.

When he stood, Patrick ran a gloved hand over his left side, smoothing out the wrinkles in his T-shirt, trying to smooth out the scars on his skin under the shirt. But he couldn't. He couldn't get rid of them, and he couldn't let Gini see them.

"No. Rules are rules. Best to stick to them." Patrick packed up the supplies he'd used, threw away the gloves, and left the bathroom. After lunch, he'd pair himself up with somebody else. He was mistaking proximity for feelings. Just because he'd spent the morning with Gini didn't mean he was ready to spend anything else with her.

He wasn't ready to spend anything else with anybody.

****

Patrick was noticeably distant through the lunch Haddy doled out from her cooler. While the others chatted and joked, he sat off to the side on one of the several wooden chairs left by the previous owners of the house. Midas lay sprawled out on the floor at his feet. Gini watched as Patrick ate his sandwich almost mechanically, as if he were counting the number of times he chewed. She thought she'd made some headway with him this morning, but apparently she was wrong. He was more closed off than ever.

What was wrong with asking if he ever broke the rules? She'd been teasing. Okay, maybe she'd been hoping. Hoping he'd take the bait. He looked as if he'd thought about it before he stormed out of the bathroom. Good Goddess, he was difficult to read. She'd never get his picture for the calendar at this rate.

When the lunch break ended, Gini decided it was time for a new strategy.

"Raina," she said. "Want to work with me on removing the wallpaper in the hallway?"

Patrick's head popped up, and Raina gaped at him. His eyes sent her a warning that Gini couldn't decode. What was he so afraid of?

"Sure." Raina slowly stood, hesitating in front of Patrick, but he nodded.

"Great. C'mon." Gini grabbed Raina by the forearm and led her to the hallway.

Soon the others meandered back to their various projects. Patrick started on another wall—one where he could see the hallway, Gini noted.

"What do you want me to do?" Raina asked. "I've never removed wallpaper before." She glanced back at Patrick.

"Find a seam and get the razor blade underneath it. Like this." Gini successfully stripped off a sizeable sheet of paper. Smoothing her hand over the area, she said, "We'll have to do something about the glue that's left behind, but let's get the paper off to start."

Raina nodded and began peeling. After a few moments of silent work, Raina peeked at Patrick again, who was ripping into more studs with his saw. His earplugs were wedged in his ears.

"You like him." Raina stood mere inches from where Gini scraped the wall.

Gini stopped working and stared at Raina.

"What?"

"My brother. You like him. I can tell. There have been enough longing glances on both your parts. I know about longing glances." She waved to Mason, who rolled a garbage barrel past them. He shot her a quick smile and continued on his way.

"I don't know wh—" Gini started.

"Save it," Raina interrupted. "Patrick could yank those earplugs out at any second. It's good you like him. I want you to like him. I also want you to know Patrick has many…layers. Layers he's thickened up over time to keep the world out. His moving here was an enormous step. I still can't believe he did it. I'm so glad he did though, and I want him to have the whole deal, you know."

Gini wasn't sure what to say. She'd expected to have to grill Raina and here she was just giving the information out.

"The house, the job, the chick. A life. It's about time he allowed himself to have one. He's always worried about taking care of my sister, Julianne, or me. He's ignored his own needs. You can fix that."

Gini swallowed loudly. She had her own things to fix. How could she fix someone else's mess? She risked a glance at Patrick still sawing, and a strange sensation passed through her. Like a cooling breeze, a melting of something inside her. It relaxed her, loosened the muscles in her entire body.

"I'm not saying it's going to be easy," Raina said. "He's a handful. No doubt about it. You probably already realize that. But he's also the most unselfish man you'll ever meet. He'll always put you first. Always."

As the saw wound to a stop and Patrick removed his earplugs, Raina slid down the hallway a little ways. She tugged at the wallpaper and sent a pastel flower-covered length to the floor. Gini stared at it as her mind processed what Raina had said.

"What's the matter?" Jonah whispered. He leaned on the ladder he was toting to the kitchen.

Gini turned to face him. His safety glasses were hooked on the neck of his T-shirt. "Nothing's the matter."

"You sure you're not...you know, mad?" He propped the ladder against the wall and slid his hand around her bicep, ready to get her out of there if necessary.

Gini shook her head. "No. Just confused, I think."

Immediately, Jonah's grip loosened. "Confused is okay." He gave her arm a light squeeze and snagged Haddy as she walked by. He waltzed her across the kitchen area, which was considerably larger now that walls had been removed.

"Hey, Patrick," Jonah said. "This makes a great ballroom!" He dipped Haddy low, and her laughter filled the house. When he snapped her back up, their lips nearly touched. Jonah spun her away from him, and Haddy sent Gini an "Oh my God" look.

Could she get Patrick to act like Jonah? Carefree and fun. Did she want him to? Was his solemn quietness what drew her to him? Jonah was an open book, what you saw was what you got. The only thing he hid was what he knew about Gini, and he only did that to protect her. Wasn't that what Raina said Patrick had been doing? Protecting her and his other sister. Was he so different from Jonah then?

Gini sifted a breath through her teeth and returned to the wallpaper. If only she could peel away Patrick's layers as easily as this truly revolting wallpaper.

****

What was Gini up to? Patrick didn't like the way she and Raina were huddled next to each other as they removed drywall screws from two-by-fours he planned to reuse. Hunched over sawhorses, they talked every so often, and Raina kept smiling at him. What was she telling Gini?

He told himself he didn't care. Two minutes later though, he picked up three two-by-fours and planned to use them as an excuse to go into the garage. Mason swung by, however, and ruined his scheme.

"I'll take those." He slid them from Patrick's grasp and carted them to the girls. Mason lingered a few extra moments, chatting it up with Raina, making her giggle. Apparently, he was over his shyness.

Patrick glanced to the kitchen area where Jonah and Haddy were tearing off drywall. Jonah paused to brush gypsum dust off Haddy's T-shirt and ended up touching way more than he needed to. It was as if everyone was on a date in his house except for him.

And Gini.

She was focused on getting those screws out, the joviality she had shown in the morning long gone. She didn't look angry, but those dimples were nowhere to be found. Was that his fault? Because he'd been a grouch through lunch. He didn't want her to be unhappy, but he wasn't used to his mood affecting anyone else's.

He made up his mind to go talk to her. After three steps into the kitchen area, however, two different cell phone rings echoed, one the standard, manufacturer's ring, the other an obnoxious, bass-heavy song. Patrick dug his phone out of his jeans' pocket, and Jonah did the same.

"This can't be good." Jonah glanced at his phone's screen. "Fire at Meadow Cliff Park." He looked at Patrick. "You must be getting the same call."

"Yeah." Patrick stuffed the phone back into his pocket and ditched his safety glasses and earplugs.

As he and Jonah headed for their cars, Mason's phone rang, a quiet span of classical music.

"Hold up. Wait for me," Mason said. "I'm getting called in too." He hopped into Jonah's Mustang.

"You'll take Haddy home?" Jonah called to Gini.

"Of course," Gini said.

Patrick hesitated for a moment at his truck and looked at the three women assembled in his garage.

"Go," Raina said. "We'll close up shop here."

"Thanks." He climbed into his truck and let Midas hop in. Within moments, only a cloud of dust remained of the men.

As he drove, part of Patrick's brain worked on what he had to do once he got to the station to be ready to fight the fire. The other part couldn't shake the image of Gini, drill squeezed between her elbow and ribs, in his garage watching him leave. When he came home tonight, the house would be dark and silent. No one would be waiting for him. No one would ask him how his day was. No one would cuddle up behind him under the covers and hold him until morning came.

No. He'd be alone. For the first time in a long time that bothered him.

****

"Must be tough to be a hero." Haddy wiped her glasses with the corner of her T-shirt. Two white spots of gypsum were left behind.

"Harder to love one," Gini mumbled. She'd worried about her father when he was chief. She got nervous if she didn't hear from Jonah after he'd gone to a scene. Did she want to add to her list of firefighters to worry over?

"When Patrick first said he wanted to be a firefighter," Raina began, "I told him he was crazy." She hugged both her arms to her chest. Her eyes closed, and Gini watched a shiver ripple down Raina's body.

Before she could stop herself, Gini reached out and rested her hand on Raina's shoulder. "You okay?"

Raina blinked several times, her gray eyes glossy and unfocused. She shifted her gaze to Gini's face and cleared her throat. A weak smile masked whatever it was she truly felt.

"Yeah. I can't comprehend how Patrick can stand to be around fire," she finally said. "It scares me to death, and it should scare him too."

Gini and Haddy looked at each other, unspoken questions written all over their faces, as Raina made her way back into the house and started cleaning up. They followed her and lent a hand. Thirty minutes later, the three of them stood between Raina's car and Gini's SUV.

"Thanks for helping my brother," Raina said. "There's so much work to be done here."

"It didn't feel like work." Haddy stuffed her cooler into the back seat of Gini's car.

"That's because you had Jonah to play with." Gini tapped her hip against Haddy's.

"We were just goofing around." Haddy drew a heart in the gravel driveway with her boot and grinned when Gini saw it.

"If by 'goofing around' you mean shamelessly flirting," Raina said.

"Shush," Haddy said. "I didn't see you telling Mason to stop following you around."

"I never tell handsome men to stop following me around." Raina winked. "Seriously though, Patrick will never say it, but having you folks around is good for him. He's a loner by nature." She deliberately caught Gini's gaze. "He needs some prodding out of his shell."

"Gini," Haddy said, "isn't shell-prodding one of your many talents?"

"Get in the car, Haddy." Gini opened her door

and turned back to Raina. "Listen, Haddy and I are organizing an event so folks—"

"Women," Haddy corrected.

"Yeah, probably mostly women, can get their Burnam Fire Department calendars signed. Would you be interested in singing at that event?"

"Me? Really?" Raina jingled her keys in her hands.

"Yeah," Gini said. "You've got a great sound. Bluesy and jazz-like. I think it would make our whole firefighter-ogling droolfest a bit classier."

Raina barked out a laugh. "Droolfest. I like the notion. Count me in."

"Great." Talking to Raina was so much easier than dealing with Patrick. Gini had trouble believing they were related. She and Jonah were so much alike. Raina and Patrick, not so much.

She fished out a business card from her purse on the driver's seat. "Here. Stop by the studio when you get a chance, and we'll talk specifics."

"Sounds good. I'll bring some samples of my music." Raina took the card and punched in the code to close Patrick's garage door. "See you around, ladies." She waved and got into her car.

"Getting in with the sister," Haddy said. "Another phase of your scheme to photograph Patrick?"

They got into the SUV, and Gini started it up. "All part of the master plan," she said, but she wasn't entirely sure what the end goal of that master plan was anymore.

Chapter Eleven

Clouds of black smoke were visible before the fire trucks arrived at Meadow Cliff Park. When they pulled into the parking lot, people were running to their cars and generally causing a monster traffic jam as they tried to leave. Six police cars screamed into the lot behind the fire trucks and dealt with crowd control by ushering cars into a single file to exit the small park.

As Patrick hopped off the truck, he caught sight of the abandoned swings. Most of them still swayed back and forth as if mothers had yanked their children from them so quickly the swings didn't realize they were without passengers. He imagined how frightened the children must have been, and his hands curled into fists inside his gloves. No child should have to be that afraid. Ever.

Jonah tapped him on the helmet signaling they were to head into the barn, which stood in the center of the park. It appeared to be the nucleus of the blaze, angry flames reaching through its roof to the gray sky above. Now that Patrick looked closer, he could see people tugging horses into the parking lot. He stopped one of them, a short, older woman wearing a cowboy hat.

"All the people and horses out of that barn?" he asked.

"Stacey Briars hasn't checked in." The woman wound and rewound the reins in her hands. "We run drills for this sort of thing, but she hasn't checked in."

"All right. We'll find her." Patrick adjusted his gear and jogged to catch up to Jonah. Midas ran alongside him. "One Stacey Briars has not checked in."

"We'll have ourselves a look then," Jonah said.

Patrick followed Jonah, who was taking the lead. Two other firefighters had been assigned to the same duty because the barn was so huge. Midas maneuvered his way ahead of them and waited for Patrick's signal to enter the barn. As fighters opened up the hoses on the blaze, all of them entered and fanned out. Patrick and Jonah went to the left with Midas while the other two went to the right. After several minutes of serious sniffing around, Midas scratched at a stall door and barked.

When Patrick caught up to the dog, he saw a young woman slouched against the door inside the stall.

"Jonah," he said. "Over here." Patrick gave Midas a quick rubbing and signaled for him to get out of the barn.

"One Stacey Briars found," Jonah said into his helmet to alert the other two fighters.

"She's alive," Patrick said after checking her neck for a pulse. He hoisted the woman up into his arms.

"Let's move." Jonah and Patrick began their exit.

As Jonah navigated his way out, a crackling noise above them sounded, causing both of them to look up. A barn rafter lost its hold and swung down. Patrick didn't have time to react with Stacey in his arms, and the thick beam nailed Jonah in the right shoulder. He lost his footing and went down to all fours.

Patrick was near enough to the exit that he handed Stacey off to a waiting EMT. He ran back inside and hauled Jonah to his feet. Though he could hear Jonah's swearing at the movement, Patrick didn't stop until they were both outside the barn and far enough from the blaze to be safe.

"Man down," Patrick said into his helmet. "Need medical."

"On the way," a voice buzzed back.

Jonah had already ripped his helmet off. "Fuck, that hurts."

"Can you move it?" Patrick helped Jonah out of his coat.

Jonah wiggled his fingers and forearm, but couldn't raise his arm from the shoulder. "Nah, I heard something snap in there when I got hit. Man, I think I'm going to pass out."

Patrick eased Jonah onto his back and sure enough, Jonah passed out. Just as well. Unconscious was the only way to face the kind of pain he had to be in. One EMT dealt with a coughing Stacey Briars, and two others secured Jonah to a stretcher, bracing his arm to his side before carrying him off.

Patrick helped one of the hose teams until the scene hissed with heat, but was free of actual flames. On his way to the truck he had ridden on, he saw Mason talking to the lady in the cowboy hat. Mason motioned Patrick over.

"Mrs. Jennison here said the barn"—he looked down at his notebook—"just 'exploded like fireworks on the fourth of July.' All of her staff was supposedly out conducting riding lessons, so the barn should have been empty at the time the fire broke out."

"Only it wasn't," Patrick said. "Stacey Briars was found inside. She's with the EMTs right now. Minor smoke inhalation, I think."

"Thank goodness she's okay." Mrs. Jennison wiped the sweat off her brow with a shaky hand.

"I'm going to need you to investigate the scene, Patrick," Mason said.

"Okay," Patrick said. "But I want to check in on

Jonah first. He got hurt back there. They took him to the hospital."

"What? Really?" Mason's face lost some of its color.

"Probably broke his collarbone," Patrick said. "You should call Gini."

"Right." Mason's expression went back to all business. "I'll get a few men to keep nosy folks out of the scene until we can come back."

"Who'd want to do this? Meadow Cliff is a place people come to relax and have fun with their families," Mrs. Jennison said.

"We'll get to the bottom of it," Mason assured her.

She nodded, her cowboy hat sliding back and forth as she did so. Clicking her tongue, she nudged the horse beside her and joined the other instructors at the edge of the parking lot.

"Seems we may have more than a one hit wonder on our hands here," Patrick said.

"I was afraid you'd say that," Mason said. "This was a much larger fire than the one on Cloudson Drive. You think Arson Mystery Guest is going to up the show each time?"

"They do love a performance," Patrick said. "That's half the thrill of setting the fire. Seeing if they can outdo themselves and what kind of an audience it'll attract."

"Sick." Mason pulled out his cell phone. "I'll call Gini and meet you at the hospital."

Patrick joined his team on the truck, whistled for Midas, and watched the blackened remains of the Meadow Cliff barn get smaller and smaller as they headed back to the station. He always wished he could do more. Putting out the fire was first and foremost, but what about afterward? What about the poor families or, in this case, the poor horses and trainers, who now had nowhere to call home base?

101

Sure, the flames were gone, but so was everything else.

Fire took so much. His own parents. His ability to look at himself in a mirror. Julianne's...He closed his eyes thinking about his sister.

Now Jonah, the first person he'd actually be willing to call a friend, was hurt. Just when Patrick thought he was winning against fire, it laughed in his face.

****

"What do you mean we can't see him?" Gini's temper was rising. The only thing keeping it at bay was her fear that Jonah wasn't going to be all right. That and her father's arm around her shoulders.

"I'm not saying you can't see him, Miss Claremont," the nurse said. "I'm saying the doctor is tending to him, then you can take him home."

"Easy, Gini," her father whispered. "There are people here. Lots of them."

The caution in his voice was clear, the warning to not get angry, and she counted to ten. When she turned back to the nurse, Gini somehow managed a smile. "I'm sorry. I'm just concerned."

"Of course," the nurse said. "I'll come back out and let you know when you can collect your brother."

Collect him? As if he were a lost wallet or something. Gini clenched her teeth as her father's hand massaged her neck.

"Here, Walter." Her mother held out a paper cup of coffee to him.

"Thanks, Liz," Walter said. "Gini, why don't we sit over there and have ourselves something to drink?" He nudged his daughter to the bright blue chairs in the hospital waiting room and pushed the coffee cup into her hand.

Gini sat and took several deep breaths. *I will not lose my cool. I will not get angry. I will only breathe.* She told herself this over and over until her muscles relaxed, and the heat of her annoyance dropped away.

"Jonah's lucky to have gone this long without a firefighting-related hospital visit," Walter said.

"You'd seen the ER at least ten times by the time you were his age," Liz added.

"Want to know what I remember most about those ten times, Lizzy?"

"What?" Gini's mother sipped her coffee.

"You bringing me muffins, cupcakes, pies, and cookies from the bakery." Walter patted his stomach, a satisfied grin on his face.

"Oh, Walter." Liz rolled her eyes, but her grin matched her husband's.

Gini looked from one parent to the other, and the last bit of anger vanished. She could never be pissed for long around either one of them. Fury didn't stand a chance when they were nearby. Love radiated off them like beams of sunlight warming everything in range.

"Feel better?" Walter asked as he patted her knee.

Gini nodded and tried a sip of coffee. Lukewarm, bitter, and a little gritty. Hospital coffee.

"I saw that face," Liz said. "It is horrendous coffee, but I've spoiled you on the good stuff at the bakery. Now you're a coffee snob."

Gini laughed along with her parents, but watched as her mother twirled a finger around the end of her hair and her father's foot tapped on the sterile white waiting room floor. They put on a hell of show for her, trying to make her feel at ease— keep her from burning the place down—but they couldn't totally mask their worry over Jonah. How selfish of her to count on them to keep her calm when they did have another child in crisis at the moment.

"I'm sorry," Gini said.

"For what, honey?" her mother asked.

Gini looked up at Liz. People often confused the two of them at a distance. They shared the same coloring and body type. Long, blond curls bounced around both their faces, and they had both been accused of walking around as if they owned the universe. Gini hoped she looked as good as her mother did when she was her age. She also hoped she'd eventually inherit a fraction of her mother's compassion and patience.

"For getting all riled up." Gini took another sip of the coffee, made a face again, and put the cup down on a table beside her seat.

"It's okay." Walter rubbed her forearm.

"No. I've got to get a better grip on myself. I'd been doing so well. I don't know what's going on lately, but I feel..." Gini glanced up and saw Patrick standing at the front desk with Mason.

"You feel what, sweetie?" Liz leaned forward.

"Umm...off balance." Gini stood without consciously deciding to and ignored her parents' voices as they called after her. She just knew she had to be next to Patrick. If she could stand next to him, she was sure she'd feel better. More centered. Less lost.

Mason turned around first. "Hey, Gini. How is he?" He gave her a hug, but Gini kept her eyes focused on Patrick whose hazel eyes studied her.

Gini took a step back. "The doctor's with him now."

"He's going to be fine?" Mason asked.

Gini nodded. "Broken collarbone. In about twelve weeks, he'll be back in business."

"Good." Mason leaned on the front desk, but pushed back to standing. "Your mother is waving me over. I'm going to say hi."

Gini stepped out of Mason's way and watched Patrick shift his weight from one foot to the other.

His hair was wet and a fresh, soapy smell hung around him.

"Were you with Jonah?" she asked.

"Yeah." Patrick stuffed his hands into his pockets. "We were doing a sweep of the barn at Meadow Cliff. On our way out, a rafter swung down and knocked him off his feet."

"You got him out?" She inched closer and drew in Patrick's scent. Cut wood and soap.

"Not without him swearing."

Gini thought of the words her brother tried—unsuccessfully—not to use.

"Thank you." Before she could stop herself, Gini was taking another step closer. Sliding her arms around Patrick's waist. Pressing herself to his chest.

It didn't feel as if he were breathing. He was so still at first. His heartbeat filled her ear, and the rhythm of it soothed her. She didn't want to let go, but realized she had to. She couldn't hold on to him. He wasn't hers.

As she loosened her grip, Patrick's arms came around her. His hands slid across her back, his fingers warm against the skin peeking from her tank top. He rested his chin on the top of her head for a moment, and Gini felt completely protected. From everything.

"Want to get some air?" Patrick stepped back so he could see Gini's face.

"Yes." Her voice didn't sound like her own.

Patrick slipped his hand into Gini's and tugged her toward the doors. Once outside, he led her to an iron bench and sat. He patted the space next to him, and Gini eased down. Patrick stretched his long legs out, crossing them at the ankles. The creases in his uniform pants made Gini smile.

"I would have pegged you as an ironer," she said.

Patrick looked down and thumbed the crease. "I've got a thing about wrinkles."

"Allergic to them?"

"Something like that." His hands rested at his stomach, and Gini watched his calloused fingers spread out. She thought about the way they'd felt against her skin a moment ago and had to look away.

"Anyone else get hurt today?" She focused her attention on the parking lot across the street.

"No. An instructor was treated for smoke inhalation, but that was it. Amazing considering the size of the fire. Mason wants us to investigate."

"Another suspicious blaze?" Patrick's use of the word *us* intrigued Gini. Did he mean they were a team? Could they be?

"Maybe. Won't know until we get photos and Midas and I dig through the scene."

"As soon as I see Jonah's all right, I'll get my cameras. I know you probably want to get in there and collect evidence."

"The evidence will be there whenever we get to it. Your family needs you right now." He stood. "Had enough air?"

When Gini nodded, Patrick took her hand again and led her back into the hospital. As they approached the waiting room, he released her hand and let her go in first. A doctor led Liz away when they entered.

"What did he say?" Gini asked. "Where's Mama going?"

"They're going to bring Jonah out in a few minutes." Walter glanced over Gini's shoulder at Patrick.

"Oh, this is Patrick Barre," Gini said. "Patrick, my daddy, Walter Claremont."

"Patrick." Walter shook Patrick's hand, but his jaw muscles tightened. Gini knew he remembered Patrick's name, that he was the one who'd caused her to set the bush on fire at the fire department.

Her father didn't forget threats to his daughter's—his family's—safety.

"Nice to meet you, sir," Patrick said.

"New to the department, right?" Walter asked.

"New to Vermont."

"Like it so far?"

Patrick hesitated for a moment. "Yes. I believe I do like it so far."

Gini knew her father was about to launch into his zillion question interview, but her mother came back into the waiting room.

"Who do we have here?" Liz looped her arm around her husband's waist.

"Patrick Barre," Walter said. "My lovely wife, Liz."

Patrick took Liz's hand, but looked back at Gini who smiled.

"Go ahead," Gini said. "Say it."

"You look just like her," Patrick said.

"No doubt I'm her mama, huh?" Liz wrapped her other arm around Gini.

"No doubt at all, ma'am," Patrick agreed.

"Now whom do you get your fine features from?" Liz cupped a hand to Patrick's cheek as only a mother could get away with.

"Suppose I'm a little of what they both were."

Liz clamped a hand onto Patrick's forearm. "Oh, honey, your parents are no longer with us?"

"No, ma'am. Died when I was sixteen."

Gini fought the urge to touch Patrick. He looked so vulnerable as he answered her mother's questions. Made sense now why Raina had said he put protecting his sisters before his own needs. He'd probably had to.

"My, my." Liz shook her head. "I hope Vermont is kinder to you, Patrick." She patted his arm. "Well, it has to be kinder if you've made friends with my Jonah and Gini."

"And now I've met you," Patrick said.

Liz giggled. "What's your favorite pastry, Patrick?"

Patrick's brows furrowed as he looked to Gini.

"Tell her and she'll make sure her bakery is well stocked with your favorite."

"I see. Blueberry muffins," Patrick said.

"Oh, Walter." Liz's face bloomed with a delighted smile. "Another blueberry muffin guy."

"Yeah, well, he better keep his hands off my muffins." Walter glanced at Gini.

"There's plenty of muffins for everybody, Walter. Be nice." Liz gave Patrick another smile, but whirled around when the doctor spoke.

"Here we are. One Jonah Claremont, slightly damaged, but still in good condition."

Jonah sat in a wheelchair, his right arm in a sling that wrapped around his torso, bracing the arm to his side. He was a little rumpled, but Gini watched three nurses at the front desk send him interested glances. He managed some winks back to them. He was going to be fine.

"Poor baby," Liz said as she took over wheeling Jonah. "Mama's going to make you soup and fresh bread."

"Because that mends bones," Gini said, causing Patrick to clear his throat to mask his laughter.

"Hush, Gini," Jonah said. "You know Ma's soup is magic."

"Ought to be," Walter said. "The way she boils it up in that cauldron of hers. The question is can she get eye of newt this late in the season?"

"You go ahead and make fun," Liz said. "When Jonah is up and around faster than is medically possible, we'll see who's laughing then." She waggled a finger at all of them, Patrick included, and wheeled Jonah to the door. "Get the car, Walter."

"Yes, dear." Walter left and Jonah held out his

hand to Patrick.

"I owe you one, man."

"Consider it payment for the walls you removed this morning." Patrick shook Jonah's hand.

"Nah, dragging my ass out of a fiery barn is worth more than that."

"I've got more work for you when you're able."

"Deal." Jonah yawned.

"Want to come to our house, Jonah?" Liz asked.

"No, thanks, Ma. I want to go home. I'm tired."

"Okay, sweetie." Liz wheeled him outside where Walter had pulled the car up to the curb. "One of us can stay with you."

"Actually," Jonah said, "I had a specific nurse in mind." He looked to Gini, who dug her cell phone out of her enormous purse.

"I'm on it, Jonah." Gini winked as she dialed. "Hiya, Haddy. Got a favor to ask you."

As Jonah let Patrick help him out of the wheelchair and into the car, he said, "If Haddy's got a nurse's uniform, this might be an excellent night. Chicks dig a man in need."

Another nurse sent Jonah a smile as she rolled the wheelchair back into the hospital.

Patrick closed the door. "Chicks just dig *you*. Period."

"When you got it, brother, you got it." Jonah grinned, but Patrick caught the wince as he shifted in the back seat.

"Yes, he asked for you," Gini said. "I swear to the Goddess, Haddy." She rolled her eyes. "Fine, hold on." Gini held out the phone to Jonah. "She doesn't believe me."

Jonah smirked and took the phone. "Haddy, are you saying you don't want to take care of me?"

Gini heard Haddy's muffled, "Jonah! You're really hurt?" While Jonah talked, Liz climbed in the passenger seat, and Walter started the engine.

Gini looked at Patrick. "You want to meet at Meadow Cliff later?"

"If you're available." Patrick's hands slid into his pockets, which disappointed Gini. After holding his hand earlier, she wanted his hands to be...available.

"Once he convinces Haddy to come over, he'll be all set. Besides, Mama will make sure he's well-fed and hydrated and medicated and whatever else her motherly instincts tell her he needs."

"She's used to tending injured firefighters, huh? Jonah told me your father was chief before Warner."

Gini nodded, thinking now about injured firefighters. *Be careful*, that voice inside her head warned.

Hush, she told it.

"Seven o'clock all right?" she asked. "I've got to stop home to feed my horses and get my other camera."

"Sure." Patrick pulled his keys from his pocket, and Gini flicked a glance to the way his fingers moved over the keys. How would those fingers feel trailing over her skin?

Chapter Twelve

Patrick stopped home and made a quick sandwich in the small kitchen, which would eventually be a tavern-like room, complete with a pool table and dartboard. He had figured the less he had to leave his home, the better. Now he didn't know if that was the right strategy any more.

He'd gutted the actual kitchen on his second day in the house, happy to have another kitchen to use in the interim. He couldn't wait to get started on the maple cabinets he'd begun to design on his laptop the other night.

Now he sat at the wobbly table alone, munching his sandwich and thinking about Gini and her family. Her mother's soft hand on his cheek as she asked about his parents. The protective look in her father's eyes as he told Patrick to keep his hands off his muffins. Gini and Jonah must feel so loved all the time.

You have love too. His sisters. He loved them both and knew they loved him, but the sense of unity that comes from an intact family was not something they had. Lost it about twenty years ago. No getting it back. Sure, his grandparents had done a fine job raising Raina, Julianne, and him, but it wasn't the same as having one's parents around. Nana and Papa were always a couple steps behind on the important matters with a generation between them and their teenage grandchildren. They did the best they could, and Patrick loved them for it.

But his grandparents were gone now. He and

his sisters were truly alone. He'd pushed that thought away, but seeing Gini's parents tonight and the way they all pulled together for Jonah left Patrick wanting. Wanting what, he wasn't quite sure.

He finished his sandwich, downed a glass of grape juice, and fed Midas. Deciding that jeans and a T-shirt would be more comfortable for crawling around a burned barn, Patrick changed out of his uniform. As he pulled off the Burnam Fire Department polo shirt, his fingers brushed against his scars. Funny how he never got used to feeling them, seeing them. He always remembered they were there, but each time he made contact with the mangled skin, fresh revulsion surfaced from deep inside him. How could anyone else ever look at him and like what they saw?

Patrick washed his face at the sink in the bathroom and slipped on a T-shirt and jeans in the bedroom he was using. It'd be awhile before the master bedroom was ready. The mattresses stacked on the floor in the smaller bedroom were lumpy, but they were a place to sleep. He'd removed the mirror Raina had hung across from the makeshift bed the other morning. Hauled it out to the garage where he figured its next step was to the debris pile. The less mirrors in the house, the better.

"Midas."

The dog trotted to Patrick's truck and waited by the passenger door. Midas was the one creature he didn't have to hide from. Midas knew all his secrets and wanted to be around him just the same.

"A dog's all a man really needs." Patrick rubbed Midas between the ears before opening the car door. When the German Shepherd jumped up into the seat, he turned and gave Patrick's cheek a solid lick. "Thanks, buddy."

Patrick slid into the driver's seat and headed for

Meadow Cliff. As he drove, he pictured Gini hugging him at the hospital. He'd been surprised by her action and more stunned at his—hugging her back. Holding a woman was not something he did. Too close, too much touching, too much at risk. The last woman he'd allowed himself to hold had ended up in his bed one moment and had made excuses for why she had to leave the next. He could have respected her if she'd said what was on her mind. That he was too damaged for her to look at, never mind touch, or make love to. He would have understood. He'd leave if he could too.

Gini's hug had been different though. She was thanking him for helping her brother. A hug of gratitude, not seduction. And yet, why had it brought all his senses to life? Made his blood run hot in his veins? Flashed pictures of her body entangled with his?

He tightened his hold on the steering wheel as Meadow Cliff Park came into view. The early evening sun sifted through the broken framework of the center barn. Nearby trees rustled in the warm breeze, some of their leaves singed to a crispy black.

Gini's SUV was the only other car in the lot. She leaned against the driver side door, that ginormous purse weighing down her shoulder. In a pair of jeans and a T-shirt that said "My Cat Is Smarter Than You" across the front, she looked so comfortable, so accessible.

So beautiful.

Patrick pulled his truck into the spot next to hers, and Midas let out a whimper.

"That's what I was thinking." Patrick gave the dog another good rubbing before grabbing his investigation kit and opening the car door. Midas crawled over him and ran around the truck to scramble to Gini.

It took all of Patrick's energy not to do the same.

****

"Hey, boy." Gini kneeled and Midas slobbered all over her cheeks, his tail wagging excitedly.

"*Asseyez*." With that one word, the dog sat back, and something fluttered in Gini's chest over the authority in Patrick's deep voice.

"Did you train Midas yourself?" she asked.

"Yes. Met him as a puppy, trained him, and got him all certified."

"Why French commands?" Not that she didn't love hearing the language roll off Patrick's tongue even if it was only one word at a time.

"Most people don't speak French out on the streets in these parts, so there's less chance of Midas getting confused. He's likely to only hear French words from me."

"What are the commands? What do they mean?"

"*Restez* means stay." Patrick whispered the words so Midas wouldn't think he needed to do all of them. "*Venez* is come. *Partez* is leave. To shake hands is *secouez*, and to smell is *sentez*. When I want him to sit, I say *asseyez*, and lay down is *couchez*."

"Makes it all sound so sophisticated." Gini smiled and wiped the cheek Midas had soaked. "Does he only work with you?"

Patrick nodded. "But he seems to like working with you too."

"Well, I like working with him." Gini scratched under Midas's chin, and he rested a large black paw on her thigh. Gini rubbed him for a few more minutes and let the dog nose around in her hair.

When Gini got to her feet, she grimaced at the sight of the barn. "I do wish, however, I could work with Midas under different circumstances. I do hate a crime scene."

"Why did you agree to photo for the police department then?" Patrick stepped onto the dirt pathway leading to what remained of the barn. Gini and Midas fell into step beside him.

"Mostly for Mason." Gini pulled her camera out of her bag and slung the strap around her neck. "He asked me and I couldn't say no."

"Did you owe him a favor or something?"

"No, but Mason is..." She puckered her lips out, drew them back in. "You can't say no to Mason. He's just always been around. Like part of my family. He and Jonah were glued at the hip as teenagers. Can't say that's changed as they got older."

"So you subject yourself to crime scenes because Mason is your brother's best friend?"

"I don't know." Gini walked quietly beside Patrick for a few minutes. "I guess I do it because Mason is *my* friend. I've been friends with him as long as Jonah has." She turned to face Patrick as they stood in front of the barn. "And the answer to the question you're really asking is no."

"What?"

The stunned look on Patrick's face was priceless. Did he think she couldn't tell what he was after?

"No, Mason and I never dated."

Gini slid under the caution tape surrounding the building, and Midas followed her. Patrick stood on the other side, and she glanced once over her shoulder. He looked so damned perfect standing there in his casual clothes.

"You coming?" Gini called.

Patrick slipped under the caution tape and wandered into the barn.

Work. Gini needed to focus on work. Not on how adorable Patrick looked or how much she wanted to wrap her arms around him again. That was a mistake in the hospital. She'd let her emotions override her logic. She had to be careful.

"I'm going to start shooting," Gini said, "but if you want photos of something in particular, let me know."

"Okay." Patrick pulled out a notebook and jotted down observations as Gini's camera flashed in the darkened barn. Though evening sunlight still filtered through the open sections of roof and wall, charred wood and soot blackened everything.

They worked in silence for about thirty minutes, staying out of each other's way. Midas sniffed and led Patrick to different corners of the barn. Gini kept one eye on the photos she was taking and the other on the way man and dog worked together. Midas would show signs of interest in an area, and Patrick would crouch to that designated spot. He'd scribble something in his notebook and pat the dog, murmuring words of praise and French commands.

How could a man with a relationship like that with an animal not want to help her with a calendar to benefit a bunch of animals? It didn't add up. There had to be something she was missing. Some piece to the puzzle that was Patrick Barre.

"Here we go." Patrick was on all fours in the corner of what used to be the last stall and shining a flashlight onto the singed floor.

"Got something?" Gini navigated over the debris to look over his shoulder.

"Yep, right here." Patrick wiggled the beam of his flashlight, and Gini pointed her camera there. She snapped a few pictures and zoomed in until she saw what he'd found.

"Another candle."

"Uh-huh. Only this one is green."

"Granny Smith apple green." Gini checked her camera screen. "I've got it if you want to bag it."

Patrick carefully scooted the misshapen ball of wax out with his pen and slid it into an evidence bag. "Midas found a gasoline trail too, but with all this hay in here, the fire didn't need it. This barn never had a chance."

"So it's got to be the same person, right? Because

of the candles?" Gini stuffed her camera in her purse and held her hand out for the evidence bag. Patrick placed it in the palm of her hand, and they both studied it more closely.

"Might be. Unless we have two lunatics with a penchant for candles." Patrick drew in a deep breath. "What's that smell?" He leaned closer to the bag as Gini did the same, and they knocked heads.

"Ouch," Gini said. "Sorry."

"No, I'm sorry. That was all me."

"No, some of that was definitely my head." Gini laughed and rubbed her forehead. Though Patrick's head had been hard, his skin was warm, so incredibly warm. She closed her eyes and focused on the smell. "It smells like chamomile."

"Chamomile?"

"Yeah, people use it to reduce stress, calm them. I toss it into a bath or a tea every now and again."

Patrick scratched more notes into his notebook and shuffled around the barn to gather a few more samples. When all the evidence was tucked away into bags, he clicked off his flashlight. The barn was almost completely dark now.

"What time is it?" he asked.

Gini pressed a button on her wristwatch, and a blue light lit up the shadows. "Nine o'clock. Wow, I didn't realize it was getting that late." Her stomach growled into the silence.

"Neither did your stomach." Patrick shouldered his kit bag and led the way out of the barn.

"I didn't get to eat before I came here. I was feeding my horses." Gini shrugged. "That's typical me. I get everyone else squared away and forget about myself." She dug around in her purse. "I think I have some crackers in here or something."

"Crackers are not dinner," Patrick said.

"I know." Gini had several ideas as to what would make a tasty dinner. All recipes included one fireman, lightly buttered. "But I've got to go home and develop these pictures. I don't have time to cook something up." She pulled out her keys and unlocked her car door.

"You should eat something more than crackers."

"Why are you so concerned about what I eat for dinner?"

"I'm not. I just think you had a long day with helping at my house, waiting for Jonah at the hospital, and then coming here. You deserve a good meal."

Gini turned around and leaned against the car to look at Patrick as he opened his truck door. Midas hopped in, and Patrick placed his kit on the floor of the passenger side.

"You cook?" she asked.

Slowly, Patrick turned to face her. "Yes."

"Okay." *Careful,* she thought. *Don't scare him away.* "Do you want to come to my house and cook me something? You know, because you're so concerned about my eating habits and because you owe me for the serious wall demolition I did at your place today."

Gini held her breath as Patrick stood frozen in front of her. Why did she feel as if she'd just rolled the dice and they'd rolled right off the table, spinning and spinning forever? Was he going to answer her? Had he heard the question?

"You want me to cook for you?" he asked.

Yep, he'd heard.

"Uh-huh. What do you say? My refrigerator is full of stuff. I'll process photos, you can mince, chop, dice, whatever. Then you can have the photos hot off the press, so to speak."

The bait was there, dangling on the hook. All she had to do was reel him in. Good Goddess, she hoped the line didn't snap.

****

Cook for her? She wants me to cook for her. At her house. Patrick turned the notion over and over in his mind. All the warning bells sounded, all the red flags waved, but only one thought truly scared him.

He didn't want to say no.

"Can Midas come?" Why did his voice sound like that of a little boy? He cleared his throat.

"Of course. If he could cook, I wouldn't even invite you."

"Real nice."

Gini laughed, and Patrick felt suddenly at ease.

"So what do you say?" Gini heaved her purse into the SUV and turned around to face him.

As he stared at her T-shirt, the way it curved to all her curves, the gears in Patrick's logical brain ground to a halt. The idea of being in Gini's kitchen—of seeing her home—caused his physical and emotional brain to take charge, which they rarely had the chance to do. They were not going to let the opportunity slip by.

"I'll cook you dinner," Patrick said.

"Great." Gini's smile lit up the parking lot, and something lit up inside Patrick. "You want to follow me?"

Everywhere you go for some reason. "Sure."

They both climbed into their vehicles, and Patrick looked at Midas. The dog glanced back at him as he did sometimes, as if he understood exactly what Patrick was feeling.

"This will either be very interesting, Midas," Patrick said, "or a complete disaster."

Midas woofed and pushed his nose into Patrick's ear. Patrick slung his arm over the dog's back and maneuvered his truck behind Gini's SUV. After twenty minutes of driving, some on dirt roads similar to the ones that led to his own place, the darkened silhouette of an old farmhouse and barn came into view. Patrick parked behind Gini and took a deep breath before getting out of his truck.

"We'll cook her a dinner and be on our way." Patrick glanced at himself in the rearview mirror as he repeated these words two more times then got out of his truck.

"You want to meet my horses first?" Gini's purse thudded as she plopped it on the porch steps.

Midas barked and started for the barn.

"I guess he does." Patrick followed Gini after the dog.

"We'll let him think he's in charge." Gini opened the barn doors, and Patrick ran a hand over the thick, wrought iron hinges.

"These are nice."

"Jonah put those on. The old ones were rusted, and the left door was leaning into the right one. When Gran owned the place, she didn't have any horses so she let the barn get rundown."

"This was your grandmother's?"

"Yep. She left it to me because I spent the most time here with her. It was like my own personal—"

"Sanctuary," Patrick finished.

Gini stopped at the first stall where a black nose peeked out. "Exactly. What made you use that word?"

"I'm considering my place to be a sanctuary too. A safe place."

"Safe. Yes, that's it exactly." Gini shook her head and looked as if she was going to say more. Instead, she opened the stall and waved Patrick over. "This is Nyx."

"Ah, the Goddess of Night." Patrick brushed his palm over the horse's nose.

"Someone knows their Greek mythology." Gini elbowed him and raised an eyebrow.

"When Raina was thirteen," Patrick began as he stroked Nyx's mane, "she was obsessed with Greek mythology. Don't remember how she got hooked on it, but she dragged me to the library weekly to look for books on gods, goddesses, and myths. She couldn't get enough of it."

"Only an exceptional brother would allow himself to be dragged to the library every week."

"I wouldn't say I was exceptional. Who else was going to take her? My grandparents hardly drove."

"You could have said no. I'm sure you wanted to be with your friends doing your own things."

Gini handed Patrick a brush and took one for herself. Nyx puffed out a breath into her hair, and she kissed the horse's face. Patrick was distracted for a moment by Gini's lips, but then started brushing Nyx's sleek black coat.

"I wasn't exactly social," he said. "I'd missed some school after my parents died when I was sixteen and couldn't catch back up with anyone after that."

Why are you telling her this? Just cook dinner. Patrick tightened his grip on the brush.

Gini brushed her way to Patrick's side. "It must have been terrible to lose your parents while you were so young." She held her hand out for the brush, but when Patrick put it in her palm, she put the brush down. She took his hand and squeezed it between both of hers. "I don't know what I'd do without my parents."

"You guys are tight. I could see that at the hospital. It was nice to see." Patrick liked to think he would have been close to his parents if they were around now.

"My parents are the best. My whole family is. They..." Gini's brows furrowed and then she closed her eyes.

"They what?" Patrick slipped his hand out from between hers and touched her shoulder.

"They're always there when I need them." She cleared her throat and walked to the stall across

121

from Nyx's. "Sometimes I think I need them too much."

"I'm sure they don't mind." *Who wouldn't come to her rescue?*

"No, they don't. And I try to pay them back whenever I can."

"Sounds like a fair system."

"Sometimes it is." Gini coaxed a beautiful white horse to the front of the stall. "This is Moon. She's my unicorn."

Patrick patted the horse where a horn would be were she a fantasy creature. A fantasy creature for a fantasy woman. He could easily picture Gini riding the horse, her golden hair streaming out behind her.

"Beautiful." Both the woman and the horse.

"Gentle as a summer breeze too. Nyx can have an attitude, but Moon here is as laid back as they come. Nothing unsettles her."

Patrick picked up the brush again and tended to Moon's coat as Gini brushed the other side. The horse didn't move a muscle, puff out a breath, make a noise.

"I wish Midas was this still when I give him a bath."

"A bit wiggly, is he?"

"There's a twenty-foot splash zone at bath time."

Gini chuckled. "I'm guessing you get wetter than he does?"

"You guessed right. In Rhode Island, I had an apartment, which didn't give me much room to play with. Should be better in the new house. More space, plus I could give him a bath outside in the yard."

"Is that why you moved to Vermont? For more space?" Gini took the brushes back and gestured for Patrick to close the stall. She led Patrick and Midas out of the barn and toward the house.

"I moved here for Raina mostly. She's been trying to get me to come to Vermont for years. She saw the fire department opening and made a good case, so here I am."

"Our gain." Gini unlocked her back door. "What about your other sister? Raina mentioned you had another."

Patrick's heart drummed in his chest. Family talk was not an area he wanted to explore with Gini. "Yes, Julianne. She lives in Rhode Island still."

"Won't she miss you?"

"Probably not." It just slipped out. The words, the tone, the emotion. He couldn't rewind and take it back either.

"Ouch." Gini flipped on a light to illuminate an oversized kitchen. Plenty of counter space spanning wall to wall, a deep sink under a set of wide windows, an old-fashioned stove, but a modern microwave. Greens, yellows, and a little bit of barn red mixed to add a country charm to the kitchen.

"Look, I—"

Gini held up a hand to stop Patrick. "You don't have to tell me about Julianne, Patrick. I can see by that muscle right there in your jaw that you don't want to talk about it. I won't push." She took a step closer to him, and he took a step back. The sunny gleam in her eyes faded a bit, but she quickly recovered. "If you do want to talk, I'll listen."

She walked to the refrigerator on the other side of the kitchen and waved a hand at it. "Use anything you want in here or in the pantry." Gini pointed to a little room off the kitchen. "Pots are in the cupboard by the stove. Dishes and glasses above the pots. Spoons, forks, knives are here." She pulled open a drawer under the island in the center of the kitchen.

Patrick wasn't sure if he should say he was sorry for stepping back. Wasn't sure if he should go ahead and unload the story of Julianne. Wasn't sure what the hell he was doing.

Gini grabbed her camera from her bag. "I'll be in

the darkroom, two doors down on your left." She pointed down the dark hallway. "Knock when the food is ready, okay?"

"Okay." He couldn't believe she was going to make it this easy. *She really isn't going to push me?* He wasn't sure how to feel about that. He was used to people pushing then having to keep his distance from them so they wouldn't uncover everything he kept locked up tightly. "Anything in particular you'd like to eat?"

"Surprise me." That radiant shine was back in her eyes as she glanced over her shoulder then disappeared down the hall.

Standing in the kitchen with Midas at his feet, Patrick's curiosity over Gini grew tenfold. What kind of a woman starts off demanding to take your picture, ends up tearing down walls in your house, photographs crime scenes, knows to back off on the family talk, and invites you to cook dinner for her in her kitchen?

The answer was simple in Patrick's mind. A woman who was up to something.

Chapter Thirteen

No pictures. No family talk. Too many rules to Patrick Barre. So rigid and armored. And yet, when Gini had hugged him in the hospital, he was none of those things. He'd held her, taken her outside by the hand, sat with her, and kept her calm. He'd been soft, gentle.

In her kitchen, however, Patrick had locked down like a bank vault. No withdrawals. No deposits. See the next teller, please. What was he protecting so vigilantly, and why did she care? She'd gone this long staying out of relationships. Kept herself busy with work, the farm, community projects like the animal shelter, and family stuff. If there was no time for men, she couldn't miss them, right?

Something about Patrick, however, made her notice her aloneness. The way he lingered in her mind had left her wanting things she'd decided she couldn't have.

"And you can't have them, idiot." Gini clipped a photo on the drying line and shook the hair out of her eyes. "He'd leave the toilet seat up one too many times, and you'd scorch the bathroom over it."

Living alone allowed her to manage her situation, and when she did have to make contact with people, she sought out the pleasant ones, people who wouldn't try her patience, test her limits, and start fights. Her family screened people before introducing Gini too. In this manner, she'd avoided clashing with the world's more difficult folks and had kept her ability under wraps. Only her family and Chief Warner knew, and Gini wanted desperately to keep it that way. She'd continue to pretend she was happy, that nothing bothered her.

That she wasn't a freak.

The universe had made up its mind. She wasn't allowed to fall in love and make a family of her own. What if her condition was genetic? Would she pass it on to her children? Would they have to hide and never be able to share all of themselves with another person?

Gini shuddered at that thought and hung up another picture. She'd eat the meal she'd foolishly asked Patrick to prepare and send him on his way. To Hell with his photograph too. He didn't want his picture taken. Fine. The calendar would still be fantastic. She'd double up somebody. Maybe Jonah. Haddy would love that idea.

When a soft knock sounded on the door, Gini clipped the last photo and pulled off her gloves. She gripped the end of the counter in the darkroom and centered herself. She could maintain her balance, enjoy a meal she didn't have to cook, and resist Burnam's newest firefighter. She opened the door, and a little of her resolve slipped away.

Patrick stood in the hallway with a dishtowel slung over his shoulder and his hands resting on either side of the threshold to the darkroom. To Gini's mind, his body filled the hallway—tall, muscled, and smelling faintly of tomatoes. She looked a little too long. She knew that. She couldn't stop, but she knew.

"All done?" she managed to ask.

Patrick nodded. "You?" He gestured with his chin to the darkroom behind her.

"Just hung up the last photo. Let's eat while they dry." Gini waited for Patrick to move his hands so she could exit, but he didn't. She didn't trust herself to squeeze by him at the moment. Didn't want to make accidental contact and scare away the control she'd summoned.

"This is where you make your magic?" he asked.

Gini glanced behind her. "When I'm working from home. You want to see?" Her stomach growled, and Patrick laughed. Damn, his face looked wonderful when he smiled.

"Maybe later," he said. "Let's get that growling bear hiding in your stomach fed first."

Later? How long did he plan on staying? How long could she let him? "What did you make?"

He slid his hands away from the threshold and let Gini go first. "Sit and you'll see."

When Gini rounded the corner and arrived in the kitchen, she stumbled to a stop in front of the table. Two places were set opposite one another with bowls of bread, salad, and pasta between them. Wildflowers sprayed color from a tall, glass vase in the center of the table, and the radio on the kitchen counter was tuned to a jazz channel. The lights overhead were dim, and Gini was touched, confused, and scared to death all at once.

"Sorry." Patrick's breath was warm on her ear. "Midas gets carried away sometimes."

Gini burst into laughter, so caught off guard by the humor. Patrick laughed along with her, and the next thing she knew, she was accepting the seat he slid out for her, placing a napkin on her lap, and holding her glass out as Patrick poured lemonade.

"I have beer or wine if you want it," she said. The smell of wildflowers and tomatoes danced in the kitchen and made the tranquility Gini usually felt at home swell. Having that serenity while a virtual outsider was sitting across the table was all new terrain. Unexplored and unpredictable. Possibly dangerous. Yet, Gini couldn't find the words to tell Patrick he had to leave.

"Lemonade is fine with me," Patrick said.

"We wouldn't want Midas to have to drive you home I suppose."

Midas lifted his head from a cozy spot he'd claimed by the couch in the living room.

"I don't think Midas plans on ever going home. Look at him. He's as comfortable as can be."

"Dogs have it easy." Gini reached for a piece of bread. "They're comfortable anywhere."

"So are cats apparently." Patrick pointed to the top of the refrigerator.

Gini looked up and stood. "Saber, get yourself down here right now." The cat squinted his eyes then stretched out each one of his limbs, giant paws wiggling. He arched his back, jumped to the counter and finally to the wood floor. He padded over to Patrick, brushed his cheek against Patrick's ankle, and slinked over to Midas. The two animals touched noses and sniffed each other. Saber circled three times and settled in a tight ball in front of Midas. The dog's head slunk back onto his paws and his eyes closed.

"Well," Gini said. "That's not how I envisioned that going down. Saber doesn't like dogs."

"Midas doesn't like cats."

"He likes mine." Gini sat back at the table and leveled her gaze on Patrick. He was still watching the animals, and Gini took in his profile. Strong jaw line with a dark, shadowy beard. Full lips, pouting a little as he considered the new friendship between Midas and Saber. Long, feathery eyelashes rimming lids squinted in contemplation.

Slowly, Patrick turned his attention back to Gini. "What?"

"Huh?"

"What's the matter?"

"Nothing. Why?"

"You look confused." Patrick parceled out salad

to each of them.

"Just surprised, I guess." Gini poured dressing onto her salad and offered the bottle to Patrick.

"Surprised that Midas and Saber are becoming friends, or surprised that I pulled this all together for you?" Patrick gestured to the table.

"Both." Gini munched on a piece of bread. "You might not be the person I thought you were."

Patrick's eyebrows rose. "I might not want the answer to this, but who did you think I was?"

Gini laughed when his face scrunched up as if he were expecting a left hook to the jaw. "I thought you were a jerk after that first day at the station."

"I had to be a jerk, because you wouldn't let up."

"About taking your picture." Gini sipped her lemonade.

Patrick nodded. "If you'd accepted my polite no, I wouldn't have gotten nasty."

"I see that now," Gini said. "You're a private guy, and I can respect that. I'm just not used to people—"

"Saying no to you. There's a word for that, you know."

"What?"

"Brat."

Gini laughed and hadn't had to force it. It bubbled out, genuine and free. "I suppose I am a brat on some level. I'm just used to getting what I want."

"Which also falls under the heading of brat."

Patrick took their salad plates to the sink when they'd finished, and Gini liked how at home he appeared in her kitchen.

He twirled spaghetti onto her dinner plate then filled his own. The bright colors of tomato, broccoli, carrot, and pepper fancied up the pasta, and he'd drizzled a light pesto sauce over it all. When Gini took a bite, she couldn't stop the satisfied hum that escaped her.

"One brat, thoroughly loving this meal," she said.

"Better than crackers, yes?"

"Definitely." Gini took a few more bites, wiped her mouth, and looked up at Patrick. "Thank you."

"No problem. It was easy to make."

"Thank you for back at the hospital too." Gini focused her attention on the bottom of her glass as she took a drink.

"Also no problem." Patrick fiddled with the fork in his hand. "It was easy to be hugged by you. And to hug you."

Gini gazed at him now and forgot all the rules as she stared into his hazel eyes swirling brown and green like running through a forest. He smiled and dove back into his spaghetti. Gini resumed eating as well and enjoyed the companionable silence that hung between them, nothing but the sound of jazz on a piano filling the kitchen.

When the food was gone and the dishes washed and dried, Gini opened the freezer and took out a container.

"I've got dessert covered," she said. "You're not allergic to walnuts, are you?"

Patrick shook his head and leaned against the counter next to Gini to see what she had. "Ice cream?"

"Yep. Maple walnut. Made it myself." She dropped three rounded scoops into a bowl and handed it to Patrick.

"Wow. Maybe you're not the person I originally thought you were either."

"You mean maybe I'm not a brat?" Gini smirked as she put the ice cream back into the freezer after filling a bowl for herself.

"Oh no, you're still a brat," Patrick said, "but you're a skilled brat."

"Thanks, I think." She handed him a spoon.

"Actually, I was looking at some of the framed pictures you have up. Are they your own photos?"

Gini nodded. "Sometimes I fall in love with a picture, so I frame it and stick it up somewhere. I've got a couple up at the studio too."

"You're good. I especially like the one of your horses with the sunrise behind them." Patrick pointed to the wall in the living room where the photo in question hung between two windows.

"That's one of my favorites too." Gini picked up her bowl and motioned to the porch door. "You want to sit outside?"

Patrick followed her, and Gini led him to the swing under the arbor.

"More of your skilled work?" Patrick ran his hand over the chains holding the swing.

"Yes," Gini said. "My latest creation actually. I love to swing." She sat and once Patrick was beside her, she pushed off the ground beneath them with one foot. The swing swayed gently as the warm summer air blew her hair back. Again, a relaxed quiet embraced them as they finished their dessert.

"That is probably the best ice cream I've ever had." Patrick clanged his spoon on the bottom of his nearly empty bowl.

"It's always a hit. Who doesn't like ice cream?"

"Raina, actually."

"Your sister doesn't like ice cream? That's just crazy. Is she lactose intolerant or something, because that I could forgive?"

"Nope. She just doesn't like it. Never has. Won't go near the stuff."

"Man, I could easily accept an all ice cream diet."

"Too bad you can't carry it in that enormous purse of yours." Patrick laughed when Gini's mouth dropped open.

"Do not badmouth the purse." She pointed her

spoon at Patrick.

"What do you carry in there? It's like a suitcase."

Gini shook her head. "A woman's purse is her treasure box. I'm not telling you what's in there. It's a secret."

"I have toolboxes smaller than that purse."

"Maybe someday I'll let you peek, but I don't know you well enough to expose my purse to you." Gini stacked her empty bowl inside Patrick's and put them both on the ground beside the arbor. She pushed them again and sent the swing rocking back and forth.

Darkness had fallen over the fields and everything was cloaked in that purpled curtain of night. As they swung, tiny pinpricks of light flashed on and off in the tall grass.

"Fireflies," they said at the same time.

"It must be awesome to create a spark like that," Patrick said.

"You think so?" Gini's chest tightened as the swing came to a stop. Creating sparks had been nothing but trouble for her.

"Yeah. It's like magic. They're attracting mates with light patterns. Isn't that amazing?"

If only her talents with sparks were so useful. "My dad used to call me Firefly when I was little."

"Because you lit up his world, no doubt."

"Something like that." Now she spent a good portion of her mental energy trying *not* to light up his world or anything else in range.

Gini rested her head on the back of the swing and gazed up at the sky where the stars were fireflies. She closed her eyes and let out a long exhale. When Patrick's hand closed over hers, she opened her eyes and rolled her head to face him.

"You okay?" he asked.

"Mmm-hmm."

Patrick slid his hand off hers, but Gini caught it

before it was gone. He stopped moving and let her pull his hand back toward her.

"I should probably go. It's getting late," he said.

"Right." Only Gini didn't let go. Her mind was working overtime to come up with a way to keep Patrick right where he was.

"Gini?" Patrick scooted closer, and Gini loved the feel of his arm brushing against hers.

"Yes?"

"It's been a long day. You should probably turn in."

She nodded but didn't make a move to get up, to put some distance between them. Instead, she stared at the sky and breathed in the wildflowered night.

"You put flowers on the dinner table." She looked at him now.

"Seemed like a nice way to finish the table off." Patrick shrugged and stretched out his legs, his hand still caught under hers. "Besides, Midas insisted. Thought you'd like them."

"Midas, huh?" Gini grinned. "That dog has class."

"He's a charmer."

"And what about you?" His hand tensed, but she was determined not to let him lock up. She held on firmly. "You're more the quiet, mysterious type, right?"

"I guess." His unease was tangible, like something sitting between them on the swing.

Gini sat up and leaned toward him. She watched as he swallowed slowly and looked at her. Enough light spilled from the back porch to illuminate the expression on Patrick's face.

"I just want to say thank you, Patrick. Is that okay?"

Patrick nodded, and Gini reached over, slid her free hand up his arm to rest at the back of his neck, and pressed her lips to his.

If starting fires had felt like an incredible fever erupting throughout her body, kissing Patrick was that times ten. She felt as if she'd been tossed into a volcano only she didn't have the faintest urge to find a way out. His lips were warm and soft, outlined with a slight scratchiness that had her insides flopping around. Maple walnut flavor mixed with a primal male seasoning Gini hadn't allowed herself the pleasure of sampling in so long.

She was cautious though. She pulled back, intending to stop before things got out of control, but Patrick slipped his hand up into her hair and started another round. He coaxed her mouth open and deepened his exploration of her. His tongue was velvet against hers, and Gini's entire body responded to his kiss, his touch. She edged closer until she could get both hands around to the back of his neck. His other hand pressed at her back, bringing her closer still.

As the control she fought so hard to maintain everyday drowned in Patrick's hold, the phone rang in the kitchen. Midas barked and they ripped apart, scuttled to opposite ends of the swing. The phone rang twice more before Gini's answering machine picked it up.

"Gini? Gini, you there?"

"Jonah," Gini rasped.

"You should get that." Patrick ran a hand through his hair and scratched at his neck where Gini's hands had been. "He might need something."

"Maybe *I* need something," Gini mumbled.

She got up from the swing, and Patrick grabbed their ice cream bowls. He followed her into the house and went to the kitchen while she grabbed the phone.

"Yes, Jonah?" She took the phone into the living room where she didn't have to look at Patrick standing before the sink, legs spread apart, head bent, ass calling out to be touched.

"Ma said you and Patrick were investigating the barn at Meadow Cliff?" Jonah's voice sounded tired.

"Yes." Gini sat on the couch and studied her bare feet.

"I need to talk to Patrick. I tried his cell, but he didn't answer. Do you know where he is now?"

"Yes." Gini chewed on her bottom lip. What was she going to tell Jonah? She never kept any secrets from him. Ever.

"What's wrong with you?"

"Nothing." Jonah was so in tune with her emotions. As if he were psychically linked to her or something. Came in handy most of the time. Not tonight. Tonight she didn't want her brother to have any clue about what she was feeling, what she wanted so desperately to do.

"Are you angry? Did Patrick piss you off? Do you need me to—"

"No, Jonah. Everything is fine."

"Why do you sound weird then?"

"Not weird. Frustrated, maybe."

"Why frustrated? Gini, what's going on?" His concern was growing exponentially, and Gini knew that in his condition he should be relaxing.

"There's no need to worry, Jonah. I'm okay. Do you want to talk to Patrick?"

Ten solid seconds of silence passed before Jonah laughed. "Patrick is at your house. I see."

"No, you don't. Now do you want to talk to him or not?" Gini took in a deep inhale. Frustration was turning into annoyance, which could easily lead to anger. She had to keep it light and not be bothered by what Jonah was thinking.

"Did I interrupt something?" Jonah asked.

"Nothing that should have gone on longer than it did, Jonah."

"I don't know about that," he said. "I think you

and Patrick could—"

"Don't, Jonah. Please, don't. We had dinner, and he's going home now unless you want to speak with him." Gini kept her voice low as Patrick put the bowls away. She didn't want him to leave, but he had to.

"No, tell him to call me when he leaves. *If* he leaves."

Gini heard the amusement in Jonah's voice. "He's leaving." She took another deep breath, got centered. "How are you doing? Shoulder hurt?"

"Like a bastard, but there's a beautiful woman here offering me drugs, sponge baths, and such. I think I'll manage."

"Only you could have fun with a busted collarbone." Gini had to laugh at her brother's outlook on things.

"You know it. You should have some fun too, Gini."

"Maybe I did. Good night, Jonah. I'll come by tomorrow, okay?"

"You'd better. Night."

After hanging up, Gini slid off the couch and went to the kitchen. Patrick was kneeling while Saber rubbed his cheeks over Patrick's fingers. She'd never seen her cat be so friendly. And while a huge German Shepherd watched no less.

"Male bonding?" she asked as she returned the phone to its holder.

"Seems to be." Patrick stood and wiped his hand on his jeans. Saber weaved between Gini's feet and meowed.

"Hush, Saber. I'll feed you in a minute."

"I should go," Patrick said. "*Venez*, Midas." He patted his thigh, and Midas got to all fours beside him. "Everything okay with Jonah?"

Gini wanted to kiss him all over again for his concern. "Yeah, he's fine. Haddy is taking good care of him." She'd probably have all sorts of stories for Gini when they talked. "He wants you to call him when you leave. Said he tried your cell."

Patrick's brows furrowed as he reached into his pockets. "I must have left my phone in the truck. I'll give him a call on the drive home."

"You want to take the photos of Meadow Cliff with you?"

"That would be great."

Gini nodded as Saber meowed again. What was that cat trying to tell her?

"Give me a minute." She disappeared down the hallway and gathered the photos from the darkroom. She stuffed them into an envelope and, thinking of Patrick's labeled file folder in Mason's office, wrote "Meadow Cliff" along with the date on the outside.

As she handed the envelope to Patrick, she said, "Thanks again for dinner. I enjoyed every minute of it."

Patrick jingled his car keys in his hands, and again Gini imagined those hands on her. Would she ever get to feel them again? Would he touch more of her next time? Would there be a next time? Could she allow one?

"I enjoyed dinner too. And the ice cream." Patrick flicked his gaze to the porch door. "And the...swinging."

Gini held her breath as Patrick closed the distance between them. She had to angle her head up to look at him, and when she did, he brushed his lips ever so lightly against hers.

Then he stepped away, smiled at her, and walked to the door.

"*Partez*, Midas."

The dog nuzzled Gini's knee and left through the door. Another second later and Patrick was gone too.

Saber meowed yet again, but Gini didn't move. She was afraid to.

If she moved, would the pleasant warmth still tingling on her lips vanish like a dream upon waking?

If so, she was quite content to remain asleep.

Chapter Fourteen

Sunday morning with orange juice, a bowl of cereal, a breathtaking mountain view, and a loyal dog by his side. What more did a man need? Patrick glanced down at the photos of Meadow Cliff spread across the table he was using in the small kitchen.

A woman with golden curls and satin lips. That's the more a man needed. The more *this* man needed. Last night, he'd come to the partially gutted building he now called home and spent at least ten minutes standing in the darkness as he reviewed the evening's events. Gathering evidence at Meadow Cliff had gone smoothly. Even cooking Gini dinner had been less strange than he'd thought it was going to be.

Kissing her, though. That's where he'd let things get out of hand. She'd wanted to thank him, and he hadn't been able to stop at just that. Once he'd gotten a taste of her, all maple walnut and female, he'd become so hungry for more. Gini had been willing to give him more too. That's what scared him. The fact that all he'd had to do was keep kissing her, and they could have easily wound up doing more. So much more.

After a cold shower last night, he'd stared at his scars in the bathroom mirror. In light of how close he'd come to letting his control slip away, his chest and left thigh looked so much worse to him. The melted flesh fourteen surgeries had not been able to repair would have repulsed Gini. Some spots an angry red, others a ghostly pale white. All peeking beneath a spider web of grooves crisscrossing his skin. He was certain one look at him would have destroyed any thoughts of physical attraction Gini might have had about him last night. She deserved perfection and that was something he could not give her.

Shaking away the pitying thoughts, Patrick focused on the photographs. He finished his breakfast and made a new file folder for the Meadow Cliff paperwork he'd filled out so far. No mistaking that both fire scenes had been started by candles with a gasoline trail. He hated to admit that it was going to take a few more scenes to be able to put all the pieces together. Two incidents were not enough to develop a pattern and uncover a path to the arsonist. In Patrick's experience so far, arsonists were characteristically intelligent people with a history of mental illness. Often, they were people who had something to hide—something that was eating them up inside. Setting fires was a release for them. A way to gain some power in a life that had made them feel powerless in some way. No one had been killed yet, and Patrick hoped it stayed that way.

He slid everything he'd done so far into the file folder and went to the bedroom. He'd called Jonah back as he left Gini's, but Haddy had told him Jonah was out cold from the drugs the hospital gave him. Patrick had to listen to Haddy's detailed description of how "damn cute" Jonah looked while he slept. He'd hung up promising to call again in the morning and trying to clear his mind of Jonah lying in bed, sleeping like a baby.

After slipping into his work uniform—it was his Sunday on-call—Patrick dialed Jonah's number.

"Jonah, it's Patrick. How are you feeling?"

"I'm feeling you're one of my new best friends, saving my life and all."

"It wasn't a heroic deed. Was I supposed to step over you and leave?"

"Oh, grumpy this morning, are we? You left my sister's too soon last night, didn't you?"

Patrick winced. He hadn't meant to sound like a sexually deprived grouch. "I left right on schedule."

"Right on whose schedule?" Jonah laughed. "I'll leave you alone on that issue. For now. You're going to the station today, right?"

"For a few hours, yes."

"Can you do me a favor? My 'Stang is in the lot there, and I'm not supposed to drive because I'm tripping on drugs right now, not to mention one-armed. I don't trust it unattended down at the station, and I certainly don't trust Gini or Haddy to drive it home for me. They don't appreciate what a delicate machine she is. Mason drives like a cop, so he's out too. And my parents would joyride all over town if I asked one of them. Would you mind bringing it by? Haddy'll give you a ride back to the station afterward."

"You're trusting a guy you just met to drive your Mustang? You sure about this?" Patrick had to admit the thought of sitting behind the wheel of Jonah's sweet red convertible was arousing. Not as arousing as sitting beside Jonah's sweet blonde sister, but damn close.

"I'm trusting a guy who dragged me out of a burning barn. I don't need to know another thing about you to know you can be trusted with my baby. There's an extra key in my locker at the station. Combination seven-twenty-twelve."

"Okay. I'm working until three. I'll drive her over after that." A little jolt of anticipation zipped through Patrick. Perhaps he could work out some of his...frustrations...driving Jonah's Mustang. It was worth a try.

He scribbled down directions to Jonah's house

and hung up. Grabbing the Meadow Cliff folder and the evidence he'd gathered at that barn last night, Patrick summoned Midas and headed for his truck. A couple of hours at the station ought to get his head back on straight. He'd focus on his incident report or whatever Chief Warner wanted him to do around the station. Get his mind off maple walnut ice cream and kissing on swings.

****

"Did you know that Jonah snores?" Haddy asked.

"Yes." Gini cut up the sandwiches her mother had sent from the bakery.

"Isn't it adorable?" Haddy giggled as she grabbed some plates from the cupboard.

"Not when you're fifteen and have to share a bed with him while on family vacation in Hawaii."

Gini remembered wanting to suffocate Jonah with her pillow as he sucked in air and let it out like a monster truck revving its engine. She had begged her parents for a separate bed, preferably in another room, but they'd said it was too expensive. That she ought to consider herself lucky she was in Hawaii. They'd had to wait until they were in their forties to go somewhere exotic and here she was, enjoying the sunshine and beaches, at age fifteen. She'd grumbled about the injustice of having to sleep with one's brother—how it would scar her fragile adolescent mind—but in the end, she had been thankful. Good thing too, for it was the last family vacation the Claremonts ever went on. Two years later, Gini had set Cameron's car on fire and everyone thought it best to stay local. The farthest she'd been was to Rhode Island for college, and even that had been a risk her family hadn't wanted to take. She'd had to beg and plead, without getting angry, of course, and finally Gini's mother had convinced her father that they had to let her live her life, had to let her go.

When Gini returned to Vermont after graduating, her parents' sighs of relief had echoed throughout the mountains.

"Well," Haddy said, "I think it's adorable. He's like a purring tiger."

"I would have said a roaring jet, but okay." Gini pushed a sandwich toward Haddy and looked around Jonah's small kitchen. His usual clutter was gone, and she hadn't once felt crumbs under her bare feet on the floor since she'd been there. "Did you clean in here?"

Haddy swiveled on the bar stool behind the island and nodded. "Uh-huh. I like Jonah and all, but I was not staying here in his filth."

Gini barked out a laugh and looked at her friend's glowing face. Haddy had never looked happier. Would she ever be that happy? Truly happy and not a happy she had to paint on each day? "You're what Jonah needs, Haddy."

"I was thinking the same thing." Jonah leaned in the doorway of the kitchen. His hair was a mess, and his eyes looked a little puffy. The gray sweat shorts and T-shirt he wore had seen better days, and he cradled his right arm in the sling bound to his torso.

Gini zeroed in on the tiny crease between her brother's brows and knew he was in more pain than he would ever complain about. "Just in time for lunch," she said. "Come sit."

Haddy popped up from her seat and slid out a chair at the kitchen table for him. He eased into it, a quiet groan escaping his lips as he lowered. Haddy dropped a kiss on his cheek and finger-combed his hair back. Another sound, quite contrary to pain, buzzed out of him, and Haddy laughed.

"How do you feel?" she asked as she stood behind him.

He leaned his head back so it rested on her

stomach. "Like if I had two working hands, they'd be all over you."

Haddy bent and teased Jonah's mouth with hers. Gini looked away and concentrated on her sandwich. Thoughts of Patrick, not erased from her memory anyway, crept to the forefront. She took a long swig of her iced tea, hoping to wash away Patrick's image, but knowing it was an impossible task.

The doorbell sounded, and Gini took that as her chance to get away from Haddy and Jonah's sappy cuteness. When she opened the door, Mason stepped inside.

"Hi, Gini. Came to check on the boy."

"He's in the kitchen getting fondled by Haddy."

Mason stopped just shy of the kitchen. "Should I leave?"

"Yes, and take me with you." Gini pushed Mason so he stumbled into the kitchen.

"Hey, Mason," Jonah said. "Sit. Have a sandwich."

"From your mom's?" Mason eyed the sandwiches.

"Only the best at Chez Claremont." Jonah arced his good arm out.

Mason sat and accepted the plate Gini gave him. "Thanks." He bit into the sandwich and rolled his eyes. After chewing and swallowing, he sighed. "If your mother wasn't your mother, I'd kidnap her and ask her to make me sandwiches for the rest of my life."

"Maybe Raina makes good sandwiches," Jonah said.

"Yeah, how was your date with her?" Haddy asked.

"She makes me dizzy."

Mason had a dreamy look on his face that made him look boyishly handsome. Not at all like Patrick.

Nothing boyish about Patrick, Gini thought. He was all man, right down to the core. Grown-up and sexier than anyone she'd ever met. Quiet, solemn, holding back part of himself from the world. She wanted to know everything about him.

She ran her index finger along her bottom lip as she pictured Patrick on her swing last night. What would have happened if Jonah hadn't called? Would she have invited Patrick to stay? Would he have accepted the invitation?

Probably not. He wasn't ready to be that comfortable with her, and she wasn't ready to test her control on her emotions. She would never forgive herself if things got out of hand, and she accidentally hurt Patrick with what she could do. She would not be responsible for another Cameron, although Gini highly doubted Patrick would force himself on her. Not his style.

Then again, she hadn't thought force was Cameron's style either. But what did she know? She had been a silly girl, mistaking physical interest and hormones for love.

"Right, Gini?"

"What?" Gini hadn't caught any of the table conversation.

"I said you were with Patrick last night," Jonah said.

Gini looked up to see three sets of curious eyes on her. "I was."

They waited, watched. Gini grew hot under her tank top and shorts. Even her bare toes sweated.

"That's it?" Haddy asked. "That's all you're giving us?"

"That's all I have to give you." Gini shrugged and finished her iced tea.

"No," Mason said. "There has to be more."

"Has to be," Jonah agreed.

"He cooked me dinner while I developed the

Meadow Cliff photos. That's it." Gini studied the crumbs on her plate. She would not look up. She would not look up so they could see there was more.

"The Meadow Cliff photos are done?" Mason asked.

Gini exhaled, relieved Mason had a work-centered brain. Bless him. "Yes. I gave a copy to Patrick and have a set for you in my purse." She got up, thankful for the diversion, and retrieved the photos. "Here you go." She placed them on the table and Mason grabbed them.

"Anything of interest?" He opened the envelope and slid his sandwich out of the way.

"Another candle, right," Gini waited for Mason to flip to the correct photo, "there." She pointed to the pale green wax blob. "Patrick bagged it. Said Midas found a gasoline trail too."

Mason nodded. "Same as the Cloudson Drive house." He stood. "I've got to talk to Patrick."

"He's at the station," Jonah said. "Then he's bringing my car by."

Mason stopped shuffling through the photos. "You're letting Patrick drive the Mustang?" His left eye squinted shut.

"Mason," Jonah said. "You're my best friend, you know that, right?"

"Thought I did," Mason said.

"Okay, so I'll be honest with you." Jonah rubbed his temple as if it caused him physical pain to say whatever he was about to say. "I don't think you can handle the 'Stang. You hit curbs and squirrels as if they're targets in a video game, as if you're aiming for them, bro. Every drive is like a chase after the bad guys."

The corners of Mason's mouth turned up into a grin. "You're afraid the 'Stang can't handle *me*. That pretty boy car wouldn't stand a chance in pursuit."

"I'll let that one go, Mason, only because I can't

146

kick your ass right now." Jonah looked over to his arm and shoulder. "But the next comment like that, and you are going down, my friend."

"You can try, Jonah." Mason tapped Jonah on his good shoulder and nodded to Gini and Haddy. "Good luck tolerating him, Haddy." He waved the envelope of photos. "Gini, thanks for these. I'll talk to you later." As he turned to leave, he scanned the kitchen. "Did someone clean in here?"

"Haddy did. C'mon, I'll walk you out." Gini grabbed her purse and leaned down to Jonah. "Get some rest and stay out of trouble, huh?" She kissed his cheek.

"What fun would that be?" Jonah raised an eyebrow and laughed when Gini rolled her eyes.

"See you tomorrow, Haddy. We have ourselves a lot of work to do with that calendar." Gini clapped her hands together.

"You have to love it when your boss considers combing through pictures of hot firefighters 'work.' Such a pleasant job I have." Haddy put one hand to her chest and fanned herself with the other.

"Don't comb too closely," Jonah said.

"I wouldn't worry, Jonah," Gini said. "I'll put Haddy in charge of combing through your shots."

"Goody." Haddy stood behind Jonah now, her hands resting on the chair back. She had that woman-of-the-house look about her.

"Guess we'll have to double up on someone's photo or do a group shot for the last month." Gini sighed.

"No luck getting Patrick's picture?" Jonah asked.

Gini shook her head. "I decided not to push it."

"Boy, he's gotten to you, hasn't he?" Haddy asked.

"What do you mean?" Gini moved her purse to her other shoulder and wrung the straps in her hands.

"It's not like you to admit defeat," Jonah said.

"It's not defeat," Gini said. "It's a change of plans. No big deal."

"Then why are you strangling your purse right now?" Mason asked as he ran for the door to avoid the smack Gini was fixing to give him.

After Mason was gone, Gini let out a breath and dropped her hands to her sides.

"I'm going now too. Good-bye."

Jonah and Haddy gave her a wave.

"No big deal," she told herself again once she was outside and getting into her SUV. So what if she was wondering what Patrick was doing right now. So what if she was picturing him driving Jonah's pretty boy Mustang through the dusty streets of Burnam.

So what if all she could think about was having him naked beside her.

No big deal.

Chapter Fifteen

Patrick finished washing the fire trucks with two other fighters then took his Meadow Creek and Cloudson Drive file folders to the station's classroom. Chief Warner had made the arson cases Patrick's top priority after making sure he didn't escape the "new guy" jobs like truck washing, of course. Patrick didn't mind those tasks, though. Like cleaning, he found manual labor meditative, purifying. Lord knew he needed some purifying. The thoughts cycling through his head about Gini were certainly less than pure. He'd figured once he'd gotten to work, the memory of kissing her would fade into the background. Sitting in the quiet of the classroom now, he knew that was not going to happen.

One taste of her and he was hooked. At least every third thought that flitted into his brain was of Gini.

"Pathetic," he said.

"Yes, a man talking to himself is extremely pathetic," a voice said behind him.

Patrick turned to find Mason in the doorway. "Oh, hey. I was looking over these photos."

Mason sat in the seat next to Patrick and plopped his own set of photos down on the table. "Gini just gave me these. So our arsonist fancies candles. That's about all we know, huh?"

Patrick nodded. "We have no clue where he or she will target next."

"I hate when the bad guys are a step ahead," Mason said. "Pisses me off."

"Me, too." Patrick fanned several photos out on the table. "Did you get the evidence I dropped off?"

Mason pulled the evidence bag out of his pocket and put it on the table. "My men missed the candles at both scenes. How is that possible?"

"They both look like globs of debris. Easy to miss. The first one I found by accident. This one I'd been looking for." Patrick gestured toward the green candle remains. "This one has a scent too." He opened the bag, and Mason held it under his nose.

"I got a whiff of it earlier but can't identify it."

"Gini thinks it's chamomile."

"I'll take her word for it," Mason said. "She would know."

"What's that mean?"

"Gini grows all sorts of herbs and flowers to use in her potions." Mason zipped the evidence bag closed.

"Potions?" Was Gini involved in witchcraft? Patrick thought back to the bush in front of the fire department the first time he met Gini. Had she done a spell or something to set it on fire? He pushed the notion out of his head. He didn't believe in magic. People didn't set things on fire by just thinking of it. Thank God.

"Yeah, you know, teas, potpourris, oils, shampoos, whatever," Mason said. "I call them potions because I saw her mixing one up once. She was in her herb garden behind the east field on her farm. She had this enormous cast iron pot that looked like a cauldron over a portable burner. Puffy, white steam surrounded her, and all she needed was a black pointed hat and a wart on her nose. I swear I heard her cackle while she stirred the bubbling concoction." Mason laughed. "Saw her make maple syrup once too. Looked like a witch then as well."

Patrick tried to picture Gini dressed as an ugly witch, but his mind kept conjuring one hell of a sexy witch. He shook his head and focused on the photos in front of him.

"So we're looking for someone with an affinity for candles, access to gasoline, knowledge of herbs, and a desire to see things burn." Patrick jotted all of these notes on a piece of paper in the Meadow Cliff folder.

"That could be a lot of people," Mason said.

"Most likely a woman, though." Patrick wrote that down too when Mason nodded his agreement.

"Is there a mental hospital nearby?" Patrick asked. "Most arsonists, especially ones that get cute with a theme like the candles, have psychological problems. You could check to see if someone has been released locally. I don't know." Patrick shrugged. "It's an avenue to explore while we wait."

"Wait for another fire." Mason looked at Patrick.

"Unfortunately, yes. So far, this arsonist doesn't seem to be targeting people. She is looking for a good burn. I'd be willing to bet she's watching as we respond to the blaze." Patrick wrote this down too and closed the folder.

"Next major fire call you guys get," Mason said, "call me. I'll get some men down to the scene right away to scout. That'll be their only job. Maybe we can find some persons of interest."

"It's the best we can do for now."

Mason grabbed his own envelope of photos and stood. "On another topic, does Raina like horses? I was thinking of taking her to Gini's for some horseback riding Wednesday night. Think she'd like that?"

"I know she would. Gini wouldn't mind?" Again, though Gini had said she and Mason never dated, Patrick wondered how deep their relationship actually went.

"Nah." Mason waved a hand. "I was with Gini when she bought Nyx, and I bought Moon for her because I lost a bet."

"A bet?" Patrick didn't like that he was relieved by what Mason was saying. He shouldn't care why this guy bought a horse for Gini. Shouldn't concern him in the least. But damn, it did.

"When we were in high school, the three of us used to go camping in the woods around Gini and Jonah's grandmother's place."

"Where Gini lives now?" Patrick asked.

Mason nodded. "It wasn't such a big farm then. More like untamed forest. Well, one night while making our s'mores around a campfire, we decided to predict what we'd be when we grew up. Jonah and Gini knew right away they'd be firefighter and photographer, respectively. I, on the other hand, had no idea what I wanted to be.

"So Gini tells me I'm going to be a cop. I completely disagree with her. I mean, we were like fifteen years old. Who knew how things would turn out? No one in my family was a cop. I didn't know any cops. I had zero interest in law enforcement." Mason smirked. "So on the day I graduated from the police academy, she raced down to me from the bleachers where she'd watched the ceremony and shouted my name. When I caught up to her, she gave me this huge congratulatory hug and then whispered in my ear, 'You owe me a horse, Officer Rivers.'

"That weekend, she took me to an auction and picked out Moon. Technically, that horse's name is Moon Rivers." Mason shrugged. "Anyway, Gini lets me ride Moon whenever I want." Mason followed Patrick out of the classroom. "What about you?"

"Do I ride?"

"No. You and Gini. You like her, don't you?"

Patrick stopped walking, panic weighing heavily in his chest. "Sure," he said, his voice strangled. "Gini's nice."

"Remember, I'm a cop. I can smell a lie."

"Look," Patrick started, "I didn't move to Vermont to find a woman and settle down. Not my life plan. I put out fires. I build stuff. That's all I need."

****

The barn display had been lovely. Just lovely. The smell of old, seasoned wood burning was much better than the newer wood on modern houses. Something to consider for future events. Scent was so much a part of the overall experience. Fire could be enjoyed by so many of the senses. That's what made it such a joy, such a pleasure to create. Not only was its red-orange glow a thing of pure beauty, but the fragrance of destruction filling the air, the heat of the burn prickling skin, and the roar of flames consuming everything in range gave her a sensory thrill beyond anything she'd known in her life.

Fire was her art, her craft, her calling. Her friend. The only one she had. The only one who truly understood her needs, her impulses, her secrets. She trusted fire. It never let her down. Never cast her aside. Never abandoned her when she was at her most fragile. It whispered words of comfort and wisdom as it rolled wherever she led it, eating its fuel with an insatiable hunger. It burned for her, to please her, to protect her, to thank her for releasing it.

And she had to release it. She'd tried not to, but that had made her sick, made her taste death. She couldn't live without the anticipation of the next blaze, the planning, the waiting, the executing. Without fire, she would shrivel and die.

The next fire had been organized. A destination picked. A time decided. A candle made. She was already feeling the thrill of seeing this one blossom. Her body grew moist, small shudders of delight echoing in her depths as the fire climbed in her mind's eye. Watching the real thing would send her body over the edge to blissful satisfaction. She would be complete when the flames soared and devoured.

Such a shame the fires could not burn eternally, could not reach from the molten floors of Hell and rip into the pristine white walls of Heaven. With the fan of angel wings, her fires could grab God himself by the neck and show him what it really meant to be divine.

****

Patrick hugged a sharp corner on his way to Jonah's. The Mustang kissed the road, her tires grabbing asphalt and not letting go. Even on the dirt roads, the vehicle flew through the dust as if nothing could ruin its dance with the street.

The leather bucket seats molded to Patrick's backside, and he'd had to hold back a moan as he sat behind the wheel. The top was down so Patrick left it that way. Late afternoon air, Vermont cooled and pine-scented, rushed into the car and did wonders to clear Patrick's mind. He could finally breathe.

Things were definitely rolling along a little too quickly for him in Burnam. His job had been kicked up a notch with the arson cases. He was further along in his house plans thanks to Jonah and company. He had been out socially and considered Jonah and Mason friends. He'd cooked dinner for a sexy, intelligent woman.

He'd kissed a sexy, intelligent woman.

Patrick shook his head as he turned onto Jonah's street. He'd have to slow things down. Get back to a schedule that was familiar to him. He didn't mind the amped up work-related things, but he wanted to take his time with everything else. Remodeling his house was something to savor and think about, not rush through just to get it done.

And the social stuff? He didn't exactly have a

roadmap for that area, but keeping gatherings to a minimum seemed like a comfortable plan. The less he allowed his circle to expand, the better he could protect himself.

As far as Gini went, Patrick hadn't expected to encounter someone like her in Vermont, or anywhere else for that matter. He'd made the decision a long time ago to walk through this life alone. Any other option opened the door to scaring a woman away again and getting himself hurt.

The Mustang galloped up a steady incline with unexpected muscle for a car of its size. He pulled into Jonah's driveway and parked between Haddy's car and a small pickup truck. Wishing he didn't need to go in to return the keys or have someone give him a ride back to the station, Patrick sat in the Mustang for a few extra minutes. He couldn't remember the last time he'd felt so out of sorts.

Actually, he could, but he didn't want to. Now wasn't the time to be thinking about his last visit with Julianne before leaving Rhode Island.

He pushed thoughts of his sister to the back of his mind and opened the car door. As Patrick made his way to the front of Jonah's house, laughter floated out the open screen door. Happy and carefree, the sound plucked at something inside Patrick and dammit, why was the next thought to enter his mind about Gini?

"Get control, man." He made a fist and rapped his knuckles on the door.

Haddy appeared on the other side of the screen door. "Hiya, Patrick." The smile on her face caused one to sprout on Patrick's. He didn't have to think about making the muscles of his face allow a smile. It just happened. What was with these people? So happy all the time and able to spread the warm, fuzzy feelings around. Patrick wasn't sure if that was a good thing or not.

"Hey, Haddy." Patrick stepped into the house as Haddy held open the screen door. "I brought Jonah's car back." He dropped the keys into her hand.

"Thanks. He was getting itchy knowing it was at the station without him."

"I can see why," Patrick said. "Driving it is an experience."

"You sound like Jonah. To me, it's just a car. Gets you from A to B. I don't see what the big deal is."

"Guess it's a Y-chromosome thing."

"Has to be, because I don't get it." Haddy shook her head. "C'mon. Jonah's in the living room with his parents. I'll get you a drink."

She ushered him toward the living room before he had a chance to decline the drink. A visit was mandatory it seemed.

"Why hello, Patrick," Jonah's mother said as soon as she saw him round the corner into the living room.

"Mrs. Claremont. Good to see you." Patrick nodded to her.

"Call me Liz, please. C'mon in and have a seat." She patted the cushion beside her on the sofa.

The look on Jonah's face—a look that said, "Please, rescue me"—propelled Patrick into a walk. As he lowered to sit next to Liz, Walter studied him from a rocking chair across the room. Jonah fidgeted in a puffy recliner perpendicular to the couch.

"How are you doing?" Patrick asked.

"He's having a little trouble getting comfortable," Liz answered.

Jonah flopped his good hand toward his mother and rolled his eyes. Patrick had to fight to keep from laughing. Luckily, Haddy came in with a drink, which Patrick used to occupy his mouth.

"I told him it's going to take some time. He's got to be patient." Liz reached over to the recliner to pat her son's knee, and Jonah smiled at her. She may have been driving him crazy, but Jonah was lucky to have his mother around to drive him crazy. Patrick would totally switch places with Jonah even if it meant a busted collarbone at the moment.

"Meanwhile, the department is down a firefighter," Walter said. "You capable of doing the work of two men, Patrick?"

"Pop—" Jonah warned.

"I'm just wondering. They're going to feel your absence, son. You're a good fighter." Walter folded his arms across his chest and steadied his gaze on Patrick.

"I work hard, sir." Patrick wasn't sure why he felt the need to defend himself to Walter. Something in the older man's eyes made him want to be considered worthy. Worthy of what? Acceptance? Praise?

Gini?

Patrick took another sip of lemonade and turned his attention to Jonah, who was shifting in the chair. Haddy got up from the sofa and grabbed one of the pillows beside her. Gently, she eased Jonah forward and positioned the pillow so it rested behind the hollow of his neck. She fluffed the pillow, and Jonah caught her arm as she walked away. Haddy stopped, and Jonah pulled her hand up to his lips. He brushed a kiss to the back of her hand then released her.

"Thanks, Haddy."

Haddy grinned and sat back on the couch.

"Such a nice girl." Liz reached around Patrick to rest a hand on Haddy's forearm. "Now if I could find a nice boy for my Gini." She grinned at Patrick and all the oxygen in the room disappeared.

"Ma," Jonah said. "Patrick's in denial. He likes Gini, but isn't quite sure what to do about it."

Patrick opened his mouth to say something,

anything, but Walter beat him to it.

"Boy doesn't need to do anything about it. Gini's independent. She can take care of herself. She doesn't need complications."

"What makes you think Patrick would be a complication?" Liz asked as if Patrick wasn't sitting beside her. "He saved our son from a burning building, Walter."

"I didn't save—" Patrick stopped when Haddy put her hand on his knee.

"She's trying to get Walter to like you," Haddy whispered.

"Why wouldn't he like me?" Patrick asked. Why did it matter?

"Gini is Walter's little girl. He won't give her to just anybody."

Patrick wanted to say he wasn't asking for Gini, but he kept his mouth shut. This conversation was making his head ache.

Jonah must have noticed because he said, "Ma, Pop." His parents both turned to him. "Let's focus on what's important here, shall we?" He angled his hand toward himself. "Me."

Liz laughed and Walter loosened the grip his arms had across his chest.

"Of course, honey." Liz got up from the sofa. "I'll heat up some soup for you." She went to the kitchen and tapped Walter as she went by. "Come help me."

With a final glance at Patrick, Walter stood and followed his wife. Patrick let out a breath he wasn't aware he'd been holding. Why did he feel as if he'd been under Walter's silent microscope?

"Sorry about them," Jonah said.

"No problem." Patrick ran his hands down the thighs of his uniform pants. "I need to get back."

"You're not still on-call, are you?" Jonah asked.

"No, but I need to get home. Got some projects on my list for tonight." Patrick stood. "Got to pick up

Midas too. Figured you didn't want him shedding in the Mustang."

Liz and Walter came back into the living room. Liz set an enormous bowl of soup on the coffee table.

"Ma, that's like a trough of soup." Jonah's blue eyes widened as he looked at the bowl.

"And you're going to slurp up every last drop of it." She turned to Patrick. "Want some, dear?"

"Oh, no thanks," Patrick said. "I've got to get home."

"Let me get my keys," Haddy said.

"I'll give him a ride back." Everyone in the room turned toward Walter, his arms still folded.

Patrick heard himself swallow. He felt like an adolescent.

"What a wonderful idea, Walter." Liz beamed and looked so much like Gini that Patrick was stunned into silence for a moment too long.

"I want to talk to Chief Warner," Walter said. "Mind if I drive you back?"

Cornered. That's how Patrick felt. As if he had nowhere to run, and the walls were shrinking toward him.

"Thank you, sir," he managed.

Walter nodded and led the way to the front door. Patrick darted a gaze back to Jonah and Haddy, who both looked scared for him.

"Have a nice drive," Liz said as she waved.

Chapter Sixteen

Patrick had to adjust the passenger seat in the small pickup truck so his knees didn't bump into the dashboard. Funny how that increase in space did nothing to lift the tightness in his chest. Cramped. Still so cramped.

Walter settled into the driver's seat and started the truck. He backed out of Jonah's driveway as if he could have done it blind-folded. As they turned onto the main road, Patrick took a quick survey of the interior of the truck. Two plastic cups half full of iced coffee sat in the cup holders between the seats. One straw had pink lipstick around it, while the other had been chewed to death. His and hers cups. Three maps were wedged in a side pocket of the passenger door next to Patrick's leg. The first was a Vermont road atlas, the second a Rhode Island map, and the third was hidden behind the second. Behind the seats, tools rattled in wooden boxes, and nails of all sizes jingled in glass jelly jars.

"Do you woodwork, sir?" Patrick threw a look over his shoulder to the tools.

"Man's got to do something when he retires, doesn't he?" Walter's eyes never left the road.

"What do you build?"

"Whatever needs building." Walter grabbed the iced coffee and slurped up a mouthful. Patrick wondered how functional that chewed up straw was.

"Like framing, or furniture, or..." Patrick let his voice trail off hoping Walter would jump in with his reply. Instead, a long minute of silence stretched on in the cab. Patrick knew he sucked at small talk, but he couldn't be this bad, could he?

Finally, Walter shook the contents of the plastic cup and put it back in the holder. "I prefer to make furniture, but I've done framing and finish work. A little plumbing and electrical too if the mood strikes me."

A Renaissance man. Okay, good. Patrick could talk intelligently about these topics.

"Jonah said you're fixing up that pit over on Hope Hill Road." Walter eased to a stop at a red light.

"Yes. She needs some opening up and updating."

"I remember when that place was being built," Walter said. "I was about ten, and my buddies and I used to run wild in those woods until our mamas were near frantic with worry. We watched every inch of construction that took place over there. We were totally fascinated by the men, the tools, the vehicles, the process." He shook his head as if coming out of a dream. "What made you buy the place?"

"The view and the woods mostly."

Walter nodded. "Nice and quiet up there. Secluded."

"Yes, sir. Very private."

"Good place to hide were someone interested in hiding." Walter turned into the station's parking lot.

"I suppose so." Patrick scratched at the back of his neck, hoping to get at the prickles there.

"You hiding, Patrick Barre?" Walter shut off the engine and angled himself to face Patrick.

He thought about saying no. He really did. Would have been the easiest answer to give, but that's not what came spilling out of his mouth.

"We all have our secrets to keep, sir."

Walter's pale blue eyes widened. "Most folks would have just said no."

"I didn't want to lie to you. Didn't feel right." Patrick shrugged and put his hand on the door handle. Before he could push open the door, however, Walter rested a hand on his shoulder.

"Maybe you're okay after all, Barre." Walter opened the driver side door and dangled a leg out. "Just don't do anything to hurt Gini, or I'll kill you."

Patrick waited for Walter to laugh, but he didn't. He eased out of the seat, closed the door, and walked to the station.

Hurt Gini? He wouldn't hurt Gini, because he wasn't getting involved with Gini. They'd shared one kiss and that was an accident. It wouldn't happen again. His reflection in the bathroom mirror told him it wouldn't happen again. It couldn't.

****

"Most people hate Monday morning at work," Haddy said.

"Most people don't have the best job in the universe." Gini held up a picture of one of the firefighters. He was bared to the waist with a leash wrapped around a well-defined forearm. On the other end of the leash was Sarge, Haddy's Golden Retriever, drinking out of the fighter's helmet.

"Tasty." Haddy held out her hand so Gini would pass the photo to her. Once she had it in her grasp, she adjusted her glasses and studied the picture. "If only we could make this calendar 3D."

"Or a touch 'n feel," Gini said. "Good Goddess, look at this one." She held up a photo with a fighter holding himself up as if he were on a pair of balance beams only instead of beams, Gini's horses were on either side of him. He balanced his palms on the backs of the horses and every muscle in his chest and arms was on display.

"You do have a gift for catching the beautiful, Gini." Haddy flipped through a pile of photos on her side of the worktable. "Where are Jonah's?"

"Here." Gini picked up a stash by her elbow and slid them across the table. "I was saving these for last, so you wouldn't get distracted and dismiss all the other masterpieces we've got here."

"Oh, I know they're all gorgeous, but there does come a time when you have to choose one specimen and admire him in greater detail." Haddy angled her head at one of Jonah's shots and licked her lips. "Did Patrick survive?"

Gini caught herself chewing on the end of a pen. She tossed the pen onto the table, reminding herself not to be like Daddy and his straws, then looked at Haddy. "Survive what?"

"The drive to the station with your father."

"Daddy drove Patrick to the station?" A sweat broke out on her forehead. She slipped off her stool and dove into her purse until her hands closed around a pack of gum.

"Yeah," Haddy said. "Patrick dropped off Jonah's car yesterday afternoon, then your father volunteered to take him back to the station."

Gini let worry seep into her veins. It was better than anger. What was her father thinking? What did he say to Patrick? What did Patrick say to Daddy?

"Oh, dear." Gini paced the length of the workroom. "You know how Daddy gets."

"Yes, I do." Haddy sat back on her stool. "And he was not being all that friendly to Patrick."

"What? What do you mean? What was he saying?" She needed to breathe. Gini flopped onto the small couch that lined the floor to ceiling window in the workroom. She kicked off her sandals and drew in several deep breaths.

Don't get angry. Daddy just wants to protect you. He knows you burned that bush because of Patrick. He doesn't know that you've...kissed and made up, so to speak.

Gini counted to ten and turned her gaze to

Haddy. "Can you tell me what my father said to Patrick?"

"Busting his balls. Like asking him if he could do the work of two men while Jonah was down for the count." Haddy toyed with a string on the hem of her shirt. "Walter may have called Patrick a complication too."

Gini let her head drop to the arm of the couch as she closed her eyes. "A complication. Like a complication to me?"

"Uh-huh." Haddy moved Gini's feet and sat where they had been. "I probably shouldn't say this, but Patrick looks like a complication worth getting complicated with."

Gini rose to her elbows and stared out the window. Complication. That was the perfect word for it. Having Patrick in her kitchen was a complication. Kissing him after maple walnut ice cream was a complication. Thinking about him around the damn clock was a complication. All of which she did not need.

Living day to day, trying to keep things from bursting into flames around her, was enough of an obstacle already. Adding Patrick to the equation was trouble. Something that would definitely tip one side of the delicate balancing act her life had become.

Her father was right. Patrick needed to stay away from her, but it wasn't her father's place to say such a thing.

"I should go to Patrick's and apologize for my father's behavior," Gini said.

"There are several ways you could make it up to him." Haddy ducked when Gini cuffed her on the head.

"I'm serious."

"So am I, Gini. I just watched you brood over Patrick right now. You're interested. Admit it. So get something from your mama's bakery and bring it over to him," Haddy suggested.

Gini stretched her gum with her tongue and snapped it. "He likes blueberry muffins."

"Excellent," Haddy said. "I read online this morning that blueberries are good for the libido."

****

Patrick adjusted the air pressure on his compressor. Time to fire up his trusty nail gun and put up some walls. He had closets to frame, door openings to erect, new rooms to define. Maybe he'd work all night. Just keep going until he dropped from exhaustion. It wouldn't be the first time he'd done that. Sometimes he got so caught up in a project that time went unnoticed. The sun could set, the moon rise, and Patrick wouldn't know the difference. There would only be the wood beneath his fingers, the vibrating buzz of the circular saw, the bang and hiss of the nail gun. All things that were familiar to him, things he had control over, things that wouldn't mess with his practical mind.

A solid night of construction would purge Gini from his system. Then he could focus on the tidy, solitary life he had been living. He was all right with that life too. Sure, it was lonely, but it was also numb. Numb was good. He'd had enough pain—physical and emotional. He didn't need any more. Didn't need to open old wounds or make new ones.

After looking over his blueprint, Patrick headed to the garage where he'd had Mason and Raina stack some of the reusable studs that had been removed on Saturday. Using his tape measure, he selected several two-by-fours long enough to frame the new master bedroom wall. He hoisted them up to rest on his shoulder and carried them to the sawhorses he'd set up as a workstation in the great room. After setting them down, Patrick measured the lengths, marked cut lines with his pencil and square, and pulled down the safety glasses resting on the top of his head. He plugged his ears and grabbed the circular saw. As it cut the studs, a flurry of sawdust sprayed like silent, wooden snow.

Patrick spent the next two hours on the bedroom wall and framing two closets. Midas checked in with him every now and again, but construction didn't interest the dog. The loud noises from the tools irritated him, and with Patrick oblivious to everything besides what he was building, the chances of getting some attention were slim. Besides, this house had plenty of little nooks for sleeping in.

As Patrick maneuvered another wall into position, his doorbell rang. Midas shot out from wherever he'd been hiding and sniffed at the bottom of the front door. Patrick lowered the wall to the floor and peeked out one of the wide windows in what would eventually be an enormous kitchen. Raina stood on the landing, a brown bag wedged under her left arm. She saw him in the window and waved.

Damn. Caught. Had to open the door now or he'd never hear the end of it.

Patrick pulled off his safety glasses and set them, along with his earplugs, on the windowsill. He brushed at the dust and cobwebs on his black T-shirt and opened the door.

"Covered in sawdust," Raina said. "How usual." She rolled her eyes and stepped into the house.

"Interrupting my progress," Patrick said. "How usual."

"Ha, ha." Raina smirked and wiggled the brown bag. "I brought Chinese, because you haven't eaten."

"Who said I haven't eaten?"

Raina leveled her gray eyes on Patrick and waited.

"Okay, I haven't, but I'm in the middle of stuff." He motioned to the great room, which now that he really looked at it, was a disaster zone. Stud ends he'd cut off and other wood scraps littered the worn green carpet. Actually, the carpet was more beige with sawdust than green at the moment. A level, two hammers, a tape measure, a utility knife, some shims, and several drywall screws left a breadcrumb trail of where Patrick had been.

"My, my," Raina said. "You've been working like an animal."

"Is there any other way to work?" Patrick picked up his notebook and crossed off some items he'd completed.

"Not for you, I guess." Raina shrugged and stepped over the mess. "C'mon. I'm hungry."

She led the way to the interim kitchen beyond the master bedroom. Patrick looked longingly at his tools, silently waiting for him to make use of them, and shook his head. His stomach growled. Maybe he was hungry now that he'd stopped working. The projects would still be there after he'd eaten and sent Raina on her way.

By the time he entered the kitchen, Raina had the containers out of the bag, silverware on napkins, and two beers on the table.

"It ain't fine dining, but it's better than the nothing you were going to have."

"I would have stopped to eat." Patrick washed his hands at the sink and dried them on a dishtowel.

"Oh, really?" Raina pulled open the refrigerator and waved her hand toward it. "Eat what?"

The empty shelves were too white. He'd cleaned the refrigerator on his first night there and had bought a few groceries. He hadn't shopped for food since, and now the refrigerator showed signs of neglect.

Staring at those empty shelves made Patrick feel empty too. If he'd had someone else living there with him—someone who needed dinner cooked for her so she wouldn't eat crackers out of her purse, for example—he'd have made sure that refrigerator was filled.

"Jesus, Patrick." Raina shut the refrigerator door and came over to him at the sink.

"What?" He blinked several times and focused on his sister's face.

"I've never seen you look so...lost." She cupped his cheek and ran her thumb back and forth.

"I'm not lost." He rested his hands on her shoulders and managed a half-hearted smile. "I'm hungry."

Patrick skirted around Raina and sat at the table. He cracked open his beer and tapped it to Raina's unopened one.

"C'mon. Let the eating commence."

Raina sat across from Patrick and opened her container of chow mein as Patrick opened his Szechwan chicken.

"Halfsies?" Raina asked.

Patrick nodded and they both removed heaping spoonfuls of their own selection. In a move choreographed over the years, they swapped half their food without spilling a single water chestnut. They ate in silence until Raina sat back and patted her stomach.

"Talked to Julianne today." She sipped her beer and set it down, drumming her painted fingernails against the bottle.

"And?" Patrick chewed slowly, carefully.

"She asked about you."

Patrick wiped his mouth with his napkin and picked up his beer. "What did she want to know?"

"If you'd been eaten by a bear yet."

Patrick puffed out a breath. "She's probably hoping for that."

"Patrick, what happened when you left Rhode Island? Why is she so mad?" Raina pushed what remained of her dinner to the center of the table.

Patrick gazed out the windows at the shadowy mountains in the distance. A line of pink clouds stretched across the sky, kissing the mountaintops and promising sunshine for tomorrow. Sunshine for him, but what for Julianne?

"She didn't want me to come here," he finally said. "Thought I was running away."

"Like me." Raina folded her arms on the table.

"You didn't run away."

"I know that, and you know that, but Julianne thinks I'm a coward."

"You came here for school and you liked it. Nothing cowardly about that. You were smart. I don't know why Julianne and I hung around Rhode Island for so long."

"Being in Vermont doesn't make it disappear," Raina said. "The memories are always right there, waiting." A shiver rippled through her.

Patrick nodded and gestured between them. "It's easier for us though, compared to Julianne."

"Easiest for me," Raina said. "I don't have to be reminded of what we lost that night in the fire every time I look in a mirror. Not like you and Julianne."

"Even I can hide that." Patrick pulled at his T-shirt. "Julianne can't hide it. Can't escape it even for a minute."

Patrick's voice cracked, and Raina slid her hand across the table to grab his.

"It wasn't your fault. I've told you this dozens of times, Patrick. You saved our lives."

"But what kind of life is Julianne having. If I'd been a little bit quicker that night, we wouldn't have still been in the house during that blast. We would have been clear of the roof collapsing, clear of the beam that hit Julianne's spine, clear of her being paralyzed, wheelchair-bound, and clear of us both being burned."

"Julianne doesn't blame you." Raina's voice was soft as she squeezed Patrick's hand.

"I blame me."

"Then it's you that has to forgive." Raina released her grip on him. "Julianne won't stay mad at you for coming here. I asked her to move here."

"I did too."

"She won't budge?"

Patrick shook his head. "She likes where she lives. Lots of nice folks around to help her. Hell, she's got more friends than we do."

Raina managed a chuckle. "I don't know. You seem to be popular in Vermont. Had that bunch over here, helping you demolish."

Patrick shrugged. "Jonah, Haddy, and Mason are kind people. Easy to make friends with."

"Yes." Raina nodded and grinned. "It's been *real* easy making friends with Mason. What about you?"

"What about me?" Patrick collected their trash and threw it in the garbage.

"You and Gini."

"You too, Raina? Everyone's insisting I feel something for Gini. You, of all people, know why that can't be true." He lifted his shirt and slapped at his scars. Raina and Julianne were the only two people he could do that in front of.

"You're the one that's decided no one can handle those scars, Patrick. You don't know how Gini will react."

"I can't take the chance. I don't want to." He let his shirt drop and rubbed his stubbly chin.

"I just hate to see you alone, Patrick."

"I'm not alone. You're here."

"You know what I mean. You have so much to offer a woman like Gini. And I'll bet she has lots to offer you."

Patrick shrugged and wiped the table down as Raina pushed in the chairs. As they walked out of the kitchen and through the master bedroom, Patrick was about to say something when Midas rushed to the front door.

"What's he—" The doorbell cut Raina off. She looked to Patrick. "Expecting someone?"

"I wasn't even expecting you."

Raina opened the door before Patrick had a chance to sneak a peek out the window. He saw Gini standing there with a basket of...good God, were those blueberry muffins in her hands? He had two urges at once. The first was to scoop Gini up into his arms and cover every inch of her with kisses.

The second urge was to run.

Chapter Seventeen

Judging by the look on Patrick's face, Gini was sure she shouldn't have come. The man looked downright pale. At first anyway. Then a soft pinkness tinged his cheeks. Was he hot? Did he have a fever perhaps? Should she check his forehead? Boy, did she want to.

"Hi," Gini said.

"Hi." Raina pulled her inside by the wrist and took Gini's evacuated spot on the landing outside. "I've got to go. See you all later." She sashayed to her car, leaving Gini and Patrick standing in the foyer.

Midas nosed around at Gini's shoes until she scratched between his ears. When she stopped, the dog whined and pawed at her hand.

"Midas, *couchez*," Patrick said. The dog hesitated for a moment, then folded his legs beneath him, resting his chin on his front paws. "*Bon.*"

"I brought these." Gini held up the basket. "As a peace offering."

Patrick's brow creased. "A peace offering? Why?"

"Heard my daddy drove you to the station. Was giving you a hard time at Jonah's. I'm sorry."

The half-smile that turned up the left side of Patrick's mouth made Gini want to strip him down naked right there. She clutched the handle of the basket until the wicker crackled in her hands.

"He was fine," Patrick said. "Threatened to kill me, but other than that, we had a lovely drive."

Gini hung her head and let out a long breath. "I told him he had to stop doing that."

"He's protective of you."

Gini nodded and loosened her grip on the basket when Patrick held his hands out for it.

"No harm done, but I'll accept these all the same. Wouldn't want to waste them."

"Then Mama would be threatening to kill you."

Gini loved how Patrick's eyes scrunched closed when he laughed. Haddy must have been right about blueberries and the libido. Gini didn't have to consume the berries to feel the starved woman buried inside her race to the surface. Race toward Patrick.

She focused on the great room behind him and stepped a little farther into the house. She hadn't meant to exactly. After all, she was leaving in a moment. No sense in straying too far from the exit. Her feet, however, insisted she investigate.

Patrick didn't try to stop her. Instead, he followed her into the great room and let her peruse his progress.

"Wow. You did so much." Gini turned in a circle to take in the master bedroom wall and closets.

"Had some energy to burn." Patrick shrugged.

Gini's gaze fell on the bend of Patrick's arm as he held the basket of muffins. She could still feel his hands in her hair, pressed to her back as they had kissed on her swing. She wanted those hands on her again. Goddess, forgive her, but she wanted him close, so close.

I have to go. These were the words Gini knew should have come out of her mouth. "Need another set of hands to put up that wall?" she asked instead.

Patrick looked to the wall still resting on the floor then glanced at Gini. Definitely a conversation going on inside his head. Gini would have paid big bucks to hear it.

"If you've got a minute, sure." He lifted the basket a few inches higher. "Let me put these in the kitchen."

Gini nodded and set down her purse while Patrick disappeared through the master bedroom. She leaned against one of the huge floor-to-ceiling windows in the great room and stared out at the darkness. Not a hint of electricity for miles. Just blackness. Thick and secretive. Sexy.

Something flickered below the window outside, and Gini smiled at the fireflies that had come to call. Their tiny lights flashed codes only the fireflies understood. Attracting mates. Isn't that what Patrick had said they were doing? Gini hoped it worked out for the insects. It wasn't easy to find a perfect mate.

"What are you smiling about?" Patrick stood next to her at the window.

"You've got yourself a firefly mountain here. Look at all of them." At that moment, dozens of glowing dots glimmered in the shadowy grass.

"Beautiful, aren't they?" His arm brushed up against hers, warm and solid.

Gini didn't move over, didn't put the necessary distance between herself and that coveted contact with Patrick's skin. Instead, she closed her eyes and pressed her forehead to the cool glass of the window. She was the one with the fever now. The one whose insides were melting into a red-hot pile of mush. If one of them didn't move soon, she'd be reduced to a mere puddle of her former self.

But she couldn't move. Couldn't give up what she'd gone so long without—the touch of a potential lover. The touch of someone who could bring her pleasure, could set free that which had been locked away. She'd gone on dates, of course, but nothing that ever made her want to have a second date. Nothing that made her feel comfortable to share herself. Her whole self, freak abilities and all. She'd kept everyone who wasn't family out of the loop, but she longed to have someone else know. Someone who didn't have to love her because they were related. Someone who would love her even though she was dangerous.

Why did she want Patrick to be that someone?

"I'm going to plant that grass you gave me under this window. Maybe it'll bring the fireflies closer." Patrick shifted so that his arm wasn't touching hers anymore. The spell had been broken, and she could think rationally again.

"That would be nice." Gini looked over her shoulder at the wall. "Want to get that in place now?"

"Sure."

Patrick walked to the foyer. He retrieved his safety glasses and earplugs from the windowsill and stopped at a toolbox for extra pairs of both for her. Gini watched the way his body moved as he walked away and came back. Everything worked as a unified whole. His long strides took him there and back in seconds with a liquid grace she hadn't seen too often on men. He was like a large wolf, scruffy around the chin with eyes that held both wisdom and sadness. Gini wanted to siphon that sadness out of his forest eyes and put something happier there.

But she wasn't the gal to do that. Patrick didn't deserve to be saddled with someone like her. A monster really. A sideshow of paranormal nonsense fit for comic books, not real life.

"Grab that end," Patrick instructed after giving her the safety glasses and earplugs, "and we'll wiggle her into her new home."

Grab? Wiggle? Gini shook her head. She was acting like a sex-starved lunatic instead of the cautious pyrokinetic she was used to.

She hoisted the wall up with Patrick and helped him slide it onto the red chalk line he'd snapped on the weathered wooden floor. Gini held it while

Patrick checked to see if the wall was level on his side. When he came to her end, he reached around her from behind to hold the level against the last stud. He was close enough that his breath tickled her neck.

"That look level to you?" he asked.

He might as well have said, "Let's take a bath together," because Gini's pulse beat in her neck as if it were trying to claw its way through her skin. She managed to steady her eyes on the bubble trapped in yellow liquid on the level.

"Right on the mark," Gini said.

"Okay, hold it still. I'm going to nail it."

Yes, nail it. Nail me. Gini cleared her throat and concentrated on keeping the wall in place.

One nail. Two. Three. Bam. Bam. Bam.

Patrick wielded that nail gun as if it were part of his hand. The compressor roared to life, and Gini jumped. Patrick laughed as he nudged Gini aside so he could drive some nails into her end of the wall. She leaned against the closet he'd framed and wondered if he had a smooth or hairy chest. She had a feeling she'd like either on him. She also had a feeling she wouldn't ever know which was hiding under that T-shirt.

She needed to go. Now. Right away.

"All set?" she asked when Patrick stopped nailing. Gini set the safety glasses and earplugs on a sawhorse and edged toward her purse on the floor.

"She's not going anywhere." He blew on the tip of the nail gun as if blowing smoke from a pistol. That one movement of his lips was enough to set off a chain of images in Gini's brain. Images of their bodies entangled, hands sliding along smooth flesh, mouths exploring curves and angles. She blinked several times, but the images remained.

"Think it's time for a muffin break," Patrick said. "C'mon." He walked past her into the kitchen.

Gini looked to the front door and back to the door Patrick had gone through. Her head swayed from one to the other as if she were watching a tennis match. Beyond one door was her quiet farmhouse where only Saber, Nyx, and Moon waited for her return.

Beyond another was a man who built things with his capable hands, who was at this moment, fueling his libido with blueberry muffins.

****

Tea. He had water and tea bags. That would be enough to make it seem as if this house was in fact a home. Unfortunately, his mugs didn't match. They never had to back in Rhode Island. When you only took one out at a time what difference did it make if they matched from day to day?

But now, it mattered. Women liked things that coordinated. Raina had once told him that it made her feel cozy when stuff matched. Staring at the two mugs now, one solid black, the other with a picture of a lighthouse on it and the words "Ocean State" spelled out in sea shells, Patrick knew cozy was a long way off.

He filled both mugs with water at the sink and opened the cupboard where he kept the tea. Patrick turned around to ask Gini if she preferred regular or green tea and found that he was alone in the kitchen.

She went home. Well, at least one of them was thinking rationally. One of them knew they couldn't be more than acquaintances. One of them didn't want to be more.

"Gini?" He felt stupid calling her name. He knew she wasn't out there.

Her body appeared in the doorway along with Midas, and Patrick's breath caught in his chest.

"Yes."

"You're still here." He cleared his throat and

177

gripped the black mug so that crushing it into hundreds of ceramic shards was a definite possibility.

"Do you want me to go?" Gini already had her gargantuan purse hanging on her shoulder.

Now that was *the* question, wasn't it? "No. I don't want you to go."

Raina's voice echoed in his head. Maybe she was right. Maybe Gini could handle his damaged skin. Maybe she would be able to look at it without thinking him repulsive. Maybe Gini was someone he didn't have to hide from.

Gini stepped into the kitchen, and her purse thudded as she dropped it by one of the kitchen chairs. The noise reverberated in the nearly empty room, and Midas came over to investigate.

"Maybe it's time you cleaned that thing out." Patrick nudged Midas away from the purse.

"I cleaned it out yesterday." Gini laughed. "Unloaded about a pound of stuff I'd collected in my travels. Now it's ready to collect more."

"What could possibly be in there that you need?"

"Okay," Gini said. "Because you had to endure my daddy's death threat, I'll give you a glimpse. Just a glimpse. No more than that."

Patrick put the mug down on the counter and came to the table. Gini sat in the chair, hoisted her purse onto the table, and dug around in it. She kept the edges close to her hands so Patrick couldn't peek inside.

"Don't pull out a camera or crackers," he said as he sat across from her. "I already know you have those in there."

"Fair enough." Gini fished around for a few seconds, and when she pulled out her hand, she held a calculator. Not a small, pocket-sized calculator, but a desk-sized one with enormous number buttons.

Patrick opened his mouth, but Gini shook her

head. "Don't say it. I know full well they make key chain-sized calculators, but I had one of those, and I could never find it in here." She thrust her free hand toward the purse. "This one I can find every time, and when I'm ninety, I'll still be able to see the display."

"Logical." Patrick tried for a serious face, but couldn't quite get past his smile.

Gini plunged her hand back into the purse, mumbled a few things to herself as her hands must have landed on items she didn't want to pull out. Patrick had a growing urge to dump the entire sack out onto the table, catalog its contents, and analyze this magnificent creature sitting across from him. What could he learn about her from what she had hidden in that purse?

The next thing Gini held up was a roll of toilet paper. "For emergency purposes. Can't count the number of times I've needed this." She set the roll down next to the calculator.

"Also a practical piece of equipment." Patrick nodded his approval. "I want to see something not so...useful."

"Not useful? Everything in here is useful in some way. Useful to me, anyway."

"Okay," Patrick said. "Keep going."

Gini only rummaged around for a second this time. She extracted her hand with her fist closed. When she opened her hand, a plastic seagull figurine perched in her palm. Patrick picked it up and turned it around in his own hand.

"I got that in Rhode Island when I started at RISD. I was feeling lonely in my dorm room. It was the first time I'd been away from my family. So I went for a walk around College Hill and ended up in this funky shop that sold Rhode Island artwork. By the register was this bin of seagulls. Something compelled me to buy one. As if I would have a friend if I took this stupid plastic bird back to the dorm with me."

"Suppose it's easier than buying a German Shepherd puppy and training it to investigate fire incidents just to have a friend." Patrick motioned to Midas, who had settled in the doorway between the kitchen and the master bedroom.

"Couldn't carry him in this purse," Gini said.

"Are you sure? I'm waiting for you to pull out Nyx or Moon next."

"I wouldn't subject them to such an undignified mode of transport."

Patrick placed the seagull on the table between the calculator and the roll of toilet paper. "What else?" He arched his neck, trying to see inside the cavernous bag.

Gini bunched up the material, protecting her treasures. "One more and that's it for tonight."

Would there be other nights after tonight? Patrick wanted to think so even if he was fooling himself.

The last item Gini produced was a Super Soaker water gun, compact model. Patrick barked out laugh when she pumped the small gun and aimed it at his chest. It couldn't be loaded. Who carried a loaded water gun in her purse?

The stream that sprayed out made a slapping noise as it soaked his T-shirt. Patrick put his hands out in front of him, but Gini kept on shooting. She aimed higher and hit his neck. Water droplets dribbled down his skin and into the collar of his shirt.

Patrick lurched out his hand and cupped his palm over the barrel of the water gun. Gini kept the trigger depressed, and water rolled down Patrick's wrist to his elbow. Finally, the gun was empty.

"Out of ammo," Gini said.

"Out of your mind," Patrick added.

Gini's shoulders did a quick bob up and down. "No doubt, but imagine walking down a deserted street and some thug tries to jump you. You whip this out and two things will happen. One, if it's dark enough, he'll think you have a gun and bolt. Two, if you shoot him with it, he'll be so stunned and confused, you'll have plenty of time to run for your life."

"Make many trips down deserted streets?" Patrick grabbed the dishtowel from the sink and wiped himself off. He hung the towel over his shoulder.

"This is Vermont, Patrick. All the streets are deserted after five o'clock." Gini gathered her revealed junk and tossed it back into her bag.

"Would you like me to reload that for you?" Patrick motioned to the water gun. "My street is a deserted street."

Gini nodded and held out the gun. *Too easy.* Patrick grabbed it and filled it at the sink. He turned around quickly and smiled when he saw Gini was still organizing inside the purse.

"Gini," he said.

"What?" She looked up as water arrowed at her head. The spray rained over her right ear and down her cheek. "Patrick!"

She got up from the chair and ran for the door, but Patrick was right behind her. He chased her through the master bedroom into the great room and to the floor-to-ceiling fireplace. Gini hugged the stones, her back to Patrick as water trickled down her neck into her tank top.

"Patrick!" she squealed again, although this time, laughter mixed with the yell of his name.

The gun finally emptied, and Gini turned around. Water had slid along her shoulders, dampening the ends of her hair. Some of the curls tightened their form, golden coils resting on her glistening skin. She held out her hand.

"Relinquish your weapon, sir," she said.

"Let me refill it." Patrick turned but didn't get far. Gini's hands gripped his arm, and he allowed her to spin him around to face her.

"I'll take my chances out there with it unloaded," she said. "Hand it over."

Patrick pouted but slid the water gun into her hand. Her fingers closed around it, and she ran her other hand through her wet hair. Patrick stepped closer and pulled the towel from his shoulder. Without thinking, he turned her around and wiped the back of her neck, her shoulders, her curls. The towel absorbed the droplets, leaving smooth, flawless skin behind. Skin so perfect it didn't seem real. Gini was a painting, a masterpiece, all skilled brushstrokes and vibrant colors.

Gini slowly swiveled around. She was only inches away from him. Close enough to reach out and taste. One step and he could have his mouth on hers again. Feel the silken press of her lips. Savor the kind of touch he never allowed himself to have. One step, and he could slip into Heaven.

But then he'd have to leave Heaven. Better not to cross that gate. Better to stay on this side of the line he'd drawn such a long time ago.

"I'd say thanks," Gini motioned to the towel, "but I wouldn't have gotten wet if it weren't for you."

Patrick took a handful of his shirt—careful not to lift it too far from his body—and squeezed the water out of it. A small puddle collected between his boots then he tucked his shirt back into his jeans. "You started it."

"You wanted to see what was in my purse, big shot." Gini took the towel from Patrick and wiped the puddle on the floor.

"I'm afraid of what else is hiding in there." Patrick studied the streaks of light blonde that started at the part in Gini's hair and disappeared into the browner blonde of her curls. His fingers itched to touch that softness.

"I think the water gun is the most dangerous item I've got." She stood and tucked the Super Soaker into the waistband of her shorts. Shaking out the towel, she closed the distance between them and pressed the towel to Patrick's chest. "It wasn't fair of me to shoot an unarmed man." She draped the towel over Patrick's shoulder.

"Next time, I'll keep my safety glasses on." What else could he use for protection against what he was feeling right now?

"If I promise not to shoot, can we have those muffins we were going to have?" Gini looked up at him. She was so right there, her face a tad lower than his, her lips reachable if he'd only bend down slightly. "Patrick?"

"Yes." He blinked several times. "Muffins. Yes." He led the way back to the kitchen and focused on the tea bags. "Regular or green?"

"Green." Gini sat at the table and waited for Patrick to microwave the tea. He placed the Rhode Island mug in front of her and took the black one for himself.

Gini picked up the mug and studied the lighthouse. "I think my seagull would like this." She blew on the hot tea and took a tiny sip. "Jonah looked tired today, didn't he?"

Patrick nodded. "He probably didn't sleep well. He's got to be uncomfortable."

"You ever break anything on the job?" Gini asked.

"No."

"Off the job?"

"Yes." He held up his hand. "Fingertip to wrist working on my grandparents' roof."

"Ouch."

Not half as bad as being burned, Patrick thought. His hand had healed perfectly. His skin, not so much.

Gini accepted the blueberry muffin Patrick held out to her. "I hope you like these."

"They look and smell amazing." Patrick examined the one he'd selected for himself. "Is this a crumb topping?"

"Uh-huh. Brown sugar, maple sugar, and cinnamon."

Patrick took a bite and his taste buds—his entire mouth—rejoiced. He finished a whole muffin before he could speak. "I've never had a muffin quite like that."

"Mama is an artiste when it comes to baking. You'll have to visit the bakery and try one of everything."

"Maybe two of everything." Patrick threw back a shot of his tea and eyed another muffin in the basket.

"Go for it," Gini said.

"You too. Help yourself." Patrick started on his second muffin.

Gini shook her head. "I don't need another muffin." She patted her stomach. "Being the daughter of a baker is not an easy life. Temptation is all around."

"You don't look like you give in to temptation often." *You look like a goddess sent to tempt me.*

"Thanks." Gini cast her gaze down, bashful-like, and Patrick nearly choked on muffin bits. He reached for his tea and washed down crumb topping. He wished it were iced tea, because suddenly the kitchen felt as if he had all his firefighting gear on. Layers of gear weighing him down and heating him up.

"You don't make a habit of eating desserts either." Gini's blue eyes rested on his face, and his temperature rose higher.

Patrick shook his head. "I don't have a sweet tooth. Blueberry muffins are the exception."

"And I've often classified them as fruit considering Mama makes sure there are berries in every bite."

"Yeah," Patrick said slowly, "I was trying to figure out what made these muffins the best blueberry muffins I've ever tasted in my life. Berries in every bite. That's it."

"She's got you under her spell now. You won't be able to eat another blueberry muffin without wishing it was one of Mama's."

Patrick couldn't argue with that. He would definitely be satisfying all his muffin needs at Liz's bakery. What other needs could a Claremont satisfy?

"What did you do today?" Patrick asked as a way of getting his mind off Gini naked.

"Haddy and I worked on the calendar." Gini's voice was quiet, careful. "It's going to be awesome when it's finished." Patrick made a pile of the crumbs in front of him. "Patrick?"

He looked up, palms on the table, ready to fight about picture taking.

"You can relax." Gini traced the outline of one of his hands with her index finger. The sensation made Patrick everything but relaxed. "I won't say I'm not disappointed you won't be a part of the calendar," she said. "I'm pretty sure the women of Burnam would pay large sums of money to see their newest fighter on display." She paused in her tracing and brushed her fingers instead over the back of his hand. If this simple touch could make his heart thud wildly in his chest, what would more than touching do?

"Or they might want their money back," Patrick said.

"Why would you say that?" Gini rested her full

hand over his now.

God, he wanted to tell her. Show her and have her say it didn't matter his body was ruined. That she wanted him anyway.

"Just being humble, I guess," he said.

"You have no reason to be humble, Patrick." Gini leaned forward. "You're an attractive man. That's just a fact."

Patrick had trouble swallowing. Attractive was not the word to describe him. Maybe it could have been had things gone differently when he was sixteen. Maybe that boy could have grown into something beautiful. But that boy didn't get the chance. Instead, that boy had become this man, an elephant man.

She should go home now. She should get up, grab that ridiculous purse, and head on home.

His mind was ready to suggest that very thing, but his body made him get up from his seat, pull Gini from hers, and lean forward instead. Lean forward until Gini's lips were right there, moistened and waiting. Patrick wasn't sure who crossed the last inches first, but wanted to thank whoever had.

Gini's supple lips teased his, gentle strokes that became firmer, more urgent as their mouths melded. His hand automatically found its way back into that mass of soft curls as her hand caressed the whiskers on his jaw. Patrick slid his hands down to rest on Gini's hips, pulling her against his body. Her hands hooked on his shoulders as she angled her head up, her lips parting to meet his tongue with her own. Hot and wet, the sensation of having something of hers inside of him brought Patrick to the breaking point. A moan from her throat made fireworks explode in his body.

Gini pulled back slightly to blaze a trail of kisses down his neck. She tugged on the right side of his T-shirt's collar and nipped at his bared shoulder.

Patrick closed his eyes and burrowed his hands into the opening where Gini's shorts didn't quite hug her waist at the small of her back. His hands glided over the porcelain skin there. The curve of her body, the swell of her firm butt delighted his calloused fingers.

Patrick was vaguely aware of movement around the waistband of his jeans, but he concentrated on sliding his hands deeper to cup Gini's behind in his palms. She let out a staccato breath and ground her hips against his. Their bodies fit together perfectly, gears meant to interlock and spin endlessly.

Gini turned her attention back to his mouth, and Patrick drank in every ounce of her. That wildflower smell wafted up from her hair, and he wanted to swim in it for an eternity.

His shirt slid from the security of his jeans, and he ripped his mouth free of Gini's before she could lift the shirt. He stared at her startled face, her hand still gripping the untucked T-shirt. Patrick backed up a step and searched his mind for something, anything, to say that would erase that shocked look from her sapphire eyes.

Patrick's cell phone echoed into the frozen stillness, and he yanked it out of his pocket.

"Hello?" He jammed his loose shirt back into his jeans and tried to listen to the voice on the other end of the line.

"Barre, Chief Warner. We got another blaze. I'm short with Claremont out. Can you pinch hit for him?"

"Of course, Chief."

"Good. I've got boys on the scene trying to contain it. It's the bookstore next to Gini Claremont's studio. You know where that is?"

Patrick cast a quick glance to Gini, and a look of concern had replaced the startled one. "I can get there, sir."

Patrick slid the phone back into his pocket and

187

rubbed his face with his hand.

"What is it, Patrick?" Gini reached out, but let her hand drop before she actually touched him.

"Another fire. At the bookstore next to—"

"My studio!" Gini rushed to her purse and dug for her keys.

Patrick grabbed her arm as she whisked by him. "You're upset. Let me drive," he said. "Tell me where to go."

Gini followed Patrick to the front door. Midas circled the foyer, ready to answer the call for help. Gini opened the door and jogged to Patrick's truck behind Midas. Within seconds, they were all in and on their way.

Patrick hoped it wouldn't be too late.

Chapter Eighteen

Gini stood on the sidewalk under a streetlight with Midas by her side. Patrick had suited up and was currently manning one of the hoses dousing the bookstore blaze. She could see from across the street that the wall abutting her studio was in shambles. If the fighters didn't get the fire under control soon, her sacred workspace was going to be toast along with all the projects she was in the middle of—the calendar, two weddings, and a christening to be exact. Thankfully, she backed up all her digital photos to an external hard drive and had the negatives for the traditional ones at home. No precious moments would be lost for her customers, but it would mean extra work to redevelop the pictures.

"Gini!" Haddy ran over. The two women hugged each other for a long, silent moment. "Mason was at Jonah's when he got called in on this. I came as soon as I heard."

"It's still mostly in the bookstore," Gini said. "It won't take long to break through that wall though."

Haddy squeezed Gini's hand and held on. "Do Sally and Phil know?"

Sally and Phil Wedson owned Pages Bookstore. They had actually owned the space next door where Gini's studio was now. She'd bought it from them about six years back and couldn't think of a better set of work neighbors. They were neat, quiet, and great at recommending Gini to everyone that came into their store. Gini had done the same for them.

Sally and Phil did not deserve what was happening. Not at all.

"I called them on the drive here," Gini said, "but they're on vacation in Alaska this month, remember?"

Haddy smacked her forehead with her hand. "That's right. Well, there's nothing they could do if they were here anyway. Only the fighters can help now." Haddy turned her attention back to the flames shooting out two shattered windows of the bookstore. A third burst and the nearest fighters shrank back with the hose.

"Patrick," Gini whispered.

"He's here?" Haddy asked. "Where?"

Gini pointed a shaky finger at the fighter holding the nozzle of the hose aimed at the center of the store. She didn't like watching him creep close to danger. It reminded her of why she avoided firefighters. One freak thing, and Patrick could be injured like Jonah or worse, dead. She looked away as a shudder wracked her frame. Haddy slid her arm around Gini's shoulders.

"It'll be okay. They'll stop the fire in time," Haddy said. "Look, Patrick is already gaining on it."

Gini peeked up and saw Patrick guiding his team closer to the building. Her chest tightened, and the studio wasn't the first thing on her mind anymore. Patrick was. She wanted him to drop the hose and come stand with her. Stand where it was safe. Where the fire couldn't reach him. Couldn't take him from her before they'd had a chance to finish what they'd started in his kitchen.

His kitchen. Why had he become so afraid when she slipped his shirt from his jeans? He had his hands down the back of her shorts for crying out loud, and she certainly hadn't minded. His palms were rough, but warm, and Gini wanted to feel them over her entire body as she touched him everywhere.

Patrick had said he was camera shy, but was he all-around bashful? She'd thought Mason had been bad, getting all locked up around women, but Patrick had been downright terrified as she'd loosened his T-shirt. She'd wanted to run her palms over his chest, feel his flesh against her fingers. Was that so wrong?

Another thunderous blast made everyone scramble back and take cover. Black smoke billowed out of a hole in the roof of the bookstore and for a moment, the fire was sucked inward. It gushed through the roof opening, and the fighters took their opportunity to slay the inferno. Three teams with hoses rushed in and converged on the epicenter of the fire, and soon what remained of the bookstore hissed in a gray after-cloud. It would have to be totally rebuilt. Nothing like books to fuel a fire.

Gini gazed at her studio, still intact, but showing signs of abuse where it met the bookstore. One wall repair and it should be fine. All her photos would be okay, but it had been a close one. To think she'd almost lost her business to the very thing she had to control daily in herself. The universe loved irony. One bad day at work for her and the studio could have been destroyed long ago by fire.

Patrick crossed the street, his helmet under his arm. Gini wanted to throw her arms around him, but knew he wasn't hers. She didn't have the right to hold him or have him hold her. She clasped her hands tightly in front of her instead, and Haddy's arm slipped from her shoulders. Midas got to his feet and wagged his tail at Patrick.

"He's ready to go to work." Gini patted Midas's back.

"He's always ready," Patrick said. His short hair was soaked with sweat, and he brushed perspiration from his forehead. "Your studio will probably need only minor repairs to that adjoining wall."

"That's what I figured. Was a close one though."

"Too close." Patrick looked back over his shoulder to the bookstore carcass. "Mason said the owners are away."

Gini nodded. "We should board up the windows and roof for now."

"Some of the fighters have volunteered to do that."

"We're one big family here in Burnam," Haddy said.

"Yeah, with one bad seed who keeps setting buildings on fire." Gini narrowed her eyes.

"We'll catch the bad seed." Mason came to stand with them on the sidewalk. "Another few minutes and we can go in." He looked at Gini's purse. "You wouldn't happen to have your camera, would you?"

"Now that's a stupid question," Haddy said. "You know she could live out of that bag for six months, easy. Of course, she's got her camera."

"Probably has two," Patrick added.

Haddy and Mason laughed.

"Catching on quick, Patrick," Haddy said.

Gini flitted her gaze from the bookstore to Patrick's face. She wanted to be annoyed at his wisecrack, but couldn't muster up the emotion, looking at the grin on his face. Even covered in sweat and smelling of smoke, he made something in her belly flutter.

"I'm going to get rid of this gear," Patrick said.

"Okay," Mason said. "I'm going to have my guys hold off on going into the scene this time. I want the four of us to have first crack at it."

Patrick walked off to one of the fire trucks. Gini had her camera out, and she sent Haddy with one of the fighters to inspect the studio.

"You okay?" Mason asked.

"Yes. The studio survived." Gini let Mason hug her, and it was like hugging Jonah. All safe and cozy. "Too bad I can't say the same for the bookstore."

Mason released her and turned to face the store. "If I know the Wedsons, they've got insurance up the ass. They'll rebuild and be back on their feet in no time."

"No doubt. It's so sad, especially if this is another arson and not an accident." Gini watched Mason's fist tighten and release, tighten and release. She rubbed his forearm. "You're doing everything you can, Mason."

He sifted a breath through his teeth. "I know, but it's frustrating to wait for enough pieces to fit together before we can come up with any suspects. This will be number three within a week's time, Gini. We've never had this many fires that close together."

"We've never had an arsonist on our hands before either. Daddy told me he can't remember the last time they had a problem with someone starting fires in Burnam on purpose."

"I did some digging around myself, and there aren't any records of arson arrests in the last forty-five years." Mason flicked the flashlight in his hand on and off. "I hate to say this," he said slowly, "but you getting any kind of vibe off Patrick?"

Now there was a question. Vibes off Patrick? Yes, a few that had everything to do with wanting to stroke every part of him.

"Vibes?" Gini hoped Mason didn't notice the waver in her voice.

"Yeah, you know, something sinister."

She couldn't stop the laugh that flooded out into the dark. "Ah, sinister isn't a word I'd use to describe Patrick. I don't know him all that well, but he's a firefighter. He works to save lives, Mason. Like you."

Sinister. No way. She could think of several words beginning with "s" to describe Patrick. Shy, soft-spoken, smart, sensual, sexy. Not sinister.

"It's just that he's the only new addition we've had to Burnam recently, and these fires started after he got here."

Gini shook her head. "It's logical, but not possible. Besides, wouldn't someone lay low for a while if they were new in town? Get a lay of the land, plan their attack? Patrick hasn't been here long enough, and he wouldn't intentionally set a fire."

"You sound so sure," Mason said.

"I am." She didn't know how she knew. She just did.

Mason glanced over to where Patrick was talking with Chief Warner. "You're right. There's nothing evil about him, is there? He's definitely the hero type."

Gini nodded. Patrick was the hero type all right. The hot, kissable, save-the-day hero type. And damn, she wanted to be saved.

****

Patrick didn't like the churning in his stomach, the constant rolling. Battling that blaze had felt too much like trying to get his sisters out of their burning home. Like if he didn't stop the fire, he'd be hurting someone important to him. He'd be hurting Gini. When had she become important? Probably the moment he'd touched his lips to hers. Now he'd had her taut ass in his hands too, and the pull toward her had increased to a perilous level.

He pulled off his gear and left it in the hands of one of the fighters to bring back to the station. His T-shirt and jeans were sweat-soaked, but they were all he had. Running a hand through his hair and accepting a towel from one of the EMTs on the scene, he fixed himself up as best he could. He stopped at his truck for his investigation kit, and was beside Gini, Mason, and Midas in front of the bookstore within a couple of minutes. Huge spotlights had been set up so artificial daylight illuminated the wreckage.

"Shall we?" Mason asked. He let Patrick and Midas go first.

"Look for the candle," Patrick said. "That's our best clue that it's the same perpetrator. Midas, *venez.*"

They traveled in three different directions. Mason to the left, Patrick and Midas straight, and Gini to the right toward her studio wall. Gini began snapping pictures, capturing the carnage on film.

After a few moments of silent searching, Mason yelled, "I found it here, guys."

Gini and Patrick joined Mason by the service door at the back of the bookstore. He shined his flashlight into a narrow closet. On the floor beneath the charred remains of shelving was a banana yellow gob of wax.

"*Sentez*, Midas." Patrick pointed to the ground near the wax.

Midas slapped his nose to the ground and sniffed along what was an invisible line to the humans in the store. He barked when he got to the end of the line, retraced the trail, and barked again. Patrick kneeled and ran a finger over a spot Midas kept pawing at.

"Gasoline," Patrick said.

"Why don't we smell it in here?" Gini asked.

"It's just a thin drizzle. Didn't need much of it with all these books for fuel. Same at the barn at Meadow Cliff. Hay is super combustible all on its own." Patrick returned to the closet. "Gini, get some shots of that." He moved out of the way then added, "Please."

Gini smirked and bent to get a clear shot of the candle remains. After shooting from several angles, she stepped back. "All set."

"May I?" Patrick held up an evidence bag from his kit.

"Absolutely," Mason said. "We've got quite a collection going."

Gini squeezed Mason's shoulder. "It's another piece of the puzzle, Mason. You'll figure it all out."

He pulled away to investigate other areas of the store.

Patrick reached a gloved hand into the blackened closet and picked up the wax blob. He waved it under his nose and inhaled.

"That one scented too?" Gini asked.

"Yes, but I don't know what it is." Patrick stood and held it under Gini's nose. This brought him close to her face, a spot he yearned to be, but shouldn't. He watched as she closed her eyes to sharpen her sense of smell. She had a little investigator in her, he thought. Knew how to not tamper with a crime scene, how to look for the details.

"Smells like lavender," she said as she opened her eyes.

"What's it used for?" Patrick slipped the wax into a bag and sealed it.

"Also used to calm, de-stress, like the chamomile."

"Okay, so our perp has an anxiety problem." That fit with the profile of an arsonist. Patrick took out his notebook and made notes.

"Or wants us to think so," Gini added.

Patrick pointed at her. "Very good. Might be wanting to set up a mental instability so when we catch our candle-lighter, he or she can plead insanity." He scribbled that into the notebook.

"It's like a sickness, huh? Starting fires." Gini snapped a few more photos then looked at Patrick. The expression on her face was solemn, haunting. The glow usually radiating from her skin was gone.

"I understand you might want to feel bad for

them, Gini," he said, "but they kill people with these fires. They may be sick, but they're also murderers."

She looked as if his words had physically hit her. He hadn't meant for them to come out with so much force, but thinking someone could actually plot to set something on fire, could flare that match to life and kill with it—well, he couldn't feel bad for someone who did that. He just couldn't.

"They are the bad guys, Gini."

She nodded and maneuvered over some debris to stand with Mason. She didn't like what he'd said. Why?

Shaking his head, Patrick made more notes and met Mason and Gini by the wide open entrance of the bookstore. Some of the fighters waited outside with plywood to board up the front of the store and the roof.

"Have at it," Mason told them. Turning to Gini, he said, "Chief Warner inspected your wall himself. Says he doesn't trust it."

"I can work from home until the Wedsons come back and decide what they're going to do."

"That's a good plan. Why don't you and Haddy gather up what you'll need while we've still got the fire department here," Mason said.

"Okay." Gini turned toward the studio.

"I'll be by the truck," Patrick said.

Gini waved a hand but didn't turn around. Patrick shifted his gaze to take in the curious look on Mason's face.

"Riding into work together now, are we?" Mason asked.

"She happened to be over when the chief called me in. She was upset. I didn't want her to drive."

"Uh-huh." Mason smiled.

"Shut up, man." Patrick didn't know why he was getting angry. What Mason was concluding wasn't off the mark. He cared for Gini. He could try to deny it, but it was becoming more difficult to do so. Knowing she was in her studio where the wall was unstable made him nervous.

"Male subject appears sensitive to his growing interest in female subject." Mason pretended to write on his small notepad.

"This isn't the time or the place to discuss this." Patrick handed the evidence bag to Mason.

"You're right. I'm being unprofessional, but I love Gini. This fire could have easily taken her place down. She could have been in there. We go around thinking we have unlimited chances to say what we want to people, but in our line of work, Patrick, we should know better than anyone that's not true."

He flicked his flashlight on to beam into Patrick's face. "Don't let your fears get in the way of what you want. What you both want." Mason shut off the flashlight and left Patrick to blink at the circle of light dotting his vision.

He hated that Mason was right.

****

The drive back to Patrick's house had been a silent one. Patrick must have been tired, and Gini couldn't stop thinking about him saying fire-starters were murderers. She knew he meant arsonists— people who used fire for malicious intent—but she couldn't help putting herself in the same category. She started fires. Sure, she didn't need matches or a lighter. She didn't need an elaborate plan. She just needed some old-fashioned fury and poof, she had fire. She never wanted to kill anyone with what she could do. That's what kept her fighting for control of her ability every day. But still, the possibility was there.

She *could* kill.

The outline of Gini's SUV came into view as they approached Patrick's house. Midas nuzzled Gini's ear, and that slosh of his tongue across her cheek did more to comfort her than anything else could have at that moment. She took the dog's black face in her hands and kissed his muzzle.

"Love you too, Midas," she said.

"He only kisses when he senses someone needs it." Patrick's voice was a little scratchy, and Gini wondered if it was from being in the bookstore or something else.

"Well, he was right on." Gini smoothed the fur on Midas's back as he licked her neck.

"You okay to drive home?" Patrick angled himself against the driver side door.

What would he say if she said no? Would he take her home himself? Would he invite her to stay the night at his house? Would he take her to his bed? Touch her? Make love to her?

Gini shook her head to clear the train of thoughts. "Yeah, I'm fine. It was a close one tonight. That's all."

"Too close. We have to catch this nutcase before someone gets hurt."

Patrick's face twisted so he looked...fierce. That was the only word that came to Gini's mind. His eyes were so dark they appeared almost brown, all the flecks of green snuffed out by his mood. Gini wanted to reach out to him, make that frustration slough off his features, but she remembered how he'd reacted to her slipping his shirt free. She kept both her hands on Midas instead. The dog didn't seem to mind.

"I'll develop the pictures first thing in the morning. Send two sets to Mason. You'll be meeting with him, right?"

Patrick nodded. "We probably have enough material to analyze more fully now. The pictures are helpful."

"Just doing what the police department pays me to do." Gini shrugged and plopped her purse on top of the crate she had between her feet on the floor of the truck. She'd filed her current projects into the crate to work on at home.

"You do it well. Looking at your pictures is like being at the scene." Patrick pulled his keys from the ignition.

"Remind me to show you more pleasant pictures sometime." Gini opened her door, and Patrick got out on his side, Midas following behind him. Patrick appeared on the passenger side and held out his hands for the crate.

"I'd like to see more of your work. The few pictures you have up in your house are amazing."

Gini grabbed her purse and handed the crate to Patrick. "Thank you. I do love my work. Not many people can say that. You love your work?"

Patrick hefted the crate to his hip and held it with one hand. "My work is…necessary. I wish I could stop fires before they started, you know?"

Gini nodded. Stopping fires before they started was critical to her having a somewhat normal life.

"Well, I watched you tonight," Gini said, "and you didn't waste a moment getting that blaze under control. It was impressive."

Patrick cast his gaze down to the crate then off into the darkness around the driveway. "Again, it was necessary." He drew in a deep breath and shifted the crate to carry with both hands. "You want this in the back?" He angled his head to her trunk.

"Yes." Gini rested her purse on the crate and fished for her keys. She felt Patrick's eyes on her as she did so. She concentrated on keeping her head bent. After a few false finds, she pulled out the keys.

"You'd be able to find them easier if—"

"I didn't carry so much in here. I know. I know." Gini dragged her purse off the crate, and Patrick pretended that a great weight had been lifted.

"Watch it, wise guy. I've got my Super Soaker in here." She patted her purse slung on her shoulder now.

"Yeah," Patrick said as he shoved the crate into her SUV, "but I happen to know it's not loaded."

Gini grinned. "You weren't with me when I gathered my stuff from the studio. I could have refilled."

"I hope you did. You've got a few deserted streets to cover between my place and yours."

Gini opened the driver side door and heaved her purse inside. "Good night, Patrick." She stepped up into the SUV before she did something stupid.

Patrick came to stand at the open door. "Good night. I'll see you." He closed the door and gave her a wave as he walked to the garage. Midas bid her farewell with a short bark and trotted after Patrick.

Gini turned around in the wide driveway and watched the garage door close in her rearview mirror.

I'll see you. Why did those words comfort her?

Chapter Nineteen

When Gini pulled into her driveway, she was surprised to find her daddy's truck parked in front of her house. She glanced at the clock on the dashboard. Pretty late for a visit. Queasiness swirled in her stomach as she hopped out of the SUV and ran to the front door.

"Daddy?" She found him sitting at her kitchen table with a glass of water in his hands. "What's wrong? Is Jonah okay? Mama?"

"They're fine, Gini. I'm sorry. I didn't mean to alarm you." He took a drink of the water and rested both of his hands at the base of the glass.

Gini puffed out a breath and went back outside for her crate. She set it on the table. "Going to be working from home for a few."

"Your mama and I were over in Montpelier. Only heard about the fire at the Wedsons' place when we got back. Figured I catch you here." Walter finished the water and set the empty glass aside. "You okay?"

"The studio will be fine. One wall will need fixing. Chief Warner didn't trust it." Gini eased into the seat across from her father.

"That's not what I asked, Virginia. I asked if *you* were okay."

Virginia? Her full name. Not good. "Well, I was afraid the fire was going to take down the studio, but our fighters are good at what they do. Come from a history of superb fighters." She patted Walter's hand.

He managed a weak smile, but it didn't reach his eyes. Something else was on his mind. He wasn't himself. He'd called her Virginia.

"Daddy, what is it?"

"There isn't an easy way to say this." Walter fussed with the fringe on the linen Gini had on the table. "I have to ask it though. I have to."

"Out with it, Daddy. You're scaring me."

Was he sick? Mama? Gini often worried about the time when her parents wouldn't be around for her.

Walter studied his hands then met Gini's gaze. "Did you...could you have started these fires?"

The cricket song outside the kitchen window rose to an almost painful level. Had she heard him correctly?

"What? Daddy, I..." She actually didn't know how to respond. She'd never been so shocked in her life. Finding out she could start fires with her emotions didn't rock her off her axis as much as having her own daddy ask her what he'd just asked her.

"Hear me out, Gini." He put up his hands. "I've been thinking on this awhile now. These arson cases cropped up after you had your encounter with that Barre character. You set the bush on fire at the station and not long after, the house on Cloudson went up in flames. Meadow Cliff followed. And now the Wedsons' bookstore."

"Right next to my own freaking studio, Daddy!" Gini shot up from her chair. She couldn't sit still and listen to this.

"That's what makes me ask the question. All these fires have been near places you are familiar with. When you were first born, we lived on Cloudson. You remember?"

Gini nodded, too stunned to do much else. She couldn't even pace. Her legs wouldn't work.

"And you took horseback riding lessons at Meadow Cliff. Now the bookstore, where you've spent a great deal of time and right next to your studio. All the locations mean something to you."

"Yes, but I haven't been angry. I know when I'm about to start a fire, Daddy. I can feel it coming. It happens fast, but I know it's going to happen. You know that."

Her father turned his pale eyes up to her face. "We haven't had any arson cases here in Burnam—"

"In forty-five years. I know."

"You haven't had an incident since Barre showed up. Who's to say he didn't start a chain reaction in you?"

"I'm to say! Me, Daddy."

"Stay calm, Gini." Her father got up from his seat and came to stand in front of her. She didn't want to look at him. Didn't want to believe he had actually accused her of starting those fires.

"I am calm." She counted to ten, listed flowers by their scientific names, recited the alphabet in Spanish, French, and Italian. She didn't want to feel the hurt, but she couldn't let it turn into anger. Hurt was safer.

"What about the scented candles at every scene? I don't need candles to start a fire, Daddy." That proved it wasn't her.

Walter's gaze swept over to the kitchen counters then to the living room. Gini had a wide assortment of candles on display. She liked candles. Never lit them, but liked how they looked on copper platters full of rocks, or in rusty lanterns, or in tall, pewter holders on the mantel of her small fireplace in the living room.

"And you make all them smelly oils from your herbs and flowers," Walter said.

"But why would I leave them at the scene?"

"To confuse maybe? I don't know, Gini. It just

seems that it could be you. It's more likely than Burnam suddenly having an arsonist. You've been among us all this time. Maybe you don't have the control you used to. Maybe Barre set if off on a new level or something."

"Daddy, Patrick has nothing to do with this, and it is *not* me. I did not start those fires." Exhaustion crashed down onto Gini, and her head pounded.

"Maybe you should come stay with your mother and me for a little while. Jonah's not in any condition to watch over you."

"Watch over me? I don't need watching." She inhaled a cleansing breath and pictured herself riding Moon through a meadow on a sunny summer day. If she got angry and started a fire right now, her father would never believe her innocence. Panic washed over her—still better than anger—but she didn't know what to do. She'd never been in this situation. Her family was always on her side. Always protecting her. Part of her knew Walter was still trying to protect her. He wanted her safe and their family secret kept secret. He also wanted the citizens of Burnam safe. Once a fire chief, always a fire chief.

"I didn't want to upset you, honey. You know I love you. We all do. I just want these fires stopped." He put the glass he'd used in the sink and turned to face her. "I'll give you the benefit of the doubt, but if there's another fire soon, I'm going to insist you come stay with us." He squeezed her arm and kissed her cheek.

The door opened and closed behind Gini. She stood in the middle of the kitchen, arms hanging by her sides, head down. She felt as if she'd been punched in the gut. Her father had never spoken to her like that. Some of the force of his words was directed at Patrick. That much she could see. Walter did not think Patrick belonged anywhere near her.

Maybe he was right. After the bush at the fire station, however, Gini had shielded herself more carefully against anger around Patrick. In truth, she hadn't needed to. The last few encounters with him had left her feeling aroused, curious, maybe a little frustrated, but certainly not angry.

Did Mama agree with Daddy? Did Jonah suspect her as well? Did her whole family doubt her control? Didn't they know her better than that?

The questions brought her to her knees. A moment later, she was curled up on the cold, wood floor of the kitchen, tears streaming from her tired eyes.

Alone. She'd never been so alone.

****

The fire department was too efficient. Extinguishing the beauty she'd created far too quickly. That entire strip—bookstore, photography studio, pizzeria, lawyer's office—all four of them should have been burned to the ground by now. Yet again, however, her work had been halted by the valiant efforts of Burnam's persistent firefighters.

Damn them. She'd watched those *heroes* descend on her flames with their hoses, ready to contain the most powerful of the elements. Their control was false, however. They could put out one fire, but that wouldn't stop her from giving birth to another. And another. And another.

She'd leave her mark on this stupid little town. Several marks. Blackened and sooty with smoke that strangled. Decimated. She was just warming up. The house, the barn, the bookstore were all tiny steps up to something monumental. Unforgettable. Colossal.

The simple folks living their simple lives here would have their eyes opened. They couldn't sequester themselves in the fairy tale they'd created in this backwoods town forever. They needed

206

enlightening. Her fires would do that for them. In the brightness of her blazes as they hungrily consumed the props these people used to fool themselves, they would see that nowhere was safe. They could try to hold onto the illusion, but she would easily shatter it.

The world was a dangerous place. She knew that better than anyone. It was her duty to make everyone else see. See how they all had nothing. That they meant nothing. Were nothing.

Just like her.

****

Gini awoke to Saber's sandpapery tongue on her cheek. She'd managed to crawl to her bedroom last night and roll into bed. She'd slept fitfully, snapping awake every couple of hours, hoping that her visit with her father had been only a dream. Looking down to her rumpled clothes—last night's clothes that she'd slept in—she knew Daddy suspecting her of starting those fires had not been a dream.

"You know I wouldn't do that, right, Saber?" She stroked the cat's thick fur as Saber kneaded her stomach with his huge paws. His eyes shrunk to mere slices as he purred, and Gini took that as belief in her innocence.

She glanced at the alarm clock beside her bed. Seven o'clock. Haddy would be there soon to work. Gini had to get up. Get ready. Only she had absolutely no desire to move. If she stayed in bed all day then she didn't have to face the fact that her daddy thought she was a loose cannon. That all the years she'd been practicing her control, managing her condition, snuffing out her anger, had gone to Hell. And, according to Walter, gone to Hell over the appearance of a new firefighter.

Her stomach flip-flopped as she pictured her father's face. It had hurt him to ask her the question, to blame her, but he couldn't possibly understand how much he'd hurt her.

Gini's pretty narrow definition of living had just gotten narrower. Maybe she had taken some risks lately. Broken some of her own rules. Allowing herself to be drawn to Patrick. To kiss him. Touch him. None of that had to do with possibly starting fires, but no good could come of it. She'd only end up hurting him. She had to get back to following her strict guidelines. Maybe make a few more commandments as a precaution. If she started a fire now, that'd be the end of it. Her father would make her stay with him. He might decide she needed to be...put away somewhere.

A full body shudder wriggled through Gini. She sat up, pouring Saber off her stomach. The cat maneuvered onto her lap and picked up where he'd left off, but Gini couldn't get the notion of her parents sending her off to an institution out of her mind. There had been a time when she wouldn't have believed they'd ever do that to her.

Now, she wasn't so sure.

Gini gathered Saber into her arms and eased off the bed. A shower. Everything would be better after a shower. Hell, it couldn't be worse.

She soaked her troubles in twenty minutes of boiling hot water and lavender shampoo. After slipping on a peach-colored T-shirt and jean shorts, Gini padded barefoot to the kitchen. She forced herself into the room and made herself toast. She chased that down with a glass of orange juice and took the crate and her camera down the hall to her home office next to the darkroom. She set up shop in there and spent the next hour developing the bookstore photos.

Back in the office, she sorted out the projects she'd taken home and picked up the phone. Mason answered on the third ring.

"Detective Rivers," he said.

"Photographer Claremont," Gini said.

Mason laughed. "My favorite photographer."

"Would you be willing to come over to get the bookstore photos from your favorite photographer? I had a late night last night and don't have it in me to drive into town."

"No problem," Mason said. "You okay? You don't sound like you."

"Who do I sound like?"

"Okay, that sounded like you." Mason laughed again. "But seriously, what's up?"

"Nothing," Gini lied. "I'm just tired."

"You didn't happen to have said 'late night' with a certain firefighter, did you?"

I wish. "No, my daddy was here when I got home, then I slept like crap." *My family thinks I'm a monster, and my heart's in a billion pieces. That's all I have to report.*

"All right. I'll be by in a few then. See you."

Gini hung up as Haddy's car pulled into the driveway. She managed to find her standard happy face and slapped it on as Haddy pushed open the door.

"Morning," Gini said.

"Hiya." Haddy carried her own crate of materials she'd collected from the studio under her arm.

"I've set us up in my office. It's small, but it'll work."

Haddy nodded. "Okay, boss." She headed out of the kitchen, but stopped at the threshold. She dug in the pocket of her shorts and pulled out a piece of paper. "I almost forgot." Haddy handed the paper to Gini. "Jonah said to give this to you."

Gini took the paper, and Haddy continued down the hall. The paper was folded into a neat triangle like the Chinese footballs Jonah used to make and get in trouble with at school when they were kids.

Slowly, Gini unraveled it until it was the size of a full sheet of computer paper. Jonah's scratchy handwriting, all in capital letters, filled a third of the sheet.

Gini,

I know what Pop asked you. He and Ma came by last night, and he told me what he'd gone and done. After I was through being rip-roaring mad at him, I let him explain his reasoning. He's just trying to protect you, us, the town. You know how he is.

I'm not saying he was right to ask you what he did, but I can understand why he did. I hope you can forgive the old man. I also hope you know I'm always on your side, Gini. Whatever you say, I'll believe. I love you. I always will.

Jonah

Gini smiled through her tears—different tears than last night—and folded the note back into its triangle. She carried it with her to the office and slipped it into her purse. Another one of her treasures.

Haddy glanced up from the photos of the christening she was formatting.

"Everything okay?" she asked.

"For now," Gini said. It was a relief to know Jonah was still on her team, but her father's accusation would not be easily erased. "Let's get some work done, shall we?"

Haddy held up a picture of the baptized baby wearing his long christening gown. His cheeks were chunky and pink, his hair a barely there blond wisp across his round head. "Is this baby precious or what?"

"Yes." Gini flipped through the firefighter calendar pictures and held up three of the bare-chested beauties. "But so are these babies."

Haddy giggled, and Gini had to join her. Yes, work would keep her busy. Haddy would keep her entertained. Gini could make it through the day.

Beyond that was still a gray area.

****

Patrick stood with Mason in the police department's conference room. Gini's photos were pinned up along a giant corkboard, and a whiteboard was filled with Mason's block handwriting.

"The gasoline trail runs east to west in all three sites," Mason said. "Forensics concludes the candles were homemade, not store bought or factory manufactured. No prints could be lifted from the globs of wax unfortunately, and the scents appear homegrown as well. No artificial ingredients."

Patrick rubbed his jaw as he studied the photos. "So we've got a real do-it-yourselfer."

"In every sense of the term."

"Appears to be a build up happening here too." Patrick examined the house, barn, and bookstore photos he'd pulled down and set on the long conference table.

"What do you mean?" Mason joined him at the table.

"This house was a small job. Just one family in possible danger. The barn is a step up in risk. Horses, trainers, and citizens plus a bigger building. The bookstore, although closed at the time, is a larger affair. More square footage and the potential of taking down the entire strip."

Patrick's hands clenched the edge of the table as he thought about Gini's studio being part of that strip, part of the damage. Luckily it had been only one wall, but the possibilities had kept him up most of the night. He'd scurried into his garage as Gini left, afraid that if he'd watched her go, he wouldn't have been able to let her. Though she hadn't fallen apart over the damage to her studio, the urge to hold her, make it all right for her, had overwhelmed Patrick.

He didn't like being overwhelmed.

"You think the next one will be bigger?" Mason's voice brought Patrick back to the conference room.

"Not only bigger, but more dramatic."

Mason rubbed his eyes. "We have no suspects, no leads, not a damn crumb here." He sat and tapped his pen on the table. "I prefer burglars and killers. They tend to leave more clues behind. They get careless. This arsonist is a God-damned meticulous genius."

"They usually are," Patrick said. "What's bigger than a strip of storefronts in Burnam?"

Mason sat up straighter in his chair as he pointed his pen at Patrick. "Umm, Groveston's Market, our only grocery store. This police station, the fire station. My God, the hospital." Mason scrawled all of these locations into his notepad. "I'll post some officers around these spots. Have them keep an eye out for anything suspicious."

"It's something to do at least." Patrick shrugged.

"Make us feel as if the arsonist isn't the only one who's plotting and planning." Mason held his hand out to Patrick. "Good thinking."

"Good thinking like a criminal is what you mean." Patrick shook Mason's hand.

"Hey, I don't care if you think like a raving lunatic as long as it helps me catch the bad guys." Mason gathered up his notepad and pushed the photos and files on the table into a haphazard pile. He laughed when Patrick cringed.

"I'm not any neater outside my office. You should see my apartment."

"I'd probably have a full-blown breakdown in your apartment, Mason." Patrick walked to the doors of the conference room.

"Wait a minute." Mason was beside him, keeping him from opening the doors. "Is Raina like you? Does she like things neat?"

"She's not as bad as me, but she doesn't like a mess either. It's how we were raised. My grandmother vacuumed every day, and my grandfather had a color-coded system for fasteners in his workshop. You know, red bins for screws, blue for nails, yellow for staples, and so on."

"Shit." Mason ripped open the doors and yelled, "Ronald, does your sister still clean houses?" He turned back to Patrick. "Catch you later, Patrick. I have to take care of some things before tomorrow night."

"Later." Patrick hoped Raina was serious about Mason, because the guy was trying so hard to get it right. And yet, it didn't appear Mason minded trying so hard. The man was ready to let a stranger come into his home and reorganize the way he lived to make Raina comfortable.

Patrick wondered if he was capable of the same thing. Could he reorganize the way he lived for someone else? Could he let some of himself go to let someone else in? A piece of him wanted to say yes. Wanted to try. But what price would he have to pay to try?

Chapter Twenty

"The Lagsten christening and the Taylor wedding albums are finished," Haddy announced at about one o'clock.

"Great," Gini said. "I've got two more pages on the Matthews wedding album and that'll be done too."

"So calendar work for the afternoon then?" Haddy clasped her hands together as if she were pleading.

"Yes, that shall be our reward for such an industrious morning."

"Fantastic." Haddy slid the two albums she'd finished into their boxes and labeled them. "Can I run by Jonah's to check on him quick before we launch into our droolfest?"

"Actually," Gini said, "can I go with you? I could use a break and owe Jonah a thank you."

"Sure." Haddy paused, an odd expression on her face.

"What?" Gini asked.

"Your parents came over late last night. I'd gone to bed, but Jonah told me they had stopped by when he came to bed." Haddy paused again as if she were trying to find the right words. "He was upset, Gini. He didn't want to talk about it, but whatever they'd said to him rattled his cage."

"I'll talk to him," Gini said. And that was all she was saying. Haddy had been her assistant for six years and her best friend for almost double that, but she didn't know every detail about the Claremonts.

Gini had come close to telling Haddy several times over the years, but always decided against it in the end. She couldn't bear it if Haddy didn't take the news well. Was there any other way to take such news? That your best friend was a pyrokinetic.

It only took fifteen minutes to get to Jonah's and Gini had turned on Haddy's car stereo in an attempt to keep the chatting to a minimum. If they weren't working then the conversation would turn personal, and Gini wasn't in the mood for such talk. Not today. Of course, every song the deejays played had a depressing, sour note to them, and Gini flipped the stereo off as soon as they pulled into Jonah's driveway.

Inside, Jonah was on the couch watching The Lord of the Rings trilogy. He was on The Two Towers, and Gini paused to admire Aragorn for a moment. The dark beard framing Viggo Mortensen's mouth got her every time. Looking at the character now, however, made her think of Patrick's beard and how it had felt when she'd kissed him. Would she be forever haunted by those kisses?

"A hobbit-a-thon." Gini sat on the couch next to Jonah, and he gave her one of his lazy smiles.

"Figured I've got nine continuous hours to kill, why not?" Jonah shifted to face Gini and winced as he did so.

"How much pain are you in exactly?" Gini asked.

"Probably not as much as you." Jonah slid his free hand across the couch cushion between them, and Gini met him halfway. He squeezed her hand then held it as Frodo and company continued their quest to Mount Doom.

"Thanks for your note, Jonah." Gini scooched closer to her brother and rested her head on his good shoulder. "I needed it this morning."

"I'm still fuming about the whole thing." Jonah shook his head as he released her hand and slipped his arm around her shoulders. "I don't—" He stopped abruptly when Haddy walked in carrying a tray of food for him. He cleared his throat and said, "I don't know what I'd do without such beautiful women to take care of me."

Haddy's cheeks pinked as she set the tray down on the coffee table. The color on her face made her look so alive, so in love. As if she were getting everything she'd ever wanted out of life. Gini wondered if she'd ever be in that happy place.

"Pause the movie for me, Haddy, please. I want to give that lunch my full attention," Jonah said.

Gini straightened up on the couch as Haddy reached for the television remote on the arm of the couch. When Haddy came in range, Jonah motioned her closer with a tilt of his head. She paused the movie—on a frame of Aragorn—and leaned down to Jonah. He planted a sloppy kiss on her cheek, and she giggled.

"Couldn't you listen to that sound for a lifetime?" Jonah asked.

"A lifetime?" Haddy and Gini said together.

"Yeah, a lifetime." Jonah nodded, his blue eyes closing in pain for a moment.

"Those are some excellent drugs they've got him on, huh, Haddy?" Gini asked.

"Excellent, yeah." Haddy's eyes were wide and totally focused on Jonah.

"No, it's not the drugs," Jonah said. "It's you, Haddy. You're like a fever consuming me only I don't want the fever to break."

"Maybe he's got an actual fever?" Haddy asked, the expression on her face changing from shocked to concerned. She reached out a hand and held it to Jonah's forehead.

Jonah closed his eyes and pulled her hand down to his mouth. A kiss to her palm then a few over her wrist up to her elbow. Gini wondered if she should leave, but Haddy had driven over there. She settled for going to Jonah's kitchen for a drink of water. She stalled for a few moments, gazing out the windows over the sink at two butterflies flitting to blossoms on a butterfly bush. Her fingers itched for her camera, but her purse was in the living room. Gini settled for a mental picture and filed the image away for a time when she'd need a calm vision to settle her.

Her cell phone rang, and she pulled it out of her pocket where she'd stuffed it. She didn't recognize the number, but figured she'd answer it. She'd had her business calls forwarded to the cell phone while the studio was closed. No sense in missing opportunities to make money. Her home office and darkroom were adequate workspaces in the interim. She could handle new jobs.

"Hello?"

"Gini, it's Willow."

"Willow! How are you?"

"Super, actually. I'm getting married."

"Congratulations! That's fantastic." Gini listened to her college roommate, Willow Greene, babble on about her fiancé, the spur of the moment proposal, the high-speed wedding plans, the honeymoon.

When she'd first walked into her dorm room at RISD, Gini had only known the name of her would-be roommate. What if Gini and Willow Greene were total opposites? What if Willow Greene made Gini angry? She'd expected a crunchy, tie-dyed wearing, granola-eating, save the world one rainforest at a time type with a name like Willow. Someone who probably had strong feelings about world issues and philosophical notions. Strong feelings and Gini just didn't mix.

Fortunately, Willow Greene had turned out to be the easiest person to get along with. Laid back and go with the flow, Willow had made dorm life at RISD a breeze. A really fun break from the small town Vermont way of life breeze.

"So you'll come and be a bridesmaid, right?," Willow said. "The wedding is this weekend."

"This weekend?"

"I know it's short notice. I haven't even sent out paper invitations. I've just been calling people. It's crazy, but Andrew and I didn't want a long engagement. We decided on a beach ceremony. His parents have a beach house. Well, beach house isn't really the right word. It's more of a...mansion."

"Mansion?" Gini felt like an idiot. Words were coming at her and it was as if they were in another language.

"Yeah, in Newport," Willow said. "Remember that night at Easton's Beach?"

Gini laughed now. "How could I forget? I haven't skinny-dipped since."

"Something about running, dripping wet, with your clothes balled up in your arms, isn't there?"

"We don't even know if those guys were cops or not?" Gini could barely get the words out she was laughing so hard. Willow joined in and the hundreds of miles between them faded away.

"Say you'll come, Gini," Willow managed around a couple snickers.

Gini turned the notion over in her mind. A weekend getaway to Rhode Island to witness the wedding of a friend sounded like just the thing she needed right now. A chance to put some distance between herself, the fires, her daddy, the temptation known as Patrick Barre.

"I'd love to come to the wedding, Willow, but how about if I do the photos instead of being a bridesmaid? You know I'm always more comfortable behind the camera, and we could consider the photos your wedding gift," Gini said.

"What a wonderful idea! Thank you, Gini. I can't wait to see you again. We have a ton of catching up to do. It's been too long." Willow gave Gini the details of the when and where of the wedding, insisted on Gini staying with her while she was in Rhode Island, and made plans for dinner when Gini arrived on Thursday night.

Gini hung up the phone feeling supercharged. She bounced into the living room where Haddy teased Jonah with grapes. The two of them stared at Gini, identical looks of confusion on their faces.

"I'm going to Rhode Island this weekend," Gini announced. "Jonah, you remember Willow Greene, don't you?"

"Sure." He snatched a grape from Haddy with his good hand and smiled at Haddy's defeated expression.

"She just called. She's getting married this weekend. Wants me to go down for the ceremony and I'll do photos for her. I'll leave on Thursday. Be back by Sunday night."

"Perfect," Jonah said. "At least one of us will have some fun this weekend."

"Hey." Haddy held the grapes out of reach. "And who said you wouldn't be having fun this weekend?"

There was a vixen-like arch to her eyebrows Gini had never seen before on Haddy's otherwise angelic face.

A slow smile leaked across Jonah's lips. "I sit corrected."

"Mmm-hmm." Haddy finished the grapes herself and narrowed her eyes at Jonah.

"I meant in my current condition," he looked to his arm still bound against his chest, "my fun is limited."

"We can work around your limitations." Haddy picked up the tray and carried it into the kitchen.

"No wonder you've kept her on as your assistant

all these years," Jonah said. "She's..."

"Resourceful?" Gini suggested.

"Yes, resourceful. That's it." Jonah had that devilish twinkle in his eyes, and Gini suddenly knew, beyond a doubt, that he was going to be fine this weekend.

"Have fun in Rhode Island, Gini," he whispered. "It's the perfect time for a trip. I'll let Ma and Pop know you've gone. Things will cool down here and everything will work out."

Gini hoped her brother was right. Cooling down was always a good idea, and things had definitely been heating up in Vermont instead. Time to blow some steam—she hated that expression—and when she came home, she could get back to the quiet little life she had been leading. The life she could handle.

****

"You have experience with animals, Barre, right?" Chief Warner asked when Patrick returned from his meeting with Mason.

"Yes, sir." Patrick angled his head down to Midas, who had trotted over as soon as Patrick had entered the station. Usually Midas went nearly everywhere Patrick did, but another fighter had offered to give the dog a bath while Patrick was at his meeting. That was an offer a man couldn't say no to. Bathing a German Shepherd was messy business even when it was a well-behaved trained German Shepherd. Now Midas's black fur was all fluffed, and Patrick hadn't gotten soaked trying to get it that way.

"Go with Fissle and Olson on this call then." The chief ushered Patrick and Midas toward two fighters suiting up. Neither fighter was moving in emergency mode, but Patrick didn't waste any time getting his own gear on and hopping onto the truck. As soon as the other fighters took their places, the truck left the vehicle bay without sirens.

"What's the call?" Patrick asked Chuck Fissle, the driver.

"It's a meow round-up," Chuck said.

"A what?" Patrick had never heard the term.

"A kitty catch," the other fighter, Willy Olson, said. "The police or animal shelter gets a call that cats have been heard or seen in some abandoned barn or cabin, one that might have structural damage. We go in and collect them. The shelter takes them in, gives them vet care if necessary, then finds them homes if they can."

"I see," Patrick said. "Does this happen often here?"

"At least once a week there's some kind of animal trouble in Burnam." Chuck eased the truck around a sharp corner and onto a dirt road. "Last week, Willy and I had to detangle a moose from maple sugar taps. Week before, old Mr. Monahan trapped a bear in his shed. We had to help...relocate the critter."

"When you live in the woods," Willy said, "you get up close and personal with nature."

"Yeah," Chuck said, "and sometimes nature ain't happy about it."

Willy pulled off his left glove and held his hand up so Patrick could see it. A half-moon of teeth impressions lined the skin between Willy's forefinger and thumb. Some of the marks had broken the skin. Others had left purpling bruises.

"Was trying to get a collie free from a wire fence she was caught on. She perceived my attempt at help to be an attack and bit me." Willy shook his head and slipped his hand back into his glove.

"Why didn't you keep your gloves on?" Patrick asked. The gloves were fire-resistant and leather lined. Strong enough to keep a burn away. Strong enough to keep teeth away.

"He had them on to start," Chuck said. "But the

dog freaked whenever the gloves came close to her. The more she struggled, the more the fence cut her up. Willy had to take the gloves off."

Patrick nodded. In Providence, he'd gone on animal calls—none referred to as a "meow round-up"—but they'd been mostly abandoned tenements with dozens of cats living in their own piss and vomit. The cats were usually passive, dehydrated, and starving. They never fought back. Some of them died in transport.

What Willy and Chuck were describing, however, sounded a bit more active. Patrick made a decision right then to leave his gloves on at all costs, freaked animal or not. He didn't need more scars.

The truck came to a stop at a dilapidated log cabin. The front door hung askew by a single hinge, creating a small V-shaped opening at the bottom. Big enough for creatures to get in and out. One of the windows was smashed, and the chinking between the logs looked like vanilla frosting someone had tasted with a finger in too many spots.

"Caller said cats have been meowing in here since Saturday night," Chuck said as he jumped out of the truck.

"Saturday night?" Patrick asked. "Why did they wait so long to call?"

"They thought someone was down here. The land's been for sale. Figured someone finally bought it and had them some cats." Willy pulled several cardboard boxes out of the truck.

"It's when the meows turned to yowls and a couple of screeches they figured they were wrong." Chuck grabbed an ax and handed Patrick an industrial flashlight. "Probably no electricity in that shack."

Patrick led the way. When he got to the door, Midas a few steps in front of him, he smelled the unmistakable scent of cat urine. Midas lowered to the ground, put a paw over his muzzle, and let out a low growl.

"*Restez*, Midas." Patrick eased the broken door out of the way and flicked on the flashlight. Cat eyes reflected back at him from every corner of the cabin, and whiny mews echoed in the emptiness.

"Jesus," Chuck said. "There's got to be like thirty cats in here."

"God, I hate cats." Willy coughed on the stench.

"I think we need our masks and air tanks." Patrick stepped back for a moment and took in a breath from outside. "Man, that's awful." His eyes had begun to tear. He shined the flashlight around the interior of the shack. "It doesn't look as if any of them are hurt."

"Probably thirsty and hungry," Chuck said. He radioed back to the station. "Fissle, Olson, Barre on scene. About thirty cats found. Need more boxes."

The station buzzed back a response that someone from the animal shelter was on his way.

"Let's start boxing them up. They all have to come out." Willy stepped past Chuck and Patrick with one of the boxes from the truck.

They spent the next ten minutes rounding up cats and settling them in the boxes they had. The animal shelter staff member had arrived and started loading the boxes into his truck for transport to the shelter's vet. When no more cat eyes reflected, the fighters exited the log cabin.

Patrick was the last to leave, and as he wedged the door back into the threshold, hoping to eliminate the opening at the bottom, a faint noise stopped him.

"C'mon, Barre," Chuck said. "This took longer than it should have. I want to go home."

Patrick ignored Chuck and tilted his head toward the cabin. Midas sidled up next to Patrick and rose to his hind legs. The dog pawed at the rounded logs, and Patrick had to back him off so he could hear.

"There's something still in there," Patrick said. He moved the door out of the way again.

"We don't have any more boxes," Willy said, "and the shelter truck just left."

Patrick stepped back into the cabin. He switched on the flashlight again and swept the beam around the single room. No cat eyes, but something scratched around toward the back of the room. Midas scurried in and made a beeline to the stone fireplace in the center of the rear wall. Patrick followed and kneeled down in front of the soot-covered hearth. The scratching was louder, but no meowing.

It sounded as if…it couldn't be. Patrick leaned over the ashes and shined the light up into the chimney. A tiny, furry face with enormous eyes peered back at him. A kitten huddled in a hollowed out section of the chimney.

"What the hell?" Patrick swiveled his body around so he lay on his back inside the hearth. Propping the flashlight beside him, he reached his arms up into the chimney. "Hey there, little one."

He slid his hands up the sides of the stone and when he offered his gloved palms, the kitten inched her way off the rock ledge without a sound. Patrick lowered his hands and cradled the small body to his chest as he slid out of the hearth.

"Son of a bitch," Willy said. "Why ain't she making a racket like the others?"

Patrick let the kitten spill out of his hands and into his lap. She was so tiny her entire body fit on his kneecap in a tight ball. "Maybe she can't make a racket."

"What, like she lost her voice or something?" Chuck asked.

"She's probably dehydrated like the others. Maybe it affected her throat or something. She's so little," Patrick said.

Despite his earlier vow to keep his gloves on, he pulled one off and stroked the matted fur on the kitten's back. She was all black with big yellow eyes and a long, skinny tail. Patrick could feel her ribs under his fingers. She wiggled a bit and when he offered a thumb to sniff, she licked it.

"Well, she likes you," Willy said.

Midas nosed around Patrick's boots until his muzzle rose to inspect the kitten. Just as his meeting with Gini's cat had been friendly, this too was cordial. Two black noses met, two quick intakes of scent, one cat nestled on his knee, one dog sitting at his feet. Acceptance. Pure and simple. Patrick wished it were that easy for humans.

"We can drop her off at the shelter on our way back to the station," Chuck said. "C'mon." He and Willy left to go back to the truck.

Patrick, Midas, and the kitten took another moment for themselves. "What do you think, Midas?"

The dog woofed softly and licked the kitten's ear.

"Yeah, I like her too."

Patrick hadn't considered himself a cat person, but this kitty—like a certain woman he knew—had worked a little spell on him that had him thinking differently.

Chapter Twenty-One

The drive to Rhode Island always relaxed Gini. As a student, she often came home on weekends to be with her family and considered the drive an opportunity to truly enjoy the picturesque New England landscape. A photographer's dream. Today was no different, and the drive did wonders to dull the pain of her father's words two nights ago. She'd avoided her parents' calls and just took off. Jonah would explain her disappearance. They would worry, but there wouldn't be anything they could do. She'd be about five hours away and on her own.

That was the other advantage to going to Rhode Island. She never had a full day to herself in Vermont. Her parents or Jonah were always checking in, inviting her over, watching her. She appreciated their concern, but it got a little suffocating sometimes. She had no room to breathe. It made her feel like a child who needed constant baby-sitting.

Gini turned up the car stereo and let the Rhode Island borders swallow her. The traffic was dense, but the fading sun cast everything in a pinkish glow, making the car windshields flicker like Christmas lights. Gini wished she could dig out her camera and capture the light on film, but once again had to settle for a mental picture. She crept ahead a few feet and waited to get on the Newport Bridge. Willow had invited Gini to stay at her fiancé's parent's beach house...or mansion...or whatever it was. Willow, her sister, and her mother were bunking in a cottage on the grounds. Sounded like a taste of the high life—something Gini wasn't used to but planned on enjoying for the weekend.

Night had fallen by the time Gini pulled into the semi-circular driveway in front of an enormous stone house. Medieval almost in décor, the mansion boasted two actual turret towers and a steeple roof above the tall front doors. A four-car garage branched off to the left, and smaller stone buildings dotted what Gini could see of the backyard from the driveway. Trees with large orange berries she couldn't identify lined the driveway while smaller flowering plants hugged the ground below the trees. Evergreens had been cut into clean spirals at either side of the front doors, and in the distance, the ocean kissed the rocky shore.

Gini grabbed her purse and leaned against her SUV, inhaling the sea-salted darkness. Burnam offered no glimpse of the Atlantic Ocean. The closest water was Gini's tiny pond, big enough to wade in with the horses and take a dip, but no good for much else. She'd definitely have to squeeze in a few hours of lazing on the sand and splashing around in the sea.

She hauled her small suitcase out of the trunk and hollered when arms whirled her around.

"Jesus, Willow." Gini's heart pounded in her chest. "You scared the crap out of me."

"Sorry." Willow pulled Gini into an embrace. "I'm so glad you're here. This is going to be so great!"

"Cheer up, Willow." Gini smirked as Willow giggled.

"I know. I'm way over the top, but I don't care." She twirled away from Gini, her long, red hair fluttering out behind her. "I'm in love. I'm getting married. It's good to be alive." She waltzed back and took Gini's suitcase. Setting it down, Willow caught Gini in a dance hold, and the two of them swing danced down the driveway.

"Oh, somebody's rusty. You're letting those lessons we took go to waste, girlie," Willow said. "Haven't been practicing?" She leaned away to study Gini's face.

"No one to practice with." Gini let her hands drop from Willow's grasp and pushed her purse back up onto her shoulder.

Willow angled her head and puckered out her lips. "No, that's not it."

"What do you mean? I can't swing dance with myself." Gini picked up her suitcase.

"No, I mean it's not that you don't have a partner." Willow narrowed her golden brown eyes. "You've got one in mind."

"Cut that out," Gini said. "You know I hate when you do that."

"Do what?" Willow took Gini's suitcase and led her onto a small path off the driveway.

"Read me like a book. It's creepy."

"Can't help it. You've met someone."

Gini shrugged behind Willow. True, she had met someone. False, she was going doing anything about it. Patrick was not her dance partner.

"Your silence speaks volumes." Willow walked up the steps of a house too big to be considered a cottage in Gini's mind.

"This weekend is about you," Gini said. "Let's keep it that way, okay?"

As Willow opened the door, she turned to look at Gini. "If that's what you want."

"I do." Gini stepped past Willow into the cottage.

"Fine, but," Willow grabbed Gini's arm to stop her, "if you want to talk, you know I'll listen."

Gini gave Willow a quick hug and that contact did more to settle her than any of her meditative tricks. She hadn't had one incident while in college with Willow, and Gini now realized it had so much to do with the kind of friend Willow had been. The kind of friend she was still today.

"Thanks, Willow."

Willow nodded. "A fast hello to Mom and Lily, then I'll show you to your room."

"Sure."

"Then, if you're not too tired, some dinner?" Willow's hopeful eyes made Gini laugh.

"I'm hungry."

Willow did a little jig in the hallway and escorted Gini into a living room furnished with a white couch, two pale blue Queen Anne chairs, and an assortment of sailboat paintings on the walls. Posh, yet simple. Homey, yet nautical.

"Nice," Gini said.

"I'm deathly afraid I'm going to get that couch dirty though. Look at how white it is." Willow thrust her arm out to the couch, and Gini had to agree the thought of actually sitting on it made her sweat. Sweat would probably stain that couch.

"That you, Willow?"

"Yes, and I've brought in a stray Vermonter." Willow put Gini's suitcase down and dragged her into the yellowest kitchen Gini had ever seen. Although it was dark outside, it seemed as if the sun were shining in the room. Seashell decorations were tastefully tucked into every nook and cranny, and Willow's mother sipped tea at a small wicker bistro set by a bay window. Her sister, Lily, munched on a cookie at the island in the middle of the kitchen.

"Gini!" Willow's mother got up from her seat. "So glad you could come on such short notice. My daughter's engagement has been such a whirlwind." She gave Gini a hug and a kiss to each cheek then stepped back. Her eyes traveled from Gini's head to her toes. "My, don't you look wonderful."

"Thanks, Mrs. Greene. You look fabulous as well."

"It's the tea. Secret formula." She winked at Gini and sat back at the table.

"Hey, Lily," Gini said. "What have you been up to?"

Lily gave a shrug that sent her dyed jet-black hair sliding over her shoulders. "Nothing. Just trapped here while my actual life is on hold."

"Lily," Mrs. Greene said. "Enough already."

"My sister thinks I'm succumbing to societal norms by entering into a binding marital contract." Willow rolled her eyes, and Gini had to stifle a laugh. Good thing she hadn't gotten stuck with Lily as a roommate at RISD.

"It's so predictable, Willow. I feel bad for the two point five kids you're going to shoot out of your vagina."

"Especially the point five," Gini said.

Willow and Mrs. Greene burst into laughter with Gini, but Lily scowled from the island.

"Lily's going to make a splendid maid of honor, don't you think?" Willow asked.

Gini opened her mouth to respond but then closed it. "I'm not touching that one."

"Wise girl," Mrs. Greene said.

"I'm going to set Gini up in her room then we're off to dinner. You sure you don't want to come, Mom?" Willow asked.

"No, I'm all set. You girls have fun catching up."

"Yes," Lily said as she spun the silver stud in her bottom lip, "have fun hob-knobbing with the epitome of economical conceit here in Newport."

"We will." Willow pinched her sister's cheek and earned herself a slap on the hand. She laughed and bent to kiss her mother's cheek. She motioned to Gini to follow her up a set of stairs off the kitchen.

At the top, Gini stopped in front of a porthole type window. She wished she could see outside, but the darkness was absolute. Not a light out there anywhere. Gini knew the water had to be hiding under that curtain of black. She couldn't wait to explore it, swim through it, wash away her troubles in it. She would let the past few days in Vermont go out with the tide and, hopefully, welcome in something fresh on the waves.

****

"You're going to keep it?" Raina's nose crinkled. "I thought you didn't like them."

"I like this one."

"What about Midas?"

"Midas likes this one too."

"He doesn't like any of them."

"Not true. He likes this one and recently met another one he could tolerate."

"Where?"

"At Gini's."

"Oh, I see." Raina's smile was smug. "You're trying to get on Gini's good side by adopting this glorified rat." She shook her head when Patrick tried to hand her the kitten he'd rescued from the cabin.

"It's not a glorified rat, Raina. It's a cat. People all over the world have accepted them as domestic pets."

"Not me. I'm afraid the thing will scratch my eyes out while I sleep." She sat on the edge of a sawhorse in the great room.

"I think a cat would have to worry about getting its eyes scratched out by you while it slept."

Raina let out a hiss and laughed. "I thought you were a solid dog man. All the way. Man's best friend and all that crap. To see you standing here, *cuddling* no less, with that fleaball is disturbing. It's like I don't even know you."

"You're right." Patrick let the kitten crawl up onto his shoulder. "If you told me I'd be owning a cat last week, I'd have said you were insane."

The kitten pushed her nose into his ear and he

231

laughed. Really laughed. The sound surprised him as the kitten rubbed her cheek along his neck. "There is something about this one, though. She doesn't meow, but the vet couldn't find anything wrong with her."

Patrick plucked the kitten from his shoulder and set her in the crook of his bent arm. She nestled in against his chest, all warm and small. She'd done the same thing this morning in his bed. Patrick had slept soundly last night for the first time in a long time. No dreams. No nightmares. When he'd opened his eyes as sunlight poured into his bedroom, the little kitten was curled into a tight circle on his bare chest. He'd watched her tiny body rise and fall as he breathed.

She hadn't been afraid to settle down on his scars. They hadn't kept her from choosing that spot to sleep. She hadn't cared. The kitten wanted to be close to him on her first night in her new home. She hadn't judged. She hadn't run. She'd accepted.

Patrick felt he owed something to the kitten for that.

Raina stood and took a step closer. She ran a finger down the kitten's solid black back. "She is cute, I guess. Now that I really look at her. What are you going to name her?"

"I don't know yet," Patrick said. "It'll come to me."

Raina nodded and looked around the great room. "So what are you working on today, Mr. Construction?"

Patrick set the kitten down on the ground and let her play with his shoelace for a moment. She bounced around his boot, swiping at the loop of string then skittering back as if she expected it to attack her in retaliation.

"Shower install, master bathroom. I started it last night." Patrick led Raina to the bathroom, and she peeked inside.

"Nice window. That's new."

"Did that yesterday too. It was too dark in here."

Raina whistled as she admired the beginnings of a corner shower stall. "You are a Renaissance man, Patrick. You try it all when it comes to construction."

"Grandpa taught me well." Patrick glanced at his grandfather's old toolbox on the floor in the bathroom. He remembered helping Grandpa make it in the workshop. "Besides, what's the worst that can happen? If I mess something up, I can always call in somebody to fix it. It's all just one big experiment."

"As is life," Raina said.

"Life is not as easily fixed."

"Shouldn't keep you from trying things, though." Raina poked him in the stomach, and Patrick backed up so she could come out of the bathroom. She strolled through the great room to the front door. Patrick followed behind her with the kitten scurrying between his feet.

When Raina reached the door, she turned around. "Don't lose track of time, okay? You'd better be ready when I come to pick you up." She wagged a long finger at him.

Patrick reached out and grabbed her finger. "Don't scold me. I haven't done anything wrong yet." He smiled as he twisted her finger slightly.

Raina kicked at his boot and pulled herself free. "Despite the new love of soft, fluffy kittens, I know you, Patrick Barre. You get your tools going, and suddenly time doesn't exist. You're in another dimension, population of one."

Patrick held his hands up in surrender. "Point made. I'll set the alarm on my watch so I'll stop an hour early. Make sure I'm all cleaned up and ready."

"I'm not trusting your watch." Raina shook her head. "I'm calling you one hour before I come to get you. I wouldn't want to be you if you don't answer the phone." She wagged her finger again and ripped open the front door before Patrick could grab her. The sound of her laughter floated in on the hot breeze.

Patrick stepped to the threshold and waved to Raina as she backed out of his driveway. A scratching noise down at his feet made him look down. The kitten pawed the casing around the door and turned her headlight eyes up to him. Patrick crouched and picked up the kitten. Setting her on his knee, he looked at her eye-to-eye. She opened her mouth and pantomimed a meow. Not even a squeak came out.

"What are you trying to say, kitty?" Patrick rubbed between her ears. "I think I'll call you Whisper." He placed his hand on his stomach and thought about the kitten on his chest this morning, on his scars. "I hope you can keep a secret."

****

Gini slipped into the turquoise dress she'd brought with her for the wedding. Satin spaghetti straps hung over her tanned shoulders. A scalloped neckline and high waist emphasized her breasts nicely. The hem of the dress reached about four inches above her knees and showcased two long legs that balanced on silver-sandaled feet. Willow's mother had piled all of Gini's hair into an intricate twist that spilled curls from the top and around her face.

Looking in the mirror, Gini was rather impressed with the outcome. She rarely got this fancified and almost didn't recognize herself. She put on dangling silver heart earrings and a matching bracelet. A couple of touch-ups to her makeup, and she grabbed her camera and dressy purse. As she picked up the tiny purse—about one twentieth the size of her everyday bottomless pit—she wondered what Patrick would say. She only had room for her wallet, phone, keys, tissues, lipstick, and a mirror in the small clutch.

See, I can downsize.

Downstairs, Willow's mother paced in the kitchen. When Gini touched her arm to stop her, Mrs. Greene looked up with tears in her eyes.

"What's the matter?" Gini asked.

Mrs. Greene grabbed a napkin from the kitchen counter and dabbed at the tears rolling down her cheeks.

"My Willow is getting married." She burst into a full sob and clung to Gini.

"That's a good thing, Mrs. Greene. You've seen how happy she is." Gini rubbed the woman's back as the tears flowed.

"I know, I know. She's walking on clouds. And Andrew is such a nice young man. He'll take care of Willow, but..." Mrs. Greene blew her nose, "who's going to take care of me?"

"Oh, Mrs. Greene, don't see it as losing a daughter. See it as gaining a son." Gini embraced Willow's mother again and gave her a quick squeeze. "I'm sure you'll be well taken care of."

Mrs. Greene nodded slowly as if she were turning Gini's words over in her head. Gini wanted to say that she still had Lily, but somehow didn't think that would be much comfort.

"It's just that since my husband passed on, Willow's been right there making sure I'm okay." Mrs. Greene wiped her eyes once more. "But you're right, Gini. Look at this cottage. Andrew turned it over to us for the week just like that. He's not even going to be here until tonight. I suppose a man that does that sort of thing won't leave me in a nursing home to rot when I'm old and feeble."

"Who says you're ever going to be old and feeble?" Gini winked and Mrs. Greene laughed through the last of her tears. "I mean, look at you.

You look fantastic in that dress." Gini waved her camera. "I just don't know how I'll manage keeping the lens focused on Willow with you looking all spectacular."

Mrs. Greene swatted a hand in the air. "Aren't you a sweetie? I always liked you, Gini Claremont." She narrowed her eyes for a moment. "Why aren't you all married off?"

Gini drew in a deep breath. *Because I have the potential to blow things up with my rage.* "Don't have the time, I guess."

"Make the time, dear. You're not being fair to the men of Vermont if you don't."

"They'll manage," Gini said.

Lily trudged into the kitchen in a violet kimono-style dress. Her black hair had been slicked back and gathered in a tight bun at the nape of her neck. Two long black sticks held the bun in place and although Gini didn't think the outfit screamed maid of honor, there was something classy about the look. Made Lily look more like a sophisticated lady than the gothic, twenty-something she really was. The only thing that ruined the picture was the hard, straight line of Lily's mouth.

"Is it almost time to get this thing done?" She pulled open the refrigerator and grabbed a can of soda. After popping the top open, Lily guzzled half the can down in one shot.

"You ruined all your lipstick." Mrs. Greene plucked another napkin from the holder on the counter and walked over to Lily.

"Do not attempt to fuss with my face, Mother." Lily ripped the napkin from Mrs. Greene's hand.

"Do not attempt to ruin your sister's day, Lily." Mrs. Greene straightened to her full height, which was a few inches taller than her daughter. Lily shrank back a bit and used the napkin and the reflective metal of the toaster to wipe the lipstick streaks at the corners of her mouth.

When Mrs. Greene turned around to face Gini, she rubbed her temples. "I feel a headache coming on."

"Why don't you go upstairs and see to Willow?" Gini said. "I'm going to get a few shots of the ceremony site before it's crowded with guests."

Mrs. Greene headed for the stairs. Gini approached the counter and leaned against it. Lily crumpled up the napkin and turned black-brown eyes to Gini.

"What?" she asked.

"Take it down a notch, okay?" It was taking a bit of effort to keep the anger at bay. Gini made a decision right then to stay away from Lily for the rest of her stay in Rhode Island to be on the safe side. "Your sister is a great person, and she deserves a perfect day. You making comments and sulking around makes it un-perfect."

Lily opened her mouth, but Gini held up a hand. "Just fade into the background. It's not about you."

Gini slipped out the French doors in the dining room before Lily could say anything. She crossed the wide patch of pristine lawn to the gazebo and chairs set up for family and friends. There had to be at least four hundred chairs by Gini's estimate. She thought of the Matthews wedding she had photographed in Burnam. Seventy-five guests tops. On the bride's family farm. Bride and groom had worn jeans and arrived at the ceremony on horseback. The reception was a barbecue.

Looking around at the mini water fountains, flowers, and candles in crystal holders set up on the round tables under hundreds of tiny lights strung through the trees, Gini didn't think ribs on the grill or jeans would make an appearance tonight. Newport was a world away from Burnam. Love would be the only common factor between Willow's wedding and the Matthews wedding, and Gini supposed that was all you needed anyway.

Not that she'd ever know.

"It's not about you either," she told herself. Shaking her head, she walked deeper into the area and started snapping photos of the decorations, the waiting gazebo, the prepped tables, the string quartet setting up, the ocean kissing the sand in the backdrop.

That shore at the edge of the property had called to her all day, but Willow had kept Gini busy with this and that. There hadn't been a free moment to steal away to the beach and test the water with her bare toes. But tomorrow. Tomorrow was another day. Willow and Andrew would be off on their honeymoon in Australia, but had said Gini was welcome to stay with Mrs. Greene and Lily in the cottage for as long as she wanted. So tempting to stay for weeks, but Gini would make do with a day, two tops. She planned to bike ride along the coast tomorrow morning and be a beach bum for the rest of the day. She couldn't wait.

Gini took a few more pictures of the grounds and caught a lovely sailboat gliding by on the water. The sun had almost disappeared below the horizon. Purple-pink streaks hovered above the dark water now, and a nearly full moon climbed to its zenith in the starry sky. The night was hot, but a soft breeze off the ocean kept it from being stifling. The air sifted through tall grasses that lined the border between lawn and sandy shore. The gentle swish was a music all its own.

"Gini!"

She turned around to see Willow leaning out a windowsill, dressed in white, several feet of stone cottage beneath her. The contrast between soft white wedding dress and rough gray rock was too much for Gini to resist. She snapped a picture, loving the play of textures.

"Come in here," Willow called.

Gini waved and walked back to the cottage. She climbed the stairs and raised her hand to open the back door. Before her fingers made contact though, the door opened. Willow clamped onto Gini's arm and yanked her inside. She pulled Gini upstairs into a bedroom and closed the door.

"What am I doing?" Willow's eyes were wide, her skin pale.

"Getting married, I think," Gini said.

"Why is my heart pounding? I don't feel right. I think I'm going to vomit." Willow sat on the end of the bed and pulled Gini down beside her. "Is it hot in here? I was cold like two seconds ago and now it's boiling in here? Are you boiling?"

"Yikes," Gini said. "Take a breath, Willow. What's happening?"

"I think I'm freaking out. Andrew called me to let me know he's at the main house and can't wait to see me, to marry me." She stood and paced in front of Gini. "Now, I can't breathe."

"Okay, okay." Gini stood too and grasped Willow's shoulders to stop her from wearing a rut in the carpet. "You're just a little anxious. You love Andrew, right?"

"More than anything."

"See, you didn't have to think twice about that answer, Willow. This is right. You know it is."

Willow grinned. "It *is* right. Andrew and I are meant to be husband and wife. I lost it for a minute there. Lily's comments just kept circling through my head, and suddenly I thought I was making a monumental mistake." She shook her head. "Not marrying Andrew would be a monumental mistake."

"All better?" Gini relaxed her grip on Willow.

"Yes. I'm ready." Willow hugged Gini as a soft knock sounded on the door.

"Willow, it's time," Mrs. Greene called.

"I'm ready," Willow said again. She took Gini's hand and tugged her to the door. "Get that camera ready. I'm going to need proof that I've actually said, 'I do.'"

****

Gini had never seen a more beautiful bride and groom. Willow looked like a mermaid in her fitted wedding dress that belled out around the ankles. Her long red hair was held back on the sides with mother-of-pearl combs. And Andrew was exactly what Gini would have picked for Willow. Tall and lean with short, sandy blond hair and trustworthy brown eyes, he had convinced Gini he was in love with Willow with the look on his face as he waited for his bride to make the trip down the aisle. As Willow had approached him, the smile on his tanned face lit up the night. He was dashing in his off-white tuxedo—a tuxedo color Gini didn't usually like. Andrew pulled it off though, looking somehow beachy and debonair at the same time.

Her camera had been busy throughout the ceremony capturing every moment of Willow and Andrew's special day. Gini had captured the entrance of the bride, the ring exchange, the kiss as husband and wife, the family and friends here to celebrate. These pictures were going to be fun to put into an album for Willow to cherish forever.

Gini found her assigned table and took a sip of water before going table to table to take photos of guests. She didn't want to miss anyone and with four hundred guests that was a definite concern. A few more sips of water and she started for the small stage where the string quartet was set up. That way she'd get some shots of the overall crowd first then delve into individual and small group photographs. She probably wouldn't get a chance to eat a bit of that lobster dinner Willow mentioned, but such was the life of the wedding photographer. Maybe she could get hers foil wrapped for tomorrow.

She approached the stage and caught the attention of the violinist in the quartet. She pointed to her camera, herself, and the corner of the stage. He nodded, never missing a note. Gini mouthed the words *thank you* and climbed the steps to the right of the stage. She grinned at the fantastic vantage point. She could see everyone at once, all the different colored dresses, all the suits, all the lights twinkling in the trees. Just lovely.

Gini lost herself in the scenery, snapping frame after frame of merry attendees. She got some marvelous shots of Willow and Andrew as they danced, kissed, smiled dreamily at one another. Seeing them made Gini believe that true love did exist. No two people could look at each other the way Willow and Andrew were and not be filled with love and passion.

Gini saw Lily talking to a short young man, both of them holding wine glasses. Even Lily was smiling, and the expression was lovely on her face. *Click, click.* Gini was pleased to have caught Lily on film looking happy. Something told her Lily didn't do happy on a regular basis. In fact, she was sort of an anti-Gini. Pissed off all the time. Good thing Lily wasn't a pyrokinetic. She wouldn't last two minutes.

Scanning the crowd with her camera still to her eye, Gini stopped on the back of a man's dark-haired head. As Gini panned down a bit, she took in broad shoulders under a black suit jacket. She continued the trip down and zoomed in on the tight ass contained in black dress trousers.

Nice, she thought. *Very nice.* She snapped two photos, maybe just for herself to look at later. No reason all the photos had to be for Willow.

Gini zoomed out and waited figuring if the back view of the man was so pretty, the front might be equally so. Why not capture the complete package? She drummed her finger on the side of her camera while the man talked to a woman in front of him, probably his wife or girlfriend. Lucky chick.

The man shifted his weight, and the woman's face filled Gini's lens for an instant. His body leaned back to where it had been, blocking the woman again. Gini pulled the camera from her eye and willed the gears in her mind to turn. To process what—or who—she had thought she'd seen.

Can't be. She blinked and shook her head, curls bouncing around her cheeks.

Gini zipped the camera back up to her eye and zoomed in on the man's head. He stepped aside again, and there was the woman. Then the man turned around, and Gini nearly fell off the stage.

"Oh. My. Goddess." Her arms lowered the camera as her mouth hung open, and she stared at the man. His eyes flicked up to the stage, and he saw her.

Patrick Barre saw her.

Chapter Twenty-Two

"Raina, are you seeing who I'm seeing?" Patrick didn't trust his eyes. Gini had to be a mirage on that stage right now. He had to be going crazy.

"Seeing who?" Raina touched his shoulder to move him aside so she had a view of the stage. "What's Gini doing here?"

"Okay, so you see her too?"

"Of course I see her, you monkey. She's right there." Raina gave him a little shove. "I think she sees you too, Patrick. Go talk to her."

"Talk to her. Right." Only his feet didn't move, and his hands were slicked with sweat.

"Before the sun comes up, Patrick. Jesus." Raina really pushed him this time, and he stumbled forward. He glared over his shoulder at his sister. She raised a hand to wave to Gini. "She's waving back. No doubt she's seen us now. You better get a move on. Don't want to seem rude." She took a step toward him.

"Do not push me again or I'll toss you into the ocean," Patrick said.

"You don't want to have to dive for the keys to drive home." Raina shook her purse where her car keys jingled. She smirked and backed into the crowd.

Patrick turned around slowly and saw Gini walking down the stage steps. She'd be in front of him in no time. He needed a minute to prepare. To put his shields up. To...do...something.

"Hey." Gini smiled and Patrick's mind cleared

out.

"Hey."

"What are you doing here?" she asked.

God, she looked amazing, her eyes an unusual blue-green against the color of that dress. A dress that fit her incredible body perfectly. Patrick's eyes were drawn to where the silky fabric brushed along the skin above her knee. He had to jam his hands into his pockets before they did something crazy.

"Andrew is my cousin," Patrick said. "What are you doing here?"

"Willow was my college roommate at RISD." Gini held up her camera. "And I'm also here on official business."

"I see." Where was a damn waiter when a guy needed a drink? Patrick's throat felt as if it were lined with sandpaper.

"I thought I saw Raina with you." Gini looked around where they were standing.

"You did. She went...somewhere. I don't know." Man, he couldn't think of anything intelligent to say. He sounded like an idiot.

"And Midas? Is he here too?" Gini smirked and raised an eyebrow.

Patrick laughed. "No, Midas doesn't do weddings. He's actually with Jonah and Haddy. I didn't think it was going to work out at first. Haddy brought her brood of dogs over to Jonah's, and Midas is more of a people person. He gets impatient with other dogs."

"Probably because they're a lot dumber than him," Gini said.

"Well, I didn't want to brag, but Midas is a genius. He's also an Alpha dog. Doesn't like other dogs taking charge." Patrick looked down and caught sight of Gini's sandals. Good Lord, her feet were sexy. He returned his gaze to her face and those spirals of hair framing her cheeks.

"Drink?" A waitress slid a tray of wine glasses between them.

Amen. Patrick looked to Gini and she nodded. He selected two glasses and thanked the waitress. As he handed one glass to Gini, his fingers brushed against hers, and the desire to touch her everywhere exploded inside him. Why did Gini keep having that effect on him?

Gini clinked her glass to his. "To Rhode Island and a night by the sea."

Patrick watched the line of Gini's neck as she tipped her head back to sip the wine. He wanted to slide his tongue over that delicate skin more than he'd ever wanted to do anything.

"Did Jonah know you were coming here?" Patrick asked after taking a sip of his own wine to clear his head.

"He did," Gini said. "I'm guessing he didn't mention it when you told him you were headed to the same wedding, did he?"

Patrick shook his head. "Must have slipped his mind."

"Haddy's too."

"Interesting."

"Quite."

"Gini!" Willow called as she and Andrew waltzed by. Andrew stopped and shook Patrick's hand.

"Congratulations, cuz," Patrick said.

"Thanks, man. You having a good time?" Andrew asked.

Patrick flitted his gaze to Gini. "An excellent time, yes."

"How about you, Gini?" Willow stood next to Gini, but her eyes were focused on Patrick.

"Great time. Got some beautiful photos for you here." Gini tapped her camera.

"Awesome." Willow glanced at Patrick. "You've met Andrew's cousin?"

"Actually, yes. In Vermont."

"Really? Do you swing dance, Patrick?" Willow asked.

"Willow," Gini warned.

"Swing dance? No." Patrick's brow furrowed as he looked from Willow to Gini.

"You should learn. Gini could—"

"Ignore her," Gini said, cutting Willow off.

"Not polite to ignore the bride," Willow sang. "Especially when she's right."

"Andrew, you better watch your wife's alcohol intake this evening. She's a little loopy already," Gini said.

"Drunk on love, girlie, and it feels wonderful." Willow threw herself at Andrew, who automatically caught her. The two of them floated away, and Gini snapped a few more photographs of the happy couple.

"That seems like a perfect match." Patrick couldn't help taking a few steps closer to Gini as her back faced him. The dress looked just as magnificent from the rear as it had from the front. He knew that superb ass he'd been fortunate enough to touch was under the delicate material of Gini's dress. Would he get to touch it again?

Should he?

When Gini turned around, she was mere inches away from him. Patrick knew he should back up. Or she should. Someone should, but neither of them did.

Gini lifted her head slightly then rested her hand on his forearm. "I've taken enough pictures for now. You want to take a walk with me?" She angled her chin toward the water.

Patrick followed Gini away from the reception, off the grass, onto the sand.

He had a feeling he'd follow her anywhere.

****

Gini had wanted to get away from Patrick. Part

of her trip to Rhode Island was to accomplish that mission. To sort out her mixed up feelings and get back in control of her quiet life. With Patrick following her down to the water right now, however, she wondered why she had wanted to be away from him.

What she wanted was Patrick.

The moment she had seen him through the camera lens, she knew she didn't want to run from him. Her body had responded to his body, but when he'd turned around and she realized it was Patrick, something else responded. Something deep inside her. Taking photographs for a living, Gini ran into many attractive people—attractive men—but none of them had awakened that empty place in her soul. She'd shielded herself from their advances, ignored their interests, and hadn't felt bad about doing so.

But Patrick. Patrick. She couldn't ignore him. She didn't want to. Gini wanted him close. Closer.

"It's beautiful here," Patrick said.

They stood together, moonlight shimmering off the ocean and casting a white glow on the sand. Gini peeled off her sandals and swiveled her feet around until they were covered with cool sand. She watched her toes disappear then looked at Patrick.

"C'mon. You too. You know you want to." She elbowed him and could make out a smile sliding across his beautiful face.

Gini handed him her camera, and he slid it into the pocket of his suit jacket. She bent, careful not to let her dress touch the sand, and untied Patrick's shoes. He didn't try to stop her, didn't move. When she'd gotten them both loosened, he lifted his left foot and let her pull the black dress shoe off. He stood solidly on his other leg, no waver at all.

"That's some balance you got there." Gini's gaze combed upward, and she enjoyed the view up the length of his body. The light green, button-down shirt he wore under the black suit complemented his dark complexion. The first two buttons were unfastened and revealed a smooth V of his neck, just a sneak peek. Gini longed for the full show.

"Tai chi. Good for balance." Patrick poised as perfectly on the left leg as Gini slid off the other shoe.

"Yoga fan myself." She pulled his socks off, handed them up to him, and cuffed his pant legs.

"Yoga's for girls."

Gini rose to her feet and stood, mere inches separating her body from Patrick's. "If you haven't noticed," she whispered, "I am a girl." She slid her hand into his.

"I noticed." Patrick trailed the fingers of his free hand up Gini's bare arm. "I can't seem to *not* notice."

Gini shivered and leaned a bit closer. Still not close enough to satisfy her.

Singing floated on the night breeze, bluesy and sensual.

"Raina?" Gini asked.

Patrick nodded. "Her gift to Andrew and Willow. She actually wrote the song and music for this one."

Gini angled her head to hear the words.
The sun will set, the moon will rise
But I'll only see the love in your eyes.
The earth will turn, seasons come and go
But my love is all you'll know...

"Nice." Gini closed her eyes, letting Raina's smooth voice carry the weight of her. She felt like flying, over the ocean, into the night. She wanted to take Patrick with her.

Gini opened her eyes when Patrick's arm came around her waist and drew her closer.

"I don't swing dance," his breath tickled her ear, "but I do slow dance."

Patrick edged them both toward the water. With the sea licking their bare feet, he turned them slowly with the music. Their bodies were like the sand, shifting, moving to fill in the gaps. His hands were firm against her lower back, and Gini felt aroused and safe at the same time. She circled her arms around Patrick's neck, her head resting on his shoulder.

They danced to four more of Raina's songs. Time lost its meaning. There was nothing but the two of them, the shore beneath their feet, and the moon overhead. Gini drank in the serenity, filled herself up.

"This is Raina's last one," Patrick said. "She'll be looking for me."

"I should be taking more pictures," Gini said.

Neither one of them released their hold on the other.

Gini leaned back a bit to look at Patrick's face. Funny how his features were sharp and clear to her, but the background behind him, everything else, was fuzzy, unfocused. Unimportant.

"I like *this* picture," she said.

Patrick pressed his lips to Gini's forehead, and she felt it all the way down to her soaking wet, sand-covered toes. He dropped another kiss on the tip of her nose and hovered, just waited, at her lips.

Gini flicked her gaze up to his. He was facing the reception area so the lights strung in the trees reflected in his eyes, illuminating those golden brown flecks swimming in the forest green.

"Patrick, please," Gini whispered.

He closed the distance between his lips and hers. Soft, warm, so gentle. Gini's entire body responded. She could barely contain the desire to crawl inside Patrick. Or have him crawl inside her. To be that close to him.

His hands pressed against her backside, fingers stroked the silky material of her dress, slipped along her contours. Patrick deepened the kiss, his mouth drinking her in.

Gini slid her hands underneath Patrick's suit jacket and up the span of his shoulder blades. She circled his tongue with her own, drawing him deeper, closer, taking more, wanting more. She broke away from the kiss only to forge a trail along Patrick's bearded jaw and down his neck with her lips. Gini breathed in his scent, somehow sawdusty though there couldn't be any on him. She wanted to check though. Check thoroughly.

A hum of pleasure vibrated in Patrick's throat as she canvassed across his chin and back up to his lips. They kissed and massaged until Raina's voice held an impossibly long note and faded on the sea breeze.

"How long are you staying in Rhode Island?" Gini's voice sounded lower to her own ears.

Patrick took a step back as if he needed to in order to form a response. "We're driving back Monday morning. You?"

"The same, I think." Gini chewed on her bottom lip, enjoying the lingering taste of Patrick she found there. "I was planning on a bike ride tomorrow morning and some beach time in the afternoon. You wouldn't…you wouldn't want to join me, would you?"

Patrick looked out over the rippling water. *Please say yes, please,* Gini thought. She didn't like the thought of not seeing him tomorrow.

"I can do the bike ride, but my afternoon might not be available."

Gini watched that cautious look wipe across Patrick's face. He was relaxed only a moment ago, and now, not so much. Did the idea of spending an entire day with her frighten him?

It would if he knew her. Really knew her.

****

"I don't know about this." Patrick slipped on a maroon T-shirt and tucked it into his khaki cargo pants.

Raina put a hand on his forearm. "Don't tuck, honey. That shirt is long enough. You're well covered, and so what if you're not."

He shrugged out of his sister's hold and finished tucking. "Don't make this more difficult, Raina."

"It shouldn't be difficult, Patrick." Raina let out a huff. "Gini asked you to join her in some fun, not solve calculus problems."

"I enjoyed calculus."

Raina rolled her eyes. "You like her, right?"

"Yeah, I like her."

"She obviously likes you if she invited you on this bike ride. Go with the flow. Have fun. You do know what that is, don't you? It's the opposite of what you normally do."

"You're being particularly tough on me this morning." Patrick stuffed his keys, cell phone, and wallet into the zippered pocket of his pants and sat on the end of the bed to put on his sneakers.

"I don't want you to screw this up with your insecurities. You're a lot more than you give yourself credit for, Patrick. Gini's seen something in you that you've lost sight of. Let her shine the flashlight on it for you."

Shine the flashlight. Sounded too much like exposing all his secrets. That's why the beach was totally out of the question. Nowhere to hide in a setting that called for minimal clothing. The beach at night was one thing. During the day, forget it.

He'd ride bikes with Gini, maybe allow a kiss or two—he'd thought of her lips all night after saying good night to her at the reception. He'd excuse himself for the afternoon and be on his way back to Vermont tomorrow. What would happen once they all got back to Burnam? Well, he wasn't entirely sure. He'd deal with that when the time came.

"I'll try to have fun, okay?" Patrick stood and

looked at Raina.

"That's all I'm asking," Raina said. "Well, that and to admit you're hot enough—every part of you—to be attractive to someone like Gini."

"Aren't you going to be late?" Patrick checked his watch and motioned to the door of their hotel room.

"Where's Julianne going? She'll be home no matter when I decide to roll around." Raina shrugged. "You going to stop by to see her?"

Patrick closed his eyes and rubbed his forehead. "Yeah, I'll go see her."

"Good." Raina grabbed her purse and put on her sunglasses. "You need a ride to meet Gini?"

Patrick shook his head and donned his own sunglasses. "I'm renting a bike downstairs at the activities desk and pedaling over to Cliff Walk where I'm meeting Gini. It's not far."

"It'll let you burn off some of that angst, perhaps."

"Ouch, again, this morning." Patrick rubbed his jaw as if Raina had punched him there.

"Sorry, sorry." Raina held up her hands. "I can't help it. I think I'm cranky because I feel all romantic and lovey-dovey after Andrew's wedding, and Mason's not here to enjoy the buzz with me." Her lips curled up into a smile as she said Mason's name.

"Oh, isn't that sweet?" Patrick said. "I think I may puke."

"Shut up." Raina opened the hotel door and let the sun blaze into the room. "Whew, hot one out here. Enjoy your bike ride." She sauntered to the stairs at the end of their row of rooms.

Patrick went the other way and headed to the main office of the hotel. After renting a bike and helmet, he bought a bottle of water and slid it into the holder on the bike. He hopped onto the bike and pedaled the short distance to the Cliff Walk. As he approached, he saw Gini sitting on the stone wall above Easton's Beach. She had on a bright blue tank top and black shorts with black sneakers. Her hair looked like rays of sunshine caught in a low ponytail. A black bike helmet sat on the wall beside her, and a silver mountain bike leaned on its kickstand in front of her. Her head was thrown back as she sunned herself, dark sunglasses hiding her beautiful eyes.

Patrick took a moment to admire the view. Spending the morning with her looking like that was going to be a challenging exercise in restraint. Good thing he hadn't agreed to the entire day option.

He coasted down the street and stopped in front of Gini. She turned her face away from the sun and smiled at him. Why hadn't he agreed to the entire day option again?

"Morning." Gini pulled her helmet into her lap and patted the space beside her. "Sit with me for a minute." She swiveled around so she faced the water.

Patrick slid off his bike and put down the kickstand. After unfastening his helmet, he hung it on the handlebars. He straddled the stone wall and sat about an arm's length away from Gini, one leg on either side of the wall. His gaze shifted to Gini's long legs dangling over the rocks that lined the beach below. She swayed them back and forth so the heels of her sneakers hit the wall and bounced away. Gini was simultaneously as cute as a little girl, her hair in springy curls, and as sexy as a full-grown woman, her physique designed to awake every cell in Patrick's body. He didn't know whether he wanted to pinch her dimpled cheeks or make love to her until she screamed his name.

Quite possibly he wanted both.

"Picturesque," Patrick said.

"Isn't it something? I love the beach this early in the morning." Gini threw her hands open wide toward the water.

"Ah, the beach. Yes."

Gini turned to look at him. "Didn't you mean the beach?" She raised her sunglasses to the top of her head revealing eyes as blue as the summer sky above them.

Patrick shook his head. "I was looking this way." He motioned toward her.

"Pretty smooth, aren't you?"

"I have a few smooth moments here and there. They happen quickly though."

"I'll be sure to pay attention. Don't want to miss any." She pulled her sunglasses back down and slid one leg over the wall so she faced Patrick. "Aren't you hot in those pants?" She rested her palm on his knee.

"No." He looked down to her hand. "I wasn't."

"Didn't bring any shorts with you?"

"Don't own any shorts."

"How come?"

Damn. He didn't owe her an explanation of his wardrobe. She didn't want the real explanation anyway.

"Don't like them."

Gini moved her hand up to his thigh and squeezed. "Doesn't feel like you have chicken legs, and you look like you tan well. Most guys who don't wear shorts either have chicken legs or are really white."

Although Patrick didn't want to talk about his lack of shorts, he had to laugh at Gini's reasoning. "You've done studies on this apparently?"

"Nothing formal. Just observations and interviews mostly." She grinned and slid her hand off his leg. "Nice color on you, by the way. Another observation." She poked a finger to his T-shirt.

"Thanks." Patrick shrank back, her finger hitting too close to what he desperately wanted to keep hidden. He angled his head toward the bikes. "Shall we?"

"Sure."

Gini stood and put on her helmet. Patrick did the same, and they both mounted their bikes. Gini looked over her shoulder at Patrick.

"Try to keep up, okay?"

"I'll do my best."

She laughed and released her hands on the brakes. Her bike took off down the hill, and Patrick only had a second to think perhaps his best wasn't going to be enough.

Chapter Twenty-Three

The rocky coastline and impressive mansions of Newport zipped by as Gini and Patrick navigated their way around the area. Gini slowed down now and then so she could ride alongside Patrick. He didn't say much and she didn't want to seem too chatty, but just being beside him made her feel...whole.

As they climbed the hill back to Easton's Beach, Gini's legs were ready to quit. She stood to give herself some extra pedaling strength, and Patrick made a noise behind her.

"You okay?" she called.

"Fine, fine. Just warn a guy when you're going to change the view like that. My heart's already pounding with this bike ride. You sent it into hyper-drive."

"I do know CPR if you need it."

Patrick made the noise again, and Gini couldn't stop the ripples of giddiness that coursed through her. She was like a kite someone had let go of, soaring higher, reaching for the sun. She'd spent so much of her life forcing herself to be happy that she'd forgotten what it felt like to actually *be* happy. Truly, naturally happy. In fact, she didn't think she ever had been happy. Not like this.

When they crested the hilltop and reached the spot they'd sat on earlier, Gini slid off her bike and removed her helmet.

"You have time for a walk to cool down the muscles?" She angled her head toward the Cliff

Walk.

Patrick nodded without checking his watch, and Gini had a feeling she might be able to kidnap him for the day. They chained their bikes together at the bike rack and turned onto the path. Gini's legs were rubber bands, but walking felt good. Walking with Patrick felt extra good.

They passed breathtaking views of the ocean to their left and The Breakers mansion on their right. Mrs. William Vanderbilt's Chinese Tea House at the Marble House mansion always fascinated Gini.

"I have at least three albums dedicated to that." Gini pointed to the ornately designed roof of the tea house. "Morning shots, afternoon shots, night shots, seasonal shots, cloudy day shots. And yet, I wish I had my camera with me now to take more."

"Wait a minute." Patrick touched her arm to stop her from walking. His fingers on her skin made her heart jump in her chest. "I thought that tiny purse you had last night was pushing it. But no purse at all? How are you managing?"

"I'm not apparently. I'm without my camera and I need it."

"Along with, and I'm just guessing here, PVC pipe cement, a wooden spoon, and..." Patrick paused, squinting one eye as he thought. "A plastic bag full of acorns?"

Gini placed her hands on his chest and shoved him back a bit. "Don't make fun. Acorns are good for making friends with squirrels."

Patrick caught her wrists and laughed. He pulled her a little closer and tucked a wayward curl behind her ear. "I'll bet you don't need the acorns. The squirrels just line up at your door wanting to be friends with you."

"Sometimes." Gini gazed at the tea house again. This was truly the best shot. Patrick in front of the tea house. Another mental picture taken. "Spend the day with me, Patrick. We can have lunch on the beach where we danced last night. Please."

Gini looked up into Patrick's face and watched him battle with his thoughts as he stared over her head to the ocean. When he met her gaze, a smile spread across his lips, and Gini let out the breath she was holding.

"I guess I am hungry." He tightened his hold on her and brushed his lips against Gini's. A quick peck, but the impact left Gini wanting so much more.

They walked back toward the bikes. Part of her was thrilled Patrick had agreed to spend more time with her. Another part was afraid of scaring him away. He had been snuggly on their walk, but she knew his mood could change in the blink of an eye. If he spent the day with her, Gini wanted the happy vibes he was giving off right now to last the entire time they were together. She made a mental note to proceed with caution, to think ahead.

"I have to return the bike first," Patrick said as they arrived at the bike rack.

"Okay. That'll give me a chance to get a lunch together. Meet me at the cottage."

Patrick nodded and unlocked the bikes. As he handed Gini her helmet, he leaned down and kissed her again. This time he was more forceful, more passionate, and Gini melted into him. He cupped the back of her neck with his palm and held her close so he could explore her mouth more deeply. Gini rested her hands on Patrick's shoulders and loved the solid, safe feeling of them under her palms.

"Mmm," Gini said when Patrick released her. "Dessert isn't supposed to come before lunch."

Patrick grinned as he put on his helmet, and Gini thought if she were to attack him right now, toss him to the ground and ravage him, at least his head would be protected.

"I'll see you in a few," he called over his shoulder.

Gini watched as his khaki-clad legs took command of his bike. When he got about thirty feet away, he stood and pedaled. Gini snapped her mouth shut before the drool spilled over her lips and down her chin. Patrick had been right. A view change like that definitely needed a warning first.

****

Patrick paced in the small hotel room. What had he agreed to? How had this happened? When did he officially lose his mind?

He marched into the bathroom and washed his face at the sink. He used the plush towel hanging on a hook to wipe away the water droplets. As he stared at his reflection, he focused on his lips. Lips that had enjoyed the sweet taste of Gini. Her flavor clouded his judgment. He couldn't think once his mouth had touched hers. She was like magic, but Patrick wasn't sure if it was white or black magic yet.

His cell phone rang, and he fished it out of his pocket as he left the bathroom.

"Hello?"

"Find anything interesting in Rhode Island?" Jonah asked. Haddy giggled in the background.

"Funny, Jonah," Patrick said. "You set me up."

"Somebody had to. It was devious, I know, but all with good intention. You're not mad, are you?"

He should be, but Patrick couldn't piece together any anger. Not with the sensation of holding Gini still so fresh in his mind.

"No. In fact, I just returned from a bike ride with your sister, and she's convinced me that I need to eat lunch with her."

Cheers and applause erupted on the other end of the line.

"All right," Jonah said. "We won't hold you up. Just one more thing. Midas wants to say hello."

Puffing breaths filled the earpiece, and Patrick had to laugh. Several short barks sounded then Jonah came back on the line.

"I believe that translates to 'Don't screw up with Gini. I like her and so do you.'"

"That doesn't sound like something Midas would say."

"I'm reinventing him."

"You better not ruin him."

"Me?" Jonah asked. "Haddy's the one who has been calling him cutesy names and feeding him from the table."

"I did not feed him from the table!" Haddy shouted in the background.

"Midas wouldn't eat from the table," Patrick said. "He knows the rules."

"Damn straight," Jonah said. "He barked at Haddy's monster, Titan, when he tried to eat my sock…while it was still on my foot."

Patrick pictured Midas disciplining Haddy's dog and nodded. "Now that does sound like Midas. What about Whisper? She okay?"

"Seems to be. She's got an appetite on her. That much I'll say. Never seen such a tiny kitty who could eat so much."

"I think she's trying to catch up after being in that cabin," Patrick said. "She hasn't meowed, has she?"

"Not even a squeak," Jonah said.

"Guess she'll talk when she's good and ready."

"When she's got something important to say," Jonah said. "Though if she's anything like the women I know, once she gets going, she won't shut up."

Patrick heard Haddy's voice but couldn't make out what she'd said. He did, however, clearly hear the muffled thud and Jonah's cry.

"Don't beat a broken man," Jonah said around a

laugh then a groan. "I'm crippled over here, and she's beating me up."

"You deserved it," Patrick said.

"Hey, that's what Haddy just said." Jonah laughed again. "All right, man. Go, enjoy my sister. Wait, that didn't come out right."

"Bye, Jonah." Patrick hung up and strangely felt better about his decision to meet Gini for lunch. Even if it was on the beach. Where everyone would be wearing swimsuits.

He'd tell her he didn't like salt water. Some people didn't like the ocean, right? Some people only swam in pools. He could be one of those people. Gini wouldn't know the difference.

A small, white lie was better than the big, black truth.

****

When a soft knock sounded on the cottage door, Gini danced to it. She'd packed a fabulous lunch and was ready for a fabulous afternoon with a fabulous man. She opened the door, and after Patrick removed his sunglasses, his hazel eyes combed down the length of her. She'd changed into her bathing suit—a bright purple bikini—and had thrown a short, white, robe-like cover-up over it. She hadn't tied it shut so it hung loose on either side of her breasts and framed her stomach and thighs. The effects must have been powerful, because Patrick stood motionless in the doorway for at least thirty seconds.

"Patrick?" Gini touched his arm.

He blinked several times and finally brought his gaze up to hers. "What just happened?"

"I'm not sure," Gini said, but she had an idea. "Come in." She tugged on his arm, and he took two steps forward into the foyer of the cottage. "Why don't you grab the food? It's in the kitchen through there, and I'll get us some towels to sit on. Meet you right back here."

Patrick nodded and moved slowly toward the kitchen. Gini laughed quietly as she climbed the stairs. She'd actually stunned the poor guy. Good Goddess, he was adorable. Now if she could keep him under her spell—keep his mood fun and light— she might get somewhere. Where she wanted to get, she wasn't quite sure. All Gini knew was that she wasn't angry. She wasn't a danger. She felt normal. Patrick had something to do with that. She wasn't having to pretend to be happy. She just was.

When she came down the stairs with two beach towels, Patrick was standing in the living room. He turned around when he heard her behind him.

"Who buys a white couch?" he asked.

"Not anyone who owns animals or drops things," Gini said. "I haven't sat on it once. I don't think Willow or her mom or sister have either. It's a scary couch."

"Damn terrifying." Patrick backed away from it with a two-handed grip on the cooler of food.

"Shall we?" As she donned her own sunglasses, Gini angled her head toward the back door and Patrick nodded.

They stepped outside into the sunshine and strolled across the grass to the shore. Patrick selected a spot not too near the water or other beachgoers, and Gini liked that he wanted the privacy. She spread out the two towels and kicked off her sandals as Patrick positioned the cooler in the sand. He eased down beside Gini and pulled off his sneakers, but that's as far as he went. Gini let the cover-up slide off her shoulders as she sat on her towel. The cover-up pooled around her waist, and she looked at Patrick. He didn't remove any more of his clothing, but raised a hand to brush his fingers along her exposed shoulder.

"You have the smoothest skin I've ever seen," he

said.

"Geranium and lavender oil in the soap I sometimes make," Gini said. "Good for the skin."

"Mason mentioned you were into potions." Patrick traced Gini's bicep and down to her forearm. The sensation left Gini breathless for a moment.

"Ah, yes. My potions. Scared the crap out of Mason once. He thought I was a witch. Didn't do much to improve his fear of talking to women." Gini laughed. "Jonah convinced Mason I wouldn't turn him into a toad."

"I think you might be a witch." Patrick eased Gini to her back. "Because I'm not sure how I got to be sitting here with you. You messed with my mind, I think."

The half-grin on Patrick's lips as he leaned over her on the towel sent Gini down a roller-coaster spiral. He barely touched her, but the closeness was so intimate, so exactly what she craved. She reached up a hand and ran a finger along the scruff on his jaw.

"You're messing with my mind right now." She raised her head and nipped on Patrick's bottom lip. He pressed both his lips to hers and teased her mouth with light pecks. Each kiss lingered a bit longer than the one before it until their lips melded together with a summer sun heat.

Patrick drew back a bit and removed Gini's sunglasses. She squinted and shaded her eyes with her hand.

"Sorry," Patrick said. "But I can't kiss you and catch my reflection in those glasses at the same time."

"Why?" Gini asked. "It's one hell of a reflection." She craned her neck up again and drew Patrick down toward her with slow, deep kisses. She closed her eyes against the sun and let her other senses enjoy Patrick. His smell, still of fresh-cut wood. His texture, scratchy around the beard, rough in the palm that held her waist, soft and wet in the lips that teased hers. His sound, the hush of his breathing, the rumble of pleasure in his throat. His taste, currently minty as if he'd brushed before coming to meet her. Gini didn't need to see Patrick to delight in his body. His essence touched her, touched her more deeply than anything—anyone—ever had.

Patrick finished up with some nibbling on her earlobe that made Gini gain a new respect for that neglected part of her anatomy. He leaned on his elbow beside her and shook his head.

"I don't know what it is about you," he said, "but I can't be around you and not kiss you."

"Nothing wrong with that." Gini took the sunglasses Patrick handed her. "I seem to have the same affliction around you."

She put the glasses back on and stared at the waves rolling onto the shore. As the water receded, the sand eroded with it, washing away seaweed, sandcastles, and footprints. Gini felt as if the water was taking things from her as well. With each retreat, the waves siphoned all the tension out of her body, all the cautious shielding she'd had to put into place just to make it through each day. A refreshed, purer Gini sat on the beach towel next to Patrick. What else was possible sitting next to Patrick?

"Hungry?" he asked.

"Starved." Gini enjoyed the way Patrick's cheeks pinked with her response. Did he know it wasn't just food she needed?

He cupped her cheek and ran his thumb across her lips. Yeah, he knew.

Gini kissed the pad of his thumb and moved on to his other fingers. Fresh beads of sweat appeared on Patrick's forehead, and he used his other hand to wipe at them.

"No swimsuit under here?" Gini tugged at the waist of his cargo pants, letting two of her fingers slip behind the band.

Patrick's hand clamped onto her wrist, stopping her from exploring any farther. "Didn't bring one with me." He scooted back on his towel, putting some space between them.

Uh, oh. Gini recognized the signs of a mood shift. The last thing she wanted was Patrick to be uncomfortable with her. She wasn't a come-on-strong kind of woman, but it seemed Patrick was ultra-sensitive to any kind of advance that involved her touching his waist. He was okay with kissing...better than okay. He was fine with touching her, but there were rules about touching him. She could play by them if it meant he wouldn't run from her.

She pulled the cooler into the spot between them. If there had to be a spot between them, it could at least be filled with food. She opened the cooler and pulled out the monster sandwiches she had created at the cottage. Gini handed one to Patrick and opened the other one in her lap. She bit into hers and watched a motorboat zip by the narrow pier that jutted into the water to the left of the beach. A person on water skis balanced behind the boat, and Gini thought they were a little too close to the shore for such activity.

She chewed quietly, letting the silence hopefully extinguish Patrick's discomfort. She stole some quick glances at him as he ate his sandwich. His jaw seemed a little tight, but overall his body looked more relaxed. Unfortunately that made her want to touch it all the more. His shoulders and chest filled that maroon T-shirt perfectly, and the line of his back as he sat on the beach towel called out for her to massage.

Gini concentrated back on her sandwich and

took another bite. She looked to the water again while she chewed, watching that boat speed by again. This time, it was closer, the rev of its motor overpowering all the other noises on the beach.

"Patrick, isn't that boat too close to—" Gini finished with a scream as the boat smashed into the pier. Mammoth splinters of wood exploded in the water as the skier's body was dragged through the shrapnel.

Patrick was on his feet and running toward the water before Gini could stop him.

****

He dove into the water because there wasn't much of the pier left intact. Patrick swam toward the wreckage with powerful strokes of his arms and swift kicks of his legs. He reached the skier as the young man's head disappeared beneath the surface of the water. A teenage girl screamed on the ripped apart deck of the motorboat as water gushed into a gaping hole in the hull. Another young man tried to calm her, but she wailed a stream of words Patrick couldn't make out.

"Life jackets," Patrick yelled, and the young man on the sinking boat nodded.

Assuming the kid would get the life jackets and take care of the girl, Patrick dove under the water and searched for the skier. He found him a few feet away, floating aimlessly. Patrick propelled himself toward the skier, but had to come up for air when something sharp jabbed his side. He broke through the surface of the water, and pulled a shard of wood from his left side. A red cloud appeared in the water, and Patrick winced at the pain.

Great, more scars. He let go of the wooden dagger, plunged back underwater, and swam to the body. Grabbing the young man under the arms, Patrick flipped the unconscious skier onto his back and kicked to the surface. The girl still jabbered in a

266

high squealy voice, and the driver of the motorboat pushed a life vest at her.

"Put it on, Vanessa!" he said as he zipped into his own.

"What about Carter?" Vanessa sobbed as she looked over the side of the boat.

Patrick waved his hand. "I've got him. Put on the vest and jump in. That boat is going down."

Something in Patrick's voice must have overridden the girl's shock, because she hurried into her vest and climbed over the railing.

"You have a buoy?" Patrick called.

The other young man disappeared from view for a moment then came back with a bright yellow horseshoe-shaped flotation device.

"Throw it to me." Patrick maneuvered his grip on the skier so he had one hand free to catch the buoy. It smacked into the water right in front of Patrick, and he quickly grabbed it. He fit it around the skier to make towing him to shore easier. The other two boat passengers jumped in and splashed along behind him.

Patrick used all his available strength to paddle them both to shore. When he felt sand beneath his feet, he stood and hauled the skier to the beach. He assessed the gash in the kid's head and felt around for a pulse in his neck. He found one, faint, but steady.

Patrick started CPR and within minutes the young man was coughing and retching up seawater. Someone on the beach must have called 911, because two EMTs appeared and took over for Patrick. One fussed around at the blood soaking his ripped T-shirt, but Patrick said he was okay with enough force that the tech backed away to tend to the more seriously injured skier.

Nodding at the applause filtering from the assembled crowd, Patrick walked away, but the girl from the boat clamped onto his arm. She shook as water ran in rivulets from her long brown hair.

"Is he...is Carter going to be okay?" A violent shiver wracked through her small frame.

"He'll be fine." Patrick turned the girl so she could see Carter answering the EMT's questions. Patrick tried to cover the hole in his shirt, but the material had been completely torn away by the pier debris. He settled for resting his arm across it but knew his skin was exposed. As the girl turned away from Carter, Patrick watched her wide blue eyes zero in on his left side.

"You're bleeding," she said and turned to get one of the EMTs.

"I'm fine. Really."

She squinted at his side and shook her head. "It doesn't look fine. It looks terrible."

It wasn't the fresh slash across his side that looked terrible. It was hardly bleeding. What had worried the girl, Patrick was sure, was the years-old ruined skin. Enough of it was in view that Patrick knew it was turning the girl's already knotted stomach. The look on her face hurt worse than the gouge in his side.

"You should get back to your friend," he said.

Patrick quickly turned around and nearly ran into Gini.

"Are you all right?" she asked.

He looked past her to the towels still spread out on the sand. If he could get to one, he'd be able to keep his secrets. Patrick started to walk around Gini, but she stepped into his path.

"Patrick."

He stacked both of his arms over his torn shirt and turned his left side away from Gini.

"Patrick, you need medical attention. There's blood on your hands." She took several steps closer to him, and he backed up.

"It's the kid's blood. I'm fine, Gini. Just go. Please."

"I will not just go." Gini had her hands on her hips now, and she didn't look happy. "You zip off to be the hero and can't admit you need some help. Let me see." She touched his arm, and he jerked away.

"I don't need any help." Patrick tried again to step around her, but an EMT sidled up next to him.

"Let's have a look at that, sir."

Patrick hesitated.

"You can't bleed all over the beach." Gini threw her hands out and let them slap against her thighs. Her hands closed into tight fists as if she wanted to hit him.

Patrick swallowed around the lump in his throat. He shouldn't have come to the beach with Gini. Too big of a risk even without the unexpected rescue. He was playing with fire, and he of all people knew better.

The EMT eased him over to the beach towels. Patrick wanted nothing more than to curl up in the towel until Gini left. But she wouldn't go. She stood over him then kneeled beside him. She was so close. Too close, but the EMT didn't tell her to move.

Blue latex gloved hands ripped the rest of his shirt away, and Gini gasped. The sound echoed between Patrick's ears and burned his heart.

Chapter Twenty-Four

Shock battled with the rising anger. Gini stared at Patrick's chest and wondered what in Hell had happened to him. Today's injury, a small slice across his left side, was nothing in comparison to the scarred flesh that spanned from the waistband of his pants up to under his left shoulder. Old scars. How long had he lived with them?

Camera shy. Gini covered her mouth with her hand as she realized what she'd been doing to Patrick. Asking him to bare his chest for a stupid calendar. Pulling his shirt from his pants without his permission. Insisting he come to the beach with her. *The beach.*

Gini shook her head and hated herself. What kind of a woman didn't respect a man's privacy? What kind of a woman thought only about what she wanted? Good Goddess, she was so stupid.

She looked at Patrick, and his eyes held so much hurt in them. Gini had a hundred things she wanted to say—a hundred apologies—but didn't get the chance.

The gazebo up on the lawn behind her erupted into flames, and Gini ran. Ran from her anger. Ran from the pain she'd caused Patrick. Ran from the fire she'd started.

Four trees went up in a red-orange fury as Gini bolted for the cottage. She wasn't using any of her calming tricks. She wasn't thinking of how to cool down. Her rage—her disgust with herself— consumed her like the fire burning the gazebo and the trees.

When she reached the cottage, she ripped open the door and stumbled inside, running headlong into Lily.

"What the fuck is happening out there?" Lily asked.

"Call 911," Gini managed. Her body was a limp rag, completely drained.

"No shit. Already did that." Lily put a steadying hand on Gini's shoulder. "Are you hurt?"

Gini shook her head. "I just...help me calm down. I need to stop the anger."

"Don't we all." Lily tugged on her lip ring then put her other hand on Gini's forehead. "You're burning up."

"Water," Gini rasped. "Get me some water."

Lily shrugged and went to the kitchen. Gini slid to the foyer floor and rested her head against the front door. She started counting, but her mind kept going back to Patrick's chest. She should have gone to him as he lay on that towel, exposed and...afraid. Told him he didn't have to hide from her. Told him he was beautiful in her eyes, because he was. But her anger hadn't allowed her to.

Something sparked in the kitchen and Lily yelped. Gini banged her head against the door and forced herself to use her techniques. She breathed deeply, recited poems, named the colors of the rainbow over and over again until the rage fizzled. Gini barely had control of it. She guzzled the water Lily had brought her.

"The toaster cord caught on fire," Lily said. "Had to throw the first glass of water on it."

Gini wiped her mouth on her arm and mopped her brow with the back of her hand. Slowly, she stood and climbed the stairs.

"Where are you going?" Lily asked.

"Home. I have to go home."

Gini gathered all her belongings and tossed them into her suitcase. She slid a gauzy skirt and tank top over her bathing suit and grabbed her purse. Her father was right. She couldn't be on her own. She wasn't safe to be around.

She was also a huge jerk.

Stifling the prickle of anger trying to push to the surface, Gini left the cottage and headed for her SUV. Fire trucks filled the semi-circular drive, and a police officer made her wait to back out. She tapped her hands on the steering wheel as she watched fighters drag hoses to the gazebo and trees. She caught a quick glimpse of Patrick being escorted by the EMT to one of the ambulances.

She should throw the car into park and go to him. Explain why she had to leave right now. Explain that she was a monster. Explain that she wanted to be with him no matter what he thought he had to hide from her beneath his shirt.

The police officer knocked on her window signaling she was good to go. Gini took one last look at Patrick, for she knew it would probably be her last, and pulled out of the driveway. The fighters would put out her blazes. Patrick would have that cut tended to. She'd go home and have her parents...contain her. She shouldn't be among the rest of the humans. Not only was she dangerous with her pyrokinesis, she was also a horrible person. Just horrible.

****

Patrick didn't flinch as the doctor stitched his side. The scarred skin around the new injury wasn't sensitive to the touch anymore. Hadn't been since the burns had healed. *If you could call that skin* healed, *that is.*

He reviewed the afternoon's events as the doctor finished up. The rescue made sense. Standard protocol on his part. Patrick hadn't thought about

272

what he was doing. He just did it. The skier, he was told, was going to be fine. Couple of gashes and a broken ankle, but other than that the kid had gotten lucky. The boat had been caught before it was totally submerged and had been towed to the nearest marina. The other young man and the girl had escorted their friend to the hospital. They were shaken up, but not hurt. The driver admitted to being a little tipsy behind the wheel of the boat. His judgment had been off, and he'd gotten too close to the pier. Stupid kids.

What didn't make sense were the fires. The gazebo and trees had gone up like firework displays. Bang. Instant explosions of flames. Patrick couldn't understand what had happened.

And then there was Gini. She made sense too. She'd taken one look at his scars and ran for it. Just as he'd known she would. She didn't want to be stuck looking at his mess. Hell, if he could run away, he would have a long time ago. But there was nowhere for him to go. He had to accept he was spoiled goods and destined to be alone for the rest of his life.

"There. All set, Mr. Barre," the doctor said.

"Thank you." Patrick slid off the exam table.

"Mind if I ask about those?" The doctor pointed to the scars.

"House fire," Patrick said. "When I was sixteen."

"I see," the doctor said. "Did you explore plastic surgery options?"

"Yes. Some of the scars are better than they would be because of plastic surgery." Patrick accepted the white T-shirt the doctor handed him. "But this is as good as they'll ever get."

"Burns are tough," the doctor said.

"Now there's a bumper sticker." Patrick offered a weak smile and left the exam room. His pants were almost dry, but when he pulled out his cell phone, it was not going to be calling anyone again. Sand was caked between the buttons and water was trapped behind the screen. His wallet hadn't fared much better.

Patrick stopped at the front desk. "Is there a phone I can use to call a ride?" He set his destroyed cell phone on the desk, and the receptionist gave him an empathetic smile.

"You saved that water skier, right?" she asked.

Patrick nodded.

"I suppose I can let a hero use my phone." Her grin widened as she pushed her desk phone over to him.

"Thank you." Patrick dialed Raina's cell phone, and she picked up on the fourth ring.

"Who is this?" she asked. "I don't know this number."

"It's me, Raina," Patrick said. "Look, I'm all right, but—"

"What happened? Oh, God. Where are you?"

"Raina, listen." He'd known she would freak. "I'm okay. Just needed a couple of stitches. Can you come get me at the hospital?"

"You sure you're all right?"

As all right as I'm going to be. "Yes. Fine. Just come."

"On my way."

Raina hung up, and Patrick thanked the receptionist for the use of her phone.

"Any time." She looked Patrick over. "Anything else I can do for you?" She arched an eyebrow.

Patrick felt like pulling up the T-shirt to save time and energy. One peek and she'd lose that seductive smile in seconds.

"I'm all set. Have a good one." He walked through the automatic double doors and sat on a bench outside to wait for Raina.

When she pulled up to the curb, Patrick eased

into the passenger seat. Raina looked at him, but he shook his head.

"Later, okay? Later."

Raina reached over and squeezed his hand as she merged back into the traffic. He wanted to get back to his woods in Vermont. Back to his Fortress of Solitude. A solitude that would probably crush him now that he knew what it was like to hold and kiss—to want—a woman like Gini. But he couldn't have her.

She didn't want him.

****

Night had fallen by the time Gini pulled her SUV into Jonah's driveway. Her father's truck was parked next to the Mustang, and Gini let out a breath, relieved that her family was all in one spot. The drive had calmed her some. Enough that she hadn't set any passing tractor-trailers on fire anyway.

Empty. That was all she felt right now. Drained of all emotion and strength.

She made it to Jonah's front door and opened it. Two things hit her right away. One was her mother's laughter floating on the air as she cracked up over something on the television. The sound enveloped Gini, pulled her into the living room, brought tears to her eyes. The second was Midas's paws scritch-scratching on the hardwood floor as he trotted over to her.

Gini kneeled and buried her face in the dog's soft fur. He licked her ear and made happy doggy noises as his tail wagged back and forth. Why weren't humans this easy to read?

"Oh, sweetie," Liz said as soon as she saw Gini. Her face went from apology mode to panic mode in two seconds flat. "What's wrong, Gini?" She was on her feet and pulling Gini into a hug.

Walter helped Jonah up from the couch, and

they joined the embrace. Gini soaked in their energy, their protection, their love.

"Gini," Walter said, "I'm sorry. I should have never—"

"No, Daddy." Gini stepped out of the Claremont group hug and shook her head. "I understand why you thought what you thought. I was hurt. I'm not going to pretend that I wasn't. What you said to me cut deep."

Walter's face contorted as he tried to keep his emotions in check. His pale blue eyes grew glossy, and he opened his mouth to speak. Gini held up a hand to stop him.

"I didn't set the fires in Burnam," she said, "but I set five in Newport today."

"Five!" Jonah and Liz said at the same time.

Walter pulled out a chair from the kitchen table and sat. He rubbed his temples and said, "Tell us what happened, Gini."

They all sat, and Gini relayed the events of the day. Every last detail right down to Patrick's scars.

"I've been such a jackass," she said. "I was pushy and unsympathetic and—"

"But, honey," Liz said, "you didn't know."

"So what did you say, you know, after you saw the scars?" Jonah had been strangely quiet throughout Gini's retelling of the episode.

"Nothing," Gini said. "I ran because I was angry and I'd set the gazebo on fire, the trees. I had to get out of there."

Jonah nodded slowly. "Before Patrick rescued the kid, you guys were...getting along nicely?"

Gini's cheeks got hot. "Yeah, we were having a wonderful time." She paused. "Well, at least I was. I thought Patrick was too, but maybe he was trying to figure out how to keep me from..." She glanced up at her parents and dropped her head into her hands. "Keep me from trying to get him out of his clothes."

"A man with bad scars on the surface probably has worse ones inside," Walter said. "You don't want to get involved in that, Gini. We have enough to deal with."

"Walter," Liz said. Her thin brows furrowed as she looked at her husband. "Gini might be the one to help Patrick with the inside scars."

Gini raised her head and studied her mother's face. "Me? No, I think Daddy's right. I'd only bring Patrick more problems. I caused five fires today, Mama. *Five*. I'm a public menace."

Walter shook his head. "Don't say that, Gini. Your control has been so good for so long. I was wrong to insinuate you'd caused the fires here. In fact, while you and Patrick were in Rhode Island, there was a fire at Groveston's Market. Mason found a candle and gasoline trail. Same deal."

Gini was sorry to hear Groveston's had been hit, but also a little relieved hard proof she hadn't set the fires existed. As far as she knew, she had to be close by for her pyrokinesis to show off its glorious power.

Jonah slid his unbound hand across the table and took Gini's. "I think Ma might be right."

"About?" Gini asked.

"About you being the one to help Patrick heal inside. Obviously, he feels like he's got to hide from the world. I thought he was just a private kind of guy, but clearly it's more than that. You ran from the anger, not the scars, right?"

"Yes," Gini said. "I was so mad at myself and maybe a little at Patrick because he wanted me to go while the EMT tended to him. The scars were pretty extensive, but..." Gini swallowed around a lump in her throat. "But I still wanted him."

"He needs to know that, sweetie," Liz said as she took Gini's other hand. "You need to tell him."

Gini pulled her hands from her mother's and brother's grips. "No. I need to leave Patrick alone.

That's what he's wanted all along. I was too busy being Miss Persistent to realize he didn't move to Vermont to be hassled. He wants his privacy. I'm going to give it to him."

"That's best," Walter said. "Best for everyone." He shot a warning glance to Jonah and Liz that Gini completely agreed with.

Haddy came in the front door toting two pizza boxes and a case of beer. "Hey, Gini," she said as she dumped it all on the kitchen island. "Thought you weren't coming back until tomorrow."

"I was done tonight." Gini glanced at the rest of her family, assured their discussion was over as well.

"Well, there's enough pizza if you're hungry." Haddy pulled out plates and napkins.

"Doesn't she look good in my kitchen?" Jonah asked, trying to lighten the mood.

"I think you mean your kitchen looks good because she's in it," Gini said. "This is officially the longest this place has been clean."

"We should send her over to Mason's," Jonah said.

"If we want to kill her, sure," Walter said.

Haddy laughed. "I saw Mason while I was out this afternoon. He hired a maid to clean his home."

"He what?" Gini asked. Somehow this day-to-day, normal conversation was doing wonders for the splitting headache she'd developed over the last hour of her drive from Rhode Island. She had a plan now. She'd stay away from Patrick. Give him his space, and she'd allow her family to keep a closer watch on her.

Haddy brought the pizza to the table, serving Jonah first with a huge smile to go along with his slice. "Patrick told Mason that Raina was like him."

For a moment, the Claremonts tensed simultaneously. *Was Raina scarred too?* Gini thought. Raina didn't seem as secretive as Patrick.

"She likes a tidy house, so Mason hired a maid to clean his man-cave before he invited Raina over." Haddy pulled out a chair and sat next to Jonah. She bit into a slice of pizza then asked, "Are Patrick and Raina back too, Gini?"

"I don't know." Gini opened her beer and busied herself with a long swig of it.

"Mason's going bananas waiting for Raina. The guy has got it bad." Haddy chuckled.

"He's not the only one." Jonah slapped a kiss on Haddy's cheek as she sat back beside him. He raised his eyes slowly so he met Gini's across the table.

Gini shook her head. She didn't have it bad like Jonah and Haddy or Mason and Raina.

She didn't have anything.

****

Patrick stretched out in his bed, stopping when the slice in his side stung, and rested his palms on his chest. He'd worn a T-shirt to bed last night, not able to bear brushing up against the scars by accident while he slept.

Sleep. As if he'd had any last night. The old nightmare of the house fire had replayed itself all night long. Over and over he'd heard his sisters' screams, the thunderous roar of the flames. Every now and then, Gini's voice had screamed along with his sisters for some reason.

Patrick's head ached.

Visiting Julianne before they'd left Rhode Island hadn't helped any. He hadn't been in the mood. He'd wanted to get home, but he'd said he would go see her and if nothing else, he was man of his word.

The visit had been rigid, full of carefully worded conversation and apologetic tones. He was sorry he'd left in a huff to move to Vermont. Julianne was sorry she'd given him a hard time. And then there had been the last thing Julianne had said to him. The thing that had also plagued him while he tried to sleep last night.

"There's something different about you." Julianne sat forward in her wheelchair, her scarred arms resting on her knees.

Patrick shook his head. "No, there isn't. I'm absolutely the same as I've been for the past million years." Some days it felt as if he'd truly been alive for that long. Today had turned into one of those days. It hadn't started out that way. Bright sunshine. Fantastic bike ride along the coast with an amazing woman. A kiss on the beach with an amazing woman. A successful rescue. And then it all went to Hell.

"I see hope in your eyes, Patrick." Julianne's voice interrupted his thoughts. "Something's changed."

He looked at Julianne then. Really looked at her. She was paralyzed and stuck in that wheelchair. Her arms, neck, and half of her face were in worse shape than his chest and thigh, and yet she was...content. She had friends. She had her book-editing work that she did from home. She had a freaking life, which was more than Patrick could say about himself at the moment.

Hope. Julianne had seen hope. Hope for what? Hope that Gini's mind would be mysteriously erased, and the memory of what she'd seen of him wiped out. Hope that he'd wake up one morning and be whole again. Hope that he wouldn't have to live out his days alone.

So alone.

Patrick shifted in bed, some of his muscles aching from the work he'd done after Raina had dropped him off yesterday. Work he'd done to stop his mind from brooding and exhaust his body. Work that had achieved neither of those things, but at least he had a partially completed ceiling in the master bedroom to show for it.

He slid his legs out of bed and sat for a moment. The house was ultra-quiet without Midas nosing around somewhere and Whisper, though she didn't meow, had added some noise with her exploring of the house. Patrick decided it was time to get his furry companions back from Jonah's then spend the day finishing that ceiling and whatever other work he could bury himself in.

After a quick breakfast—why did he have an overwhelming desire for blueberry muffins this morning?—Patrick dressed and headed to Jonah's. Haddy's car wasn't next to the Mustang when he pulled into the driveway, and he figured she was probably working over at Gini's. Good. The less people he ran into today, the better. He'd collect his pets and be on his way.

Jonah answered the door in a pair of sweatpants with a hole in the knee and a Burnam Fire Department T-shirt. His arm was still wrapped to his chest and evidence of a beard framed his mouth and jaw.

"Haddy doesn't groom you as well?" Patrick teased. Something about seeing Jonah made him want to attempt to be social.

"I ain't letting any chick, no matter how gorgeous she is, near my face with a sharp object." Jonah stepped aside to let Patrick in. "Besides, I think Haddy likes the scruff."

Midas galloped over and as soon as Patrick patted his own chest, the dog rose to his hind legs. Man and dog hugged their hellos while Whisper climbed Patrick's pant leg.

"What a reunion," Jonah said. "You'd think I treated them horribly while you were gone."

"I know you didn't, but Midas likes his routine, and Whisper here," Patrick plucked the kitten from his jeans, "she's just getting used to people." If she was anything like Patrick, Whisper would never get used to people.

"Well, they weren't any trouble at all, and I'd be happy to sit for them anytime." Jonah scratched behind Midas's ear as the dog sat between him and Patrick.

"Thanks. Appreciate it, but I don't think I'll be heading out anywhere for a while." Patrick was aiming to sequester himself in the woods, only coming out for work and necessities.

"Not a good time in Rhode Island?" Jonah sat in a kitchen chair, and Patrick saw how tired he looked.

"You sleeping at all?" Patrick asked as he sat in the chair Jonah had pushed out with his foot.

"On and off. Can't get comfortable, but we weren't talking about me," Jonah said. "We were talking about you."

Patrick shrugged. He so didn't want to have this conversation with Jonah of all folks. "The wedding was fine. My cousin, Andrew, looked truly happy with his new wife, Willow."

"I met Willow a few times." Jonah winced as he repositioned in his seat. "Nice chick. She and Gini got along well in school."

The mention of Gini's name had something aching inside Patrick.

"Look," Jonah started, "I'm going to poke my nose where it may not belong, but that's never stopped me before." He offered Patrick a grin and rested his good arm on the table. "Gini told me about yesterday's events."

Patrick winced. He'd been hoping Gini hadn't mentioned anything to her family. Hoping that she'd be the only one that knew his secret.

"Can I see?" Jonah's voice was soft, compassionate, as if he wanted to understand and wasn't merely interested in seeing the freak show.

Before Patrick could over-analyze and change his mind, he untucked his T-shirt and slowly pulled it up until two-thirds of his chest was exposed. The bandage over yesterday's gash covered some of the scars, but most of them were out there for Jonah to see.

Jonah's expression didn't change. The compassion that had been in his voice was still written over his features. He didn't rear back in disgust, or dart from the room. Of course, his mobility was limited, but Patrick had a sense that wasn't why Jonah hadn't reacted as he'd expected him to. As Gini had.

"When I was in college," Jonah began, "I volunteered at the hospital's burn unit to remind myself every fire I didn't fight my hardest at was a chance for someone ending up in that unit. I didn't— I don't—want anyone to wind up there." He gestured to Patrick's chest where the T-shirt had fallen back into place. "What happened?"

Patrick told Jonah the entire tale, from start to finish, and when he was done, he felt as if he could tell Jonah absolutely anything. Jonah had listened, not judged, not tried to make him feel better, not said anything meant to be comforting but sounding trite and useless. Patrick had never told anyone the complete version of what had happened all those years ago. He'd never imagined it could feel so...good to tell someone.

"Shit end of the stick, brother," Jonah said, "but it's not who you are. It doesn't define you or what you can and can't have. You can't allow those scars to keep you from being with my sister."

"She takes pictures of beautiful things everyday for a living, Jonah. How could she stand to look at this? At me?"

"There are different kinds of beauty, and you shouldn't decide for Gini."

"She's already decided. She ran once she saw what I'd been hiding."

"You sure you know what she was running from?" Jonah's blue eyes—eyes so much like Gini's—held Patrick's gaze.

"Of course. What else would she be running from?"

"Talk to Gini, man," Jonah said. "Please. Just talk to her."

Chapter Twenty-Five

"We've got the wedding pictures you took this weekend," Haddy said, "and the calendar. That's it."

That was enough as far as Gini was concerned. She didn't want to look at either of them. Both were reminders of what an incredibly insensitive person she was, but Willow and Andrew deserved pictures to remember their beautiful wedding, and she'd promised the animal shelter the calendar fundraiser would be an enormous success. She'd fulfill her commitments even if it made her feel wretched to do so.

What she wanted to do was head over to the animal shelter and spend some time with her animal confidantes. They'd listen and calm her as she tended to their needs. They'd make her feel as if she weren't the most annoying person alive.

"I booked the hall over by Beaver Pond for the calendar signing while you were in Rhode Island," Haddy said, reading from her notebook. "As long as there isn't a fire at the time, all the fighters we photographed agreed to sign calendars. I'm going to call Raina this afternoon and see if she can still be our musical entertainment."

Gini lowered her head. Hearing Raina's name made her think of Patrick. Patrick, who she'd spent last night trying to forget. Forget the feel of his lips. The amber specks in his evergreen eyes. The pain she'd caused him by pushing him when he didn't want to be pushed.

"Gini, did you hear me?"

Haddy's voice registered in Gini's brain. "What? No. Sorry, what did you say?" Gini shook her head and tried to focus.

"I said are you going to tell me what's causing that permanent crease between your brows?" Haddy tapped her pencil to Gini's forehead. The quick poke made Gini blink.

"Have I always been an asshole?" she asked.

"What?" Haddy pretended to clean her ear with her pencil. "Where did that come from?"

"Do I always think about just me? Am I so out of touch with what other people want?" Gini looked at her friend. If anyone would know, it'd be Haddy. They spent so much time together working and hanging out. Haddy didn't know everything about Gini, but she knew the most next to her family. And maybe Mason.

"You've always been a fantastic friend to me, Gini Claremont. The best." Haddy put down her notebook and pencil and came to stand in front of Gini. She adjusted her glasses and smoothed the front of her shirt. "You were the one who encouraged me to own up to my feelings for Jonah. I wouldn't be happy right now if it weren't for you. And think of all you do for your family and the animal shelter and... Lord, Gini, I could go on all day." She threw her arms around Gini and squeezed.

"Thanks, Haddy." Gini's voice wavered as she hugged her friend back. "I needed that."

"Anytime. It's what I'm here for. Now tell me why you asked me that."

Gini did, leaving out the fires she'd set in Newport, of course. When she was done, Haddy let out a long breath.

"How do you know he doesn't want to be with you?" she asked.

"Haddy, would you want to be with someone who got on your nerves like that?" Gini gathered up her camera and marched to her home darkroom. Haddy followed.

"Did Patrick say you got on his nerves?"

"He didn't *say* it. He didn't have to. He wants to be left alone."

"*You* think he wants to be left alone, but you don't know that for sure." Haddy put a hand on Gini's shoulder. "I think it'd be an awful shame if you two weren't together because *you* decided what Patrick wanted instead of asking him."

Gini shrugged.

"Talk to him, Gini. If you don't, I might change my answer about you not being an asshole."

"Hey," Gini said. "That was harsh."

"Maybe, but if I have to use some tough love on you so you'll wake up, I will." Haddy turned on her bare feet and padded noiselessly back to the office.

Gini stood in the darkroom, tracing the contours of her camera in her hand. Patrick's secret was out, but hers was still hidden. It had to stay that way. She couldn't think about what she wanted—that'd be selfish, and she didn't want to be that anymore. She had to think about everyone else. Her family, her friends, the town. Her secret was much worse than Patrick's. Her secret could kill.

****

The market affair had thrilled her. It had been a challenge planning such chaos, tending to every detail, timing it all so brilliantly. The fire department had been a little slow in showing up, but she'd known they were two fighters down. Smart to keep one ear to the town gossip. One fighter had been injured in her barn blaze, the other was out of state. She hadn't thought two men would make such a difference, but it had. The market fire had burned longer and wider than any of her Burnam projects yet.

That would change. The next fire would be an

event to remember. A fitting prelude to her final masterpiece in this backwoods town. She'd visited the next site just this afternoon. There'd be too many things for the fighters to think of in order for them to work effectively. They would never be able to save everyone and the building itself. Total chaos.

She smiled as she thought of the perfection in her planning. She wished she could have photographs to remember her ingenuity. A scrapbook of her creativity. The newspaper clippings would have to suffice. They were grainy and black and white, but they were better than nothing. Her work had to be catalogued, remembered, repeated.

****

"You were right." Mason invited Patrick into his office. "Our fire enthusiast targeted Groveston's, something bigger than her previous hits."

"None of your men saw anything unusual in their patrols?" Patrick asked. He'd gone home with Whisper and Midas to find two messages blinking on his answering machine. Not having his cell phone was going to be an inconvenience he'd have to rectify as soon as possible. Mason wanted him at the police station to talk over the latest arson site, and Chief Warner was calling with the same request. Patrick had left Whisper to guard the house, but Midas was by his side as he sat in Mason's office.

"Nope, not a thing." Mason ran a hand through his hair and tapped a Marvel Comics pen on his desktop. "She's winning, Patrick, and it's making me crazy."

"We're on to her though. She did strike some place we'd predicted. Eliminate anything from the list that's smaller than Groveston's Market and double up the security at the bigger places. Midas and I will go scout out the market right now. See if there's anything that got missed." Patrick stood, and Midas rose to all fours.

"Good." Mason followed Patrick to the door. "I've got a call to Gini. One of my guys took some shots, but she's got a better eye than he does." He looked at his watch. "She's probably there now."

Patrick swallowed though his throat was tight, so incredibly tight. He nearly choked on his own saliva. He definitely wasn't ready to see Gini. He doubted she was ready to see him either. She probably never wanted to set eyes on him again.

"Listen," Mason said, "I'm heading to Wolf's Pub later tonight to see Raina. She's playing there. Haddy is bringing Jonah, because he's losing his marbles staying inside." Mason laughed, and Patrick wanted to join in, but was too busy piecing together where Mason was going with this conversation. "I need something to keep me from losing it over this arsonist business. Why don't you and Gini come by, have a drink with us?"

Patrick didn't answer right away. He wasn't sure what to say. How do you tell your friendly neighborhood detective that the woman of your dreams and a good friend of his doesn't want to get involved with you because you're grotesque? Because you're too disgusting for words?

He drew in a deep breath through clenched teeth. "I've got a lot of work to do at the house tonight."

Not exactly a lie. Patrick did have a ton of jobs waiting for him at the house. A limitless array of tasks that needed doing. Enough to keep him busy for a lifetime if need be.

"Well, consider stepping out for a few, man. All work and no play makes for one cranky bastard." Mason slapped him on the back.

"I'm not a cranky bastard," Patrick said, but as the words came out he sounded exactly like a cranky bastard.

"Not yet." Mason saluted him before turning to

go back to his desk.

Patrick stood in front of the main door of the police station thinking about Jonah telling him to talk to Gini and Mason cautioning him not to become a curmudgeon. He shouldn't be worrying about seeing Gini actually. All his secrets were out on the table. He didn't have to hide anymore. She'd seen it all, freaked, and bolted. She'd be the one uncomfortable about seeing him. Not the other way around.

He was sure Gini would be careful not to look at him. He couldn't be certain, however, that he wouldn't steal a few glances at her.

****

The arsonist had done a number on Groveston's. Gini worked her camera overtime trying to capture all the destruction. Amazing that no customers had been seriously hurt. A few cases of smoke inhalation and one broken arm when an older woman slipped on her way out of the blaze. No one had been burned.

No one had suffered as Patrick must have when he had gotten burned. Gini shivered though the late August heat seeped into the market through the broken front windows. With scars like the ones he had, Gini imagined his physical pain to be excruciating. And yet, he risked additional burns every time he entered a building on fire.

Did that make him crazy or a hero?

Gini didn't think Patrick was crazy. She thought he was possibly the bravest person she had ever met. Facing a force as ruthless as fire on a regular basis to protect people from the fate he had endured. She didn't know the details of his situation of course, but imagined he must have lost his parents in that blaze that had left him scarred. Had he said he lost them when he was sixteen? That was a long time to be hiding.

She should know. Gini had only been a year

older when she found out she could set fires with her anger. She'd been hiding for as long as Patrick. Hiding parts of herself from the world, parts she didn't want people to be afraid of.

Shaking her head, Gini turned her attention back to her photos. The entire produce section of the market was nothing but a heap of ash. Those poorly constructed fruit and vegetable stands made of cheap lumber were no match for the angry flames. She zoomed in on what had been a fresh flower display area. Gini remembered making some of the bouquets when she was in high school and had worked at Groveston's a couple hours a week to earn a little cash. It had been a peaceful job, one her father had gotten her.

"Flowers are serene," he'd told her when he brought home the application. "I talked to Paul Groveston and too many folks start disputes at the register. That wouldn't be good for you, but putting bunches of flowers together in the back will be perfect."

She'd filled out the application and started the job two afternoons later. Worked there until she set off to Rhode Island for college. Looking at the blackened tin buckets that formerly housed the bouquets, Gini couldn't find the serenity in flowers right now.

She raised her camera and focused in for another shot when a bark stopped her. She knew that bark and the footsteps that followed. Gini had hoped to be in and out before Patrick came to investigate. She wanted to give him the space he wanted. She wanted to not get angry with herself all over again. She wanted to not start any more fires.

"Midas, *venez.*" Patrick's voice was low, authoritative.

Slowly, Gini turned around, prepared to what? Apologize for bugging Patrick? For coming on way too strong when he just wanted some peace and quiet? For being Gini Claremont, Queen of the Self-Absorbed Pyrokinetics?

Luckily, Patrick had wandered into the meat section of the market by the time she'd turned around fully. She caught a glimpse of his flashlight beam on the ceiling and took a moment to center herself. The anger was right there, ready to spill, ready to ignite. She had to finish up and get out before her secrets were revealed too.

Gini headed down the book and magazine aisle not as badly destroyed as the front of the market. The fire department must have contained the blaze before it had reached the last third of the building. Some of the hardcover books were still intact, but the magazines were masses of soaked paper. She snapped photos of the shelves and when she angled her camera up to the last shelf, something caught her eye. A book was wedged between the drop ceiling and the top of the bookcase. Gini couldn't read the title because the spine was facing inward. She looked around for something to stand on, but the aisle contained only debris.

After slipping her camera around her neck, Gini set her foot on the bottom shelf and tested its strength. It didn't creak or crumble under her weight, so she slid both feet onto it. She bounced a little, and still the shelf didn't budge. The book was out of her reach, so she moved up to the next shelf using the bookcase like a ladder. When she got halfway to the top and her fingers closed around the book, the shelf she was on split in the center.

Gini braced herself for the floor's impact on her backside, but it never came.

Two solid arms cradled her body instead, one at her shoulders, the other behind her knees. Patrick squeezed her body to his, and Gini breathed in that fresh-cut wood scent infused in his skin.

"What were you doing?" he asked.

Gini held up the book. "I found this," she said. "It seemed out of place wedged up there." She pointed to the top of the shelf.

Patrick lowered her legs and let his other arm slip from her shoulders once she was steady on her feet. Gini took several steps away from him so she could think. The distance didn't help. Her thoughts were all jumbled as the feel of Patrick's skin against the back of her knees lingered. She'd never wanted to touch someone as much as she wanted to touch him.

Stop it, she warned herself. *He wants his space, not you crowding him.* She straightened out the front of her T-shirt, backed up a little farther, and looked to the book still in her hands.

"It's an animal book," she said. "For kids."

Patrick donned a pair of latex gloves, and Gini silently berated herself for getting her fingerprints all over the book. She hadn't thought that far ahead. She'd been too busy thinking about Patrick. Frowning, she held out the book, and Patrick took it.

"Where are the kids books usually located?" he asked.

Gini thought about it for a moment, visualizing the way the aisle used to look. She pointed across from where she'd found the book. "That bookcase over there on the bottom three or four shelves."

Patrick pulled an evidence bag from his kit. "So someone had to move this book. Put it purposely up where you risked your life to get it."

"I thought it might have been important," Gini said. "I couldn't see the title, so I had to get closer."

"You could have called me over. I was right here." Patrick zipped the evidence bag closed.

"I didn't want to disturb you," Gini said.

"You mean you didn't want to set eyes on me or be anywhere near me." Patrick crouched and balanced the book on top of his kit.

"No," Gini said. "*You* don't want to be anywhere near me. I'm just giving you the privacy you've wanted all along."

"What are you talking about?" Patrick raised those forest eyes on her, and Gini felt her heart speed up.

"Since you came here, all you've wanted was to be left alone. I've been so incredibly annoying asking to photograph you, wanting to..." She let her eyes drop to his chest. "Wanting to touch you, have you touch me."

"You don't want that anymore though, do you? Not after you saw my secret, right? I mean, you ran away pretty quickly." Patrick stood and rested a hand over his left side as if he were protecting himself.

"Wait a minute," Gini said slowly as she took a step closer. "You think I ran from that? From your scars?" She pointed to his chest.

"You wouldn't have been the first to do so, Gini. I know they're wretched. I can hardly look at them, and I've lived with them for so long. I would have preferred to keep my secret and not have you run from me."

"Patrick." Gini took another step forward, close enough now that she could reach out and take his hand. She didn't, but she wanted to. "That's not why I ran."

Patrick narrowed his eyes at her. "Of course it is. It's a tough secret to keep, Gini, but it's a harder one to learn."

"You're not the only one with secrets, Patrick." Gini did take his hand now, and he looked down, confusion written all over his features. "I ran because of me, not you."

"I don't understand," Patrick said.

Gini sucked in a breath and heard Haddy's voice

294

in her head. *Talk to him.* Suddenly that seemed like exactly the right thing to do.

"You think those scars would keep me from wanting to be with you?"

Patrick nodded.

"Well, then. I guess you don't think that much of me. I'm pushy, irritating, and selfish, yes, but shallow and cruel, no. At least I try not to be. I like you, Patrick. In fact, I think I more than like you." Gini paused to shoot a quick glance at his face. His brows were furrowed as he chewed on his bottom lip, listening to her, but clearly still confused as if her words weren't in a language he understood.

"I ran away at the beach because I was angry. Angry at myself for not respecting your desire to be left alone and maybe a little angry at the fact that you wanted me to go."

"I didn't want you to see...me." Patrick's head bent as he gestured to his side.

Gini gripped his chin so he had to look at her. "I ran because I didn't want you to see me either, Patrick."

"What do you mean? You're absolutely perfect." His finger traced the line of her jaw, and Gini closed her eyes. That simple touch was enough to make her insides flutter.

"I'm a monster," she whispered.

Patrick shook his head and cupped her cheeks with both hands now. He opened his mouth to say something, but Gini shrugged free of his grasp.

"No," she said. "I know your secret, and it doesn't change a thing about how I feel about you. You should know mine so you can decide."

Patrick shoved his hands into the pockets of his jeans. "Okay, that's fair. So tell me your secret."

"I need to show you." Gini looked around. "But not here. Come to my farm. It'll be safer there."

"Safer? Gini, just tell—"

"Patrick, please. If I tell you, you won't believe me. You're going to have to see. Come to my farm, please."

The desperation in her voice must have convinced him, because Patrick picked up his kit and looked around. "Okay. Are you done here?"

"Yes."

"Let's go then." He turned around and led the way out of the aisle. "Midas, *venez*." The dog trotted to the front of the market and exited with them. Patrick faced Gini as they stood beside their vehicles. "Show me whatever it is you have to show me," he said, "and then let's get this evidence and your pictures to Mason."

Gini nodded and climbed into her SUV. She watched Patrick's truck turn onto the road behind her in her rearview mirror. He was definitely coming to her farmhouse to see what a spectacular light show she could put on. She pushed away all the little voices in her head—ones that sounded like her daddy's. Patrick's secret had been revealed. It was only fair to reveal her own. Reveal it and see if he could still want her.

If he could maybe love her.

****

Patrick parked his truck behind Gini's in her driveway and wondered what the hell was happening. Did Gini actually say she still wanted him even after seeing him? Did she say she more than liked him? Did she mean she loved him?

He rested his forehead on the steering wheel until Midas pushed his nose into Patrick's cheek.

"You heard her too, right, buddy?" Patrick rubbed the dog's muzzle. "I'm not imagining things, am I? She did say she wanted me."

Midas let out a short bark and nudged Patrick toward the driver side door.

"Okay, I'm going." Patrick opened the door, got

out, and let Midas jump out after him.

They met Gini at the barn where she was unlocking the doors. She went inside and grabbed a hose, which she handed to Patrick. He took it as she hefted a block of hay up onto her shoulder.

"Follow me," she said.

They stopped by the house to attach the hose, and Gini made Patrick stretch the hose out as they walked to an open field by her small pond.

"Gini, what—"

She waved a hand at him. "Just let me do this. Then you can say whatever you want to say, do whatever you want to do. Even if that means never seeing me again."

Patrick wanted to tell her he didn't want that. No matter what she was about to show him, he wanted to see her again. And again. And again.

Gini set the hay down by the water's edge. "The hose is a precaution," she said. "Be ready to use it."

Patrick nodded, not sure why he'd need to use a hose.

"Piss me off," Gini said.

"Excuse me?"

"Get me mad, Patrick. Come on. Say something truly awful." Gini widened her stance, bracing herself, as she stared at the hay block.

"Gini, I don't understand." What was she trying to show him?

"Tell me you don't want me," Gini said. "That'll get me good and angry."

"I don't...I don't..." Patrick sifted a breath through his teeth. "Gini, I can't say that. I've never wanted anyone as much as I want you."

Gini's smile made Patrick's knees weak. He dropped the hose and took a step toward her.

"No, wait," she said, still smiling, almost laughing. "I've got to show you this, Patrick. Pick up the hose and give me a minute."

Patrick did as she said and watched as her eyes closed. She looked like a goddess standing in the field with the sun shining off her golden curls, her beautiful face turned up to the sky, a light breeze pressing the front of her shirt to her breasts.

She was an angel.

The hay block burst into flames, and Patrick squeezed the hose on as Gini kicked the bale into the pond. The fire hissed to an end as the hay sunk below the water's surface. Slowly, Gini turned around to face Patrick.

"Did you..." Patrick's voice cracked and he cleared his throat. "Did you *do* that?"

Gini nodded and sank to her knees in the tall grass. Patrick released the hose and ran to her. She was so pale, and a sheen of sweat coated her forehead. He gathered her into his arms and picked her up. She didn't say anything as he carried her to the house. Little shudders rippled through her body, and Patrick squeezed her closer.

"Keys," he said as he stepped up onto the back porch.

Gini pointed to her purse on the steps. Patrick set her down in one of the rocking chairs on the porch and retrieved her bag. He set it in her lap, but she shook her head.

"You." Her voice was barely a whisper.

Patrick slid his hand into her purse and sifted around a travel alarm clock, a wrench, a cake decorating tip kit, and a packet of cucumber seeds before his fingers closed around Gini's keys. He tried the keys in the lock until he found the right one then scooped up Gini and brought her inside. Midas wiggled in after them, sniffing at Gini's dangling feet.

"Midas, *couchez.*" The dog sank to his belly by the door, a whimper his only sign he wasn't happy about Patrick's command.

Patrick eased Gini onto her couch, propping up her head on one of the throw pillows. Saber jumped up onto Gini's stomach and rubbed his cheek along her neck.

"What can I do?" Patrick asked.

"You've already done it," Gini said. "You came to me even after seeing what I can do, what a freak of nature I am. Why aren't you afraid of me?"

Patrick studied her face. Somewhere in the back of his mind, he knew she could be dangerous with what she could do, and yet, he couldn't tear himself away from her.

"I'm not afraid of fire, Gini. I hate what it did to my family and me. What it does to everyone it touches, but that's why I became a firefighter. So I could stop it, control it." Patrick kneeled beside the couch. "You only start fires when you're angry?"

Gini shifted Saber to the cushions and rolled to her side to face him. "Yes."

Patrick pushed her hair back from where it had pooled at her neck. "Then I guess I'll have to make sure you're always happy." He leaned in and brushed his lips against hers, quick and light at first, then slow and hungrily.

Gini shifted to make room for him on the couch. He climbed up one leg at a time until he was atop her, their bodies pressed against one another.

"You make me happy, Patrick. I don't have to pretend to be happy with you. I just am." Gini slid her arms around Patrick's shoulders as she parted her legs so one rested on either side of his hips.

Patrick nipped at her ear and down her neck until his lips met hers again. They teased and tasted until Patrick thought he was going to explode with need. He wanted Gini, every fire-starting molecule of her.

"Want to make me even happier?" Gini pushed gently on Patrick's shoulders so there was a little space between them. Patrick wasn't particularly fond of that space.

"I want to make you the happiest you've ever been in your life," he said.

Gini slid up to a sitting position. "Come with me." She wiggled out from underneath him and held out her hand.

Patrick let her tug him to his feet. Gini led him down the hallway past her darkroom, her office, to the doorway at the end. She nudged the door open with her foot and pulled him inside.

Her bedroom lay in afternoon shadows before him. The bed was an enormous king-sized with a barn wood headboard and frame. It was exactly what he'd thought about making for his own bed once he'd gotten the master bedroom finished.

Gini eased onto the harvest orange bedspread and leaned back on her hands. She bent her legs so the heels of her feet rested on the edge of the mattress. Her blue eyes and smile sent the invitation.

All Patrick had to do was accept.

Chapter Twenty-Six

She didn't think he was going to come to her. Patrick stood in the doorway of her bedroom, a look on his face caught somewhere between arousal and fear. Was he having second thoughts about wanting her now that he knew she was a human match?

Gini let one of her legs dangle off the side of the bed. Any minute now she'd have to walk Patrick to her front door and say good-bye. He wasn't going to make love to her. He had changed his mind. She could tell.

When Patrick walked deeper into the room, pushed her shoulders down so her back rested on the bed, and crawled up the length of her, Gini nearly screamed in victory. She wrapped her arms around his back and pulled him down to her. She wasn't letting him get away. Not today, not ever.

She trailed kisses along his cheek to his ear then forged a path down his neck, up his whiskered chin, and finally to his waiting lips. The kiss was hot, deep, and full of longing—years of stored passion ready to overflow. Gini wanted to bathe in that passion, let it run in rivulets over her skin. She nipped on Patrick's bottom lip and slid her hands up into his hair.

They kissed until a sound rumbled in Patrick's throat, so masculine, so able to turn Gini's insides into a bubbling Vesuvius. He sat back on his heels and straddled her thighs. The view from where she lay had her depths clutching with need. Patrick's eyes were black suns with leafy green coronas as he stared down at her. His Burnam Fire Department polo shirt was still tucked into his navy uniform pants as if he were a present waiting to be unwrapped.

Gini placed her palms on his chest, and his ribs expanded as he took in a swift breath. "Did I hurt you?" she asked.

Patrick shook his head. "No. I just…it's only…no one's touched me in so long."

Gini sat up and brushed her lips against Patrick's as she ran her hands down his bare arms. He shuddered and pulled her closer, feasting on her mouth with hungry strokes.

"Let me touch you, Patrick. I want to touch you. All of you." Gini looked into his eyes as she tugged at his shirt. He didn't stop her as the bottom hem cleared the waistband of his pants. She slid her hands under the shirt and pressed her palms to his flesh. Bumpy and cratered, the skin on his left side was actually smoother than she'd expected. Her fingers grazed the bandage where he'd been hurt during the beach rescue, and she pictured Patrick running off to save those boaters. He hadn't hesitated at all. Just jumped into action. Gini fell a little deeper on that thought.

She slowly raised his shirt until he shrugged the rest of the way out of it. The shadows in her bedroom had multiplied and though she wanted to see him, she didn't turn on the light. There were more ways to see than with her eyes.

Patrick must have had the same notion, because he made no move to turn on a light either. Instead, he traced swirls onto her thigh and caressed the patch of stomach he'd exposed by lifting her tank top. He ran his lips along her collarbone, pushing aside the thin straps of her shirt to clear a path for his mouth's journey along her skin. When he rid her of the tank top, he let out another noise, low and satisfied.

"You're so beautiful. So beautiful." He dropped kisses along the edge of the bright blue lace bra corralling her breasts then he freed them, let them spill into his ready hands.

Gini arched her back, pressed her breasts into his palms as his touch brought her nipples to tight buds. When his mouth closed over one of her breasts and his tongue flicked over the sensitive tip, she forgot everything. Her name. Her address. Her ability to have intelligent thoughts and form words. There was only Patrick touching her, making love to her, and he was everything she needed.

****

Her hair smelled of wildflowers, and her skin tasted like ripened summer peaches. Patrick could feast on her for the rest of his life and never tire of her flavor. In fact, his craving was only growing the more he drank her in.

Gini's hands were on his scars. He knew that, but he could barely feel them there, that skin having lost most of its sensitivity to touch. She hadn't moved her hands since removing his shirt, hadn't recoiled at the feel or sight of his ruined flesh. Instead, she kept her right palm pressed to his scars while her other hand worked on unzipping his pants.

Patrick stopped her so he could investigate her breasts more. The feel of them filling his mouth made him mumble in appreciation to whatever deity had created her. Such perfection had to be applauded.

Small noises escaped Gini's throat as he swept his lips between her breasts and caught the other one in his mouth. Feeling her body wriggle beneath his own in what he hoped was pleasure sent a jolt of electricity throughout his system. He was going to have her. Today. Now.

Patrick slid Gini's shorts and underwear off so

she was naked on the orange bedspread. Her skin nearly glowed in the shadows of her bedroom.

How could someone so flawless be content with someone like me? It didn't seem possible, but there Gini was, smiling up at him, working on the zipper of his pants again. She wanted the full show and was handling what she'd seen so far. If the heat coming off her body was any indication of how much she wanted him, he'd better hurry out of his pants.

Once Gini got the zipper down, she peeled the sides away from his hips. She edged the pants down until they gathered at his bent knees. She did the same to his boxer shorts. Patrick watched as her brows lowered. She either didn't like what she saw or felt sorry for him. Patrick held his breath and maneuvered the pants and boxer shorts off his legs.

Gini traced a line from the scars on his chest over his hips to the scars on his thigh. "You've been through so much, Patrick. We both have." She slid her hand over to the soft, unblemished skin covering his erection, and firecrackers went off in Patrick's body.

His head lolled back as Gini coaxed him to greater lengths. All the blood in his body rushed to fuel the fire she was starting. He had a fleeting thought she could literally set him on fire, but that thought vanished the more she stroked him. Being set on fire would be worth it if it meant having Gini touch him like this. Her hands were both gentle and demanding, priming him, getting him ready to fill her needs. And oh, did he want to fill them.

Patrick tested her center with his fingers, dabbed into that sweltering moistness, and Gini let out a growl that made his head swim. She was a large feline stretched beneath him, soft yet muscular, playful as a kitten yet hungry as a tiger. He kissed a trail from her belly button through the valley of her breasts, taking the time to nibble at her throat. A buzzing purr vibrated beneath his lips as he continued the expedition up to her mouth. She kissed him as if she wanted to devour him.

"Now, Patrick, please." Gini pulled him down so their bodies pressed together, his rough flesh against her silk.

Patrick kissed her once more then plunged into the inferno between Gini's legs. She cried out at first, and he froze. Not easy to do when all he wanted was to drive himself deeper, be a part of her.

"Are you okay?" He rose to his elbows and looked at Gini's face. Her eyes were glossy, dreamy.

Gini nodded. "I never...I never did this before." She turned her head away and closed her eyes.

Patrick nudged her face back to him with a finger to her chin. When she opened her eyes, they were full of uncertainty.

"Neither have I." He took her hand and rubbed it along his left side. "This happened when I was sixteen before I'd had a chance to...do this with anyone. I only tried once to have sex after the scars, and that ended..." He couldn't finish.

"That ended badly," Gini said.

"She couldn't deal with it. Maybe I couldn't either."

"The first time I started a fire," Gini began, "I was seventeen. My boyfriend tried to force himself on me. I wasn't ready. I said no. He didn't want to hear it. Ticked me off, so I accidentally blew up his car." She let out a breath. "I was so scared I'd hurt someone that I never let anyone get that close again."

"You're not scared now, are you?" Patrick began to edge himself out of Gini, but she clamped her hands around him, digging her fingers into his back.

"Not at all. I want this, Patrick. Do you?"

"More than I've ever wanted anything."

Gini slid her hands down to cup Patrick's

bottom. She pulled her hips away slightly then edged them back toward him, fitting him neatly inside her.

Patrick's mouth dropped open, and his heart raced in his chest. Before he could recover, Gini rolled him to his back. Her satiny bottom crested his hips, and each adjustment she made in her position sent Patrick into a hazy bliss. The borders of his vision blurred, music sounded in his head, his body became weightless.

He was flying.

Gini's hair tickled the unscarred portion of his chest, his neck, his face as she leaned forward and rocked her body back and forth. This rhythm was one he'd never forget, one he wouldn't be able to live without. His body and Gini's were two halves of a whole, links in a chain. Patrick felt as if he were under a spell, an ancient love magic changing his view of the world, sprinkling stardust over the darkness he'd been lost in for so long.

Gini let loose a breathy sigh as she increased her strokes. She brought Patrick to the edge of sanity, and he fought not to release himself too soon. He matched her movements, sensual synchronicity. Their bodies rose and fell as one. Patrick could no longer tell where he ended and Gini began. They were a circle, fused by passion, bound by love.

Love? Yes, that was the word he meant. Patrick just now realized he'd loved Gini from the first moment he saw her in the fire station. How could he not love her? She was amazing in every sense of the word. Like no one he'd ever met or would meet again.

Gini's body shuddered atop him, and when Patrick looked up at her face, he could hold back no longer. They climaxed together, her body hot and shaking above, his body slick and piercing below. When he let go, spilled himself inside her, Gini's legs tightened on either side of his hips, and a throaty laugh filled the bedroom. The sound of it made Patrick burrow himself deeper into her heat until she collapsed onto his chest. Her hand rested on his scars, and he placed his hand over hers.

All those years searching for a way to rid himself of the scars and all he'd needed was Gini.

****

"Here we go." Gini breezed into her bedroom toting two heaping bowls of maple walnut ice cream. "I added a surprise to yours." She handed one bowl to Patrick, who sat up in her bed and leaned against the headboard.

"Blueberries." Patrick smiled, and Gini got heated up all over again under her light summer robe.

"Picked them from the garden." She climbed into bed next to Patrick with her own bowl.

"You've got everything you need at this farm." Patrick shoveled a spoonful of ice cream into his mouth.

"I do now." Gini dropped a kiss on Patrick's cheek before scooping up some ice cream as well.

Patrick shifted the bowl to his left hand and slid his right arm around Gini's shoulders. He pulled her closer and kissed her temple.

"I never knew it could be like this, Gini," he said.

"Perfect?"

"Yeah, perfect."

Gini met Patrick's mouth as he lowered his head toward her. Funny how maple walnut ice cream tasted better on his lips. Of course soapy suds in the shower they'd taken together before resettling in her bed had also tasted pretty damn good. Patrick had shied away a little when Gini had turned on the bathroom lights over the vanity, but she'd prodded him toward the shower with red-hot kisses and whispers of how attractive he looked to her.

And it was true too. Although he had stood naked in the middle of the bathroom, bright lights hiding nothing and every scar from chest to thigh revealed, Gini found Patrick breathtaking. She saw strength in those scars.

"I was thinking," Gini began, "although I can easily see how I could be happy forever, if I were to get angry and you know, accidentally start a fire, you'd be the best equipped to put it out and keep everyone around me safe." She looked up at him and twisted a curl between her fingers.

"I am professionally trained," Patrick agreed. "You'd be in capable hands." He raised an eyebrow, and Gini smirked.

"Those hands definitely have many talents." She thought about how he'd touched her, gentle yet strong. She'd felt totally safe, totally...loved. Good Goddess, she *did* love Patrick. He now knew everything about her, more than her own family knew. He knew her secret and also how to make her growl like a lioness.

Gini dove back into her ice cream to cool off. If this wash of heat kept up, she'd be able to turn off the furnace in her house all winter. Nothing like a man in one's bed to make everything warm and cozy.

Saber jumped up into Gini's lap and sniffed at her ice cream. Midas, lounging at the end of the bed, raised his head to see what the cat was up to. Saber slinked over to Patrick and nudged his arm until he made room for the cat next to his thigh. Saber sniffed at Patrick's bowl, which was empty by now, circled three times, and rubbed his cheek against Patrick's exposed waist.

Gini watched as Patrick's eyes softened to a mossy green-brown while Saber, clearly unruffled by the scars, nestled closer. When one furry paw stretched to rest against Patrick's stomach, Saber closed his eyes and leaned his head on Patrick's thigh. Patrick closed his eyes too, and Gini itched to take a picture to keep with her always. To remember the happiest day of her life.

"Animals are so accepting." Patrick's voice was raspy.

"That's why I like helping at the Burnam Animal Shelter," Gini said. "Every time I go there, I feel like I can be myself. I don't have to pretend. The animals don't care I'm a freak. They just care that I'm there to scoop their poop, give them a bath, feed them, or cuddle with them. Love them."

Patrick nodded. "The shelter means a lot to you."

"It's been there when I needed a place to hide."

Patrick's lips puckered out and drew back in, creating a slight dimple in his right cheek. Gini pressed her lips into that indentation and felt a smile edge across Patrick's face.

"Get your camera, Gini," he said.

"What?" Gini almost dropped her bowl of nearly finished ice cream. She fumbled around with it, her spoon clanging loudly against the ceramic. "What did you say?"

"Your camera. Get it. You can have a picture for your calendar."

Gini's mouth opened and closed as she sputtered around for words. Patrick's hand on her forearm settled her.

"As long as you take it from the right somehow. I obviously don't want any of this in the picture." He gestured to his left side.

"I can do that." Gini jumped off the bed and stopped abruptly at the bedroom door. "Are you sure, Patrick? You don't have to do this."

"After hearing the way you talked about the animal shelter? Seeing your face as you thought about it? Yeah, I'm sure. It's for a good cause, and you are a fantastic photographer. I'm sure you can make even me look presentable."

"The camera does all the work, Patrick. And it doesn't lie. You'll see. You are presentable. More than presentable. Damn gorgeous."

She bounded out of the room in search of her camera before Patrick changed his mind. When she returned, Patrick had his uniform pants on and was walking around the bedroom holding Saber. He was saying something to the cat, but stopped talking once Gini entered. She wished she could ask Saber later what Patrick had told him, but that cat refused to gossip.

"How about if we take Saber and Midas out to the barn?" Gini asked. "There's still enough light outside for a wonderful dusky shot."

Patrick followed Gini down the hall through the living room to the back door. Midas trotted ahead and picked a spot Gini would have selected herself. Honeysuckle vines climbed the back of the barn, offering a splash of yellow against the red painted wood. The setting sun cast a pinkish curtain of light over the area. Just perfect.

"Over here." Gini tugged on Patrick's arm, and he let her position him. She angled him so his left shoulder leaned against the barn, casting everything he didn't want exposed into the shadows. He still held Saber, and the cat's fluffy body covered most of his chest, so even the unscarred half was hidden. Sunlight kissed Patrick's muscled shoulders and arms, however, reminding Gini again of his strength.

Midas sat at Patrick's feet, poised and picturesque—a symbol of duty, loyalty, companionship. He was a sleek black wolf and Gini clapped her hands. Sex *and* photos. Could this day get any better?

"You guys all look fantastic," she said. "Don't

move a muscle." She held up her camera and centered the three of them. Gini had offset many of the other fighter pictures to add variety and interest to the calendar, but she had to center Patrick. He was the focal point. No mistaking it. He was *her* focal point. Thinking that made her insides do a happy dance.

Is it possible that I'll never be angry again? That I'll never have to worry?

Gini shook her head and snapped photos. She clicked the shutter until Saber squirmed in Patrick's arms and jumped down. Neither Midas nor Patrick had moved an inch.

"I don't know how to thank you, Patrick." She held out her hand, and he took it. "I do know your picture in the calendar will make a difference to all those animals at the shelter." She reached up on her toes and kissed Patrick. He circled his arms around her waist, and they fell into a passionate game of tongue tag.

As Gini's mind and body were drifting on a cloud, Patrick ripped his mouth from hers.

"How big is the animal shelter?" he asked. "Is it bigger than Groveston's Market?" He stepped back from Gini.

"The shelter is huge, but with all the animals we service in this area, we still need to expan—"

"Come on." Patrick cut her off and walked around her toward the house.

Gini ran to catch up. "Where are we going? Patrick, what's wrong?"

"Nothing's wrong yet." He opened the back door and ushered Saber, Midas, and Gini inside. "Be right back."

Gini watched as Patrick jogged to his truck and pulled out his investigation kit. He dumped it on her kitchen table when he came back inside. After fishing around for a moment, Patrick extracted the evidence bag containing the children's book they'd recovered from Groveston's.

"What if this is a clue?" Patrick tapped the bagged book with his finger. "What if it points to the next target, Gini?"

The blood drained from Gini's extremities causing a general numbness. "The shelter. You think the shelter is the next hit?"

"It could be. It's bigger than the market, and this lunatic keeps upping the stakes. It would be a tough place to fight a fire, too, with all the animals and equipment."

"We have to tell Mason." Gini headed for the bedroom on shaky legs to get dressed. Patrick was right behind her, and he was all that was keeping her from coming unglued.

Chapter Twenty-Seven

Raina's voice filled Wolf's Pub as Patrick led Gini to Mason's table. As they approached, Jonah looked up and waved with his good arm. Haddy turned her head and smiled, one of her eyebrows raised. She poked Mason and pointed toward Patrick and Gini. A grin washed across Mason's face when he saw them.

"Decided to join us, huh?" Mason asked. Both he and Jonah looked down to where Patrick was holding Gini's hand, and their smiles grew wider. Haddy's eyes were fixed on Gini's face, and Patrick was certain they were using female telepathy to tell each other that sex had occurred. He couldn't worry about what he and Gini showing up together meant to these people. He was about to ruin their evening, and he had to do it quickly.

"Mason, we found this at Groveston's." Patrick held out the bagged animal book, and Mason took it.

"A kid's book? What's special about a kid's book? Groveston's sells a bunch of these." Mason looked at the book. "How did this one not get ruined though?"

"It was wedged above the shelves," Gini said. "I saw it up there when I was taking photos."

"We think it's a clue," Patrick added.

"The animal shelter might be the next target," Gini said. "You need to send more police. We need to go there."

Mason pulled out his cell phone, and Haddy helped Jonah to his feet.

"We're coming too," Jonah said. "I may be one-armed, but I got me two functional eyes."

"I got me four." Haddy tapped her glasses.

"You should be taking it easy, Jonah," Gini said.

"He stopped taking it easy about two days ago," Haddy said.

"You can't keep men like us down." Jonah glanced again to Patrick and Gini's joined hands. "Right, Patrick?"

Patrick half-smiled. "I guess not. Not when there's so much to do in life."

"Did those words just come out of Patrick Barre's mouth?" Raina asked as she sidled up beside her brother.

"They did." Patrick eyed Raina and waited for a wisecrack.

"Interesting." Raina winked at Gini, then slid her gaze to Mason. "What did they say to you that's causing that little crease between your brows, gorgeous?" She pressed her finger to it, and Mason caught her wrist, pretended to bite her finger off, and then paced away as he talked into his cell phone.

"Rivers here. Need available units to report to Burnam Animal Shelter ASAP. No sirens." He snapped his phone shut and rejoined the group.

"Raina, we've got a lead on the arsonist's next target thanks to your fantastic brother here," Mason said.

"Don't forget Gini. She found the book." Patrick gestured to Gini and rather liked the feeling of being part of a duo. An entirely new yet comforting feeling. Gini smiled, but Patrick could tell her mind was focused on the shelter. Her worry over the animals only made him want her more if that was possible.

"So I guess this means you're bailing on me?" Raina knocked her fist lightly against Mason's chest.

"Sorry, but if we can head this whacko off before he, she, or it strikes again, that will be a good thing,"

Mason said.

"It's what I get for going for the hero type this time." Raina shook her head, but stepped closer to Mason. She gave him a kiss on the cheek and said, "Be careful."

"Always." Mason kissed her once on the lips and led the way out of the pub. Jonah and Haddy followed right behind him.

"You be careful too," Raina said to Patrick. "I'd like to see that glow coming off the two of you last." She laughed and walked toward the stage to continue her set.

"Does everyone know we had sex?" Gini whispered.

"I was going to ask you that." Patrick squeezed her hand and tugged her toward the door. "It doesn't seem that anyone minds that we did."

"They may have been the ones to get us to do it." Gini laughed as they jogged to Patrick's truck. Midas barked a greeting as they opened the doors and hopped inside.

"You could be right," Patrick began as he started the truck and pulled out behind Haddy, "but in your bedroom...that was just us, Gini. What we wanted. What we needed."

"What we deserved," Gini added.

Patrick held his hand out, and Gini slid hers into it as Midas nuzzled her cheek. All of Patrick's senses sharpened with Gini beside him as if a part of him had been awakened. A part that had been asleep for what felt like centuries. She had cleared the cobwebs from his locked closet of a heart, cleaned the shelves, and filled them with something new and soft and cozy. He could get used to this feeling.

****

Although Gini wanted to get to the shelter and make sure the animals were all right, she wasn't too eager to let time with Patrick sift through her fingers. Making love with him had thrown open the shutters and let the sun into her careful little life. Suddenly things were possible. A normal existence was within her grasp and all because of Patrick. She didn't want to waste a moment of that normal existence. She wanted to make every second count.

They pulled up behind Mason's car at the shelter as Gini finished her call to the shelter's director, Josephine Crateski, to update her on their suspicions. Unfortunately, the director was in Paris with her husband for two more days. Gini assured her she'd take care of everything. Hell, she'd spent nearly as much time at the shelter as the director.

The outside floodlights were on in the front, and a few dim lights glowed inside where Gini knew the small animals were penned. She dug around in her purse for her keys. Patrick shined his flashlight into the landfill of her handbag.

"Thought this might help," he said.

"Shut up." Gini increased her efforts to locate the keys. Every minute she spent foraging was a minute the animals could be in danger. "Here they are!" She held up the keys in triumph and got out of the truck. She followed Patrick and Midas to Mason, Jonah, and Haddy. Squad cars stalked into the parking lot on silent tires. Several uniformed officers exited the cars and reported to Mason.

"Check back doors first. That seems to be our arsonist's preference. Look for candles, gas trails, signs of forced entry. You all know the drill." Mason pulled a walkie-talkie from his belt and handed it to Jonah. "You and Haddy stay out front in Haddy's car. Call me if you see anything suspicious."

"Roger that, Detective Rivers." Jonah took the walkie-talkie, and Haddy helped him into her car. She got in the driver's side and gave them a thumbs up. Gini felt better about Jonah being secured in the vehicle away from the building.

"Gini, you let me in the front door here," Mason said. "Then if the perp isn't here, you work on keeping the animals calm. They know you."

"Got it," Gini said.

"Midas can go in first," Patrick said. When Gini opened her mouth in protest, Patrick held a finger to her lips. "It's what he's trained to do, Gini."

She swallowed her comment and nodded, though the thought of sending the dog into possible danger unsettled her.

"Patrick, you're with me," Mason said. "I'll follow Midas. You stay behind me and keep a sharp eye." He pulled his gun from a shoulder holster and motioned for Gini to unlock the door.

Gini's hands shook as she attempted to fit the key into the lock. She had to remind herself several times to calm down. Good thing fear didn't make her start fires.

When she finally got the door open, Patrick said, "*Sentez*, Midas." He gave the dog a little nudge, and Midas entered the shelter, nose to the ground. Mason swept his gun around in the dim interior and signaled for Patrick to follow him.

The animals began to meow, bark, neigh, hiss. Gini stood by the front door, not at all liking the fact that one of her best friends and the man she'd just decided she loved were heading into possible trouble. If anything happened to them, she didn't know what she'd do. Mason was family, and Patrick was what her life had been missing all this time. She would never be the same now that she knew him, had made love to him. She didn't want to be the same. She liked this new and improved Gini. One that knew true happiness and didn't have to work so hard at faking it anymore.

It felt like forever before Mason popped his head out. His voice made Gini jump.

"Nobody's inside, Gini. Just the wicked smell of gasoline and some pissed off animals. See what you can do about the critters."

Gini stepped inside, the scent of gasoline nearly choking her, and went to the cats first because they were making the loudest racket. Patrick stood in front of the cages, holding Midas by the collar as the dog barked and whipped his tail around.

"He's telling us there's gasoline over here," Patrick said over the noise. "We know, boy. We smell it too."

Gini dropped her purse on a counter and ran to the cats. "Oh, Patrick! The cages are soaked with it." She reached a hand inside and touched an orange tabby. "Good Goddess, the cats are covered with gasoline too." She shielded her nose with her hand and coughed.

"Sick and twisted," Patrick said. "We have to catch this nut job before someone gets dead." Midas struggled in Patrick's grip. "I know, boy. You found the gasoline. *Bon. Bon. Asseyez.*"

Midas sat for an instant, but popped up again to bark at the cats. "I'm going to put Midas in the truck," Patrick said.

Gini didn't say anything. She was still looking at the wet, matted fur on all the cats. About twenty of them. How could someone pour gasoline on kittens? She couldn't imagine even having the notion.

Patrick's hand on her shoulder jarred Gini out of her paralysis. "Hey, I'll help you wash them off. They'll be okay, Gini. None of them are hurt." He gave her a quick hug and pulled Midas to the door.

Wash them off. Right. That's what we'll do. Gini had needed Patrick to take charge because her mind kept picturing someone spraying defenseless animals with gasoline with the intention of setting them on fire. A full body shudder coursed through her, but also propelled her to fill the large sink at the counter with warm sudsy water.

When Patrick returned, Mason was with him. Both of their faces were grim.

"What?" Gini asked. "Are Jonah and Haddy okay?" Soapsuds crested over the counter as the sink overflowed.

Patrick shut off the water and tossed a towel on the floor at Gini's feet.

"Jonah and Haddy are fine," Mason said as he opened the windows to let out the gasoline smell. "They're heading in to give us a hand with washing these critters." He gestured to the meowing cats then held up an evidence bag. "One of my guys found this at the back door."

Gini stepped toward Mason, though she didn't remember making the decision to do so. Mason placed the bag in her hand. A purple candle, completely intact, sat inside the bag. Though it was the first non-melted candle they'd recovered, it had an odd shape.

"Definitely homemade," Gini said. "Does it have a scent like the others?"

"Open it. Just don't touch it," Mason said. "We may be able to lift prints off this one because it didn't burn yet."

Gini unzipped the bag and the smell assaulted her nostrils. Sharp, woody, heavy, more powerful than the gasoline. "Hmmm." She sealed the bag and handed it to Mason.

"Do you know what that scent is?" Mason asked.

"I've smelled it before." Gini's eyes watered from the gasoline scent, and she reached for a tissue from the supply shelves behind her. "I can't identify it right now with the stink of gas in here." She couldn't focus on anything besides the cats. "I'll think on it."

Mason nodded. "Two more of my officers reported snapping of twigs off to the east after we entered the shelter. They chased a bit, but couldn't find anyone. I've ordered a full sweep of the woods. More officers will come with lights. There are foot impressions in the mud by the back door as well that might help us."

Gini prepared to respond, but a strangled sob came out instead. She used the tissue in her hand to catch the tears, but she couldn't stop. Mason folded her into his arms, and Gini leaned her forehead on his shoulder.

"Shhhh," Mason whispered. "You and Patrick kept this from being a disaster, Shutterbug. You did good. None of the other areas in the shelter are in this state. Just the cats. We're steps closer to catching this jackass because of you."

He was right of course. Gini knew that, but she couldn't get a hold of herself. She thought about how scared the cats must have been, heard their wails now, and was overwhelmed.

Mason peeled her back and took a fresh tissue. Dabbing at her cheeks, he said, "Come on. Let's get these kitties cleaned, okay? I've still got men posted outside, and Chief Warner is sending a truck and some fighters over just in case. No one's getting close to this shelter that doesn't have authorization. Give me a number for one of the vets, and I'll get someone to call. These cats should probably be examined after they're cleaned."

As Gini nodded, Patrick replaced Mason and raised Gini's chin until her eyes met his. He dropped the softest of kisses onto her tear-stained lips, and without saying a word, he made Gini feel better. His touch, his presence, calmed and soothed her better than any of the stupid techniques she'd been using to manage her anger. Patrick pulled her into an embrace and held her for a few moments.

"Who's the least likely to scratch our eyes out?" he asked as he tugged her toward the cages.

Despite her tears, Gini had to laugh. "Bella in

the top right cage. She's as gentle as they come."

Patrick opened that cage, and a pure white cat rubbed his hands as she meowed. He lifted her out and followed Gini to the sink where she threw another towel to the floor on the suds that had overflowed. Jonah and Haddy came in as Patrick lowered Bella into the water. The cat squirmed, but Patrick kept a firm grip on her until his hands and the cat were covered in suds.

"Haddy," Mason said, "you and I will clean the cages while Patrick and Gini clean the cats."

Haddy nodded as she got a chair for Jonah. "And Jonah can cuddle the cats before we put them back in the cages. He's so good at cuddling." She planted a kiss on Jonah's forehead.

"A+ in Cuddling 101 right here, folks." Jonah aimed a thumb at himself.

Gini looked at her friends and her brother, all of them willing to endure the horrid gasoline smell to pitch in and help these animals. She felt like crying again, but happy tears this time. Lunatic arsonists didn't stand a chance with people like the ones in this room around.

****

Sick and twisted? No. Those fools had it all backward. They were the twisted ones thinking they could stop her. Thinking they could contain the fires she unleashed. They'd known where to look this time. Had finally caught on. Found her candle, discovered her gasoline. But they had not caught her. They weren't good enough. She'd easily disappeared into the woods after hearing that self-absorbed fighter call her sick and twisted.

There was nothing wrong with what she had done. She'd enjoyed the sound those cats made as she doused them in the sweet nectar of fuel. Their wails were music, helpless cries rising in harmony. She could have listened to it all night, but she had a timetable to follow. She was right on schedule too until that cop and firefighter interfered. What right did they have to destroy her plans? To interrupt tonight's performance? To make her waste all that gasoline?

No right. No right at all. And then to call her names too. She was not sick and twisted. She was doing the best she could with what she had. She'd planned bigger and better fires each step of the way. No easy feat. Yet, where were the congratulations? The praise? The gratitude?

They were too wrapped up in their perfect little lives to notice. Well, she'd make them notice. She'd planned the final fire for Burnam's school complex. Kindergarten to high school all in one sweet location, one monumental target. Hitting a town's children always made a grand finale.

But the more she thought about it, the more a new plan took shape in her mind. It had been about teaching the entire town a lesson on how they had no control over their petty existences. Now, she wanted to narrow her focus. Zoom in on particulars. Teach one man a lesson he'd never forget.

That firefighter would regret calling her sick and twisted. It would be the last thing he did.

****

"And I thought giving Midas a bath was a challenge." Patrick mopped the puddles on the floor of the shelter. His front was soaked, and Gini's tank top was plastered to her chest and stomach. He didn't exactly mind that—the view was spectacular—but he wished they were alone so he didn't have to keep his hands to himself.

"Cats and baths don't mix," Gini said, "but then again, cats and gasoline don't either." She took the last kitten from Jonah's lap and put it back into its freshly cleaned cage.

"Listen," Jonah said. "Not a meow of protest

now. They may not have liked the man-handling or the water or the impromptu vet probing, but they're happy now. And it doesn't stink so bad in here anymore either."

Gini took Jonah's hand and gave it a squeeze. "Thanks, all of you."

"We're here to serve and protect, Miss." Mason tipped an imaginary hat. "That includes cats." He tapped Gini on the nose and put away the bucket and sponges he had used to clean the cages.

"After the calendar signing, I'm cooking you all dinner at my farm, and I won't take no for an answer," Gini said.

"We wouldn't say no," Jonah said. "I will not admit to saying this out loud later, but your cooking is better than Ma's."

Patrick watched the sunshine come back into Gini's face at her brother's compliment. He'd been worried tonight's events had lowered a storm cloud, thick and heavy, over Gini. She hadn't said much as they scrubbed those poor kittens until they were soaked all the way through. She didn't react when one of them scratched a sizable slice onto her forearm. She just pinched the fur at the cat's neck and rinsed him off mechanical-like while blood edged the cut.

Looking at her now, though, Patrick was sure she'd be all right. They had done a good thing here tonight. Stopping the fire was major. Catching the sicko would have been nice, but they were on to her. They had more clues to work with and lots of officers on the case now. It was only a matter of time before Burnam's arsonist was securely behind bars or in a padded room.

"I'm taking Jonah home," Haddy said. "He's had enough excitement for his first time out of the house."

Jonah awkwardly got to his feet, and he stopped

Haddy before she left to put the chair away. "I think I have room for a little more excitement tonight," he whispered loud enough for everyone to hear. The wink that went with his words was so incredibly Jonah, and Patrick warmed at the fact that he could recognize that about his friend.

"You'll be asleep by the time I pull out of this parking lot," Haddy teased.

"We'll see about that." Jonah followed her out the door of the shelter with a wave to Gini. "See you later."

Mason checked on his officers posted outside then poked his head back inside. "They're going to keep watch, but I don't think our perp will be back here tonight."

"Especially if our arsonist saw us here," Patrick said. "She'll move on to her next target."

"Which, in theory, will be bigger than this place?"

"In theory, yes," Patrick said.

"We're running out of bigger places," Gini said.

"Which means the arsonist is almost done with Burnam," Patrick said.

"Which means we need to catch her before she leaves." Mason ran a hand through his hair. "I've got some evidence to analyze. I'll talk to you guys later." He walked to the door, but swiveled around before leaving. "You guys make a good team."

Team? Patrick turned the word over in his mind as he looked at Gini. She was still soaked, and now they were alone. In three steps he was standing in front of her, his hands wrapping around her waist, cold, wet cotton pressing against his forearms.

Gini slid her hands up to his shoulders and laced her fingers at the back of his neck. *Team.* Yes, Patrick definitely wanted Gini on his team.

He brushed his lips against hers, and her body sunk into his as she kissed him back. Patrick pulled some of her curls away from her neck and sampled the soft skin there. Gini let out a murmur of pleasure, and Patrick's insides bubbled.

"You must be exhausted," he said.

"Actually, I'm wide awake." Gini shrugged. "Adrenaline rush from wanting to help the cats, I guess." She let her hands drop and took a step back. "You have some demo work at your place we could do to unwind?"

Patrick held in a sigh. *Okay, she officially became the perfect woman.*

Chapter Twenty-Eight

"She doesn't meow at all?" Gini held Whisper up for closer inspection.

"Not a squeak," Patrick said.

"That's sad." Gini nuzzled the top of the kitten's head with her chin. Whisper swiped a paw out at one of Gini's loose curls, and Gini laughed. "My, you're a cutie, and now you have a good home."

"It'll be better once everything is done and the dust settles," Patrick said.

"I meant she's got a good home because she has you." Gini put Whisper down and leaned against the wall she had helped Patrick put up the last time she was at his house.

"Midas hasn't run off to find a new owner, so maybe you're right." Patrick walked over to Gini and rested a hand on either side of her, corralling her against the wall.

"Well, he knows he's got the best. Why would he look elsewhere?" Gini loved the way Patrick's eyes darkened in color when he looked at her. As if he'd never seen anything so interesting. She felt less and less like a fire-starting freak and more and more like a woman. A woman in love.

"What do you want to work on?" Patrick asked.

Now there's a question, Gini thought. All she wanted to work on was getting Patrick out of his clothes. She had a feeling Patrick wouldn't necessarily be opposed to that idea, but also knew he was a man who liked to ease into things. Some construction work would let them release what they'd seen at the shelter. Gini could still hear the cats wailing in her mind and needed a little time to clear that out of her system before she could concentrate on pleasuring this incredible man standing in front of her.

"What's next on your list?" Gini placed her hands on Patrick's chest and watched his eyes close for a moment.

"List?" he mumbled. "What list?" Patrick lowered his head to Gini's. He teased her lips with light kisses until Gini's hands slid to Patrick's waist. She hooked her fingers on the pockets of his pants and pulled him toward her. When his hips neared hers, the drive to feel his flesh against her own was maddening. Gini feasted on Patrick's mouth and he on hers until she was ready to erupt.

"If you seriously want to do some demo tonight, we'd better get to it," Gini whispered. Her voice was breathy and low. "Then we're so getting back to this." She pecked him lightly on the cheek.

Patrick shook his head as if he were waking from a dizzying dream. "I've got some strapping to hang on the master bedroom ceiling to get it ready for drywall. If you cut and hand it to me, I can nail. We'll be done within the hour and can get back to *this.*" He slipped a hand up the back of her neck into her hair and pulled her close for another kiss.

"Deal." Gini could barely get the word out after having Patrick's lips on her with such passion, such desire.

"I'm going to change," Patrick said.

No need to change. You're perfect. Gini enjoyed watching Patrick walk out of the great room toward the bedroom he was using. She busied herself with setting up the miter saw on Patrick's sawhorses and hauling the bundles of strapping from the garage to the great room. After doing that, she wasn't even a little less turned on. In fact, touching his tools, waiting for him to come back, thinking about the feel of his lips, his hands, made her arousal skyrocket. By the time, Patrick strode into the great room dressed in jeans with a hole in the right knee, scuffed work boots, and a black T-shirt, Gini was ready to drop kick him to the carpet and ravage him.

"You okay?" he asked as he turned on the compressor and attached his nail gun.

"Yeah, but let's work fast."

Gini licked her lips, donned a pair of safety glasses and earplugs, and took up her post at the miter saw while Whisper and Midas took off for a quieter corner of the house. They worked like a well-oiled machine, Patrick calling out measurements, Gini cutting and bringing him strapping. Using the nail gun, Patrick popped the boards into place, and as promised, within the hour, the master bedroom ceiling was prepped for drywall.

"Mason is right." Patrick propped his safety glasses up onto his head and pulled out his earplugs. "We do make a good team."

"Don't tell Mason he's right," Gini said, removing her glasses and earplugs. "That's the kind of stuff he lives for."

Patrick pretended to zip his lips closed as he unplugged the compressor and disconnected the nail gun. Gini unplugged the miter saw and swept up the sawdust she'd created with her cuts.

"Good Goddess," she said. "I love the smell of sawdust."

"Plenty of that over here." Patrick held a shovel to her pile, and Gini brushed the dust into it.

"You getting sick of it?"

"I don't mind being in the middle of a project," Patrick began, "but there are so many projects here I feel a little overwhelmed sometimes. I mean, I have a functional bathroom, bedroom, and kitchen, but it'd be nice to have a place to kick my feet up and watch some TV." He grinned at her. "You know, a place to cuddle up with a beautiful, blond photographer at the end of the day."

"Something to shoot for," Gini said around a smile. "Just for the record, though, I'll cuddle with you anywhere, anytime."

Patrick closed the distance between them. "Good to know." He brushed some sawdust off her shorts. "Care to get cleaned up with me?"

"Love to."

Patrick rubbed his hands together like a child ready to play with a new toy. Gini delighted in the fact she *was* the new toy. She followed Patrick to his bedroom and let out a squeak when he turned around quickly to scoop her off her feet. He dropped her onto the mattresses he was using as a bed and pinned her hands down.

"You're not dirty enough yet for a shower."

"You going to get me dirty?" Gini surprised herself by falling so easily into the foreplay talk. Her mind had never worked that quickly before, but with Patrick, feeling sexy was natural.

"That's the plan." Patrick slid his hands under her tank top and in one swift motion, he pulled it over Gini's head and arms.

Gini grabbed a handful of Patrick's T-shirt and did the same. Within moments, she was looking up at Patrick's naked body, tracing canyons of skin on his chest and loving every inch of him.

****

Patrick watched Gini's fingers trail across his chest then searched her face for signs of revulsion. Hints that she was merely pretending to handle his messy physique. He still saw nothing of the kind. Gini's eyes were blue pools, her lips curved into a delicious grin. She appeared to be enjoying the view as much as he was.

How can this be? Patrick couldn't understand

her acceptance of him, or her desire for him. It was contrary to prior experience. Even he had trouble looking at himself, yet she lay below him, smiling and pulling him closer. Touching him like no one had ever touched him. He felt as if he'd slipped into some alternate version of reality, some backward world where up was down, left was right.

Patrick slid one hand beneath Gini and rested on the other arm. He kneaded the muscles between her shoulder blades. She wiggled herself up toward the head of the bed so her thighs brushed along Patrick's erection. Her skin was so hot, so smooth, and Patrick could barely support his weight as he hovered above her.

Gini's legs parted and when Patrick buried himself into her wet heat, every one of his systems shot to full power. Her velvety folds surrounded him, hugged his length so each trip a little deeper was like swimming in feathers. The more Gini climbed toward release, the more Patrick teased her limits. When she cried his name over and over, her voice gone ragged in arousal, he gave into every facet of the pleasure she gave him. Their bodies flowed together like the ocean and the horizon. No beginning, no end. Just that purple line where water meets sky and all things seemed possible.

Patrick rolled to Gini's side and slowly slid out of her. Her breath caught in her throat, and he laughed into the side of her neck.

"I couldn't have said it better myself." He nipped at her earlobe.

Gini shifted to her side and caught Patrick's lips with hers. She drove him back to heaven with the silken sweetness of her mouth. He couldn't get enough of her. He'd made love to her twice in one day, and yet he wanted more. He wanted to do nothing but make love to her.

"Patrick Barre, I'm so glad you came to

Vermont. I've been waiting all this time for you." Gini cuddled up closer, her hair tickling Patrick's chin.

"I've been waiting too, Gini. You've unlocked some pretty secured doors here." He tapped his chest where his heart beat overtime only for her.

"I haven't exactly been an open book to everyone around me either." Gini shrugged.

"Who else knows what you can do?" Patrick asked.

"Just Mama, Daddy, Jonah, and Chief Warner, for safety's sake. I never told Mason or Haddy. I didn't want them to be afraid of me."

Patrick nodded his understanding. "You balance being social and hiding well. I've always come off looking like a jerk when I hide from people. But you, everybody likes you in this town."

"Some folks in Rhode Island too," Gini added with a smirk.

"Let's not forget them." Patrick swirled a finger along the rim of Gini's ear.

"As long as I stay happy, even if just on the surface, I'm not a danger to anyone," Gini said. "It's exhausting trying to let every annoyance roll off your shoulders, though. Acting as if nothing brings you to the breaking point can often bring you to the breaking point."

"You ever meet anyone who has the same ability?" Patrick asked.

"Nope. It's either just me, or we're all experts at hiding our troublesome talent." Gini twisted a coil of her hair around a finger then raised her gaze to Patrick's. "I did try searching for others like me, but then wondered what I would do if I did find someone. Would we meet? Swap stories? Would they be more powerful than me? Would they be crazies? Would I become a crazy? I decided assuming I was the only one was safer."

"Probably wise." Patrick watched Gini's eyelids blink slowly, as if slumber was a real possibility. "C'mon. Let's shower." He slid to the edge of the mattresses and pulled Gini to a sitting position beside him.

Gini's hair was a spray of golden curls about her dimpled cheeks. Some curls bounced above her pert breasts, while others coiled around her shoulders and curtained her neck. Patrick had to hold her until the sun rose. He had to.

"Will you stay, Gini? Please." Patrick looked at his hands resting on his kneecaps as he waited for her reply.

"Like you could get rid of me now." She elbowed him as she stood. On long, lean legs, Gini paraded her naked loveliness to the bathroom.

Patrick raised his face to the ceiling and sent a silent thank you into the cosmos. Then he scrambled to his feet and joined Gini in the bathroom. Her peals of laughter when he grabbed her bottom mixed with the steam from the hot water she'd turned on.

Intoxicating. That's what she was. And Patrick was drunk. Good and truly drunk.

****

"Look what I've got." Gini waved her prize in front of Haddy's face as her friend entered the home office.

Haddy reached for it and when her eyes registered what she was looking at, she let out a hoot. "No freaking way!"

"Yeah freaking way," Gini said.

"When? How?" Haddy sat across from Gini, one of the shots of Patrick with Saber and Midas on her lap.

"Yesterday. I was talking about the animal shelter after we..." Gini cleared her throat, but Haddy didn't give her a chance to recover.

"Had sex. Go on." Haddy smirked and adjusted

her glasses.

"Made love, I was going to say." Gini tapped her pencil on Haddy's knee.

Haddy shrugged. "Anyway...finish the story."

"He suddenly told me to get my camera when Saber cuddled up to him."

"That cat is good." Haddy raised an eyebrow. "But more importantly, is Patrick good?"

Gini rested her head on the back of her chair and twirled around in it. She went for two more spins before stopping to face Haddy again.

"I'll take that as a definite yes."

"More good news," Gini announced. "Chief Warner called this morning and said we can move back to the studio."

Thirty minutes later, Gini and Haddy were settled in the studio with calendar parts strewn about the worktable. Haddy was at the computer, cutting and pasting, aligning and cropping, drooling and fantasizing.

"I can't wait until Jonah's all healed up." Haddy studied Jonah's photo, Mr. May. "He's lethal with one arm. Two arms should rock my world."

Gini laughed and angled her head at the picture of Patrick she'd chosen for July. The setting sun caught the reddish-brown highlights in his hair, and Saber's light fur was a wonderful contrast to Patrick's dark coloring. Midas had an intelligent tilt to his nose as his brown eyes looked straight into the camera.

She traced a finger on the photograph along Patrick's exposed arm where he supported Saber against his chest. The curves cut into his bicep made Gini's heartbeat race. She couldn't wait to see Patrick again. To touch him. To make love to him.

They'd held each other all night, and in the morning, waking to Patrick's steady breathing behind her made Gini feel complete. As if this was how life was supposed to be. Peaceful. Content. When she shifted to face him, Patrick's eyes slowly opened, one at a time. Gini had scooted closer, fitting herself in the circle of his arms, feeling the warmth of his body against hers.

A hot blush shot to her cheeks as she thought about peeling Patrick out of his clothes tonight and feeling him inside her again. They fit together as if they'd been made for one another. All this time she'd been convinced her life was destined for solitude. For nothing more than flirting glances with men. She'd never expected to find someone she could actually tell her secret to. Someone who would love her even after finding out she was a monster.

"Give me that picture," Haddy said, "and I'll scan it in." She pulled on the edge of it, but Gini couldn't make her hand release the photo. Haddy peeled Gini's fingers away from the glossy borders. "Jeez, you can have it right back, Gini."

"No." Gini shook her head and sat on her hands. "Don't give it back to me, because I'll only look at it all day, and we've got stuff to do here."

While the computer spit out draft copies of photos and calendar grids so they could play with layout, Haddy's cell phone rang. She dug it out of her purse and checked the caller.

"Jonah." The smile that accompanied her brother's name made Gini squeeze her friend's hand.

Haddy squeezed back and stood. "Hey, Jonah." A pause as Jonah responded. A giggle as Jonah undoubtedly said something dirty. "I'll come by at lunch, you nut."

Gini watched Haddy walk to the other end of the studio and gave her some privacy. She collected the printouts from the computer and organized them on the worktable. Hot firefighters on the top row, corresponding month grids below each specimen. Starting at January, Gini examined each photo all the way down to December—a tough job, but someone had to do it.

Haddy had surrounded each picture with an appropriately themed border. Snowflakes for January and the scarf-wearing fighter. Hearts for February and a chocolate-toting fighter. Shamrocks for the red-headed firefighter posing as Mr. March. April had raindrops and umbrellas with a fighter Haddy and Gini had soaked with the hose. Beads of water glistened on his well-defined chest.

May had Jonah sitting in Gini's garden, flowers bursting into bloom behind him while Haddy's dog, Titan, sat beside him. Suns encircled Mr. June's picture while Patrick set July on fire within a honeysuckle vine border. September had apples and a fighter up in a tree, Saber in a basket below him as if waiting for the apples. Leaves surrounded Mr. October. Pumpkins for November, and holly for December.

The entire calendar looked amazing, and Gini knew Burnam's women would single-handedly fund the improvements to the animal shelter. The animal shelter they had saved last night. Gini ground her teeth, but quickly thought of Patrick in suds up to his elbows as he gently washed kittens. She filled with such warmth that the tiny spark of anger trying to spill to the surface was snuffed. A single thought of Patrick, and she was calm.

Would he always have that effect on her? Good Goddess, she hoped so.

****

Patrick vacuumed out the last of the fire trucks and put away the vacuum. He'd jumped at that particular task when Chief Warner called out duties. Figured he'd have plenty of time to think about Gini while he reached into every nook and cranny of each truck.

Gini. Man, waking up next to a woman like her

had been something he'd never thought he'd experience in this lifetime. She hadn't run away. Hadn't changed her mind about him. Gini had stayed the entire night, her smooth body against his rough one. The wildflower scent of her hair had infused his dreams. Dreams that in no way involved the night he'd lost his parents. Gini had chased that nightmare away with her caresses and kisses, with her very presence.

"Barre!" Chief Warner called.

Patrick looked up from where he'd stowed the vacuum. "Yes, sir?"

"I've been calling you for at least thirty seconds. That's too long, boy," the chief said, but a smile tugged at his lips.

"Sorry, sir." Patrick skirted around the trucks and walked to the chief's office.

"If you're done with the trucks, spend some time on the arson cases. You can use the classroom."

"Yes, sir."

Chief Warner turned to go back to his office. Before he entered, however, he leaned against the doorframe and studied Patrick. "Good job on figuring out the next target was the animal shelter. Rhode Island's loss is Vermont's gain."

"Thank you, sir, but I had help."

"Yes, I heard. Help of the leggy blond flavor." Warner raised an eyebrow. "You be careful with her, son." The chief waited a heartbeat before adding, "She's different."

"One-of-a-kind, sir." Patrick gave a knowing nod of his head, and Chief Warner's eyes narrowed.

"As long as you know what you're getting into."

"I do."

"Okay, then." Chief Warner smiled. "Very good." He disappeared into his office.

Patrick headed for the dorm where he'd stowed his copies of the arson files in his locker, but stopped when he heard laughing in the vehicle bay. When he looked over, he saw Jonah standing with some of the fighters. As Patrick walked over, Jonah's smile widened.

"Hey, man," Jonah said.

"Escaped again?" Patrick shook Jonah's hand.

"Haddy went to work, and for some stupid reason, my house is not as fun as it used to be without her there."

"Not our Jonah!" one of the fighters yelled.

"Someone finally got her claws into him? How? When?" another asked.

"It's just not possible." A third fighter shook his head in disbelief.

"How will we live vicariously through you, Claremont, if you settle down with just one woman?" the first fighter asked.

"Sorry, guys," Jonah said. "It had to happen sometime." He looked at Patrick. "And I'm not the only one getting serious, am I, Patrick?"

"Something in this Vermont air, I guess." Patrick shrugged and slipped his hands into his pockets.

"Or in my sister's maple walnut ice cream." Jonah elbowed Patrick with his good arm.

"Could be."

The rest the fighters went absolutely still as they stared at Patrick for a few awkward moments. Finally one of them broke the silence.

"Wait. A. Minute. *You* and Gini?"

Patrick nodded. No sense in denying it. He could feel his cheeks grow hot just having the phrase, "You and Gini," bounce around inside his head.

A loud whoop echoed over the circle of men. Claps on the back, handshakes, congratulations. Patrick was stunned. He'd never encountered such camaraderie. He was more surprised at how much he enjoyed it.

"These two are taking all the good ones," Chuck said.

"We'll have to branch out to New Hampshire," Willy added.

Another round of laughter filled the vehicle bay as Jonah nudged Patrick away from the group.

"Hope you don't mind I let the cat out of the bag about you and Gini. Those guys have been pining after her for ages. It felt good to let them know she was taken." Jonah stopped Patrick in front of the chief's office. "She is taken, isn't she?"

Patrick puffed out a long breath. "I hope she thinks so."

"Got it pretty bad, don't we?" Jonah teased. "Good. I don't want to be the only lovesick dope in town."

"There's always Mason," Patrick said. "I talked to Raina this morning, and I think she's hooked him in her net too."

"Chicks." Jonah shook his head, but his blue eyes glinted with amusement. He shifted his gaze to something behind Patrick. "Here comes my keeper for today."

Patrick turned to see Jonah's father walking toward them and stiffened at the sight of the man. The last words Walter had spoken to him involved the word *kill*. Patrick thought of Gini's secret, and the pieces clicked into place. Of course Walter would be protective of his daughter. Of course he wouldn't want anyone coming around and rousing Gini into a fury.

And hadn't he done just that? A couple of times. The bush in front of the station. The gazebo used in Andrew's wedding. The trees as she ran off the beach. Those were all because he'd ticked her off. Shut her out. How could he have been such an ass to her? He'd make it up to her. Tonight. Several times.

"Barre," Walter said.

338

"Mr. Claremont. How are you?" Patrick felt like a teenager trying to make a good impression on a real grown up. Probably too late for this grown up. Walter had made up his mind. He didn't want Patrick anywhere near his daughter.

"Warner told me you helped keep the animal shelter from being torched. My Gini's shelter." Walter stood with his solid legs hip distance apart and his arms folded across his chest. His posture screamed, "Retired firefighter. Don't mess with me."

"Gini found evidence at Groveston's that made me think the shelter was next." Patrick pulled his hands from his pockets and wiped his sweaty palms on his pants. Walter's pale blue stare never left Patrick's face.

"My girl's good to have around," Walter said.

"Yes, she is."

"You like having her around?"

"Very much, sir."

Walter leaned closer and flitted his eyes around the station. All the other fighters had scurried off to their assigned duties. In a low voice, almost inaudible, he said, "You think you can handle her?"

Patrick glanced at Jonah, who nodded. Patrick pulled up a corner of his uniform shirt, exposing a fraction of his scars. "If she can handle me, I can handle her."

Walter's eyes slid down to Patrick's side. Like Jonah, he didn't flinch. Instead, Walter's hand slowly extended toward Patrick. "Fair enough, kid."

Patrick took Walter's hand and with a firm handshake, they arrived at neutral ground.

Chapter Twenty-Nine

"Best to spread the fighters out, don't you think, Haddy?" Gini surveyed the Beaver Pond Hall. They'd spent the last two days printing up calendars and advertising the signing event.

"Yeah," Haddy said. "We don't want to have all the women mob one location trying to get autographs."

Gini nodded and directed the high school students she'd enlisted to help to place six tables around the perimeter of the hall.

"Two fighters to a table ought to work," she said.

The students carried out her orders while she and Haddy set up a table where the calendars could be purchased. They decorated the hall walls with Gini's photographs of the animals the shelter serviced. Gini knew all the critters by name and if she had room at her farm, she would have adopted every last one of them. Even the one snake that lived at the shelter. It freaked her out a little at first, but Slithers was a sweetheart even if he did eat cute little mice. Whole.

"Looking good in here."

Gini looked up from where she was taping a picture of a white rabbit to the wall. The fluffball was on its hind legs peering into a black top hat. Gini loved that picture and hoped to sell it and the others she'd already hung to bring in additional money for the shelter.

"Hey, Raina." Gini put down the tape and crossed the hall. "Will this piano be okay?" She put a hand on an old piano at the front of the room.

Raina's mouth dropped open as she moved toward the piano. "Is that...oh my God, is that a Steinway Duo-Art Pianola Grand?" She caressed the glossy amber-colored wood finish and shuddered. "Circa 1923?"

Gini shrugged. "Yeah. Is that good?"

Raina barked out a laugh. "It's like a pianist's dream, Gini."

"Sorry. I don't know the difference. That piano has been here forever, but it's all in tune and totally functional."

Raina sat on the bench and closed her eyes. Her fingers hovered over the keys, and Gini wondered if Raina was channeling the spirit of some great pianist. When her eyes opened, Raina played a quick ditty that had a deep rich sound.

"Wonderful," Raina breathed. "Perfect for some of the more sultry songs I have planned. We'll set this place on fire."

I hope not, Gini thought. "Do you need anything else?"

"No. This will more than do it." Raina rummaged around in the tote bag she had on her shoulder. "Here's what I have planned."

Gini glanced down the song list and approved of the selection. "You're going to be a great addition to the evening, Raina. Are you sure we can't pay you?"

"I'm sure. Contrary to popular belief, I do like animals. I just don't want any in my home." Raina smiled. "Besides, I talked to my brother this morning, and I owe you. Big time."

"Owe me?" Gini sat on the bench beside Raina. "What do you mean?"

"He's never sounded so...alive." Raina rested her hand on Gini's shoulder. "I thought the move here would be good for him, but it's been more than good. It's been fantastic. Because of you, Gini.

"Patrick's been so private, so closed up since our parents died and he was…" Raina let her voice trail off as she searched Gini's face. "Since he was hurt. He's been hiding for so long."

"Are you…were you hurt too?" Gini asked.

Raina let the short sleeve linen shirt she wore over her red tank dress slide off her shoulders. Raising her left arm, she revealed a thin strip of scarred skin along the back of her bicep.

"I got off easy." She slipped the shirt back to her shoulders. "Patrick wasn't so lucky, and our sister, Julianne, even less so."

Gini's chest ached as she thought about Patrick getting burned. He deserved only good things. She would try to bring him good things. She would try so hard.

"Seems his luck has changed, though." Raina elbowed Gini.

"Mine too." Gini stood. "I'll leave you to your setting up and practicing. Thanks again."

"Being trapped in a room full of hot firefighters and their shirtless photos is thanks enough, Gini." Raina gave her a wink. "Though I think the next calendar should be police officers. Detectives, specifically."

"I'll see what I can do."

Gini and Haddy finished setting up while Raina tried out her songs. From the look and sound of things, the night was going to be superb.

"Do we know how to organize a fundraiser or what?" Haddy slung her arm around Gini's shoulders.

"It sure looks like we know what we're doing." Gini scanned the room, looking for anything they'd missed. She couldn't find anything, but she felt as if something were out of place.

"C'mon," Haddy said. "We need to get ourselves ready now. Big night ahead of us."

Gini let Haddy edge her out the door and into the afternoon sunshine. An autumn-like breeze hinted at what was soon to come to the mountains of Burnam, but for once, Gini didn't mind that the summer was winding to a close.

After all, she now had someone to keep her warm.

****

Patrick slipped into his dress uniform, still navy blue, but with a button down shirt instead of a polo shirt. Gini had asked all the fighters to come in uniform for the signing, and naturally they had all agreed to whatever she asked. He thought about the reaction of the men when they heard that he was with Gini.

With Gini.

The words still made him want to jump around the house and sing—two things he hadn't done since he was sixteen. Two things he thought he'd never have a reason to do again.

He finished buttoning his shirt and went to the interim kitchen to feed Midas. After the dog slopped down his grub, Patrick called him to the small deck outside and brushed the dog's black coat until it looked like sleek sealskin. Gini had insisted Midas come to the signing.

"He's just as beautiful as all the other males in the calendar," she'd said. "Plus, he's so well behaved."

Midas licked his cheek as Patrick changed the dog's collar to a black leather one with silver spikes.

"There you go. Now you're ready to sign some calendars."

Midas let out a short bark and when Patrick led him inside, they found Whisper digging in a plant Raina had given him.

"Whisper, no." Patrick waited for the kitten to jump down from the large pot, but she totally ignored his command. "Midas, you've spoiled me, boy." Shaking his head, Patrick plucked the kitten off the pot, and her limbs flailed about in all directions. Her tiny mouth opened, but still no sound came out. Patrick pushed his nose to the cat's.

"You have to learn that no means no, Whisper."

The kitten put a paw on Patrick's cheek, no claws, just soft pads, and Patrick laughed. "Nice try, but I'm not that easily won over."

Unless you have blond hair, blue eyes, and lips that trump any dessert on the planet.

When Patrick placed her on the ground, Whisper climbed the pot again. This time Patrick said no and Midas let out a bark. The kitten stopped for a moment then continued her climb. When Patrick said no again, but louder, and Midas threw a little growl into his bark, Whisper edged down from the pot, her tail low between her back legs.

"Good girl." Patrick crouched and rubbed the kitten between the ears. Her eyes closed as she pushed her head into Patrick's fingers.

Patrick patted his thigh. "*Venez*, Midas."

Midas padded to Patrick. "*Bon*. Good boy. We'll have Whisper trained in no time. Maybe she speaks French too." Patrick rubbed the dog's muzzle until he had two pets at his knees enjoying the scratchings. "We're doing all right here, aren't we guys?"

The doorbell rang, and Patrick stood. He peeked out the window and saw Gini. He couldn't stop his smile. "Now we're doing *more* than all right."

He opened the door and took a full forty seconds to enjoy the view. Gini wore a black, sleeveless dress with black sandals whose thin straps weaved over her delicate feet. Her hair was a mass of blond curls about her face, and the silver beads around her neck were knotted between her breasts. His eyes zoomed in on that particular region, and the cool night air didn't feel so cool anymore.

"Are you finished?" Gini teased. "The more you look, the less time you have to touch."

"Good point." Patrick stepped aside and gestured for Gini to enter. When she did, he backed her against the wall by the front door and descended upon her lips. She let out a giggle when he moved onto her neck, winding his hand around the beads as if they were a leash. His other hand pressed on her back, drawing her closer, holding her against his body.

"Raise a hand if you don't want to go to the signing now," Gini said.

"Signing? What signing?" Patrick mumbled as he licked at her earlobe. He was losing himself in her scents, her textures, her everything.

"You look wonderful in that uniform. So unfortunate I have to share you with the rest of the town tonight." Gini rose to her tiptoes and explored Patrick's mouth until he let out a grizzly bear of a growl.

"Sharing sucks." He inched up the hem of Gini's dress and ran his palm along her thigh. Patrick drowned in the hot breath Gini released into the curve of his neck.

"Patrick."

Hearing her speak his name made him feel as if he belonged to her, and God, he wanted to belong to her. Right now. All night.

Forever.

Patrick eased aside Gini's panties and fingered her scorching folds. When she didn't stop him, didn't tell him they didn't have the time for such things, he caught her mouth with his and plunged his fingers into her volcanic center. Her breath caught in her throat, and Patrick pressed his lips to the pulse in her neck.

With shuddering sighs, Gini tightened her hold

on Patrick's shoulders. Her muscles spasmed around his fingers until her body went limp in his arms. After a moment of ragged breathing, Gini inhaled deeply and placed her hands on either side of Patrick's face.

"Thank you." She brushed her lips lightly against his. "Your turn?"

"Later." Patrick couldn't believe he had the discipline to say that when what he meant was, "Right now, please." He rested his palms on the wall behind Gini and looked into her blue eyes. "It'll give me something to look forward to."

"I'll make it worth the wait." Gini cupped his erection through his pants briefly, and Patrick let out a moan. "Why don't you grab some more comfortable clothes for when we have dinner at my place with the gang after the signing?"

"Okay." Patrick pushed off the wall and turned down the hall.

"Patrick?" Gini called.

He backed up a couple of steps. "Yeah?"

"Maybe you want to bring anything else you might need to…you know…stay the night with me?" Gini twirled a curl around her index finger, and a wash of heat flooded over Patrick's entire body again.

"Sure."

Gini's smile could have sustained a million galaxies. It shed light into his once dark world. It warmed the chill of loneliness. It made Patrick feel indestructible.

****

Everything was set. The candle in place. Gasoline drizzled. The target would be inside soon. There would be other casualties. Necessary casualties. This town would finally understand the power of fire. Its rage. Its beauty. Its ability to reduce evil to ash.

Sick and twisted? No. She didn't think so. Brilliant. Yes, that's what she was. An absolute genius. Everyone inside would see. They'd know as the flames rose around them. They'd understand they had been living a lie. A happy little lie that now seemed so ridiculous. If they'd only opened their eyes sooner, they would have seen the world for what it was. Not warm and fuzzy, but cold and hard. An unforgiving place full of judgment and neglect. A place where true happiness could not exist for long.

Watching that fighter now as he walked into the hall, she could tell he thought he'd found true happiness. He was wrong. She'd show him that. He thought her to be delusional, but it was he who was not seeing the truth.

Truth would come to him tonight. In flames that stretched toward the skies, his blindness would be burned away as he took his last breaths.

****

Gini, Patrick, and Midas were the first ones to arrive at the hall. A slight chill slithered up her spine as Patrick guided her inside. He stopped walking and looked at her while Midas sniffed the ground at Patrick's feet.

"You okay?" Patrick asked.

She squeezed his hand. "Yeah."

Gini glanced out into the darkness surrounding the hall. The moon's reflection off Beaver Pond captured white light rippling on the watery surface. "For a moment, I felt like...I don't know...like someone was out there."

Patrick's eyebrows lowered as he edged Gini toward the door of the hall. "I'll take a look around. Midas, *restez*." He started to slip his hand from hers, but Gini held on tightly.

"No. Come inside with me. It was nothing. I'm just being silly."

Patrick nodded, but scanned the darkness before

347

letting Gini pull him inside the hall. Midas followed behind them, but not before casting a glance into the silhouetted woods.

"Wow," Patrick said. "Looks wonderful in here. You guys worked really hard."

"Thanks," Gini said. "Between pictures of cute animals and calendars of hunky fighters, I'm hoping to sell out of both and raise an amazing amount of money for the shelter."

"If anyone can do it, you can." Patrick dropped a kiss on Gini's nose.

"With the help of said hunky fighters." Gini pulled Patrick into a hug. She brushed her lips against his as the door opened behind them.

Jonah walked in with Haddy beside him. He was wearing his dress uniform as well with his arm still in a sling. The scruff he'd been growing around his chin had been shaven away and his hair neatly styled.

"Now there's the Jonah I know." Gini ran a hand along his chin.

"Haddy promised not to sever my head, so I let her shave me. She has a surprisingly steady hand."

"It's not that much different than peeling a potato," Haddy said.

"Are you calling me a potato head?" Jonah asked.

"Maybe." Haddy stepped out of Jonah's reach.

"I'll get you later." Jonah wagged a finger at Haddy.

"I'm counting on it," Haddy teased. "C'mon. I'll take you to your table, Mr. May."

Jonah winked at Gini. "Nice work in here, sis." He followed Haddy across the hall and eased into a seat.

"He looks like he's doing better," Patrick said.

"I think Haddy has a lot to do with that." Gini watched her friend fuss over her brother.

"Nothing like a beautiful woman to raise a man's spirits," Patrick said.

The way Patrick's hazel eyes combed down the length of Gini left her feeling as if he'd caressed her, but he hadn't laid a hand on her. His simple gaze stirred her body, brought her to life.

"Where do you want me to sit?" he asked.

"You and Midas can go to the table after Jonah's. I made you Mr. July."

"Why July?"

"My birthday is in July," Gini said.

"I'll have to remember that."

"Yes. Yes, you will." Gini smirked and nudged Patrick toward his table. Midas trotted over to Jonah. "You also need to remember that no matter how many women throw themselves at you tonight, you're coming home with me."

"Don't want to go home with anyone else, Gini," Patrick said. "Just you."

Just you. Patrick's words filled her with peace— a peace she didn't think possible for someone like her.

She watched Patrick walk away and knew that women would definitely *try* to get his phone number at least if not a date with him tonight. But he was hers. He actually wanted to be hers. The thought sent her heart skyrocketing.

Only the door opening behind her pulled Gini from her Patrick-watching. Raina glided into the hall in a long red dress that tied around her neck like a halter top.

"My Goddess," Gini said. "You look stunning, Raina."

"Figured I should try to be as fun to look at as the man candy you'll have here tonight. Give the men something to look at." Raina grinned. "Plus, I can't wait to see the look on Mason's face when he gets a glimpse of this number."

"Fortunately we'll have trained CPR professionals—twelve of them—on hand to resuscitate him when he goes into shock."

Raina laughed and headed for the piano. Several other fighters arrived and took up their posts around the hall. Guests wandered in shortly thereafter, and soon the hall was full. Raina's voice and piano playing wafted over the crowd as folks mingled and chatted, drooled and giggled.

Gini's parents came in and gave her huge hugs.

"My, my," Liz said as she fanned herself with her hand. "Either I'm having a hot flash or those fighters are steaming up the place."

"Try to contain yourself, Liz," Walter teased. "I used to look like them back in the day."

Liz patted her husband's cheek. "You still do to me, sweetie."

Walter kissed Liz's hand and led her to a seat. Gini watched them and finally understood what they must feel for one another. She hadn't truly got it before. Now she had it herself. Her mother's belief in soul mates made perfect sense now. Yes, Patrick had a risky job, but Gini had to love him just the same.

Her gaze swam across the crowd and connected with Patrick's. Three women were standing in front of his table, chatting it up, but his attention was on Gini. A wash of heat crept over her face as she smiled at him. When he smiled back, Gini regretted the dinner invitation she'd extended to the gang. What she wanted was to drag Patrick back to her farmhouse and make love to him until the sun came up. Now she'd have to feed people. Talk to them. Laugh with them and kick them out before she got to touch Patrick the way she wanted to. The way she needed to.

Letting out a sigh, Gini headed for the sales table where Haddy had set up shop and had been selling calendars since the first guest had arrived.

"Selling like bottled water in the desert," Haddy said. "Sheer brilliance, Gini Claremont. Sheer brilliance."

"I've got a few good ideas now and then." Gini patted herself on the back. "I'm going to get things formally started at the microphone now."

"Okay. I'll keep selling, boss."

Gini corralled Chief Warner, who'd come out to support his men, and Josephine, the director of the shelter, now back from Paris. She tugged them both to the front of the room over by the piano. Raina wrapped up the song she was singing, and the room quieted. Gini stepped to the small podium she'd set up.

"If everyone could take a seat, we can get started in a couple of minutes."

As people meandered to the seats, Gini's attention yet again circled toward Patrick. Yet again, he was staring at her, all of his focus on her and no one else. If she didn't get to touch him soon, Gini was sure she'd lose her mind. Or maybe she'd already lost it.

Either way, she didn't care as long as her evening ended with Patrick in her arms, in her bed.

****

She was so beautiful up there with her smile dimpling her cheeks and her long, toned legs stretching down into those sexy sandals. Patrick couldn't wait to slide them off her feet and free her from the rest of her clothing. Gini was undoubtedly the most amazing person in the room. Looking at the photos she'd taken for the calendar and the pictures of the animals decorating the hall, Patrick appreciated the talent Gini had with a camera. She had an artist's eye and maybe a magician's hand, because everything she photographed looked absolutely perfect. He didn't recognize himself standing with Saber and Midas in his calendar picture. Was that actually a *smile* on his face?

"I'm next," a voice sang in front of Patrick. "Hello, Mr. July."

"Hi." Patrick took the calendar opened to his month and uncapped his pen.

"Can you make that out to Cecilia Bennette?" the woman asked. She proceeded to spell the name for him.

Patrick signed the calendar. He focused on the letters forming his name as he wrote them because he could feel the woman's eyes on him. Made him uncomfortable and he didn't want to look up to catch her ogling.

"You're my favorite picture," Cecilia said. "The others are nice, don't get me wrong, but you…" She let her voice drop off. "You're something."

Taken. The word popped into Patrick's head, and he had to smile at the notion. He was taken. Taken by that fantastic woman still up on the stage waiting for everyone to get to a seat.

Patrick slid the calendar back to Cecilia. "Enjoy your night," he said.

"Oh, I am. That Gini Claremont sure knows how to throw a fundraiser. I can't wait to see what she comes up with next." Cecilia giggled and walked away.

Me neither, Patrick thought. The mere idea he'd be around to *see* what Gini came up with next excited him. He was thinking in future terms when it came to being with her. He glanced back to the stage and was bothered by the bodies between Gini and him. If he could send them all home right now, he would. He just wanted to be alone with her.

"Looks as if everyone's almost settled," Gini said into the microphone. "I'd like to welcome you to the first ever Burnam Firefighter Calendar Signing." She hooked her arm through Chief Warner's and looked up at him. "Hopefully it won't be the last."

Chief Warner grinned. "That's up to the men."

Gini gestured to the tables of fighters set up around the edges of the room. "What do you say, fellas? Was it too dreadful posing with dogs, cats, horses, birds, and the occasional rabbit?"

"Not for you, Gini," Willy called out.

She shot Willy a killer smile that had Patrick's insides bubbling. How could a mere smile have that effect on his body even when the smile was directed at someone else?

"A special thanks to all the test dummies...I mean, fine, upstanding firefighters for helping me and the Burnam Animal Shelter. We will be able to do quite a bit with the money we raise tonight, don't you think, Josephine?"

"Absolutely," Josephine said. "I know the animals would thank you themselves if they could. Your support means so much to each of them and to the staff at the shelter. We shall proudly display your calendar in our shelter and always remember how you suffered the trials of being treated like supermodels to help us."

Chuckles sifted through the crowd, and Gini stepped back to the microphone.

"Don't forget to enter your name in the raffle to win a dance with one of the fighters. Twelve lucky women will get the chance to sashay across this floor with a hero. Enjoy yourselves, folks, buy calendars and animal photos, and thanks again."

A round of applause filled the hall then died off as people headed back to the tables to get their autographs and enter the raffle. Patrick lost sight of Gini when she stepped away from the microphone and got swallowed by the crowd. He craned his head, but couldn't find her.

"Looking for your next admirer?"

Patrick focused on the woman standing in front of his table. Petite, thin, almost sickly so, with short, spiky black hair. Her skin was grayish, her eyes a strange shade of blue, nearly violet. Her mouth was full, but the corners were angled down in a permanent frown. She reminded Patrick of a sad fairy.

"Hello." Patrick watched the woman's jaw tense slightly then release.

"Evening." She set a calendar on the table and flipped to Patrick's picture. "Nice photo."

"The photographer's a genius." Patrick smiled, but the woman's facial expression never changed. Her lips kept their downward arc. The purplish eyes narrowed as they stared at Patrick's face. He waited for her to say something, but she merely watched as he picked up his pen, its tip hovering over his picture.

"Would you like this made out to someone in particular?" he asked.

The woman shook her head. "Just your name will do it."

As Patrick signed his name, Midas rose from his spot beside him. He sniffed at the woman's shoes, up her leg, around the back of her, and let out a deep bark that had the conversation in the hall quieting for a moment.

"*Couchez*, Midas."

The dog lay down, but he continued growling at the woman.

"Sorry, about that." Patrick closed the calendar and handed it back to the woman. "Have a nice…" He stopped when she tucked the calendar under her arm and walked away without letting Patrick finish.

"Nice manners, huh?" Chuck, Mr. August, elbowed Patrick.

"Maybe Midas offended her or she's in a rush to get other signatures." Patrick shrugged, but as he watched the woman, he noticed she didn't stop at any of the other tables. Instead, she headed for the

354

front doors, her slight body easily weaving through the dense crowd. He lost sight of her for a moment then saw the door open and close. Midas let out a short bark and sidled up next to Patrick. A bit closer than he was before.

"How's it going?"

Patrick shifted his gaze to take in Gini leaning on the table in front of him. In that position, he could see down the front of her dress, catch a glimpse of her full, round breasts contained in a black bra. Did she know the effect she had on him?

Chuck cleared his throat and stood. "I'm getting a drink. You want one, Patrick?"

Patrick didn't take his gaze off Gini. "No, thanks."

Gini followed his eyes and smirked. "A preview," she said after Chuck left. "You like?"

"Very much." Patrick met her gaze now, and the noise of the hall dropped away. The smells of the crowd vanished, replaced by that heavenly wildflower scent that was unmistakably Gini.

"Who was that last chick?" Gini asked.

Patrick blinked and pulled himself out of the play-by-play scene running in his mind of what he was going to do to Gini when he finally got her alone tonight.

"I don't know," he said. "I was going to ask you. She didn't give a name. Just wanted my signature."

"Maybe she's your number one fan," Gini said.

"I was hoping that title belonged to you." Patrick grinned as he ran his index finger over Gini's hand resting on the table.

"I consider myself a groupie. Has more of a devoted connotation. As if I'd follow you anywhere."

"Would you?"

Gini puckered her lips out and looked up to the ceiling as if she were considering her answer. When her gaze leveled with Patrick's, she slowly eased forward and kissed him.

"You know, Mr. July, I think I would follow you to the moon and back."

Patrick looped the dangling beads of Gini's necklace around the fingers of his left hand and tugged her closer. He caught her lips with his and collected another kiss.

"I can't wait to go home with you," he said.

"That makes two of us." Gini maneuvered the beads out of Patrick's hand and glanced over her shoulder. "I better move along. Your line is getting rather lengthy."

She blew Patrick a kiss and walked away on those magnificent sandals. When she reached Haddy at the sales table, she immediately sparked up a conversation with an older woman purchasing a calendar. Only the sound of the next person wanting an autograph tore Patrick from his admiration of Gini.

"Did I hear talk that you're from Rhode Island?" the woman in front of him asked. Beside her stood an enormous bear of a man with his arms folded across his Harley Davidson T-shirt. Clearly, the woman had dragged him to this event. Clearly, he wasn't happy.

"Yes. You heard right."

"My daughter lives in Rhode Island now. Could you make the calendar out to her? I'm going to send this to her. I know the gals she works with will get a hoot out of these pictures."

"Sure." Patrick took the calendar, found his picture, wrote the name the woman told him, and signed his own name.

"Thanks. If only Gini could have figured out how to make there be more than twelve months in a year." The woman laughed. The man standing beside her did not.

Patrick nodded toward the man, and the man

nodded back, but that was the extent of their interaction. The woman collected her calendar and moved on to the next table. The man followed her wordlessly.

"Can we say jealous?" Chuck whispered, now back with his drink.

"Huh?" Patrick turned to look at him as the next person in line handed him a calendar.

"Old Finneas Yasberg. You know, I think this is the first time I've seen him without a shotgun held lovingly in his hands."

"Now that you mention it," Patrick said, "he looked familiar. I think he was poking around on my land the other day. Had a beagle with him whose nose never left the ground."

"That would be Haggis, his hunting dog."

"Isn't haggis sheep guts or intestine or something?" Patrick's stomach did a sick flop as he thought about it.

"Yep. Tastes as good as it sounds too."

"Why name a dog that?"

"Dog has a fondness for sheep. Never picks up the trail of deer, or moose, or bear. Always sheep."

"People don't generally hunt sheep, do they?" Patrick asked.

"Nope," Chuck said. "Hence, the ever-present sour look on Finneas's face. He's wanted to get rid of the dog for ages, but Helen won't let him. He's stuck with the dog. And Helen, for that matter."

Patrick slipped the bit of town lore into his mental filing cabinet. If he were truly going to make a life in Burnam—one look back at Gini at the sales table confirmed he was going to attempt it—he should start getting to know the people and their stories. After all, he'd signed up with the fire department to keep them safe. He should know whom he was protecting.

"Tough having all these lovely ladies giving you

attention, ain't it, boys?" Gini's father asked as he rested a hand on Patrick's shoulder.

"You remember how it is, Walter," Chuck said. "They can't resist the uniform."

"Put puppies and kittens in your hands, and it isn't any surprise they're lining up to eyeball all of you. Gini is a marketing genius," Walter said.

"She gets that from me," Liz said as she sidled up to Walter.

"No one else can push pastry out the door like you," Walter agreed.

Gini's mother beamed a smile at her husband. "Hand getting cramped?" she asked Patrick. "Your line has been the longest."

"It's because I'm the new guy." Patrick fiddled with the pen cap while there was a lull in his line.

"No, dear," Liz said. "It's because you're adorable." She cupped his chin.

Normally, Patrick shied away from letting people touch him. Easier to keep his distance if he didn't let them into his circle. Easier to keep his secrets. Being with Gini these last couple of days, though, had definitely thawed something inside him. *Thawed* wasn't the right word.

More like melted, Patrick thought. His self-constructed walls, thick and insulated against the world, had been melted by Gini's touch, by her acceptance of him, by her choosing to be with him even though he wasn't perfect. He hadn't thought about his scars or about hiding from folks over the past few days.

"Oh, he *is* adorable," Chuck said, his eyes rolling as he pretended to swoon.

"You shush," Liz said to Chuck. "Or there'll be a sudden shortage of apple turnovers next time you come into the bakery."

"You wouldn't." Chuck grabbed Liz's hand.

"I most certainly would." Liz tried to contain her

laughter.

"Sorry, Mrs. Claremont."

"That's a good boy." Gini's mother patted Chuck on the back. She turned back to Patrick as he signed another calendar. When he was finished, she bent so she was close enough to whisper in his ear. "You'll take care of Gini, won't you?"

Patrick looked up into Liz's eyes, ones as blue as Gini's, and knew she'd been looking for someone to take care of Gini for a long time.

"We'll take care of each other," Patrick said.

Liz squeezed his hand as a single tear rolled down her cheek. Never had Patrick felt so important.

Chapter Thirty

"We're rolling in dough." Haddy accepted payment for several calendars. "People aren't buying one or two, Gini. The last four customers bought six apiece and your animal photographs are flying right off the walls."

"Sweet. I have to say I didn't think it would be *this* successful."

"No one's ever done an event like this before around these parts. People had to come and check it out." Haddy picked up a calendar and flipped through the pages. "And one glimpse at these pictures is enough to have the stingiest of folks forking over their cash."

"I think we should volunteer to make the fighters lunch one day next week. We have to do something to thank them for their time."

"And muscles," Haddy said.

"True. Let's not forget the muscles." Gini glanced toward Patrick and saw the way her mother was beaming at him. What was he saying to her? Why did she look as happy as Gini felt?

"What's on the menu for tonight?" Haddy asked.

"Thought we'd grill up some chicken. Picked corn and the fixings for a salad this morning. Pasta. Sangria is chilling in the fridge as is some beer."

"Sounds good," Haddy said. "Can't wait."

Can't wait until you all go home, Gini thought. *So I can have Patrick all to myself.* She wasn't sure she'd make it much longer. Yes, she loved the turnout at the signing. Yes, she loved all the money they were raising for the shelter. Yes, she loved the way the fighters looked on display in their uniforms.

But mostly, she loved Patrick.

As this thought bounced around in her head, Gini realized it was the first time she had felt this way about any man. True, she'd thought she'd been in love with Cameron when she was a teenager, but she didn't know what love was back then. Sure, Cameron had given her attention and had treated her well until that night in his car when everything literally went up in smoke. But what she felt for Patrick right now, in this very moment, was enormous, deep, and expanding the more she thought about him.

"Gini?" Haddy tugged on her arm.

"I love him." The words tumbled out, and they felt so right as she said them.

"Oh, Gini." Haddy threw her arms around Gini's shoulders. "I've never seen you this happy. Go tell Patrick what you just said, what you feel. Don't wait."

Gini nodded and squeezed Haddy's hand. She took three steps toward Patrick's table where he'd just signed the calendar of the last person in his line. He looked up and smiled at her. She took another three steps and Midas blocked her path. He pushed his nose into her hand, then let out a short bark and backed up a few feet. Midas pressed his nose to the floor and paced in a small circle before coming to Gini again. He went through the entire routine a second time.

"Midas," Gini said, confused by the dog's weird behavior. "What are you doing, boy?" As Gini tried to skirt around the dog, Patrick got up. His face lost its smile as he neared the dog. When he was close enough to reach out and touch Gini, a voice boomed over the conversations and Raina's music.

"Fire!"

Everyone went as still as stone. Talking stopped. Music ceased. All movement in the hall ended.

And then there was panic.

"We have to get out!"

"The fire is at the back door."

"Head for the front doors!"

"Everybody move."

Patrick grabbed Gini's shoulders. "I want you to get out of here. Go. Now. Take Midas with you." He turned to the dog and pointed to the door. "*Partez*, Midas."

Gini shook her head, but Patrick spun her around. Midas nudged her toward the doors.

"Gini, please. I'm going to help the rest of the fighters get everyone out. I don't want to worry about you being in here still. If something happened to you..." Patrick shook his head, and Gini touched his cheek.

"I feel the same way about you. I want to stay with you."

"You'll be better on the outside, keeping everyone organized and away from the building until we see what's going on here."

"C'mon, Gini," Jonah said, tugging on her arm. "Patrick is right. We'll be of better use on the outside."

Gini let herself be pulled away from Patrick. She ushered Haddy, Raina, her parents, and several other Burnam citizens toward the front doors of the hall. She couldn't count the number of times she looked over her shoulder, searched the room for Patrick. He was among the other fighters corralling people away from the blaze now raging at the back door.

Two fire trucks were in the parking lot outside, and some of the fighters scrambled over it, donned gear, unraveled hoses. Gini kept a close watch on who came and who went, but she didn't see Patrick.

"I grabbed the money and as many unsold calendars as I could," Haddy said. "What the hell is happening?"

"Fire at the back door, apparently," Jonah said.

Gini watched her brother pace back and forth, upset at not being able to help the other fighters. His pacing reminded her of Midas.

Midas. Fire. Back door.

Thoughts snapped into place like the pieces of a puzzle, and Gini ran.

"Gini!" Jonah called, but she was already around the side of the building. Dark woods surrounded the hall. The light of the moon overhead and the orange glow of the fire burning ahead lit her way. Still, she didn't see Mason until she ran right into him.

"Whoa. Easy." Mason supported Gini with his hands on her biceps. "You should be running the other way, Shutterbug."

Gini pulled free of his grip. "It's her, Mason. She's here. Your fire-loving lunatic is here."

"Where?" Mason swiveled his head in all directions as his hand went for his gun.

"I don't know, but I'll bet you anything there's a candle at that back door and a gasoline trail outside. Midas was acting weird, but I didn't know what he was trying to tell me. And..." Gini paused and took a deep breath. "What is that?"

Mason inhaled too. "Whatever it is, it's wretched. It's not gasoline."

"No, but it's familiar." Gini closed her eyes and focused everything she had on that smell filling her nostrils. She clamped onto Mason's arm. "It's the scent on the last candle you found. It's..." Gini snapped her fingers as she searched her mind. "It's patchouli, but as if the leaves have been burned or mixed with something harsh this time. Patchouli, like the other scents on the candles, is for relaxation, but making it smell like this is—"

"Totally *not* relaxing," Mason finished around a cough.

"The scents indicate our arsonist's state of mind, Mason," Gini said. "Cinnamon, chamomile, lavender, and patchouli all combat depression."

"I thought cinnamon was an aphrodisiac."

"It is, but maybe that's what she's depressed about," Gini offered. "That she has no one to love."

Two more officers emerged from the back of the hall. "Looks as if the fighters got everyone out, Detective. They're all waiting out front."

"Search the group," Mason said. "Look for anyone you don't recognize and hold them for questioning."

The officers jogged to the front of the hall, while Mason turned toward the back. "I'm going to look for a candle once they have that blaze under control. I want you to go to the front with the others and stay safe, Gini."

Gini nodded. "Be careful, Mason." She ran to the front and searched the crowd for Patrick. She found her family, Haddy, and Raina, but no Patrick.

Haddy touched her shoulder. "He's probably battling the blaze out back."

"Right." He wouldn't stop at getting everyone out of the building. He would want a hand in putting out the fire too. As Gini sifted out a breath, accepting that Patrick was in his gear, protected, while he extinguished the flames, her eyes settled on something by the front door.

Midas.

The dog was on his hind legs, scratching his claws furiously along the door, as if he were digging. Digging for his best friend.

"Patrick!" Gini yelled.

****

Patrick thought everyone had gotten out. He

was on his way out as well when the front doors slammed shut.

"Help..." a faint voice called.

Patrick whirled around, his eyes combing over the empty hall. Overturned chairs lay haphazardly on the floor. Raina's song sheets were strewn over the piano keys and bench. Some of Gini's animal photos were on the floor, footprints marring their beauty. And at the back of the hall, flames caught curtains and walls on fire.

"Help me."

The voice was so soft Patrick could hardly tell where it came from.

"Hello?" he called. "Where are you? Tell me where you are and I'll get you out."

No answer.

Part of Patrick's brain told him to leave. Get out while he could. Find Gini and Midas and let the fighters in gear come in to investigate and put out the fire. Another part couldn't abandon someone who might be still in the hall.

"Hello?" he said again.

"I'm stuck." The voice sounded like a child's, but Patrick didn't remember seeing any children in the crowd tonight. Those calendars weren't exactly G-rated.

He stepped away from the doors, and with one eye on the smoke filling the back of the hall, Patrick crouched to look under the tables. No one. He opened the doors of the bathrooms, a small kitchen area, an office. Still not a soul around.

Water spraying the back of the building outside was a comforting sound, but the temperature was rising and more smoke sifted in along the ceiling.

"Where are you?" Patrick shouted.

"Right here," a voice said directly behind him.

Patrick turned around. The thin, violet-eyed woman sat on the piano, a lighter flicking on and off in her right hand, a red, 5-gallon gas can under her left.

"Got a candle?" she asked. When Patrick didn't answer right away, a disturbing smile slid across her chapped lips. "Not to worry. I have one. No scent on it this time. I put the scent outside to toy with your fighters and cops, but for us inside, well…death has no scent. Unless you count the gasoline."

She tapped the gas can, then plunged a bony hand into the pocket of the gray hooded sweatshirt that hung unevenly off her shoulders. She pulled out a candle, black this time, and held it out to Patrick.

He made no move to take it, and he watched the woman's jaw tense as it had when he'd signed her calendar.

"What's the matter?" she asked. "Don't fraternize with 'sick and twisted' people?" She slid off the piano. "No, you're probably too busy with your pretty blonde and her brother and that stupid cop. You're all so *comfortable* in your little worlds."

Patrick watched her strange eyes dart around the room. Was she high? And why did she harbor such disdain for him? What had he done to her?

"Stopping fires that were meant to burn is so selfish," she said.

Okay, Patrick thought, *she's mad I put out her fires.* What could he do to make her not mad? To distract her long enough to get out? To keep her from dumping that gas can and lighting that candle?

A faint bark sounded from the other side of the front doors. Midas had made it out with Gini. He'd get help.

But would help come in time?

"Why would you want to burn this place down?" he asked. Get her talking was the only plan he had at the moment.

"Because I can," she said.

Patrick waited for her say more, but she was

apparently a woman of few words. Damn.

"People were just having a good time here," he said.

"Exactly." She let her heels rest on the keys of the piano so a disjointed melody clanged into the hall. "A frivolous good time while there are people in the world with nothing."

"It was a fundraiser," Patrick said. "Raising money to help the animal shelter, which you also tried to burn down."

"And you also stopped from burning down," she added. "I've only gotten to enjoy three full blazes in this stupid town. The house and the barn burned nicely before you got to it, and the market was a lovely performance, because you weren't here."

How did she know that?

"You prematurely ended my bookstore show," she continued, "and the animal shelter. To think I doused those oversized rodents in gasoline for nothing. Waste of fuel."

Patrick's hands clenched into fists. "What kind of a person does that to cats?"

"Me. I'm the kind of person that does that. Sick and twisted. Remember? That's what you called me." She slid off the piano, the lighter flicking on and off more rapidly now.

"You were at the shelter?" Patrick asked.

"Yes. And I heard what you called me. You have no business judging me. Putting me into one of your neat little categories. You or the cop. He can go to Hell too. You both need to be taught a lesson. One you'll never forget, or perhaps the last one you'll remember. Either way is fine with me."

She picked up the gas can and unscrewed the spout. Instantly, the smell of gasoline mixed with the scent of burning wood. She poured the contents of the can in sloppy lines all over the piano. Raina would have cried to see the piece treated that way.

Patrick recognized it as an antique and had watched Raina's fingers on the keys tonight. She'd caressed the black and ivory keys, closed her eyes, sang her best.

Patrick glanced behind him at the flames still raging at the back of the hall. They hadn't progressed any farther into the room, and he had to assume the fighters were winning the battle against it. That would only further infuriate this nutcase bent on teaching him a lesson.

Patrick searched the immediate area for something he could use as a weapon. The only thing he came up with was a broom leaning against the wall in the tiny kitchen area. While the sicko hummed and positioned the black candle on the floor in a puddle of gasoline, Patrick sidestepped his way to the broom. One hand closed around the handle, and he picked it up. He shifted his grip down near the bristles. He wielded the broom like a baseball bat and walked toward the woman.

She was a lightweight, couldn't weigh more than a hundred ten pounds. One solid swipe to the head and she should go down. Patrick hated the thought of smashing her skull, but he was out of options. He didn't want to kill her, just knock her out for a while. If she lit that candle, they were both finished. In her pouring, the leg of her pants had gotten saturated. She'd go up in flames within seconds. His own boots were covered in gasoline because he'd stepped all over it, and the smell was starting to make him dizzy. He also didn't know how close people were standing outside the front of the building. He wouldn't risk them. Wouldn't risk Gini.

Gini. She'd been walking toward him before the fire had broken out. The smile and expression on her face had been full of joy. She'd looked as if she were about to tell him something. Something important. Would he ever get to hear what that something was?

God, he hoped so.

Choking up on the broom handle, Patrick took four steps closer to the arsonist as she screwed the cap back onto the gas can. He ratcheted his arms back, the broom ready to connect with the back of her head. At the last second, she ducked. Patrick's swing completely missed her and because he'd put all his strength into it, he stumbled forward a few feet.

"I could see your every move in the mirror," she said, pointing to the one hanging on the wall. "You're going to have to do better than this." She shook her head and tossed the lighter from hand to hand.

"Look, why don't you move on to the next town, huh?" Patrick leaned on the broom, trying to think of his next move. "You've put on a nice show here. We're all impressed. Time to give some other folks a turn."

"As if your cop buddy will let me leave now." She shook her head, her odd-colored eyes disappearing behind her lids for a moment. When she opened her eyes, the fire at the back of the hall reflected in the blacks of her pupils. She looked possessed. "If you fellows are going to stop my mission here, I'm going to at least go out in a blaze of glory." She laughed at her own joke, the sound more maniacal than pleasant.

"You can go out in an inferno for all I care," Patrick said, his patience all used up, "but I don't want to watch."

"But you must. I've given you a special invitation. I would have liked to have the whole town in here, but alas, they'll have to enjoy the festivities from the outside." She turned in a circle, her hands thrown up in the air. "Do you think anyone will miss you?"

His answer to that question a few weeks ago would have been short. Raina and Julianne would have missed him. That would have been it. Now, however, the list had gotten longer. Jonah had befriended him immediately, and Mason had trusted his input on the arson case. Haddy had welcomed him into the group as well. Gini's mother had shown him nothing but kindness, and her father was even coming around.

And Gini. Patrick thought she'd miss him if he died tonight. They'd found each other. Shared their secrets, their bodies, their hearts. Dammit, he loved her, and he wasn't going to let this psychopath keep him from loving her.

"A few people will miss me, yes," he said.

"Tragic, isn't it?" The woman's face twisted into the saddest expression Patrick had ever seen. "No one will miss me. No one." Her hands trembled, her grip on the lighter precarious. Tears collected in her eyes as she dropped to her knees into a pool of gasoline.

The lighter clicked as Patrick launched himself forward.

Chapter Thirty-One

"She's going to light it!" Gini screamed. The front doors wouldn't open. She'd tried, but they wouldn't budge. Fighters had started to hack away at them, but it was slow going. The doors were reinforced steel because the hall had had problems with vandals in the past due to its secluded location. The fighters wouldn't break them down in time.

Gini pressed her face to the window at the front of the hall, and Midas barked like a rabid wolf. Raina called for Midas, but the dog was inconsolable. Mason tried to pull Gini away from the building, but she shrugged out of his grip and did the only thing she could think of to save Patrick.

She got angry. Gini let loose all her control. She targeted the second back door, away from the fighters, away from the people gathered at the front, away from the man she wanted to spend the rest of her life with.

The door exploded outward with a thunderous boom. Inside, the woman Patrick wrestled with screamed at the sound. Her head whipped to the source of the eruption, and Gini watched Patrick yank the lighter out of her hand. He hauled the slight woman over his shoulder and bolted for the front doors.

Gini heard Patrick trying to open the doors, and she ran to them, calling the fighters off and willing Patrick to come out safely. Moments passed by in slow motion as Gini's mind scrambled for something else she could do to help. If Patrick went to either of

371

the back doors, he'd have to run through the fire. The windows of the hall were custom made with three panes of shatterproof glass in each one to protect against vandalism. The front exit was jammed.

Patrick was trapped. The only person who had ever managed to make her truly happy was going to die if she didn't get him out of there.

Gini searched the parking lot. Her gaze settled on one of the fire trucks. Mason was still trying to drag her away from the building, his hands ultra-tight on her arms now.

"Gini, please!" he yelled. "It's not safe here!"

"Mason, let go of me." She managed to free herself again and dart to the fire truck. Her father was right behind her as she stepped up the side of the truck and opened the door.

"Gini, what are you doing?" Walter asked.

"Keys, Daddy. I need keys."

"Get down from there. I don't know what you're—"

A tree catching fire behind them cut off Walter's words.

"Calm down, Gini," Walter said.

A car burst into flames at the far end of the parking lot. "I can't calm down. Patrick is going to die in there if we don't give him a way out." Gini's heartbeat pounded in her ears, and she felt lightheaded. She couldn't rein in the anger swirling inside her. Anger that someone would try to take Patrick's life. Take him away from her.

"Get. Me. The. Keys." Each word sifted through Gini's teeth as the sign for Beaver Pond Hall blew up in an orange cloud of fire.

Walter ran off toward the back of the hall and when he returned, he stepped up into the truck where Gini sat behind the wheel.

"Move over," he said.

"Daddy, I—"

"Gini, do it." He pushed her over until there was enough room for him to hop into the driver's seat. "I'm going to aim for that corner." Walter pointed to the hall. "I'd like to tell you to get out, but I know that's not going to happen, so brace yourself."

Gini focused on the bricks making up the corner of the hall they were targeting. The fire truck roared to life and in the parking lot, Gini's mother, Haddy, and Jonah pushed back the crowd. Her father put the truck in gear, backed up a few more yards, and gave it some gas.

The nose of the truck buried itself into the building with a horrible scraping sound, and Walter threw it into reverse. As the truck backed up, bricks fell like concrete rain. Wood splintered and fell.

An exit was born.

As soon as the truck was clear of the building, Gini jumped down and ran to the opening. Mason caught her before she plowed inside. Jonah blocked her path as well.

"Where is he?" Gini shouted. "Where is he?" She tried to push past Mason and Jonah.

"I'll go in," Mason said. "Wait here." He nudged her toward Jonah, who used his good arm to hold on to her.

Gini struggled, but Jonah didn't let go. "Gini, you're hurting me."

She stilled. "I'm sorry, Jonah. I just need to see him. Why hasn't he come out?"

"Mason will get him," Raina said as she came to stand beside Gini. Her face was pale as she stared at the crumbled corner of the hall. "He has to be okay. Has to be." She didn't blink, but Gini saw the quiver in her bottom lip.

Gini slid her arm around Raina, half to console Patrick's sister, half to console herself. Raina leaned into Gini, and together they waited for Patrick to appear in the opening.

If he didn't, Gini hoped her parents had a nice asylum picked out for her.

****

"Patrick!"

Yes, that was his name. He recognized it. That had to be a good sign.

"Patrick, where are you, buddy?"

Mason, he thought, but he couldn't get his lips to form any words. And what was pinning him to the wet floor?

No, not just wet. He took in a strained breath and smelled the gasoline. His uniform was soaked with it, his hands slick with it and something else. Patrick forced his eyes open and a ceiling spun in dizzying circles. He clamped his eyes closed and steadied his breathing as his stomach flip-flopped. When he opened them again, he stared above him until the grid of acoustic tiles snapped into place and stayed there. He pushed up onto his elbows and took in the body strewn across his lap.

The arsonist. Patrick reached a hand out and touched her neck. Her pulse still drummed in her neck. Alive. He made a move to turn her over and caught sight of the blood on his right hand. As he sat up all the way, a blinding pain screamed through his head. He raised his left hand to the back of his head and felt the warm moistness of a fresh wound.

As his mind put the pieces together, a shadow fell over him.

"Oh, thank God. There you are," Mason said.

Patrick squinted up at Mason and the two firefighters flanking him. "Arsonist." He gestured to his lap, and the room went black.

****

Haddy joined Gini and Raina, a hand on both of them, as medics rushed into the hall with two stretchers. The sound that came from Raina's throat before she crumpled to the ground mirrored everything churning around inside of Gini.

"Can't be," Raina whispered. "He can't be."

Gini went to her knees, both arms around Raina now, holding on. The anger had fizzled away, replaced by sadness so great, Gini felt as if someone had gutted her like a pumpkin. Carved out anything that mattered, any life, and left it splattered on the sidewalk for the pigeons to eat.

No one would ever mean as much to her as Patrick.

She squeezed Raina tighter as the other woman cried, her own eyes inexplicably dry. Further proof she was dead inside. And to think Patrick had let her take his picture and had agreed to sign calendars because the shelter meant so much to her. He'd done it for her. Now he was gone.

It took several moments for Gini's mind to register the sound around her as applause. Raina shook within her grip, but Haddy tugged them both to their feet.

"He's out, Gini," Haddy said. "Look." She pointed to the rubble at the corner of the hall.

Gini stood and pulled Raina up as well. Two medics were toting a stretcher past the hall debris, and Midas made a beeline for them. When she saw a hand reach out to the dog from the stretcher, Gini ran too.

"Patrick!"

Midas bolted toward her then back to Patrick as if to say, "I've found him. He's okay."

The medics paused to let Gini grab Patrick's still outstretched hand. When her fingers closed around his, she felt complete. Life spilled back into her.

She looked at his hand. "You're bleeding."

"Got a nasty bump on the head," one of the medics said. "We're going to take him to the hospital. Couple of stitches, and he'll be fine."

"I think I slipped trying to get to the other corner of the hall. The floor was covered in gasoline, and I was carrying our arsonist friend." Patrick shrugged and winced.

"Not easy being a hero." Gini leaned forward and pressed a kiss to Patrick's forehead. "I love you, Patrick."

His grip on her hand tightened as a smile tugged one side of his lips up. "I love you, Firefly."

Gini loved the sound of the old nickname. Loved hearing Patrick say it. Made her feel as if what she could do was a gift, something beautiful. Not a curse, or something to be afraid of. She'd used her ability to help Patrick. Well, her ability and an enormous fire truck.

"Come with me?" Patrick asked.

Gini nodded and followed the medics to an ambulance. She stopped when EMTs emerged from the hall with a second stretcher. Mason jogged to catch up to them.

"That's her?" Gini couldn't believe such a tiny woman could have caused so much trouble in Burnam. She touched Patrick's arm as a way to calm the anger threatening to ignite something.

"Yes." Mason glanced at the notebook in his hand. "Lara Farnswell, according to her driver's license. I'm going to run the name when I get back to the station. Something tells me she's got a story."

"Is she hurt?" Patrick asked.

"No," Mason said. "But she's babbling on about lessons and fire being the most powerful of the elements. She's nuts and needs to be under close observation. Figure the hospital with a couple of guards ought to do it for now. As long as she can't start any more fires, I'm happy." He signaled for the EMTs to take her to another waiting ambulance and ordered one of his officers go with them.

"I'm going to start processing her while you're

getting pieced back together." Mason laid a hand on Patrick's shoulder. "And then, Gini, tell me you're still going to feed us."

"Definitely. We need to celebrate that our arsonist is caught, and all our heroes are alive." Gini's voice cracked a bit on the word *alive* as she looked at Patrick.

He gave her another smile before the medics slid the stretcher into the ambulance. Mason helped Gini up behind them, and Midas jumped up as well. The dog covered Patrick's face in sloppy doggy kisses.

"I'll take Raina to the station with me then to Gini's," Mason said. "Gini's mother is calming her down right now."

"Thanks, Mason," Patrick said.

Mason nodded. "See you in a few." He closed the ambulance doors and pounded on them.

Gini focused on Patrick's face. She cupped his cheek, and his eyes closed for a moment as he pressed farther into her hand.

"Say it again," she whispered as she bent over him and ran a finger over his lips.

"I love you, Firefly." He kissed the tip of her finger. "Right now. Always."

"That better not be the head wound talking." Gini pursed her lips and narrowed her eyes.

"Nope," Patrick said. "It's just the truth."

Chapter Thirty-Two

Other than the remains of a slight headache, Patrick felt wonderful seated at Gini's dining room table and surrounded by friends. Gini had taken him to his house so he could clean up and feed Midas and Whisper. He'd ended up spending more time kissing Gini than anything else, but he considered that time well spent. They'd brought Midas and Whisper back to Gini's house because Patrick wasn't planning to return home tonight. He was planning, instead, to love every single beautiful inch of Gini Claremont.

He watched her as she and a finally calmed Raina brought food to the table. Everything about Gini was perfect. The gold curls collected into a low ponytail at the base of her smooth neck. The dancing light in her blue eyes. The upward arc of her berry-flavored lips. The sexy curve of her waist in the fitted green T-shirt and jeans she'd changed into. And beneath her physical attributes was a woman of strength, intelligence, compassion, and talent. She was everything he never knew he needed, but now couldn't live without.

In fact, everyone gathered around the table was someone he'd miss if they were gone. His sister. His buddies, Mason and Jonah. Haddy. Gini's parents. Each of them had broken through his defenses and changed him for the better.

His life was...full.

"I brought blueberry muffins, Patrick." Liz set a pitcher of sangria on the table. "You might have to fight off Walter for them, however."

Walter shook his head. "Nah, the kid's earned them." He held up his beer and nodded at Patrick.

"Thank you." Patrick gestured with his lemonade, having foregone alcohol due to his head already aching.

"Enjoy, son." Walter took the dish of pasta Haddy handed him.

"So did you make a formal arrest?" Jonah asked Mason.

"Yes. Ms. Farnswell, apparently the last Farnswell, as her entire family was killed in a car crash about six years ago, has staged similar performances in five other New England towns. Always candles and gasoline. Always starting small and working up to a grand finale. Two of my men found notes among her things at this rundown cabin she was living in while in Vermont. Apparently, she changed her last show from the school complex to the Beaver Pond Hall."

"The school!" Liz gasped.

"She changed because of me," Patrick said.

All eyes turned toward him. "What do you mean?" Jonah asked.

"She was at the animal shelter. She heard me call her sick and twisted. Tonight's show was meant to get back at me." Patrick shifted his gaze to Mason. "She wasn't too fond of you either."

"Probably likes me even less since I've arrested her, but I'm used to not making friends with the criminals."

Mason rested his arm on the back of Raina's chair, and she leaned toward him. Patrick let some of the responsibility he had always felt for his sister slip away.

Mason will take care of her. For as long as Raina would let him. Patrick knew Raina got bored easily. He loved his sister, but she went through men like paper towels. Maybe it would be different with

Mason.

"You want me to cut that for you?" Haddy asked as Jonah struggled with his chicken. She didn't wait for an answer. Instead, she picked up a knife and fork and cut into the meat.

Jonah used his free hand to tug on Haddy's hair as she leaned across him to reach his plate. He winked at Patrick with an "I've got it made" look on his face.

For the first time in his life, Patrick knew what his friend meant. Gini sat beside him and just having her close by made his pulse speed up. All of his senses were tuned into her. Her wildflower scent was still discernible over the barbecued chicken. The hand she rested on his forearm under the table was warm and soft. Her laughter made him feel buoyant, as if he could float on the clouds.

"Despite the turn of events this evening," Liz began, "did you make what you'd hoped to make for the shelter, Gini?"

"Thanks to Haddy grabbing what she could, yes, we raised more than I'd hoped," Gini said.

"The first order of business should be a security system for the shelter," Mason said.

"And updated smoke detectors," Jonah said.

"And sprinklers," Patrick added.

"I'll put all that on the list," Gini said as she saluted all three of them.

Patrick felt better knowing that a place Gini frequented would be well protected. He couldn't be with her everywhere although he totally wanted to be.

He spent the rest of the evening enjoying the food and the company and thinking about what he wanted. He wanted to finish his house. He wanted to protect the town of Burnam from fires. He wanted to go snowmobiling in the winter with Jonah and Mason. He wanted to eat Liz's blueberry muffins from sunrise to sunset.

Mostly, though, he wanted Gini. Wanted his life to revolve around making her happy.

As if knowing he was thinking about her, Gini turned around from the sink where she and Haddy had been washing dishes. A slow smile crept across her face, dimpling her left cheek and stirring Patrick's insides.

"Patrick, does your head still hurt?" Gini's eyes locked onto his and told him to go along with whatever she said.

"Yeah," he said. "The drum solo in there rages on."

"Oh, you poor dear," Liz said. "Everybody, we should get a move on. Let Patrick rest."

Patrick looked back to Gini and almost laughed out loud at her satisfied grin.

"You're good," he mouthed.

Gini did a little half-bow and walked to the door. Within ten minutes, everyone had said their good nights and be wells, and Gini and Patrick were finally alone.

"Impressive." Patrick sat on Gini's couch, and she crawled into his lap.

"I know how to clear a room in an emergency," she said, "and this qualified as an emergency. I couldn't be held responsible for my actions if I didn't get to touch you immediately." She teased his lips with soft, quick kisses.

"You can touch me all you want." Patrick slid his hands up the back of her neck into her hair.

"You'd better mean that." Gini snaked her hands under Patrick's shirt and freed him of it. "Because I intend to leave no portion of you untouched."

****

Gini stood in her kitchen, her barefoot tapping to a happy tune only she could hear. A tune she had in her head—her heart—because of Patrick. Right now he waited for her on the swing outside. She never thought she'd have anyone besides family waiting for her. Now she had this wonderful man, his dog, and an extra kitten to love.

How did I get so lucky?

The knife sliced through the grapefruit and sent the two halves rolling away from each other. Gini picked them up and plopped each half into its own bowl. Her gaze slid to the drawer under the island where she stored the plastic wrap and she smiled. Saber meowed from his position between her feet.

"Yes, that's right, Saber," Gini said. "I've finally found a man to share my grapefruit with."

The cat rubbed her ankle and purred.

"Yes, I've also found someone who can make *me* purr."

Gini thought of how happy her friends were too. She'd never seen Mason so comfortable around a woman. Raina had erased his shyness, brought him out of his shell.

Haddy was the best thing to ever happen to Jonah. Gini just hoped the relationship would continue after Jonah was healed. She knew her brother. He was a natural flirt. He loved women. Would he be content with just one? Time would tell.

Gini picked up the two bowls along with her copy of the calendar and carried everything out to the swing. In the pool of light spilling from the back porch, Patrick gently rocked the swing back and forth. Midas and Whisper were in the grass at his feet, and Saber darted through the darkness toward them. Gini handed Patrick one of the grapefruit halves.

"Thanks," he said.

"I figured some fruit would help us replace the energy we used." Thinking about making love with Patrick had Gini's heart galloping in her chest all over again.

"Something tells me we're going to be eating a great deal of fruit." Patrick ran a finger down Gini's forearm, and her entire body buzzed at the caress.

"Fine by me."

Patrick leaned closer and brushed his lips over Gini's. Though they'd just had amazing sex—like cosmic, wobbling-planets-off-their-axis sex—Gini felt she could go another round or two...or ten. She didn't think she'd ever tire of Patrick's touch, his kiss, his ability to make her feel freaking incredible.

He was an answer to her prayers, a wish come true, a gift. A miracle that left her breathless.

****

Breathless. Looking at Gini under the moonlight stole his breath away. Everything was better with her beside him. The night air smelled sharper, as if someone had buried Patrick in wildflowers. The cricket song sounded happier, as if even the insects knew the night was special. Even the grapefruit—normally no match for his beloved blueberries—tasted like fruit from Eden. All because of Gini.

"Sign mine?" Gini held out her calendar.

Patrick set his bowl on the swing beside him and took the calendar.

"Hang on a minute," Gini said. "I forgot a pen." She popped up and jogged back to the house. She returned to the swing with her gigantic purse and opened it on her lap. "I have a pen in here somewhere." She buried her hand in the purse up to her elbow.

Patrick opened his mouth, but Gini stopped him with a finger to his lips.

"If I don't find it in a minute's time, you can say your wisecrack."

"Fair enough." Patrick pressed a button on his watch, and its screen lit up blue. "One minute. Go."

Gini grumbled, but intensified her search in the purse.

"Forty seconds." Patrick slid his hand to Gini's neck then up into her hair.

"No distracting. That's cheating." Gini wiggled to the edge of the swing and continued her hunt.

"Twenty seconds…" *God, she's adorable foraging around like a squirrel.*

"Here it is!" Gini held up the pen as if it were an Olympic gold medal.

"With seconds to spare," Patrick said. "Well done."

He took the pen and opened the calendar to July. He wrote over the boxes in large print, then stared at the words, shocked he had written them. He who had resigned to being along forever. But it felt right. The words looked right, and he wanted what they said. He closed the calendar before Gini could peek and held the pen over her open purse.

"Good luck, brave pen." He made a faint screaming sound as the pen dropped into the bottomless pit of random, but apparently necessary, items.

Gini elbowed him. "Shush, you. Everything I need in life is in this purse."

"You'd better get a bigger purse then," Patrick said.

"Why?" Gini looked up, meeting his gaze.

"Because I want to be something you need in life, Gini." Patrick opened the calendar and angled it toward her.

"Marry me," Gini read aloud where he'd written on the calendar. Her eyes widened, as did her smile, and Patrick held his breath. "Oh, Patrick!"

She launched herself onto him as her purse fell to the ground. Its contents thudded to the grass as she hopped into his lap and kissed him until he could barely remember his name.

He pushed her back slightly to see her face. "Is that a yes?"

"Yes. Yes. Yes." Gini punctuated each yes with a kiss. "I love you."

"I love you."

As they enjoyed another round of memory-erasing kissing, a loud meow sounded from the grass.

"That wasn't Saber." Gini climbed off Patrick's lap.

"No," Patrick said. "It was Whisper." He slid off the swing and got to his knees in front of the kitten. She meowed again and when Patrick picked her up, a dot of light flew out from under her paws.

"She caught a firefly," Gini said with a laugh.

Patrick brought Whisper to the swing and sat. "So did I."

He slipped his arm around Gini's shoulders and pulled her close. She fit there perfectly as if she had been made especially for him.

Perhaps she had, and now they would share a lifetime together.

A word about the author...

By day, Christine DePetrillo teaches and inspires young writers. By night, she writes, writes, and writes. She loves hanging out with her characters and watching their tales unfold.

Her stories are meant to make you laugh, maybe make you sweat, and definitely make you believe in the magic of love.

Visit her at:
www.christinedepetrillo.weebly.com